Brides of OHIO

Brides of
OHIO

*Three Historical Tales of Love
Set in the Heart of the Nation*

JENNIFER A. DAVIDS

BARBOUR BOOKS
An Imprint of Barbour Publishing, Inc.

Yankee Heart ©2011 by Jennifer A. Davids
Wounded Heart ©2011 by Jennifer A. Davids
Restored Heart ©2012 by Jennifer A. Davids

Print ISBN 978-1-63058-152-7

eBook Editions:
Adobe Digital Edition (.epub) 978-1-63409-343-9
Kindle and MobiPocket Edition (.prc) 978-1-63409-344-6

All scripture quotations are taken from the King James Version of the Bible.

This book is a work of fiction. Names, characters, places, and incidents are either products of the author's imagination or used fictitiously. Any similarity to actual people, organizations, and/or events is purely coincidental.

Published by Barbour Books, an imprint of Barbour Publishing, Inc., P.O. Box 719, Uhrichsville, OH 44683, www.barbourbooks.com

Our mission is to publish and distribute inspirational products offering exceptional value and biblical encouragement to the masses.

Member of the
Evangelical Christian
Publishers Association

Printed in the United States of America.

Contents

Yankee Heart

Dedication

I would like to thank the Ohio Historical Society, Slate Run Living Historical Farm, and the Columbus Metropolitan Library for helping me with all the historical information needed to write this book. Many thanks to my husband, Doug, our two children, Jonathan and Grace, my extended family, and my church family for supporting me as a writer. And last but never least, a great deal of thanks to my Father in heaven. Thank You for giving me the honor of being Your scribe.

This book is lovingly dedicated to my grandma Minnie and my great-aunt Jennie. You both were Ohio to me and are dearly missed.

Chapter 1

Katherine Eliza Wallace looked around her with wide eyes as she stepped off the train. Rising over the top of the tiny railway station were the false fronts of buildings, their painted signs announcing the Ostrander Hotel and Decker's Dry Goods. Yet another store advertised furniture notions to her left. But it wasn't the sight of the simple country shops that caused her to stare. A light snow was falling, the first the South Carolinian had seen in the twenty-two years of her life.

Her companion watched her with a gentle smile. "I've missed snow," she said as she also watched the tiny flecks of icy softness swirl through the air.

Katherine turned to look at the woman, slightly embarrassed. "It's lovely," she declared in her soft Southern drawl. Then she shivered in spite of her warm wraps. "But my, it's chilly!"

The older woman chuckled. "It'll be spring in a couple of weeks. I warned you it would be different than living along the Congaree."

"I don't mind." Katherine's face grew pensive. "You know I had nowhere else to turn."

Mary grasped her hand. "Welcome to Ohio," she said with a grin. "Ten to one it'll be warmer tomorrow and then freezing the day after." They laughed.

A shrill cry rang out, and they turned toward it. "Mary O'Neal!" A graying, scarecrow-like woman was bearing down on them from the direction of the dry goods store.

Katherine looked at Mary nervously.

The older woman smiled reassuringly and smoothed back a strand of Katherine's dark hair, tucking it back into her bonnet. "It'll be fine," she whispered and turned to the new woman's outstretched arms. "Ruth

9

Decker!" Mary smiled as she gently returned the strong embrace. "It's so good to be home."

Grasping her friend by the elbows, Ruth smiled back as she examined Mary's face.

"We thought you might be here soon. I'm so glad. We heard about General Sherman's march. The *Delaware Gazette* said he went right through where your plantation stood." She drew a little closer to Mary. "Did the general. . .burn your house down?" She finished the last sentence in a sort of loud whisper.

"No, he was very good to us while he and his officers stayed at the house."

Ruth gasped and her eyes became so large, Katherine thought they looked just like those of the tree frogs that were so common in her home state.

"Mary O'Neal," she gasped. The train began to leave and her voice rose above the laboring engine. "You met General William Tecumseh Sherman and didn't tell me straightaway!" She picked up one of the carpetbags Mary had set down on the platform. "Now you just come with me and tell me everything!" Mary gave Katherine a droll little smile, and they picked up their other bags and followed.

With the train gone, Katherine got a glimpse of the rest of the town. The tall spire of a church rose up further down, and across the street and a block or so closer was a brick schoolhouse. Several other homes dotted the rest of the town, and in the distance she heard the distinct sounds of bleating sheep.

"A purebred sheep dealer a street or two over," Mary explained.

They stepped up onto the wooden boardwalk outside the dry goods store, and Katherine noticed there was a post office just around the corner. Evidently it was also taken care of by the Deckers, for Ruth stuck her head in as they passed to tell her daughter, a young lady named May, to mind the counter; she would be "back in a bit."

The walkway ended at a stone-lined path, at the end of which stood a quaint whitewashed two-story house. Quicker than a body could say "knife," Ruth Decker had them out of their wraps and sitting in her elegant little parlor sipping tea out of a china service she claimed her grandmother had brought over from Ireland.

"Now," Ruth said as she came into the room with a plate of cookies, "tell me everything." She sat down next to Mary and took her hand.

Mary smiled gently at her friend. "If you don't mind, Ruth, first I would like to introduce you to my dear friend, Katherine Wallace."

"Good heavens, where are my manners?" Ruth leaned over and patted Katherine on the leg. "I am so sorry, dear. I was caught up with seeing Mary again."

"Please don't give it another thought, ma'am," Katherine said softly. "I'm pleased to make your acquaintance."

Ruth started at the sound of the young woman's gentle accent and looked at Mary.

"Katherine's family owned the plantation next to ours, Ruth." Mary calmly took a sip of tea. "The Wallaces. I'm sure I wrote you about them."

Ruth looked at Katherine a moment longer. "Oh, of course. Yes. How do you do?"

Katherine noted the cooler tone to the woman's voice and flushed slightly as she took another sip of tea. It wasn't the first time since they had passed the Mason-Dixon Line that she had been snubbed in such a way. But it hurt just the same. She lightly fingered the long, thin scar that lined her left jawline.

"For man looketh on the outward appearance, but the Lord looketh on the heart."

The verse sprang into her mind of its own volition, and Katherine remembered it as one Mary had quoted after a particularly bad incident in Springfield, west of Ostrander. Katherine felt her face cool a little and, dropping her hand away from her jaw, took mind of Mary and Ruth's conversation.

"You mean General Sherman used your house as his headquarters!" Ruth was gushing.

Mary smiled. "Well, not exactly. He and his staff simply stayed the evening. We gave him what we could, and he provided Katherine and me with a horse and wagon, which got us up to Lexington. There was no catching a train so far south. He'd ruined the lines."

The tree frog eyes appeared once more. "You traveled from South Carolina to Lexington, Kentucky, all by yourself! Mary O'Neal, wasn't it dangerous?"

"No." Katherine spoke now with a soft voice. "There are many refugees on the roads these days. We had a great deal of company on our way here." She looked at Mary. "I'm afraid General Sherman has made many a family homeless."

Ruth gave her a sharp look and then turned to Mary. "What is the general like?"

"He's a bit rough, but he's a good man," Mary said with a sympathetic glance at Katherine.

When Sherman's army had arrived at her family's plantation, they destroyed everything, including burning the house to the ground. Katherine and her aunt Ada had fled to the O'Neals', whose plantation was mostly spared when General Sherman discovered it housed a fellow Ohioan. Her aunt had been quite indignant over that fact, but Katherine had been very glad her friend's home had been spared.

"My people were so happy to see him," she said. "He remarked that many former slaves clamor around him as if he were Moses."

Ruth looked at her friend with reproof. "I still can't believe you and John actually owned slaves. How could you, coming from a family like yours? Your people have been abolitionists for years."

Mary patted Ruth's hand. "Well, you know my husband's inheriting the place was quite a surprise to us. We had intended on freeing our people and selling the land, but a stipulation in the will demanded the plantation couldn't be broken up. It would have been given over to a distant cousin we knew to be terribly cruel. So we thought it best to keep it." Mary smiled at Ruth. "We were kind to our people and kept them well cared for."

"And you were the least popular family for it." Katherine smiled broadly. "Folks said they would turn on you because of your kindness."

Ignoring Katherine's comment, Ruth clasped Mary's hand once more. "Dorothy told us about John and Thomas. We're so sorry."

Katherine looked compassionately at her friend. The mention of the loss of Mary's husband and son had brought a strained look to her face. Her husband, John O'Neal, and their son, Thomas, had sneaked north and joined the Union army not long after the surrender of Fort Sumter. John had been with a Pennsylvania regiment and Thomas with one from New York State. Thomas had perished at Chancellorsville; John only two months later at Gettysburg. With her son and husband gone, Mary had longed for family and decided to abandon her plantation and return to Ohio where her sister, Dorothy, lived along with her three sons. Dorothy's husband had died before the war, and other relatives had either gone west or passed on.

Katherine frowned as Ruth prattled on about who else in Ostrander had lost loved ones in the war. Couldn't she see how tired Mary was and how sad the news made her? When the woman finally paused to draw breath, Katherine spoke up. "Shouldn't we be getting along to your sister's farm, Mary? You said you wanted to go there directly, seeing how it's been so long since you had a letter." Mary shot her a grateful glance.

"Oh, of course," Ruth exclaimed. "I've been keeping you! I'm so glad you're on your way to Dolly's. It's been at least two weeks since I've seen her here in town."

"Two weeks?" Mary immediately rose and made for their wraps, which hung on an oak hall tree near the door.

Katherine followed her lead.

"Well yes. Elijah Carr was coming to get her mail—"

"Mr. Carr has been coming to town for my sister?" Katherine started at the stern look on Mary's face as she handed her things to her.

"Well yes, to get the mail and buy a few things." Ruth looked in wonder at Mary's confused look. "Toby ran off and joined up nearly two years ago. With Jonah and Daniel gone fighting, she needed the help."

Mary paled and leaned back against the door.

Katherine thought she might faint and grasped her arm.

"Oh Mary, I'm so sorry!" Ruth exclaimed. "I thought you knew! I was sure she'd written—"

"Hush up!" Katherine snapped. Seeing Mary so distressed made her sharp. Ruth stopped her chatter, but Katherine could feel her eyes on her as she began to rub Mary's wrists. "Mary, are you well?"

Taking a deep breath, the older woman nodded. "May we borrow your horse and buggy, Ruth? I need to see my sister."

"Of course!"

⁂

At least the woman is efficient, Katherine thought as she tooled a little black buggy down the road out of town.

It hadn't taken Ruth Decker long to get them going. She had even offered to get a boy to drive them, but Katherine had insisted on performing the task to the woman's great surprise; she hadn't seemed to believe her capable. *Two weeks ago she would have been right,* the young woman mused.

The trip up from the South had forced Katherine to learn and do things she had never done in the whole of her privileged life—like driving a horse and wagon and cooking over an open flame. She was glad to have learned them. She'd never felt very comfortable having others do things for her or being prim and proper as was expected of a Southern belle. She was glad she was becoming more self-sufficient, particularly now.

Ruth had given Mary her sister's mail for the last two weeks, and she knew Mary would want to look at the correspondence in private, meager though it was. There were a grand total of three letters in the bundle, two of them from Daniel, one of Dorothy's sons, and one from someone whose name Mary hadn't recognized. Katherine had noted it was from a Union officer and hoped it wasn't bad news. She wasn't sure how much more Mary could take today. Her friend now flipped through the letters one at a time, her steel blue eyes pensive and a loose strand of ash-blond hair tickling her face, trying in vain to gain her attention.

"Maybe you should open one," Katherine suggested softly.

Mary glanced at her and looked as if she might refuse.

"I'm sure your sister wouldn't mind."

Biting her lip, Mary opened one of Daniel's, the most recent one. "He's in Petersburg, Virginia, with General Grant." She breathed a small sigh of relief. "He says homesickness is all he's come down with in the last month."

Katherine nodded and sent up a prayer of thankfulness. Sickness was such a problem in the army camps of both sides that it was feared almost as much as combat.

Mary looked at the other letter from the unknown Union officer. "This is dated before Daniel's," she muttered. She turned weary eyes to Katherine. "It may be about Jonah. . . . I. . .can't. . ." She raised a hand to her eyes.

"Then don't," Katherine said. "You're so tired. . .I regret suggesting it."

Mary tucked the missives in her reticule and looked around. The familiar scenery seemed to soothe her, and Katherine sensed her tension ease and a little of her weariness fall away.

The road they traveled down had trees thick on both sides, and every now and then a squirrel, not long from a winter nap, dashed in and out of the leaves. The snow had not lasted long at all, having only served to make a light coating on bare patches of grass and frost the sides of the road.

When they rolled past a neatly kept brick church, Mary mentioned that was where her family had attended since before there was even a building to meet in. She sincerely hoped Katherine would enjoy Mill Creek Church.

Katherine bit her lip and glanced out away from Mary's eye. *I know I'll enjoy it, but will the church enjoy me?*

She thought back over their visit with Mrs. Decker. Were people like Ruth Decker the kind of folks she had to look forward to? In spite of the woman's chilly behavior, she regretted being so sharp right before they left. And comparing the poor woman to a tree frog! She felt the color rise slightly in her cheeks. *I ought to be ashamed of myself.*

Katherine was hoping to start a new life here, far, far away from the one she had left behind in South Carolina. Ohio was to be her home now.

I surely got off on the wrong foot with Mrs. Decker, Father. Help me to behave better the next time we meet.

"My, but Mill Creek is high."

Katherine started at the sound of Mary's voice. She had been so lost in thought she had not noticed a rushing sound that was quickly becoming a roar. They were approaching a creek—Mill Creek, according to Mary.

Katherine stopped the horse for a moment to look. The creek was a tumult of rushing water running quickly past them as if on serious business that would not wait. The spring thaw had made the waters run high and fast. It seemed slightly smaller than the Congaree, the waterway near the plantation where she grew up. But according to Mary, it wasn't called Mill Creek for nothing. It powered more than one mill along its banks.

A covered bridge spanned the creek, and Katherine urged the horse forward. Not long afterward they came to a crossroad, and Mary instructed her to turn east. After crossing the creek once more, the trees began to thin and Katherine noticed Mary's face take on a gentle, happy look, much to her relief. The creek was on their right, and the road now followed the base of a gentle slope. As they rounded a slight corner, the rear of a farmhouse came into view.

"There it is," Mary murmured.

Katherine pulled the buggy up the sloped driveway and turned to see a kindly, cozy-looking farmhouse. Painted a simple white with a slate roof, a little dormer window capped the square front porch. The pine-green shutters on the windows were open and welcomed all to come in. Smoke was rising from one of the twin chimneys that rose from either side of the house, and Katherine found herself longing to sit before its fire away from the chill.

"This isn't right," she heard Mary say. "Dolly wouldn't stand for the farm to be in such a state."

Confused, Katherine turned and saw that her friend was looking out at the scene in front of the buggy. She had been so absorbed admiring the house that she hadn't noticed the rest of the farm. The yard and other farm buildings were in poor condition. More than one rail in the garden fence was broken. The barn door was standing half open, and several chickens, loose from the coop, wandered here and there.

Before Katherine could say a word, Mary was out of the buggy and in the house.

Katherine looked around for a place to leave the horse and buggy, eager to follow. But Ruth's horse, a gentle old mare, had already raised one hoof and appeared to be dozing. She secured the brake and followed Mary into the house.

Finding herself in a little entry hall with stairs in front of her, she was unsure where to go. To the right was a charming little parlor with rose-print wallpaper, comfortable-looking chairs, and a sofa; a dining room with a long, sturdy table and chairs lay to the left. Mary was nowhere to be found.

"Katherine?"

Hearing her friend's call, Katherine immediately ascended. Halfway up she heard the worst coughing she had ever heard in her life, and the sound made her dash up the last few steps. There were several doors to choose from at the top. All were closed save one. She entered the room and nearly gasped at the sight of a woman in bed, covered with a handmade quilt. Her face was drawn and pale, and it grieved Katherine to come to the conclusion that this was Dorothy Kirby.

Mary sat on the edge of the bed trying to urge her sister to drink from a cup. "The fire's low. Go through the dining room and there should be some wood in the kitchen."

The tightness in the older woman's voice gave Katherine speed, and she flew down the stairs as directed to the kitchen in the rear of the house. The wood box had several logs in it, and seizing a few of the thicker ones, she lugged them back upstairs. It didn't take her long to get the fire going again.

She turned to find Dorothy looking at her. She swallowed hard. It felt like a walnut with its green spring husk still attached was trying to go down her throat. Would her presence alarm the sick woman? Dorothy couldn't possibly know who she was.

She started to step out of the room when Mary motioned for her to come near.

"Pneumonia," Mary stated as she approached.

"Is that Katherine?" A catch grew in Katherine's throat at the sound of the poor woman's hoarse, weak voice.

"Yes, but hush now," Mary soothed. "We'll save introductions for later, Dolly."

But the woman shook her head. "Been praying for her. Like you asked." She made an attempt to give Katherine a weak smile but began to cough again.

"Maybe she'll quiet down if I leave." While gratified that Mary had asked her sister to pray for her, Katherine was more eager to let the woman rest.

Mary shook her head, seemingly resigned to something Katherine was unwilling to consider.

"Toby...," Dolly began.

"I know. He's fighting."

Dolly shook her head and looked toward her night table.

Mary took the letter lying there and read the first few lines and then handed the letter to Katherine.

Toby had died at Cold Harbor, Virginia, a little less than a year ago.

"Jonah?" Mary's voice was barely above a whisper.

Tears smarted at Katherine's eyes as she watched Dolly shake her head.

Mary bit her lip and drew the letters from Daniel from her reticule. "Daniel's all right. He's in Petersburg."

Her sister nodded and closed her eyes. Her breathing was ragged for a minute or two. It became shallower and shallower, and Katherine gently grasped Mary's shoulder as Dorothy Kirby left to go to her reward.

Tears flowed freely down Katherine's face as she sat down on the edge of the bed and held Mary as she sobbed.

Oh Father, she prayed, *dear Mary has lost so much. Keep Daniel safe and let this sad war come to an end. Soon.*

Bootsteps sounded on the stairs, and Katherine rose, standing protectively over Mary who still sat on the bed. A huge, gruff-looking man filled the doorway, and fear gripped Katherine as she saw the rifle in his hand.

But Mary knew the stranger. "Mr. Carr," she said calmly, far more calmly than Katherine thought her capable of just a few minutes after her sister's death. The older woman stood, handkerchief in hand.

Surprised, he said the name almost under his breath. "Mary O'Neal!" Clearing his throat, he took his straw hat from his head. Long strands of gray hair tumbled clumsily into his eyes, and he immediately pushed them back. "Mrs. O'Neal, I—I wasn't expectin' you."

"I understood from Ruth Decker you were helping Dolly run the farm."

Mr. Carr nodded. "Yes, that's right. Since that rascal Toby took off."

"I'll thank you not to speak ill of the dead, Mr. Carr."

"Sorry," he mumbled gruffly and nodded toward the bed. "How's your sister?"

"Mrs. Kirby has passed," Mary said softly as she turned back to her sister. As she did so, Katherine thought she caught a brief gleam in Elijah Carr's eye.

"If you want to gather up a few things, I'll wait outside for you." His voice strained not to sound eager.

"What on earth for?" Mary asked suddenly, turning from her sister.

"Well. . . ," he began hesitantly. "Thing is. . .Dolly promised the farm to me."

Mary stared at him. "I'm quite sure that must be a misunderstanding. Dolly would never give up this land. Joseph always intended it for the boys."

"Jonah and Toby are gone, Mary. Died fighting the war."

"But Daniel is still alive and well, Mr. Carr." She walked up to him. He towered over her, but she paid him no mind. "I read a letter from him this morning. He's with General Grant in Petersburg."

"Daniel always had a head for book learnin'. He was already an instructor over at that college of his. He was never a farmer. Dolly said, with Jonah and Toby gone, he would most likely sell me the land."

"Dolly said that?"

"She surely did."

Mary looked at him carefully. "Be that as it may, whether or not to sell the land to you is for Daniel to decide. And until he comes home, we'll stay right here and keep the farm going."

Katherine took a step forward to stand right behind Mary, backing up her words. She grasped the older woman's hand and squeezed it. She had no idea how to run a farm, but she was more than willing to try.

Her movement attracted Mr. Carr's attention, and he looked at Katherine as if just noticing her. "Who are you?" he asked gruffly.

With a pounding heart, she raised her chin. "My name is Katherine Wallace, sir."

At the sound of her voice, Mr. Carr glared at Mary. "What do you mean bringing a filthy little secesh up here? Dolly most likely died of shock from you letting her step foot in her house."

Mary glared right back at him. Secesh, short for secessionist, was a word they had both heard spoken in anger far too often since coming north. Mary thought it a cruel name, but Katherine felt it was an accurate one.

"Miss Wallace is my dear friend, and I had my sister's permission long ago to bring her here." She crossed her arms over her chest. "Dolly would have more of a fit if she could see the state the farm is in right now."

Mr. Carr looked uneasy. "Been hard," he finally muttered. "When she took ill, she insisted on stayin' here. I've been goin' back and forth to take care of my lands, too."

"So you were at your farm all morning?"

Carr looked at Mary rigidly. "Had business up in Delaware this morning that wouldn't wait." His excuse that he'd had to drive nearly nine miles to the county seat clearly did not convince Mary. "She made me go," he said defensively. "Said she'd be just fine."

Mary's shoulders fell wearily. She seemed either out of arguments or too tired to continue sparring with him. She turned and sat down next to her sister's still form. "I guess I should thank you for being so neighborly after Toby left. Thank you."

Mr. Carr approached her, giving Katherine a hard look as he brushed by her.

"I'm sorry Dolly's gone. Let me take you back to my house. You could stay there a spell. . . ."

"No thank you. We have the farm to look after."

The man gritted his teeth in silent frustration.

"But if you would be so kind," Mary continued, "as to take Ruth Decker's horse and buggy back into Ostrander, I would appreciate it. And please call on Reverend Warren on your way by Mill Creek Church. I need to lay my sister to rest."

Mr. Carr nodded and, without so much as a glance at Katherine, left the room. Presently they heard the distinct sound of a wagon pulling away from the house.

"Father, forgive me for disliking that man," Mary murmured.

Katherine looked at her questioningly, but her friend said nothing more.

Instead, she leaned forward and folded Dolly's arms across her waist. She then grasped the patchwork quilt and gently pulled it over her sister's body. "We'll talk later, Katherine. For now, we need to get ready for Reverend Warren."

Chapter 2

Katherine tossed in her bed for what seemed like the hundredth time. In spite of all she had done and been through today, sleep refused to call on her. Too many thoughts ran through her mind.

To begin with, Mary had insisted on her using one of the unused rooms upstairs. One of her nephew's rooms. It hadn't seemed proper, but where else would she sleep? The barn? She supposed it simply felt odd to be sleeping in a man's bed. Mary had thought she would be most comfortable in Daniel's room and insisted he wouldn't mind. She would have felt much more comfortable in Dolly's room, but that would need airing out. *And besides*, she thought, *Mary should have her sister's room.*

Mr. Carr had spoken to Reverend Warren as Mary had asked, for the reverend and his wife, Minnie, soon arrived to help her with all the arrangements. They had been kind and sympathetic toward Mary, but the couple seemed to keep Katherine at a polite distance. At least they were a tad warmer than Ruth Decker.

She played with a thread in the quilt that covered her. She had kept herself busy in the kitchen while Reverend Warren spoke to Mary, and she had rounded up the loose chickens while Mary and the reverend's wife laid Dorothy out in the parlor. Making herself as scarce as possible was all she could think of to avoid the discreet coldness of the couple. In light of their behavior, alongside Ruth Decker's, she could only imagine how people would treat her at the funeral on Saturday.

She rolled over and stared at the ceiling. When she had insisted on coming north with Mary, she had not really thought about how people would treat her. In retrospect, she realized she had latched on to the silly notion that the North was a sort of wonderland where everyone was warm and friendly and welcomed strangers with open arms. How could she help it? Mary had been the standard she had used to measure all Northerners.

The anger and suspicion Katherine aroused had come as shocking as a slap on the face. The instant any Northerner heard her voice, it was assumed she was either a secessionist or, worse, a Southern spy.

I was a fool to think people would assume otherwise. Mary warned me it might be this way, but I was so happy to be coming to the North. . . . Why shouldn't people be suspicious? The war certainly isn't over yet. Oh why didn't I just stay put?

She put a hand to her eyes and sighed deeply. She couldn't stay and live a life she didn't want with a family who had never wanted her.

Andrew Wallace, Katherine's father, had never forgiven her for not possessing her mother's beauty and vivaciousness. His only daughter's shy and studious spirit only irritated him. As far as he was concerned, her only value to him lay in whom she married. Her brother, Charles, had always blamed her for their mother's death. Annabelle Wallace had died giving birth to her. And her father's sister, Aunt Ada, had always contended that it was downright shocking that the Wallace family could have conceived a drab little nothing like Katherine.

But God opened a wide window for her when the O'Neals became the Wallaces' neighbors the year Katherine turned thirteen. John O'Neal had inherited a prosperous plantation and was connected to a very old South Carolinian family. Therefore, they immediately had standing in the community despite the fact they were Yankees.

She and Mary had become fast friends at the picnic held to welcome them, and when Katherine was sent off to school in Columbia, she corresponded regularly with Mary. The older woman became the mother Katherine had always longed for. It was Mary whom she confided in, Mary who led her to a deeper relationship with Christ, Mary who had shown her the ills of slavery.

Katherine smiled sleepily. *Thank You for my dear friend, Father. Thank You for bringing us here safely. . . .* She yawned as weariness crept over her. Folks here would surely come around once they got to know her. Closing her eyes, she drifted off to sleep.

The crack of a whip shot though the air, and Katherine started at the sound of it. Dropping her book, she ran through the house and into the kitchen.

The cook grabbed her as she tried to race out the back door. "Don't be goin' out there, Miss Katherine!"

"Who is it, Clarissa? Who's being whipped?"

Before the woman could answer, the crack of the whip and a scream rent the air.

Katherine pried loose and tore out of the house. She half ran, half stumbled down the slope toward the whipping post her father kept in full sight of the sad shacks that housed the Wallace slaves.

Another scream tore through her heart, and Katherine suddenly realized who it was.

"Chloe," she whimpered as the post came into view. Without thought for herself or the state of mind her father was surely in, she ran to her friend and stood between the poor young slave woman and the long black whip. Her eyes rose to the man holding it, and she gasped to see it was her father and not the overseer as she had expected.

Her father swore and yanked her out of the way. Katherine fought, but he was too strong. He shoved her into the hands of the overseer, who stood nearby, and Andrew Wallace continued his vicious attack.

Katherine wailed, and when her father finally stopped his brutality, he turned and backhanded her. Searing pain shot through her jaw, and she soon felt blood trickling down her neck and onto the fine French lace of her morning gown. With a shaking hand, she reached up and touched the gash his signet ring had made.

"Next time," he roared as she sobbed, "it will be someone else tied to that post. You hear me?"

"Katherine, do you hear me?"

Katherine awoke to find Mary sitting at the edge of her bed, gently shaking her awake. She reached for her jaw. It was wet. She pulled her hand away and saw not blood but tears, which fell free and fast down her face. She looked up at her friend. Moonlight reflected in Mary's motherly eyes and brought the young woman out of her nightmare.

"Chloe?" Mary asked gently.

Katherine nodded, and the older woman handed her a handkerchief.

"I'm so sorry I woke you," she said as she propped herself on one elbow to dry her face.

"Don't worry yourself over that."

Mary smoothed Katherine's hair, tucking in loose strands that had come loose from her long braid. "Seems like you had that dream a number of times on our journey back."

Katherine lowered her eyes.

Mary put a finger beneath her chin and lifted her face until their eyes met. "God knows you had no intention of doing what you did. His Son's blood covers all sin."

"But what about Chloe? I never got to tell her how sorry. . ." Fresh tears filled Katherine's eyes.

"I'm sure wherever she is, she has forgiven you."

Katherine nodded, but even though she knew Mary was right, she still felt guilty. She had only wanted the best for Chloe, the young slave woman who had been her only friend through her lonely childhood. Teaching Chloe how to read had been Katherine's way of setting her free. Katherine, then sixteen, hadn't really cared that it was against Southern law. Her father may have controlled the young woman's body, but Katherine knew if she was educated, at least her mind could go wherever she wished.

How could she have been so foolish as to have let her emotions get the better of her? But the things her father had said that evening at dinner. . . Even now his horrid, ugly words rolled back and forth in her mind, causing her to shake with anger. If only she had kept her tongue, Chloe would never have been beaten senseless and Katherine would have no scar to mar her face.

She sighed and looked at Mary. Chloe hadn't been the only one affected by her rash actions. "How did Thomas take it when I left?" she ventured. Her father had sent her off to Charleston for six months after the incident.

Mary hesitated. "It was hard for him."

"I'm sorry, Mary. I'm sorry I hurt your feelings. . .and Thomas's. Father said you bewitched me."

Mary said nothing, and Katherine knew she was trying not to say what she felt. She had hoped Katherine would one day truly become her daughter by marrying her son.

That had been Katherine's hope as well, but any chance she may have had with Thomas was dashed when her father forced her to break off all communication with the O'Neals. And he made arrangements to make sure it would stay that way. For the past seven years, Katherine had no contact with them until the night she and her aunt were forced to find refuge with Mary after their house had been destroyed.

"That's all water under the bridge now," Mary said finally. "I just hope your father and your brother made their peace with God before the war took their lives."

"I hope Aunt Ada does the same," Katherine said thoughtfully. "I'm going to write to her and let her know I'm safe."

"That would probably be best. Maybe you'll be able to reconcile with her."

"I'm afraid I've burned that bridge." Her aunt had disowned her when Katherine insisted on going north with Mary rather than accompanying her to Charleston. "I've never seen her so angry, not even after. . .Chloe."

Mary sighed. "Well, we should be getting back to sleep. Lots to do tomorrow." Mary rose and pulled the quilt over Katherine. Her face fell a little. "I guess we'll both be posting letters. I have to write to Daniel. He and Dolly were close."

"I'll keep him in my prayers."

Her friend gently smiled her thanks and went back to her room.

Katherine rose and, in spite of the chill of the room, stood in front of the window. She looked up at the moon and watched its soft light gently play on the bare trees outside her window. Sending up a quick prayer, she asked God to comfort Daniel Kirby's heart when he heard the news of his mother's passing.

As she turned to go back to bed, she noticed piles of books on the floor with more stacked on a rough-hewn table. She longed to see what tomes Mary's nephew possessed, but she knew if she started looking at them now she would never get back to sleep.

She climbed into bed. *Help me sleep well, Father, so I can be a help to Mary tomorrow.* But as she laid her head back, she found herself fingering her scar. She rolled over, trying not to drown in the guilt that washed over her.

Chapter 3

Appomattox Courthouse, Virginia
April 9, 1865

C onfederate general Robert E. Lee stepped out the door of the borrowed farmhouse belonging to Wilmer McLean. While his horse was being rebridled, he pulled on his riding gloves and, seemingly without thought, plowed his fist into his other hand several times. He didn't seem to notice the numerous Union officers, who were waiting in the yard, rise respectfully at his approach. The arrival of Traveler seemed to wake him, and with great dignity, he mounted the gray horse.

At that moment, Union general Ulysses S. Grant, to whom Lee had just surrendered his forces, approached him and tipped his hat.

Major Daniel Kirby was among the officers waiting outside the house when Lee came out. He and the others around him followed Grant's example.

Lee returned the act of respect and courtesy in kind and rode off with his aide, Colonel Charles Marshall.

Daniel looked after the valiant general with sympathy. He had fought hard and bravely for his cause, and while Daniel knew that cause had been terribly wrong, he still felt such valor should be respected and honored. Gunshots, a victory salute, suddenly rang out, and the twenty-five-year-old snapped his head around in consternation. *It's over; they are our countrymen again. We shouldn't humiliate them.*

It was as if General Grant had read his thoughts, for he quickly ordered all celebration to cease. He, too, saw no need to crow over their prisoners. As he turned, Daniel caught the general's eye and gave him a small nod of approval. Grant gave him a wink and the barest of smiles as he went back into the McLean house.

"Let us pray the peace in the next few months is as respectful." Daniel turned to see General Joshua Chamberlain mounted on his horse,

26

Charlemagne, standing next to the fence.

He walked over to the general, leading his own horse, Scioto, behind him. "I know that's how the president wants it, sir."

Chamberlain nodded. "Unfortunately, not everyone up North is very pleased with the prospect." He pulled a letter from his wife out of his pocket. "Fanny writes that people are eager for reprisals, revenge."

"If there is that type of bloody work, there won't be peace for long," Daniel replied grimly.

The general nodded in agreement. They both gazed down the road General Lee had just ridden down.

"'Rejoice not when thine enemy falleth, and let not thine heart be glad when he stumbleth,'" Daniel softly quoted.

"Amen." The general turned to look at the young major. "Have you heard from your people recently?"

Daniel looked up at the general, his face suddenly quite sober. He indeed had received word from home—an unexpected letter from his aunt Mary. It had come just as the siege at Petersburg had ended and they had General Lee on the run. There had been no time for him to reply or even think about it until this very moment. He took the letter out now and looked at it gravely.

"What is it?" His friend's voice sounded small and far off.

"I could use some coffee," Daniel heard himself reply.

"Mount up and let's have some then," Joshua said quietly.

Putting the letter back into his pocket, Daniel mounted Scioto and followed the general to his encampment, not far from town. They didn't speak, and Daniel was glad.

Joshua always seemed to know when to speak up or remain silent. Like the time they had first met, a day or so after Fredericksburg, at the beginning of the war. It had been a horrific battle, and Daniel still winced at the mere thought of it. His regiment, the 4th Ohio Infantry, had lost a shocking amount of men. The platoon he had been charged with had nearly been wiped out. Joshua, then a lieutenant colonel, had called to him as he aimlessly wandered through the army's encampment and invited him over to his campfire. Daniel had approached him warily, wondering if he was about to be reprimanded for the loss of his men. He had only been a first lieutenant at the time. But the superior officer spoke not a word about the battle and instead asked about Daniel's schooling, having heard he had graduated from Ohio Wesleyan and had taught there before the war. He asked about the university and talked about his own years as a professor of rhetoric at Bowdoin College in his home state of Maine, and their friendship began. Joshua never treated him like an underling while they were off duty, and they watched out for one another in battle. They had saved each other from certain death more than once. Daniel was proud to have such a man as a friend.

They eventually reached Joshua's tent, and Daniel soberly read his aunt Mary's letter while his friend made the coffee. When he had finished, he looked up to find Joshua seated at the small table he used to lay out military maps. Two tin mugs of coffee sat in front of him, and Daniel sat down and took a sip of the harsh brew. He looked at the general. "It's from my aunt Mary."

Joshua's brows knit together. "I thought she was in South Carolina."

Daniel shook his head. "When General Sherman went through, she made her way back up to Ohio. When she got back, she found my mother dying from pneumonia."

He covered his eyes with his hand. The war was coming to a close. Death, his close companion of four years, was supposed to have fled, yet here it was still, leering at him with its hideous pale face. He'd been through some of the bloodiest and most brutal battles of the war, yet this was harder than any of them. *Lord, give me strength.*

"I'm truly sorry for your loss," he heard his friend say quietly.

Daniel abruptly took his cup and went to the tent flap, where he finished his coffee in one large gulp, welcoming the heat of the liquid. It helped stop the tears from forming in his eyes. If he was going to succumb to grief, he wanted to do it in private.

"You need to go home, Daniel."

He had a dozen arguments ready, but they died on his lips. While the war still raged further south in parts of North Carolina and Alabama, Lee's surrender had been the beginning of the end. It was only a matter of time now. At any rate, the Army of the Potomac, which the 4th Ohio was a part of, wouldn't see any more action.

His aunt had also sent word that his brothers were dead, but Daniel had already known. He had been at Cold Harbor and seen Toby lining up with a Pennsylvania regiment. He'd been shocked to see him. It had been decided at the beginning of the war that Toby would stay home and help their mother keep up the farm. He'd had every intention of finding the nineteen-year-old after the battle and figuring out a way to get him home. But there had been no chance. His brother died that very day, and having no heart to break the news to their mother, Daniel requested that Toby's commanding officer write to tell her the news. And as for Jonah, one of his older brother's fellow soldiers had written him. His body had never been found, but the man had been positive he had seen Jonah fall in the midst of battle, mortally wounded. With his mother and brothers gone, the farm was his responsibility now. *Like Pa always wanted,* he thought grimly. He turned back to Joshua. "General Grant is most likely still at Mr. McLean's house."

Joshua rose from his chair. "If he's not, we can ride on to head-quarters."

Daniel slowly nodded and, putting down his cup, followed his friend out of the tent.

Chapter 4

Saturday, April 15, 1865

Katherine walked down to the edge of the drive and stopped, raising her face to the bright spring sun. With closed eyes, she allowed the rays to play and dance on her face before steeling herself to the chore ahead.

She was headed into Ostrander to check on the mail and buy a few things at the mercantile. Mary had written Daniel almost a month ago, and there was still no word from him. And with General Lee's surrender a scant two weeks ago, her friend had become terribly worried.

Katherine looked back at the sweet little farmhouse and checked her desire to go back inside. She had to do this because Mary could not undertake the task herself. *Grant me strength, Father.* Making sure her bonnet was straight and readjusting the basket on her arm, she turned and started to make her way down the dirt road.

Her first month in Ostrander had been interesting to say the least, starting with Dorothy Kirby's funeral. It seemed as if the entire township had shown up and crowded into the Kirby parlor. Unfortunately, the viewing hadn't been going on for five minutes when she sensed very clearly she was not a welcome addition to the community. With some there was a tangible, yet polite coldness, and they kept their distance. With others it was an occasional barb or remark she was sure to overhear.

Ruth Decker had even pointed out a few people Katherine should take great care to stay away from. "Oh, there's the Hoskins," she would say. "Their son died at the Rebel victory at Bull Run." Or "There goes Estelle Perry. The Rebs killed her husband at Gettysburg."

But by far the worst comment the woman made concerned a young widow only a few years older than Katherine. Dressed in black, the young woman had seemed so quiet and grave sitting all alone in a corner of the room that Katherine had forgotten herself and made her way over to see if she needed anything.

"Are you quite all right, ma'am?" Katherine asked. She was going to ask if she wanted any coffee, but the words died on her lips at the long stare the young woman gave her. Abruptly, she got up and left the room.

"Adele Stephens." Katherine turned to see Ruth Decker standing beside her and shaking her head sadly. "Such a shame. Her husband was captured and killed when he tried to escape." She grasped Katherine by the arm and drew her closer. "They say it was a South Carolinian who did the filthy deed," she hissed.

"Excuse me, Mrs. Decker," Katherine murmured and rushed outside to see the young widow pull away in a worn-out buggy. She was sure the woman had been crying. Later she learned Adele Stephens resided in town with her young son, an eight–year-old boy named Jacob.

Now, as she brushed her fingers lightly across her jaw, Katherine could only hope they would not meet today in town. *Father, please bring peace and healing to Mrs. Stephens's heart.*

She was drawing close to Mill Creek Church. As she approached, she looked around. No one seemed to be about, and she quickly slipped through the gate to the graveyard behind the little brick building. She quickly walked through the rows until she came to Dorothy Kirby's grave. Although Mary hadn't asked her to stop, Katherine had felt she should just to be sure it was neat and tidy. The weather had finally decided it was spring a few weeks ago, and everything was blooming. She wanted to make sure a stray weed hadn't sprouted.

Delicate new grass was creeping up the soft mound of dirt in front of the gravestone, and Katherine decided to come back once her task in town was completed. Maybe some spring flowers would brighten her resting place. There might be some blooming closer to the creek.

As she rose, her back protested, reminding her of the hard work she and Mary had been doing to keep up the farm. The work was substantial and constant; Katherine deemed it a miracle they were even able to keep up. Mary had laughed and quoted Ecclesiastes, the verse about how two were better than one.

Katherine had gone to bed exhausted every night the first few weeks. But she was gradually becoming accustomed to her new life. Under Mary's care, the blisters that formed on her hands soon healed and formed tough calluses. And she was beginning to wake herself in the early morning rather than Mary calling for her. They would do the daily chores and then set about whatever needed to be done that day. Repairing fences, boiling down maple sap into syrup and sugar, spring cleaning—there was always something to do.

In fact, things had been twice as busy since they had started getting the fields ready for planting. Mary had gone through Dolly's papers when they aired out her room and discovered she had written down what would be planted and where. Katherine had wondered why Mary had been so glad to find the slip of paper until the older woman explained crop rotation to her.

They had started plowing for corn and oats, but the day before yesterday there had been an accident. Mary had tripped and badly sprained her ankle while they were plowing the oat field. She could not put weight on it at all, but somehow Katherine had managed to get Mary back to the house.

Unfortunately, they got no more work done that day, a sore blow to their schedule. To make matters worse, Elijah Carr had come calling the next morning while Katherine was doing the chores. They had been forced to leave the plow in the field all night, and Mr. Carr had noticed.

"Saw you left your plow out," he'd said as he leaned against a stall door. "Think the field will plow itself?" He chuckled.

Katherine had clenched her jaw and was grateful her hands were busy so he wouldn't notice how they shook. "Mrs. O'Neal took a fall yesterday, Mr. Carr." She filled the horses' feed boxes with grain. "I was tending to her the better part of the afternoon."

"Well, I'll take my team out to your field and finish it off then."

Katherine stopped her work to look at him. "Whatever for?"

Carr's eyebrows raised in surprise. "Who else is going to plow up that field, Miss Wallace? You?"

"Certainly." She quickly walked around him and grabbed a pitchfork. "Your offer is very kind, sir, but I can manage it myself."

The man's face darkened, and it was all Katherine could do to stand her ground until the overbearing man left without another word.

When Katherine finished, she went inside to discover Mary hobbling about the kitchen with the use of a homemade crutch. "I found this upstairs," she explained.

"Mary!" Katherine cried. "You shouldn't even be down here. I was intending to bring breakfast up to you!"

Mary had managed to start the coffee and the bacon on the black cookstove at the rear of the kitchen. Mornings were still cool enough that they hadn't yet started cooking in the summer kitchen out behind the house. Katherine had been surprised at the need for one. She hadn't realized summers could get so hot this far north.

"Well, I have to admit I'm tired and sore," Mary said as she leaned against the worktable in the middle of the kitchen. "But once I sit a spell, I'll be right as rain. We'll be a little slower plowing today...."

"Oh no, you don't! I declare I never saw the like!" Katherine put her hands on her hips and gave Mary a defiant look. "You are staying right here! I have every intention of finishing up that field myself!"

"Is that what you told Elijah Carr?" Mary asked with a small smile.

"You saw him, then?"

"He left here with a look that would spoil milk."

"Before it left the cow," Katherine added. She gently grasped Mary by the arm. "Let me finish breakfast. You go sit at the table in the dining room."

While they ate, Mary had mentioned they were drinking the last of the coffee. "I'm sure you won't let me make the trip into town tomorrow." She chuckled and Katherine smiled. It was Friday, and they had been going into Ostrander every Saturday if only to check the mail. "We could manage without coffee, but"—her face had become etched with concern—"I'm eager to see if Daniel has written yet."

Katherine was so deep in thought, the buildings of Ostrander came into view sooner than she expected. She stopped not far from the Decker house, which was situated behind their store on the southern edge of town.

Ostrander's dislike of her hung darkly over her head. This was the first time she would have to deal with the townsfolk without Mary. Their previous trips into town had been tolerable for Katherine due to her friend's presence; people simply ignored her in favor of speaking to Mary. But what would happen today now that she was by herself? What would happen if she met Elijah Carr?

"But perfect love casteth out fear." Yes, of course. God's love surrounded her, and He would surely give her all the strength she needed. And as for everyone else, *"A soft answer turneth away wrath."* Mary always seemed to have a verse ready for any and every occasion, and Katherine had found herself beginning to fall into the same habit.

She smoothed the front of her green floral print dress and adjusted her bonnet. Squaring her shoulders, Katherine walked briskly up to the door of the post office, determined to be as nice as possible to whomever she encountered.

Entering, she saw that May, Ruth Decker's oldest daughter, was behind the counter. The girl was a little younger than Katherine and looked at her with wide eyes.

"Good morning, Miss Decker," Katherine said in her kindest, sweetest voice.

The girl nodded.

"Is there any mail for Mrs. O'Neal this morning?"

May shook her head.

"Well, thank you kindly." Katherine turned away reluctantly. She was almost at the door when a small voice stopped her.

"Are you going anywhere else in town today, Miss Wallace?"

She looked around, surprised that May had actually spoken to her, and stared at the girl for a moment or two. "I have some shopping to do at your parents' store," she said finally. "Why?"

The girl bit her lip and wrung her hands. "Folk are out of sorts today. You'd be better off heading home."

Katherine tilted her head and stared at the girl. "Whatever for? What's happened?"

"P–President Lincoln. . . ," May stammered. "They say. . .they say he's dead."

Katherine could feel the blood rush from her face at the young woman's words as she stared at her. *Oh Father, no!* "How? When?"

"I don't know. Pa got the message over the telegraph early this morning."

"Then I must speak with him." Katherine turned to leave.

"Oh Miss Wallace, you shouldn't."

Ignoring May's plea, Katherine left the post office and rounded the corner. She all but flew into Decker's Dry Goods. A crowd of people had gathered, mostly men, but here and there a farmer's wife stood sobbing into a handkerchief. Oblivious to all, she made her way to the counter behind which stood Mr. Decker. "Oh Mr. Decker," she said breathlessly, "what has happened to the president?"

Mr. Decker, a gray-haired man with a long face, gave her a stony look. "Why should you care, Miss Wallace? He wasn't your president."

Katherine stood there for a moment, ready to protest with all her heart, until she noticed the dead silence in the room. She turned to see those gathered giving her hard, long stares. Catching sight of Elijah Carr, she felt her knees go weak.

He glared at her. "You'd best be on your way."

"But the president..."

"He's not your concern, secesh!" Carr's voice was loud and harsh.

"There's no need to speak to her like that, Elijah," someone said from the rear of the store. "After all, Mrs. O'Neal trusts her."

"And I don't," Carr shot back. "For all we know, she knew the man who murdered President Lincoln." He stepped forward and towered over Katherine. "Your pa owned one of those big fancy plantations. You were quite the Southern belle, I hear. You ever meet John Wilkes Booth?"

Katherine felt the hair stand up on the back of her neck. She swallowed and began to stammer. "I—I..."

"Not sayin', eh? Well, maybe you'll be able to tell the county sheriff."

"No," she breathed. "I—I never knew him. I don't want any trouble." She backed away from Carr, and her eyes darted around the store.

Near the back, she caught sight of Adele Stephens's black dress. The young widow's eyes were red, and she held a white handkerchief in her hand.

Katherine stared at her and tears began to well. "I'm so sorry," she muttered before leaving the store as quickly as she could.

Her tears and the bright sunshine temporarily blinded her, which was why she all but ran over the young man walking down the boardwalk toward the store. She gave a little cry as strong arms grasped her own as they collided.

"Whoa!" he exclaimed in surprise.

Katherine looked up into a pair of soft green eyes, which were intently surveying hers from beneath the broad brim of a Union slouch hat. Dark blond hair curled slightly at the collar of his jacket, and while she was uncertain of his rank, she had seen enough Union soldiers on her way to Ohio to know he was an officer. In spite of a thin, unkempt beard, he was quite handsome. And quite tall.

A tear escaped and slid down her cheek.

His brow furrowed in concern. "Are you all right, miss?"

Katherine merely nodded in reply. In light of her reception in the mercantile, she had no desire to open her mouth and give away her undesirable origins to—of all people—a Union officer. She could only imagine the look on his face when he discovered she was a Southerner. Looking down, she struggled with the strings of her reticule, searching for her handkerchief.

The young officer released her. "I suppose it is a day for tears."

Catching the sad note in his voice, she looked up quickly, realizing he was referring to President Lincoln. She nodded once more.

He tipped his hat. "May God help us all, North and South," he said gravely.

His comment caught Katherine completely off guard, and she stared after him for a moment as he walked away. He stepped into the mercantile, and she walked out of town surprised to be hearing such a thing from a Union officer.

Chapter 5

Daniel rode Scioto out of Ostrander with a considerably heavier saddlebag. Coffee, tea, crackers, even some candy—everyone in town was so glad to see him and so sorry over the loss of his mother, he was lucky to get away without one of Mr. Henderson's purebred sheep in tow. A small smile touched his lips. *What a sight that would have been.* But the humor he normally would have found in the picture faded quickly. Too much had happened for him to laugh over anything right now.

General Grant had only been too happy to discharge him once Joshua had explained the situation. The great man had shaken his hand, offered his heartfelt condolences, and thanked Daniel for his service. Joshua had helped him pack and ridden with him back to Petersburg, where the army had a military train depot. The whole trip back to Ohio had been uneventful, a blessing that gave Daniel time to process the news of his mother's death. He reflected, prayed, and read parts of the battle-worn Bible he had preserved and protected through the war. His mother had been one of the most faithful women he had ever known; that she was alongside her Lord, he did not doubt for a moment. But he would miss her kind and gentle presence for a very long time.

Yet just as he was beginning to come to terms with his mother's passing, his world was once again shaken. Upon arriving in Marysville that morning, a town in the adjacent county west of Ostrander, he decided to ride Scioto the last nine or so miles. The horse had ridden most of the way up in freight cars, and Daniel knew his mount would be eager for exercise. He was just tightening the girth on his saddle when a general uproar erupted outside and within the telegraph office. The news quickly ran up and down the streets that President Lincoln had died—killed by an assassin's bullet. Daniel initially found it very hard to get specifics. All of Marysville was in complete turmoil. Eventually he learned of the terrible crime John Wilkes Booth had committed—the single gunshot to the back of the president's head, the wild leap onto the stage at Ford's Theater, and the escape somewhere into the Maryland countryside.

He had ridden to Ostrander in a daze. Daniel had been a great admirer of Abraham Lincoln, and by the end of the trip he still could not believe his president was gone. Lincoln had been a good and just man who, like Daniel, abhorred slavery. As Scioto loped along, he pulled his leather glove off and flexed the hand the great man had once clasped.

When Lincoln had traveled from Springfield, Illinois, to Washington, DC, on the way to his inauguration in 1861, he made stops in several cities, including one in Columbus, Ohio's state capital. Daniel, then a student at Ohio Wesleyan in Delaware, had made the trek down to see him. Long lines of people stood in the statehouse's grand rotunda waiting to meet the future president. The instant their hands touched, Daniel had been doubly glad Lincoln had been made president. Like his father, Daniel took his first impression of a man from his handshake. The firm, strong grip of Lincoln's hand confirmed all the good things he had heard about the president-elect. No one better could have led the country through the war. And no one better would have led it down the road of peace.

He brought Scioto to a halt. *I don't understand, Lord. What will happen to the country now?* It took Daniel a moment or two to quell the feelings of grief and anger that welled up before he nudged his horse forward.

He looked around him as he rode, and the beauty of his home state surrounded him like one of his mother's quilts. He felt some of his grief and weariness recede. Elm, ash, oak, and maple trees rose like giants on either side of the road. And mixed in with them all, particularly close to the creek, were buckeye trees.

Daniel had carried a buckeye nut in his pocket throughout the war. Some folk thought carrying one was good luck or could ward off whatever ailed the bearer, but he had never held to such silly notions. To him the small brown nut with its large round white splotch was a reminder of home. He pulled it out now and looked at it. In the fall, when the nuts fell from the trees, it had been all-out war as he and his brothers pelted each other with them. But they had always been careful never to bring one near the livestock or the dinner table. While they might be good food for squirrels, the nuts were poisonous to most animals and to people.

Jonah had taken a buckeye with him, also. He had carved his initials in it.

Daniel had laughed at him. "Afraid someone will take it?" He'd chuckled as he watched his brother carving at it with his pocketknife.

Jonah had soberly glanced up at him before returning to his work. "If something bad happens, they'll know it's me."

Grimly, Daniel put his buckeye back in his pocket and looked around some more. The spring sunlight danced down through freshly bloomed leaves, and bright rays of light hit new grass as it poked up through last year's fallen leaves. Squirrels darted and played, running partway up a trunk and, seeing him, dove back into the underbrush. And far back from the road, where the trees grew thicker, Daniel caught sight of a buck with a full rack of white antlers. Even the dust Scioto's hooves were kicking up was wonderfully familiar—plain brown dirt. No more red Virginia clay, which refused to wash out of his clothes.

At length, Mill Creek Church came into view. He stopped out in front and gazed at the little brick building for a moment before dismounting. He tied Scioto to the graveyard fence, and as he looked out over the rows of gravestones, he stared in surprise. Kneeling over his mother's grave was the same young woman he had bumped into in Ostrander. He quietly came up behind her and saw she was arranging flowers on the mound.

"There you are, Mrs. Kirby," she said, leaning back. "Pretty as a picture."

He wasn't sure which surprised him more, her presence or her accent. Who was she, and why on earth was this young Southern woman placing flowers on his mother's grave? He was about to ask when she spoke again, still unaware of his presence.

"We still haven't heard anything from your son, ma'am. Mary's so worried. She wrote him almost a month ago." She rose and brushed the dirt from the skirt of her dress. "God willing, Daniel's all right. I'll keep him in my prayers."

Daniel couldn't help but smile at her kindhearted gesture and spoke without thinking. "Thank you."

With a shriek, she whirled around and stood face-to-face with him. Well, almost face-to-face. He hadn't realized how petite she was earlier.

Other than that, it was hard to forget such a pretty face. Granted, she wasn't the Southern ideal of beauty with flashing blue eyes and honey-blond hair, but she did remind him of a picture of a simple English maiden in his copy of Bullfinch's *The Age of Chivalry*. There was an appealing sweetness to her face with its pert little nose and soft lips. Auburn hair peeked out from beneath her brown, low-brimmed bonnet, and she was staring at him with a large pair of the most incredible eyes he had ever seen. They were a kaleidoscope of green, brown, and amber.

"Daniel?" she asked in surprise. She looked down, her cheeks suddenly red. "Do excuse me, Captain. . . ."

"Major," he gently corrected.

She winced. "*Major* Kirby."

He gave her a long look before suddenly remembering a portion of his aunt's letter he had merely skimmed over, being so preoccupied with the news of his mother's death. She had spoken very highly of a young woman who had come north with her from South Carolina. "Are you Miss Katherine Wallace?"

Her eyes remained wide as she nodded. "How did you know. . . ?"

He gave her an apologetic smile as he removed his hat. "My aunt mentioned you in her letter. I'm very sorry I frightened you."

"That's quite all right, Major Kirby. I'm. . .very glad you're home safe. Mary's. . .been so terribly worried."

He frowned and regretted he hadn't at least sent them a telegram before he left. "I'm afraid I received Aunt Mary's letter right as the siege at Petersburg ended. There was very little time to do anything. Then General Lee surrendered. . . ."

"Of course! I. . .I understand perfectly, Major Kirby." Although her voice shook, it was gentle and reassuring. "And I'm sure Mary will as well."

Daniel looked at her curiously. She had to be one of the very few daughters of the Confederacy he had met who had not instantly hated him on sight. A Southern woman's zeal for the cause was almost legendary. He had been spit on, snubbed, and bad-mouthed any number of times. And unlike other young ladies he'd met, Northern or Southern, she made no attempt to flirt with him. In fact, judging by the way she stumbled over her words, she seemed painfully shy.

"I hope—I hope you don't mind, sir," Katherine said, rousing him from his thoughts. "I thought flowers might cheer your mother's resting place."

He stepped forward to look at his mother's grave. "Aunt Mary saw to the headstone," he stated.

"Yes, they put it up just a few days ago."

He saw the flowers Katherine had arranged were a small spray of purple violets, the sort that bloomed near Mill Creek this time of year. He turned back to see she had edged away a little to give him some privacy.

"Thank you for seeing to Ma's grave. Violets were always her favorite."

"There was n—no time"—she quietly stammered, her face flushing red once more—"for me to get to know her well. But she seemed like a very kindly Christian woman." Her eyes softened. "I'm very sorry for your loss."

Daniel knelt down and ran his fingers over his mother's name carved in the simple granite headstone. Her gentle face filled his mind, and he closed his eyes against the sudden onset of tears. After a few minutes, he rose and, as he donned his hat, looked over at Katherine, who was dabbing at her eyes with a handkerchief. "Miss Wallace, you mentioned how concerned my aunt is about me, and I would like to get home right away. Would you mind riding with me? My horse is very well behaved."

Her eyes turned to saucers, and she looked at him hesitantly. "Are you sure *you* don't mind?"

He smiled broadly, hoping to set her more at ease. "Of course not." Gently taking her by the elbow, he guided her over to the fence where Scioto stood.

Seeing him, her shyness ebbed a little. She quickly walked through the gate with a smile and stroked his neck. "What a beautiful animal! What's his name?"

"Scioto."

"That's the name of the river Mill Creek flows into, isn't it?"

"Yes, that's right."

"I haven't seen the Scioto yet," she explained. "Mary and I came through Cincinnati, and I did see the Ohio River. I must say I agree with President Jefferson. It is the most beautiful river on earth."

He blinked and looked at her with raised eyebrows. "You've read *Notes on the State of Virginia*?"

She blushed twice as hard as before, obviously embarrassed. "I'm afraid I've been looking through your books, Major Kirby. I hoped you wouldn't mind. . . ."

"No, not at all."

This young woman was one surprise after another. She smiled demurely, and as he helped her into the saddle, he found himself looking forward to getting to know Katherine Wallace.

Chapter 6

H ow awful for Mrs. Lincoln!"
Katherine patted Mary's hand. They were sitting at the dining room table, she and Daniel on either side of the older woman. It seemed a shame to spoil his homecoming, but they both knew the report of the president's assassination would not wait.

Her friend paled so terribly at the news that Katherine suggested Mary go lie down, but she gently declined and turned toward her nephew. "Who could have done such a thing?"

"John Wilkes Booth," Daniel said quietly.

"I still can't believe it," Mary murmured. "Poor, poor Mrs. Lincoln. How did it happen? Have they captured him?"

"The president was at the theater last night," he replied. "Booth came up behind him. . . . It was a head wound." As Daniel spoke, Katherine blanched and put a hand to her mouth. Mary did likewise.

"Booth's on the run"—his voice turned low and his face darkened—"but the army will get him."

"What will happen now?" Katherine asked. "Will this make the war last even longer?"

Daniel's grave face softened as he looked at her.

"Yes." Mary turned toward her nephew. "Will you be called back into service?"

"No," he replied reassuringly. "I've been discharged from the army." He looked at both of them for a moment before continuing. "I feel the war is as good as over. General Lee started something that cannot be easily stopped. And people in the South look up to him. If he sets the example, many will follow."

Katherine nodded while Mary embraced her nephew. While the news of the president's death had shocked her, she was very glad to have Daniel home. A great deal of worry had lifted from Mary's face when they had walked in earlier, to Katherine's great relief. As they reminisced, she quietly rose and set about emptying the young major's saddlebags.

He was without a doubt the handsomest, kindest man Katherine had ever met. She had been frightfully nervous sitting so close to him on the ride home, as she had very little experience with handsome young men. Apart from Thomas, of course. It had been so much easier with him; their relationship had existed chiefly through correspondence. She'd been to numerous balls, of course, but her shy ways and odd coloring meant she had been little more than wall decor, much to her aunt's and father's displeasure.

Words had failed her as she rode home with Daniel. Happily he asked her questions about the farm and Mary, and he was so kind and polite that her nervousness eased a little. She told him about what they had been doing over the past month, including how Mary had sprained her ankle. But she had not said anything about Elijah Carr's desire to buy the farm. She'd felt that bit of information was best left for Mary to explain.

Katherine glanced over at the young major. She had to admit to being quite surprised that a Union soldier could have such a generous attitude toward Southerners. His voice had been full of respect as he had spoken of General Lee, and he seemed genuinely concerned for the welfare of the South, judging by what he had said to her in town. Even now he was telling Mary the concern he felt over people's desires to punish the South for the war.

She gathered a few things in her arms and carried them to the kitchen. As she set everything down on the worktable, the last thing left in her hand was the coffee Deckers sold. The sight of it was a forceful reminder of the town's attitude toward her. *Daniel is kind, but the South got what it deserved.* The thought caused her to bite her lip, hard, and she set down the coffee to finger her scar. She didn't mean that. *It's only right that everyone up here should treat me poorly after how I betrayed Chloe.*

Blinking away the tears pooling in her eyes, she continued her work. After putting everything in its place, she walked back into the dining room to see what else Daniel had brought home.

"I'm so glad you were able to find him," Mary was saying. She looked up at Katherine and gave a sad smile. "Daniel was able to find Toby and give him a proper burial."

Katherine looked at the young major. He was deep in thought, and weariness hung heavy in his eyes.

"I couldn't get to Jonah," he said slowly. "He was with the Army of the Cumberland. I was sent word he fell at Kennesaw Mountain in Georgia." He patted Mary's hand. "I'll travel back down to Virginia in a few months and bring Toby back home. Ma would've wanted him buried with her and Pa." He looked out the window for a few minutes before turning back to his aunt, his face grave.

"What is it, Daniel?" Mary asked.

"I got to see Uncle John just before Gettysburg," he said quietly.

Mary's hand went to her throat, and Katherine was sitting beside her in an instant. Her friend's eyes shone very bright as she listened to her nephew.

"He was fine considering he had just gotten over being sick," he whispered. "It was very good to see him."

Katherine felt her own throat go tight, not only for Mary's sake but also at seeing how terribly it affected Daniel. He looked as if he had suddenly aged ten years, his face was so still and grave.

"My friend Joshua, Uncle John, and I—we ate together a few nights before we followed General Lee into Pennsylvania. Ma had sent me some food." His eyes were nearly beet red as he looked at his aunt. "I found him...later. Buried him." He quickly excused himself.

A few moments later, Katherine heard the creak of the pump out behind the house. She swallowed, uncertain of what to say.

Mary simply sat there lost in her own memories, a broken yet bittersweet look on her face.

"Mary," she whispered.

Her friend looked at her and smiled through her tears. "I'll be fine, dear," she whispered back. "Please, make sure Daniel's all right."

Katherine nodded, rising from her seat. Walking into the kitchen, she could see the young major through the window. He was standing next to the pump in the little brick courtyard situated between the house and the summer kitchen. His hair and face were damp, and he was staring out over the hills and fields beyond the house. She hesitantly opened the simple screen door.

It creaked slightly, and he turned around.

"Can I get you anything, Major Kirby?"

He shook his head and turned away, resuming his scrutiny of the farm.

Katherine stepped out onto the porch, uncertain what she should do. After a moment or two, he spoke. "Is my aunt all right?"

"She's fine."

"I shouldn't have told her."

"No!" Her vehemence caused him to turn back to her in surprise. "I mean. . .it was the only news she's ever heard of John. It was terribly hard to get a letter across the lines. She only heard of his death through a friend of a friend." Her voice suddenly caught in her throat. "I only wish you had seen Thomas, too."

He looked at her curiously. "Were you close to my cousin?"

"I. . ." What should she say? That day on the front veranda played out in her mind, and all she could see were Thomas's hurt-filled eyes as she flippantly told him she was no longer interested in socializing with either him or his family. "I cared for him," she whispered, her eyes darting away.

Daniel walked up to her. "I'm sorry."

She looked up. What had it been like for him, all these years, seeing nothing but death and destruction? How many times had he marched men toward their deaths, and how many lives had this horrible war forced him to take? He had already buried a brother and an uncle, but had there been others? Four years of combat rested so plainly upon his features that she forgot to be shy and impulsively grasped his hand with both of hers, sensing he needed to feel the warm touch of life.

The look on his face was a mixture of surprise and gratitude as he placed his other hand over hers. He opened his mouth to say something when they heard the sound of a buggy coming up the drive.

They immediately returned to the dining room and found Mary struggling to rise from her seat. Katherine urged her to sit back down as Daniel went to the front window, parting the white curtains for a better look. Having settled her friend back into her chair, she joined the young major at the window.

A black buggy had pulled up in the driveway, and a well-dressed gentleman was climbing out. Her heart sank as she saw who was with him. It was Elijah Carr.

"What on earth is Ma and Pa's lawyer doing here with Elijah Carr?" The young man turned to look at Mary.

"He believes you're willing to sell the farm to him," Mary said, her voice quiet.

Daniel frowned as a knock came at the front door. He turned to Katherine and gave her a little smile. "Would you please see them into the parlor, Miss Wallace? Tell them I will be with them shortly."

∽

As Katherine went to the door, Daniel knelt down in front of his aunt and spoke quietly. "Ma told Mr. Carr I would sell the land to him?"

"Yes," she replied softly.

Daniel sat there for a moment. Since before Ohio had become a state in 1803, the farm had been in the Kirby family. His father had been very determined that his sons follow in his footsteps and farm the land just as his father had. It had disappointed him greatly that Daniel had favored books over sowing a field. Daniel had always resented his father trying to force the farm on him, especially when Jonah, his older brother, had been a born farmer and preferred it over anything else. And Toby had been the same way. Why should it matter if Daniel did not want his share of the farm?

Because Pa saw books as a waste of time, not real work. He couldn't see how a man could make a living reading books all day.

He rose and looked in the direction of the parlor. Ironically, now that Toby and Jonah were gone, their shares of the farm now belonged to him as stipulated in his father's will. And he didn't want any of it. He already had a position to return to at Ohio Wesleyan. His mother had known that. She had always understood his love of learning and his desire to teach.

But to sell the land to Elijah Carr? True, he was a good farmer, but he seemed to think that since his family helped found the county, the entire county should belong to him. He owned most of the land along Mill Creek. Except the Kirby farm.

Pa would roll over in his grave if I sold the farm to him. Of course, he'd roll over in his grave if I sold the farm to anyone.

"He'll give you a good price."

Daniel looked down at Mary. His aunt was of the same opinion of him as his mother. "I know." He gave her shoulder a gentle squeeze before walking out of the room toward the parlor.

Katherine was standing in the hall between the two rooms, her dainty face distressed.

"Are you all right, Miss Wallace?"

She looked up at him. "Yes, Major Kirby, thank you." Before he could ask more, she retreated to the dining room.

Frowning, he continued on into the parlor and was immediately greeted by Elijah Carr.

"I'm real sorry about your ma," he said as he shook Daniel's hand.

"Thank you," Daniel replied stiffly. He looked over at Mr. O'Conner and offered his hand. "It's good to see you again."

The lawyer gave him a small smile as he took Daniel's hand. "Good to see you, too. Your ma was a lovely Christian woman. She'll be missed."

"Thank you. Is your son well?"

"Yes, we missed you helping him with his studies. Too young to join up, of course."

"He was better off. I suppose you heard about Toby?"

"Yes. Very sad. Eliza and I are so sorry for the loss of both your brothers. We—"

Mr. Carr cleared his throat. "I don't believe Mr. O'Conner came clear over from Delaware to talk family."

Daniel glanced at him with slightly narrowed eyes and nodded. "No. I understand you brought him here on business. Why don't we have a seat?"

Once they were settled, Mr. O'Conner spoke. "Daniel, I've been told you're willing to sell Mr. Carr the farm."

"Yes, I've been told the same." Daniel rested his eyes on Carr.

The man looked back at him confidently, not at all bothered by the younger man's statement. He settled back in his seat and smiled.

"I've heard the folks up at that college over in Delaware. . . What's the name?" he asked.

"Ohio Wesleyan," Daniel replied.

"That's the one. Anyway, they're wantin' to make you more than just an instructor now." A grin produced folds of wrinkles on either side of the older man's face. "News of you rescuing a bunch of our boys from the Rebs made its way up here. They're talking about making you a professor."

Daniel thought his heart might leap straight out of his chest, but he quickly reined in his excited emotions. "Well, I'm sure the story was greatly exaggerated. It was only about five men."

"Six as I heard tell it."

"One of the Confederates got Nate Stephens as he tried to make a run for it," Daniel replied quietly. "We tried to go back for him, but the gunfire was too thick."

Carr shook his head sadly. "Shame. His wife couldn't keep up with the farm. I forgave the debt provided she returned the land to me."

Daniel looked away from Carr, irritated. Nathaniel Stephens had not only been one of his men but a good family friend. Their farm had been his and Adele's dream. He had rented the land from Carr several seasons before the war. Jonah had helped him plow up the numerous rocks and build a small frame house. Their son, Jacob, had been born there. Nate had made a good profit even those first years, according to Jonah, so much so Daniel couldn't quite believe he still owed on the property.

Carr spoke, interrupting his thoughts. "Look here, Daniel. You're all set over at the college. If you sell the farm to me, I'll give you a fair price. With the money, you can set you and your aunt up real nice over in Delaware." A look of pure hate crossed his face. "And you can send that little secesh packing back to where she came from."

Daniel's irritation quickly morphed into anger. No wonder the young woman had looked upset as she left the parlor earlier. Whatever issues Elijah Carr had in the past with Southerners, he had no right to take out his rage on such a considerate young woman. He clenched his fist, fighting the desire to strike the greedy, hateful look out of Elijah Carr's eyes. A quick prayer for calm and guidance caused his hands to relax, and the tightness in his chest began to loosen. He looked over at his parents' lawyer. "What's the value of the farm right now, Mr. O'Conner?"

Mr. O'Conner scribbled a figure on a scrap of paper and handed it to Daniel.

He looked at it and knew Carr was right. He could find someplace quite nice in Delaware for himself and his aunt. And while he had no desire to send Miss Wallace "packing," if she had family she would rather be with, he could afford a train ticket for her to just about anywhere.

His heart pounded. He had loved his time at Ohio Wesleyan; his years there as a student and the brief time he had been an instructor at the institution had been very rewarding. He had always dreamed of one day becoming a professor. As much as he admired his family's dedication and hard work on the farm, he knew in his heart farming wasn't his path. In his prayers he had always come away with the feeling that becoming a professor was in line with God's will.

This is *Your will, isn't it, Father?*

Daniel nearly gasped out loud at the unmistakable prodding he felt from his Lord.

Looking up, he saw Elijah Carr's eyes now held a glint of triumph in addition to the hardness and greed that usually rested there.

He rose. "I'm sorry, Mr. Carr," he said quietly. "This farm has been in my family's hands for two generations. I feel obliged to keep it that way."

Chapter 7

Katherine opened her eyes. It was still dark, but she could hear the sound of the birds' quiet chirpings as they greeted the coming day. She smiled sleepily as she sat up in bed.

The wildlife here was refreshingly different than what she had grown up with—no green anoles scurrying up the walls, no tree frogs making a shocking amount of noise in the evening. And the insects seemed tiny compared to those in South Carolina. She supposed it must have something to do with the weather. It was so much crisper here, not heavy and damp, although Mary had told her summers here could get just as hot and humid. Best of all, her friend had laughingly assured her there were absolutely no gators in Mill Creek. Alligators were a regular danger on the Congaree, and she had never been permitted to go too close to the river.

Mill Creek was therefore an endless source of fascination for her. She especially enjoyed one particular place along its banks where large rocks provided a perfect place to sit and pray or just enjoy God's creation.

As she pulled on an old work dress she had borrowed from Mary, she remembered it was Sunday. The lighthearted feeling she had woken with ebbed a little. She and Mary hadn't planned on going to services today with her ankle so bad. But with the president's death, surely everyone would be attending church. It wouldn't be proper to stay away.

Her mood sobered further as her thoughts turned to Daniel and the aftermath of his conversation with Mr. Carr. She hadn't heard all of it, having been going in and out of the kitchen, but she and Mary had both overheard his refusal to sell the farm. The words had then become rather heated. The young major had kept his temper, but Mr. Carr had to be all but forced to leave.

Daniel had gone out to the barn after that, and she and Mary did not see him until supper. He had not said much except to explain to his aunt it would have been downright sinful to sell anything to a man so greedy. After they ate, he gathered a number of things from his room and, after insisting that Katherine continue using it, mumbled something about the barn. She assumed there was a shed of some sort he was making do with, and she felt bad she had chased him from his room. They did not see him for the rest of the evening.

She quickly twisted her hair into a loose chignon. Had he stayed away because she had been so forward earlier? What had she been thinking grabbing on to his hand like that? Daniel Kirby must think her the most brazen woman he had ever met. But the memory of those war-weary green eyes made her wonder what she would have done differently.

She shook herself. *Stop being so silly! He's bound to have left some pretty young thing behind who's been pining away for him,* she thought as she slipped downstairs. If that was the case, it was no wonder he had stayed away. He seemed too much of a gentleman to allow a young woman to get her hopes up. *Besides, what would he see in a drab little thing like me?*

Lighting a lantern, she silently hurried out of the house and walked over to the barn. If she was quiet, she should be able to get through the chores without waking him.

The Kirbys' big red barn was nestled into one side of the hill. The upper floor was level with the ground on one side, while on the other, the stone basement, where the horses and cows were kept, was exposed. The upper level stored hay, grain, a wagon, and a four-wheeled carriage. A shed for sheep was built onto the south end of the barn, and the pigs had a separate sty north of the building.

Katherine descended a set of stairs near the hay mow to feed the stock. When she had finished, she lingered outside Scioto's stall to admire the animal. He was a beautiful mahogany bay Morgan without any white markings that she could see. And his size matched that of his master's. The horse paused to nudge her shoulder gently with his nose, and she smiled and gently patted his neck as he returned to his feed.

"He likes you."

Katherine gave a small gasp and turned around to see Daniel standing at the bottom of the stairs, a sheepish grin on his face. "I'm sorry. I really shouldn't keep doing that."

She placed her free hand on her chest. "I must admit you do have a way of sneaking up on a body."

"A necessity of war." His smile waned as he spoke, and Katherine silently chastised herself. He joined her at Scioto's stall and rubbed the horse's neck. The lamplight fell fully on his face.

"You shaved," she blurted out, and immediately felt her face turning four shades of red. She lowered the lantern slightly to dim the view of her face.

His smile returned, and he rubbed his face. "I never cared for a beard, especially during planting season. Gets too hot."

"Oh." She swallowed and searched for something to say, but he spoke first.

"About yesterday. . . ," he began. He stopped for a moment, and Katherine held her breath. He was going to bring up her brazen behavior, she was sure of it. She was shocked when he apologized. "I'm sorry for the way I behaved yesterday after Mr. Carr and Mr. O'Conner left. I hope I didn't upset you and Aunt Mary."

"Oh, th–that's quite all right, Major Kirby," she stammered. She was relieved when a cow lowed from her pen. "I really should be getting to the milking."

"I'll help. I've been up for a while now. Seen to the sheep and the swine."

"I hope you slept well, Major Kirby," Katherine said as they made their way toward the row of sweet-faced Jersey cows. "I'm terribly sorry you had to sleep in a drafty old shed."

"I wasn't in a shed." A small smile crossed his handsome face. "And actually, it was the best night's sleep I've had in a long while."

"Then where on earth did you sleep?" Her gaze wandered curiously to the spare stall next to Scioto.

He chuckled. "I didn't sleep there either. Come here, and I'll show you."

Katherine followed him to the area that separated the horses and cows where a straw mow and the barn's root cellar were situated. He stepped inside the cellar, and she saw that one of the bins had been pushed off to the side to reveal a trap door. Daniel pulled on the door's iron ring and took the lantern from Katherine. He lowered it down the hole far enough for her to see a small room, complete with a cot and a small shelf.

"You cannot mean to tell me you slept down there last night, Major

Kirby!" she exclaimed. "All shut up in a hole in the ground?"

He raised the lantern out of the trap door and shut it. "I left the door open while I slept," he reassured her. "I only shut it this morning so no one takes a bad fall."

Katherine's brows knit together. "If I had known this was where you intended to sleep. . ."

"It wouldn't have made a difference." His eyes held a gentle firmness, and the light from the lantern highlighted their soft green depths.

She bit her lip and looked back down toward the door, glad for the dim light. "What is it doing here in the barn?" When he didn't answer right away, she turned to see him looking sober. "I'm so sorry. Perhaps it's none of my business."

"No, it's not a secret. Not anymore." He paused. "My family's farm used to be a stop on the Underground Railroad."

Katherine's eyes widened and her heart began to pound hopefully. "Can I ask. . . Was there ever a young woman named Chloe here? She escaped during the summer of 1860."

"No." Daniel stepped out of the root cellar, and she followed hesitantly, startled at the gruffness in his voice. He stopped by the cows' stalls and after hanging up the lantern, picked up one of the milking stools that sat nearby. "By then it was just a hole in the ground." He walked into a stall and sat down. "Time we started the milking."

∞

In the silence that followed, Daniel could feel Katherine's discomfort. As she quietly settled down to work in the stall next to his, he regretted being so abrupt. She seemed nervous enough around him already, and this surely wouldn't help. After all, she hadn't asked him anything anyone else wouldn't have asked. But his foolish betrayal of a runaway slave when he was ten was still a sore spot for him. *It wasn't her fault my emotions got the better of me back then.*

Within a few minutes, the urge to apologize was overwhelming. He was about to speak when her soft voice carried over from the next stall.

"Chloe was one of my father's slaves. She and I were the same age, and we grew up together. Her mother was a house servant, so she was always nearby. Her father had been sold off not long after she was born. I had never seen slaves as anything other than automatons doing our housework, planting our fields, making us money." She paused briefly. "I had even come to see Chloe that way. Mary taught me they were people, no different than I, with hopes and dreams and feelings and faith. I saw then how horribly wrong slavery was, and I so wanted to do something. Your aunt was teaching her slaves to read. Secretly of course. Back then it was against the law. So I began to teach Chloe how to read. Mary told me not to, and I should have listened. When my father found out. . ."

Her voice caught, and Daniel rose from his stool and looked over into the next stall.

The young woman sat there small and shrunken, holding a hand to her face, the milking only half done. The cow twitched her with her tail, but she didn't notice. "My father whipped her and sold her off." He could see the tracks her tears had made in the soft light. "I heard she escaped, but I never found out anything more." She stopped and, looking away, began to wipe at her face. "Do excuse me, Major Kirby."

He dug into his pocket and handed her his handkerchief. "I was ten. Some boys were teasing me, and I blurted out our secret. The man we had in hiding at the time almost didn't get away. Fortunately, the law never found the hiding place, or else my father would have been fined and possibly hauled off to jail. We couldn't take in any more runaways after that. The risk was too great for them and us."

Her now-dry eyes were filled with compassion as she looked up at him.

"I never found out what happened to him either." He and Pa had asked after the man for months afterward, as discreetly as they could. He hadn't been seen anywhere else in the township, and they had been unable to go ask anyone further north. It had been harvesttime and all their attention had been needed at the farm. Daniel had resumed the search himself when he was at Ohio Wesleyan, but the man had never given them his name.

Thoughts of his alma mater gave him an idea. "You said Chloe escaped in 1860?" he asked Katherine tentatively.

"Yes," she said hopefully. "In June. She was sold to a man in North Carolina."

"Not many slaves from there made it up our way." Since the Appalachian Mountains lay between the Carolinas and Ohio, most runaways from those states generally trekked through Virginia and Maryland into eastern Pennsylvania and up into New England. "A friend of mine from the army might be able to help. I'll write to him and see what I can find out." Joshua Chamberlain knew several people who were active in abolitionist activities, including Harriet Beecher Stowe.

"That's very kind of you, Major Kirby, to go to so much trouble."

Daniel smiled at her continued formality. "I'm no longer in the army," he said. "And before you say it, Mr. Kirby was my pa. I would really rather you called me Daniel."

Her kaleidoscope eyes regarded him shyly. "Then perhaps you should call me Katherine."

Chapter 8

Daniel tugged at his uniform as he sat in church with his aunt and Katherine later that morning. He hadn't really wanted to wear the outfit and draw attention to himself, but his Sunday best did not fit him quite right. Poor food and occasional illness during the war had thinned him a bit. Well, home cooking and farmwork would soon cure him.

Thoughts of plowing and planting poked annoyingly at his thoughts, and he returned his attention to Reverend Warren's sermon. The minister was extolling President Lincoln's virtues and exhorting the body to have faith in these uncertain times. When he quoted Proverbs 3, verses 5 through 6, Daniel rolled the verses over and over in his mind. *"Trust in the Lord with all thine heart; and lean not unto thine own understanding. In all thy ways acknowledge him, and he shall direct thy paths."*

His eyes strayed to the wooden cross hanging on the wall behind the pulpit. He couldn't understand the path the Lord was having him take. He had been so sure being a professor was the role he was to play in God's will. And now he was suddenly supposed to farm? Had he missed something? Had his desire to learn and his love for books clouded his judgment? After all, his preference for books had nothing to do with his abilities as a farmer. He was, in fact, a decent farmer. Not as good as his pa or Jonah, but he could easily make a good living at it. Perhaps that fact, Pa's opposition to his schooling, and his now owning the entire farm was God's way of telling him something he hadn't really wanted to hear.

The reverend concluded his lesson, and the body rose to sing a closing song.

Daniel turned slightly to see if Adele Stephens and her son were still back in the second-to-last pew. They were. Daniel was determined to speak to Adele about Nate and the land she had given back to Elijah

Carr. Happily, Carr did not attend church in Ostrander. In fact, as far as Daniel knew, he didn't attend a church at all.

When the song concluded, he turned and saw Adele and Jacob had disappeared. He frowned and started to move out of the pew when he was stopped by Reverend Warren and his wife.

"It's good to see you, Daniel," the older man said as he shook his hand.

"Thank you, sir." Daniel nodded to Mrs. Warren. "Ma'am."

"We're so sorry about your dear mother," the gentle lady said.

"Thank you. Sir, when things are more settled, I intend to go back down to Virginia and bring Toby's body back home."

"Of course. We'll have a special service for him."

"It's so good to have you back safe," Mrs. Warren said. "If you'll excuse me." She walked over to Mary, who was already surrounded by several ladies.

Daniel glanced back toward the door.

"Are you looking for someone in particular?" the reverend asked.

"Yes, Adele Stephens. She was here for services, but I don't see her and Jacob now."

"Ah yes, she seems to be slipping out early lately." Daniel noticed the man's gaze rest briefly on Katherine, who was standing quietly off to one side. His eyes turned toward the window. "Why, there she is now, climbing into her buggy."

Daniel saw she was just settling into her seat next to her son and, excusing himself, hurried outside. He rushed around the corner to where the young widow was just taking up the reins. "Adele!"

Adele and her son looked back. The young boy smiled and waved at Daniel, but his mother quickly turned around and directed her horse onto the dirt road.

Daniel watched them ride off. He couldn't blame her really. It had to be hard for Adele to see him—the man who had failed to rescue her husband. Being an honest man, Daniel had carefully, yet tactfully, explained Nate's death. He had known Adele; she would have wanted to know. *I should have gone back for him.* But even as the thought crossed his mind, the horrible image of Nate being mowed down by Confederate bullets reminded him he would only have died with his friend, leaving the surviving men to face possible recapture.

Out of the corner of his eye, he caught sight of the shoulder decorations on his coat, which indicated his rank. They had made him a major for saving those men. He'd rather have Nate alive and still been a captain. He turned to find Katherine standing a little ways behind him.

"Do you know Mrs. Stephens well?" she asked.

He walked over to her, trying to read the expression on her face. "Yes, her husband was under my command in the war."

"Oh."

She looked as if she wanted to say more, but Ruth Decker came up at that moment. Smiling, she gave him a hug. "Daniel, I'm so glad you're home!"

"Thank you, Mrs. Decker," he replied.

"I saw poor Mary this morning. Said she sprained her ankle. Do you need me or May to come out and help tend to her?"

He looked at her in surprise. "Thank you, but Miss Wallace has been doing a fine job." He glanced over at Katherine, whose eyes were lowered.

Ruth glanced at her with pursed lips. "Oh yes," she replied. "I forgot about your guest." She sidled over to Katherine. "I imagine with the war nearly over, you'll be leaving us soon. Won't that be a shame?"

Daniel frowned at the clear note of sarcasm in the woman's voice. He found it hard to believe Ruth Decker had been one of his mother's oldest friends.

He watched Katherine lift her eyes to the woman and calmly answer her. "I'm afraid I have no more family to return to, Mrs. Decker. Mrs. O'Neal assured me I could stay with her as long as I wanted."

"Well, Mary is the picture of hospitality, but I'm sure you must have misunderstood," Ruth said pointedly. "Surely you can't mean to say you have no one you could live with. I mean, you can't keep burdening Mary and Daniel. They run a farm, not a hotel."

Katherine looked away with a clenched jaw and reddening cheeks.

Enough was enough. "You're quite right, Mrs. Decker, we are running a farm," Daniel said. "And Miss Wallace has been a great help. She was taking care of things all by herself after Aunt Mary sprained her ankle. I've never seen the farm look better."

"Oh...well...." The woman faltered. She turned to see her daughter helping Mary down the church steps. "May, how considerate of you." Giving Katherine a reproving glance, she walked over to them.

Daniel gave Katherine's elbow a squeeze, and she looked up at him gratefully. "That was very kind of you," she said. "But I only looked after the farm for a day and a half before you came home."

"And you did a great job." He smiled.

Mary was waiting at the carriage, and as they started to walk over, several people came up and offered their condolences to Daniel. He was gratified by their kind words about his mother and brothers, but he could not help but notice they simply ignored Katherine. One woman even elbowed her out of the way. First Ruth Decker, and now this? At first Katherine stood quietly off to the side, but she eventually walked over to the carriage where Mary was still waiting. It was several more minutes before he was able to join them.

He glanced over at Katherine several times on the way home. She acted as if nothing was wrong, but she was very quiet during lunch and then after helping Mary into the parlor, decided to walk down to the creek.

He joined his aunt in the parlor. After several attempts to read a psalm or two, he looked up to find Mary asleep in the high-backed easy chair, her ankle propped up on a settee. He smiled nostalgically. Dorothy Kirby had always insisted on comfortable pieces of furniture in her parlor, and that particular chair had been one of her favorites. In fact, Pa had often woken her as she sat in it on Sunday afternoons. He rose and rescued his aunt's Bible, which had been threatening to fall off her lap.

He wandered over to the window and watched the breeze gently bend the branches of the trees along the creek. His thoughts turned to services that morning, and he shook his head. He could hardly believe the behavior of the people who had been such good examples to him as he grew up. He couldn't recall a time when new people had not been made to feel welcome. When Adele and her brother, Erich, had come to Ostrander, the church people had gone out of their way to help them settle in. They had paid no mind to the newcomers' German accents. But apparently Southern accents were a different issue altogether. He ran a hand through his hair. He was sick of hate and anger. Coming home should have relieved him of that.

The little mantel clock rang the hour. Katherine had been gone for a while now. He frowned. He found he didn't like the idea of her being down by the creek all by herself, especially if she was upset.

In spite of how forward it was, the way she'd held his hand yesterday had been endearing. And just at the moment he needed to be reminded of life, not death.

He looked out the window toward the creek. He had a good idea of where she went—the place where he and his brothers had always gone fishing. Daniel glanced over at Mary, who was still asleep, and quietly left the house, making his way out to the barn. There wasn't much hope of catching anything this time of day, but drowning a few worms was just the excuse he needed to make sure Katherine was all right.

∽

It had been all Katherine could do to make it home from services and through lunch. As soon as she had helped settle Mary into her chair, she made her way across the road to the creek. Pushing her way through the trees, she sank down next to a large mossy rock. Without thinking, she reached for her scar as her chin began to quiver. She had thought by this time at least one or two people would have warmed up to her. But folks were as cold as ever, even more so after what had happened to the president.

Ruth Decker's snide comments echoed loudly in her ears, but her breaking point was Adele Stephens. Katherine had dared a glance back toward her and her son when services had ended. The young widow had such an empty, bitter look on her face that Katherine could now not erase the image from her mind. She leaned over the rock and, burying her head in her arms, wept.

It wasn't supposed to be this way, Father, she prayed. *Is it me? Am I just naturally some sort of pariah?*

How long she sat there sobbing she didn't know. But when a warm hand laid itself on the middle of her back, she was still so upset she didn't resist being scooped up into strong arms and letting her head rest on a broad shoulder.

Several minutes later her tears began to ease, and a handkerchief was thrust into her hand. She looked up to see warm green eyes gazing into her own and shyly took a step back.

Daniel released her, although his hands still rested on both her fore-arms. "Are you all right?" he asked.

Katherine nodded, not trusting herself to speak.

"You're sure?" She nodded again, and he gently urged her down onto the rock he had pulled her up from. "I'm going to try to catch our dinner."

Katherine watched as he took his fishing pole and, baiting the hook with a worm from an old rusty can, cast his line out into the swirling water. The rush of the creek filled her ears and rays of sunshine poked though the green, leafy roof, dancing here and there as the wind played through the trees. She took a deep breath. The air had a wholesome, earthy scent. Sitting there taking in the rhythm of God's creation helped her bring her emotions back in order.

Daniel looked over from where he sat at the edge of the creek. "Feeling better?"

"Yes, but you must think I'm the type to cry at the drop of a hat."

He chuckled. "I have to admit I'm beginning to wonder if I should go buy more handkerchiefs."

"I'm sorry."

"Don't apologize. I'm only joking. You don't seem like the weepy type." His face grew serious. "Have people at church been behaving like that since you came here?"

Katherine hesitated. She didn't want to seem like a gossip or a snitch, but neither did she want to lie. Fingering her scar, she looked down.

She heard him give an exasperated sigh. "Katherine, I'm sorry you've been treated so poorly." He paused. "I want you to know this isn't like any of them."

"I know," she replied. "But I can't blame them for feeling the way they do. The war has been hard on everybody."

"That doesn't give them the right to treat you badly. No one should be treated like that by the body of Christ. It doesn't matter if they're from the North or the South, saved or sinner." He looked out over the creek for a moment before turning toward her once more. "I'm going to take this to Reverend Warren."

Katherine bit her lip. "Mary wanted to do the same thing weeks ago. I persuaded her not to."

"Why?" He frowned.

She looked down at her lap. "Folks already think of me as a spoiled Southern belle. A rebuke won't change their opinions of me. It will only make it worse."

"What they are doing is wrong in God's eyes." She turned to find him standing with his arms crossed and a look of gentle consternation on his face.

He was right. Even if she could talk him out of going to the reverend, she would be letting these people remain in sin.

"Whosoever doeth not righteousness is not of God, neither he that loveth not his brother." The verse rang in her head. *But Father, it will only make matters worse,* she prayed desperately. But the Lord's call was clear. And in her heart she knew He knew what was best. She looked at Daniel miserably and nodded.

He crouched down in front of her. "Don't look so worried," he said with a small half smile. "Trust God to work it out."

An hour later, she, Daniel, Mary, and Reverend Warren were seated in the parlor discussing the situation. Katherine looked at the clergyman warily as he took in all that Daniel had said. He was an older gentleman, slender with round wire-rim glasses and light brown hair. His generous sideburns were streaked with gray. He looked like a strict headmaster of a boarding school, but Daniel had told her Paul and Minnie Warren were two of the kindest people he knew. She looked away. If that were true, she had yet to experience it.

"Daniel, Mary," the man finally said, and Katherine looked at the reverend once more. "You know how greatly your family is respected, not only in the church but in this community."

They both nodded.

"But I have to question your judgment in bringing Miss Wallace here."

Katherine felt her face burn.

Mary pursed her lips.

Daniel's face hardened. "Excuse me, Reverend," he said, his voice surprisingly calm, "but I can't quite believe what I'm hearing. The Word clearly states—"

"I'm not refuting the many scriptures you brought to my attention," he declared with a raised hand. "I just don't think you realize how deeply the war has affected the church and the community." He gave both of them a firm and steady gaze. "The members of Mill Creek Church were very proud to have had so many of its young men go off to fight. But over half of those young men will never return. It has hardened many a heart. And now you're asking them to accept someone who represents the cause of all this."

"You know as well as I do this war was caused by the way the North reacted to things just as much as anything the South did," Daniel retorted. "Need I mention Bleeding Kansas?"

Katherine remembered her father speaking of the bloody battles between antislavery and proslavery settlers as they fought to decide if Kansas would be a free state or a slave state.

"I know that. I only mean for you to understand that it may take a very long time for them to come to accept Miss Wallace, if they do at all."

"If they do at all?" Mary cried. "You can't be serious."

"You haven't been here, Mary. These aren't the same people you and John said good-bye to. Adele Stephens hasn't been the same since Nate passed, and she's been slipping out early ever since Miss Wallace began attending."

Mary, who sat next to Katherine on the sofa, grasped her friend's hand tightly in both of her own. Katherine was too stunned and saddened by the man's words to notice.

Reverend Warren rose.

"So you won't do anything about this?" Daniel's voice was hard as he also stood to face the reverend.

The man's face was strained as he put a hand on the younger man's shoulder. "I never said that. I will address the congregation as gently as the Lord will enable me." He turned to look at Katherine. "Miss Wallace, I can tell you are a sister in Christ, and I am sorry if Minnie and I have hurt you in any way." His face grew longer as he continued. "You see, my nephew, Andrew, was wounded in the war, and although his injuries healed, his mind never did. My brother is talking of taking him to an asylum."

"Paul, I'm so sorry," Mary breathed.

"We'll keep him in our prayers, Reverend," Daniel said quietly. "Thank you for coming." He left to walk the clergyman to his horse.

Katherine turned to Mary. "Was the reverend close to his nephew?"

"Andrew was planning on following his uncle into the ministry." Mary's eyes glistened.

Daniel slowly walked into the room and sank down into a chair. "I had no idea."

"Your mother never wrote a word about Andrew or how bad the church's losses were," his aunt murmured.

"You know how Ma was. She hated giving anyone bad news." Daniel ran a hand through his hair, and a heavy silence settled over the room.

Katherine looked at Mary and then Daniel. A thought had been growing on her heart for some time now, and she suspected the idea was not far from their thoughts as well. "I shouldn't have come," she said softly.

They stared at her.

"I'll go back to South Carolina as soon as it can be arranged."

Chapter 9

Daniel started at her words and watched his aunt pale.

"No!" Her voice rang out. "I won't have it!"

"Mary, it's for the best." Daniel could tell by Katherine's eyes she wasn't as resolute as she sounded. He tried to catch her gaze, but she looked down at her lap. "I know where Aunt Ada is, and if I apologize. . ."

"No!" Mary repeated and stomped the floor with her good foot. "I won't have you going back to a family whose only value you are to them is who you marry." Her eyes snapped, but her voice took on a gentler tone as she continued. "And I won't have you returning to people who would do this to you." His aunt pointed to the scar along Katherine's jawline.

He'd noticed it before but had assumed it was the result of a childhood injury. Jagged and ugly, it looked entirely out of place on her sweet face. A family member had done that to her?

She glanced at him and raised her hand to cover the blemish.

His aunt grasped Katherine's hand and pulled it away from her face. "This is your home now," she said firmly. "I won't hear of you leaving."

"Neither will I," Daniel declared. If that was how her family treated such a sweet-natured girl, there was no way he would let her return to them.

Katherine frowned and looked at Mary. "But what about the church and everyone in town?"

"God can soften even the hardest heart." His aunt smiled. "We'll pray for them. Right now if you like."

At Katherine's nod, they joined hands and Daniel led them in prayer, asking the Lord to bind up the wounds of war and heal people's hearts.

"Thank you, Daniel," Mary said. "It's time we started supper." Grasping her crutch, she rose and made her way toward the kitchen.

Katherine rose to follow her, but Daniel stood and laid a gentle hand on her arm. "How did you get that scar?"

She reached up and laid her fingers against her scar before she answered. "I was trying to protect Chloe from my father's whip. He struck me, and his signet ring caught the edge of my jaw."

"I'm sorry. And I'm sorry Reverend Warren's visit wasn't more encouraging."

Katherine bit her lip. "I wasn't entirely surprised. People have been through a lot over the past four years." A shy look passed over her face. "Thank you for praying with me."

"We can pray every evening if you'd like," he offered.

She smiled gently. "I'd like that."

Feeling a little foolish, he watched as she went into the kitchen. In his mind, he had hoped the peace that had begun at Appomattox would quickly spread to every heart in the Union. But the wounds of war ran deeper than he had imagined. He hadn't realized how being away for four years had made him so out of touch with those back home.

Bits of Mary and Katherine's conversation floated in from the kitchen.

Real peace needs to begin somewhere. As far as Katherine was concerned, he resolved to be an example to those around him and go out of his way to make sure she always felt welcome in his home.

∞

A few days later, Katherine and Daniel were going about planting the kitchen garden next to the house. Over the past couple of days, Daniel had been plowing the fields set aside for corn and oats, but as he had told Katherine and Mary at dinner last night, the newly turned earth needed to dry out before he harrowed. "If nothing else, the kitchen garden can get planted," he'd said, running a frustrated hand through his hair.

Planting was going to be a problem. Katherine and Mary were more than willing to help, but with Mary's foot still on the mend and Katherine so inexperienced, he would be lucky to get everything done on time. He would have hired some farmhands, but with so many young men still in the army, help was in short supply. And those few who were available had already been hired out until the fall.

A good many of them had been snatched up by Elijah Carr. *He's still hoping to get the farm one way or another,* Daniel thought as he fetched the gardening tools from the shed connected to the summer kitchen.

His face must have betrayed the anger he felt, because Katherine stared at him as they met on the way to the garden. Her kaleidoscope eyes were large with surprise. "Is everything all right?" she asked tentatively.

"I'm sorry. I was thinking about Elijah Carr."

Her dainty face grew thoughtful. "I've often wondered about him." They walked through the garden gate and began a row of carrots. "Has he always been. . . ?"

"Angry, greedy, and hateful?"

"Well. . .yes."

Daniel straightened from covering up the seeds she was dropping and leaned against the hoe. "Elijah Carr's brother and his family moved to the Kansas Territory just when everything was beginning to heat up. He was antislavery and got into a fight with some proslavery men. He was shot to death, and his wife and son were left homeless when the men burned their house down."

"What happened to them?"

"Don't know. Carr doesn't talk about them, and no one's ever asked."

A wave of compassion washed over Katherine's face. "That poor, poor man," she breathed. "No wonder. We should keep him in our prayers."

Daniel stared at her. His mother had always told him and his brothers to pray for Carr, to take his pain into consideration and not hold his actions against him. But her words had fallen on deaf ears. Elijah Carr's many attempts over the years to get the farm had hardened their hearts.

Seeing the look on his face, Katherine paused. "I'm sorry," she said. "If you don't want—"

"No, I'm just ashamed of myself," he said softly. "I should have the same compassion for Carr as you do."

"Oh Daniel," Katherine said gently, "he's always been a thorn in your family's side. It's only natural—"

"Exactly. Only natural. We're called to be like Christ. We're not called to give in to our sinful natures. Keep me in your prayers, too. Pray that I can see the man instead of the sin, as you can."

Katherine blushed and quickly returned to dropping seeds in the soft earth.

Over the past week, she'd slowly become comfortable around him, but she still never failed to blush furiously whenever he paid her a compliment. From what he'd learned about her family, he imagined compliments had been few and far between. She didn't talk about them very often, but his aunt had told him a great deal.

He shook his head. And he thought *he* had been a black sheep! He watched as she dropped another seed in the ground. From what his aunt had told him, she'd learned a lot since coming north. And not just about housekeeping and farming. Since her arrival, she had read a number of the books in his collection and had been very happy to talk with him about what she'd read. She'd attended one of the finest schools the South had to offer, but her father had only allowed her enough education to make sure she would make someone a charming wife. Daniel could hardly imagine her being the matron of a plantation, not with her intellect and hatred of slavery. *She deserves a much different life than that,* he thought.

Katherine was now waiting for him at the end of the row, looking toward the barnyards where the cows and horses grazed. He joined her, and she turned and shyly smiled at him. Her family may not have appreciated her, but he certainly did. As he looked into her unique eyes, he could certainly understand how Thomas had come to care for her.

The sound of a buggy drew their attention to the drive. Mary stepped out the front door as it drew to a halt. A slender older gentleman with a Vandyke beard and wearing a frock suit climbed out. He removed his tall beaver-skin hat, and Daniel immediately recognized James Harris, his old professor from Ohio Wesleyan.

"Professor Harris," Daniel said as he walked over. He wiped his hands on his handkerchief before extending his hand, wishing he was a good deal less dusty. "This is a pleasant surprise."

The older man smiled broadly and shook his hand vigorously. "Daniel, it's very good to see you home safe." He peered over Daniel's shoulder to look at Mary and give her a gentle smile. "Mary. . . ," he began and then seemed to remember propriety. "Do excuse me. Mrs. O'Neal, how good to see you."

"James," Mary half scolded, "you've been too close a friend of our family to be formal." She limped over and gave the professor a warm embrace.

Daniel did not fail to notice the slightly reddened cheeks of the old bachelor as they parted. "I heard about both your losses," the professor said. "I'm terribly sorry."

"Thank you," Mary replied quietly. "How is your nephew?"

As they spoke, Daniel turned and found Katherine standing off to the side. He saw the apprehension on her face and smiled reassuringly as he walked her over to his old instructor.

"Professor Harris, may I introduce another good friend of our family, Miss Katherine Wallace. Katherine, this is Professor James Harris."

"How do you do, Professor?" Katherine murmured.

"Miss Wallace, it is very good to meet you," the gentleman said with a tip of his hat. "How nice to hear a Southern accent again. I taught at a Southern university before I came back home to Ohio Wesleyan. What part of the South do you hail from?"

Daniel could not help but smile at the look of surprise on Katherine's face. She'd been so used to people snubbing her as soon as they heard her voice. It was good to see her taken so off guard by his professor's kind comments.

"Why, South Carolina, sir," Katherine said. She paused as a small smile gradually appeared. "On the edge of Lexington County near the Congaree."

"Katherine was our neighbor, James." Mary smiled, grasping her friend by the hand.

"And what a charming neighbor she must have been." The professor's smile faded, however, and he looked at Daniel. "You've heard about the president, of course."

He nodded. "Is there any more news? I won't get to Ostrander until the day after tomorrow."

"Not about Booth, but they have announced there will be a funeral train traveling from Washington, DC to Springfield. Mrs. Lincoln insisted he be laid to rest in Illinois. Our own Governor Brough and John Garrett of the Baltimore and Ohio Railroad were put in charge of organizing the trip." He reached over and laid his hand on Daniel's shoulder. "They say he'll lie in state in several cities along the route they've arranged. Columbus is one of those cities."

Daniel felt his mouth go dry. "When?"

"A week from this Saturday, the twenty-ninth." The professor gave his shoulder a squeeze. "I remembered how you and some other students went down to meet the president when he passed through before his first inauguration. I thought you would want to know."

Daniel looked down. More than anything he wanted to say good-bye to his president but. . . "I'm very glad you came to tell me, sir," he said, looking up at the professor. "But I can't afford to take even a day away from the planting."

Professor Harris looked at him soberly. "The board got the letter you sent with Mr. O'Conner," he said.

Daniel nodded. His parents' lawyer had been good enough to deliver his letter of resignation to the university after his visit to the farm with Elijah Carr.

"I took the liberty of speaking to him. He said you heard about our offer. I had hoped—"

"I'm sorry, sir. I can't," Daniel replied, looking away.

The professor looked at his former student sadly, and Daniel hoped Dr. Harris wasn't going to try to change his mind. Turning down the university's offer was hard enough. He was relieved when his mentor simply extended his hand.

"It was very good to see you again," the professor said. He then nodded to Katherine and Mary. "Miss Wallace, Mary."

As the professor's buggy rolled down the road, Daniel walked down the drive and across the dirt road. He soon found himself at the bank of Mill Creek. He stood there for several minutes before picking up a large stone and heaving it into the rushing water.

"I don't suppose You're going to tell me why, are You?" he prayed aloud.

He sat down on a low rock near the creek bank and ran his hands through his hair. The urge to ride over to Elijah Carr's farm and accept the man's offer to buy the farm was so overwhelming he actually stood up.

A professor! They want to make me a professor, Father!

But in spite of his plea, he felt the Spirit close the door on his dream. He quickly walked over to a solid buckeye tree and plowed his fist into the rough bark.

A small gasp caused him to turn around. Katherine stood just inside the shadow of the trees, her eyes wide and a hand to her mouth. She rushed over and looked at his hand.

The skin on his knuckles had broken and blood oozed from the wounds. She looked up at him, her small brow furrowed, and he immediately felt sheepish. He gently pulled his hand from hers and walked over to the creek. Kneeling down, he washed his hand off and sat back down on the rock, avoiding her eyes. He was ashamed that he had lost his temper and that Katherine, of all people, had witnessed it.

She knelt down beside him, her simple work dress billowing out around her, and grasped his hand to take another look at it. "This will need tending to," she said. Her gentle voice didn't hold even a hint of reproach. "We should cover it up in the meantime. Where's your handkerchief? Mine's too small."

Daniel pulled it from his back pocket and looked away. He felt her gentle hands wrap up his wound and felt even more like a heel. "Thank you," he murmured when she was done. She released his hand, but he grasped her fingers and squeezed them. "I'm sorry you saw that," he said, finally daring to look at her.

Her face was soft, and an understanding smile graced her face. "It's all right."

He released her hand and looked at the makeshift bandage on his own. "Professor Harris was going to offer me a position as a professor at Ohio Wesleyan."

"I gathered as much."

"You're wondering why I don't just sell out and accept it, aren't you?"

"Mary told me your father was bound and determined you become a farmer. She thinks since your brothers are gone you're keeping the land out of respect for him."

"I would sell this farm in a heartbeat to Carr or anyone else who would give me a fair price for it, but. . ."

"The Lord is telling you otherwise," she finished.

Daniel stared at her, and she blushed and looked out toward the creek.

"You're such a godly man, I can only imagine the reason you're doing this is because God is guiding you."

Daniel laughed hollowly. "If I'm such a godly man, why was I about to ride over to Elijah Carr's and accept his offer?"

"You wouldn't have."

He threw a pebble into the creek. "You're right." They sat there for a moment or two watching the creek swirl by.

"If your pa wanted you to be a farmer, then how did you come to be at Ohio Wesleyan?" Katherine asked tentatively.

"Pa died of a heart attack when I was fourteen. After he died, Ma insisted I sell my share of the farm to Jonah and go. She was the one who understood me. Only Jonah wouldn't take it."

"Why?"

"He felt Ma and I were betraying Pa."

Daniel remembered how angry his brother had been. When his first term at Ohio Wesleyan was over, he'd stayed in Delaware with Uncle John and Aunt Mary instead of going home. They had owned and run a mercantile there before his uncle inherited the plantation.

"He forgave Ma eventually, but he and I never really reconciled."

He looked over at Katherine to see her beautiful eyes large with sympathy. He found their speckled depths comforting, and he allowed himself to become lost in them for a minute or two. They reminded him of the way the trees looked along the creek in the early fall.

Chapter 10

Katherine blushed and looked down at her lap, wondering why he would pay so close attention to her bizarre eyes. She had always thought of them as her worst feature. Her father had always called them "perpetually confused" since they weren't really one color or another.

She could feel Daniel's gaze still on her, and a warm feeling grew in her chest. Why did he give her so much of his attention anyway? He couldn't possibly think her *that* interesting. Could he? She had to admit she enjoyed their evening conversations. They reminded her of the letters she and Thomas had exchanged while she was away at school.

Thomas. She would always miss him, always care for him. But what she had felt for Mary's son was nothing compared to what she was now beginning to feel for her nephew. How could she help it? He was kind, a very godly man. . .*and far too handsome for a drab little nothing like me. He can't possibly think of me as anything more than a friend.*

Glancing up, she saw he was now looking out across the creek. She felt her breath catch as she took in his handsome features.

Closing her eyes, she bit her lip. *Oh Father, please take these feelings from me. I know I once dreamed of loving and being loved, but it was never anything more than a dream.*

"Are you all right?"

Katherine started and looked at Daniel. The look of worry in his green eyes caused her heart to pound so hard she was afraid he'd hear it. "I–I'm fine. Why do you ask?"

He reached over and pulled her hand away from her jaw. She hadn't even realized it had strayed there. "Because you only do that when something is bothering you," he said, his fingers curling around hers.

Coherent thought refused to form in her mind, and she closed her eyes. "I. . ."

Suddenly harsh shouts came from the direction of the farm, and Katherine and Daniel immediately jumped up and raced toward the house. As they approached, Katherine could hardly believe the scene being played out on the Kirbys' front porch.

Elijah Carr stood towering over Mary, a switch in his hand. She was glaring at the man with young Jacob Stephens standing just behind her.

Katherine gasped as Daniel forced his way between his aunt and Carr, anger hardening his face. "What's going on here?" His voice was surprisingly calm.

"Nothing that concerns you, Kirby," Carr growled. "If you and Mary just step aside, I'll deal with this vandal here myself."

"I didn't do anything," the young boy cried out. "I just wanted to see my home again. Those windows were broken when I got there."

"It ain't your home. That's my legal property."

"No, it's not. You stole it from me and my ma after the Rebs killed Pa."

"You just shut your mouth before I tan your hide."

"Enough!" Daniel hadn't shouted, but his voice was so rough with anger Katherine jumped. With one swift movement, he grabbed the switch out of Carr's hands. Snapping it in half, he tossed it away. "As long as Jacob is on *my* property, you won't lay a hand on him."

"He was trespassin' and broke out the windows of that house his pa built," Carr said. "I—"

"Whatever he's done, send me the bill and I'll pay for it." Daniel glanced back at the boy. "He can pay back what he owes working for me."

"Tore up a couple rows of corn going after him."

Daniel glared at him for a second before going out back to the shed. He returned with a small cloth bag of seed corn, which he all but threw at Carr. "I'm sure that will cover your loss. Now get off my property."

Carr walked away from the porch and down the drive, glaring at Katherine as he went.

She ignored him and rushed over to Mary. "Are you all right?"

"I'm just fine," Mary said calmly. "But I'm afraid Jacob got a taste of that switch."

Katherine looked down to see an ugly red welt on the young boy's hand. "Oh, you poor thing!" As Mary stepped aside, Katherine knelt down and gently lifted Jacob's hand to look at it. "Please let me tend to this for you."

The boy looked at her in wonder. "Are you really a Johnny Reb?"

"No," Daniel said sternly. "She's the kind young woman who's going to bandage up your hand just as soon as you apologize to her and tell me what happened."

Shamefaced, the young boy looked at Katherine. "Sorry, ma'am." He turned to Daniel defensively. "I just wanted to see our old house. Mr. Carr found me there and chased me because he thought I was throwing rocks at the windows. But I didn't do anything. I just wanted to look. The windows were busted when I got there."

"Why were you trespassing on Mr. Carr's land?"

Jacob shuffled his feet, his brown eyes cast downward. "Sometimes I forget what Pa looked like. When I go back to our old house, I remember."

Katherine rose and bit her lip, trying not to choke on the sudden onset of tears and guilt. Her hand itched to touch her scar, but she clasped them together tightly against her waist. *Boys from South Carolina made this child fatherless.* Then another stinging thought crossed her mind. *What if it had been someone under her father's command? Or Charles's?*

Daniel reached over and rested his hand on the top of the boy's dark mop of hair. "It's all right, Jake. I understand. I know your ma well enough to know she wouldn't raise you to do a thing like that." His voice had lost its stern tone, and he looked at Katherine. "I'll go on with the garden while you fix him up. Send him on out when you're done."

Jacob looked up hopefully. "You mean it? I'm going to be working here?"

Daniel raised his eyebrows. "You do understand this isn't going to be easy or fun?"

"I know, Mr. Kirby." Jacob looked at him as seriously as an eight-year-old could look. "There's no school since everybody's planting, and I'm tired of wandering around town. I want to be a farmer like my pa."

Katherine watched a wave of guilt pass over Daniel's face. "You can work here so long as it's all right with your ma."

A huge smile lit up the youngster's face, and he looked at Katherine and Mary.

Katherine mustered up a smile. "I believe there might be some peppermint candy somewhere about the house. Isn't that so, Mary?"

"Yes." Her friend smiled. "Why don't we go take a look?"

As she went to follow Mary and the excited young boy went into the house, Daniel grasped Katherine's hand. "I almost forgot about my hand," he explained and then flashed an impish grin. "I like peppermint, too."

"Well, I suppose. As long as you behave." Katherine found herself unable to resist playing along, but she quickly reminded herself friendship was all there could ever be between them. *Handsome men like Daniel Kirby don't fall for women as plain as me.*

∞

Daniel was hitching the team up the next morning as he waited for Jacob to arrive. He hoped Adele would let the boy work in spite of Katherine's presence. And his. After all, he had failed to protect the life of her husband, and now he was asking her to trust him with Jacob on a daily basis. Farming wasn't the same as going off to war, but it certainly had its own share of dangers.

Sweat was already beginning to form on his brow. It was going to get warm today. He looked up at the sky in frustration. He was well behind where he should have been at this point in the season.

He shook his head. Jonah wouldn't have gotten behind, even without help. His older brother had been a gifted farmer. He could make every bit of sunlight count for something.

His hand ached as he pulled on a strap, quickly reminding him of Professor Harris's visit. A prayer rose in his mind, but he bit it back. *What's the use?*

Katherine came out of the house just then and walked out to the poultry yard on the other side of the garden. Daniel watched as she stepped into the chicken coop to collect eggs. She'd seemed reserved yesterday evening in the parlor. Even Mary had commented on how quiet she'd been. She'd given the excuse she was tired and left for her room earlier than usual, before they'd had a chance to talk.

He heaved a long sigh. It was going to be a long day today with or without help. He hoped she wouldn't be too tired to talk tonight. Their conversations in the evening were a lifeline, a connection to something now lost to him. *At least He hasn't taken that away,* he thought. *At least not yet.*

He was just about to take the horses out to the fields when Jacob arrived. And he wasn't alone. The boy was walking up the drive alongside a wagon carrying three freemen, one of whom Daniel instantly recognized.

"Simon Peter!" he exclaimed as he strode over to them.

The wagon springs creaked with relief as the man climbed down. He was a sturdy, muscular man, a head or two taller than Daniel.

Unperturbed by the man's height, Daniel looked up at the man with a grin. "Are you still the tallest man in the county?"

"Sure as you're the second tallest," the man joked back and slapped Daniel on the back. "You remember my boys, Aaron and Michael?"

"I sure do," Daniel replied as the two young men climbed out of the wagon to stand next to their pa. Daniel greeted them and glanced in the back of the wagon. A plow, harrow, and other farm equipment lay in the bed. "What's all this?"

"Well, my youngest, Jeremiah, he's been working with them colts of Professor Harris's, training them and all, and he comes home yesterday and tells me the professor says you're trying to work all this land by yourself." The man's normally good-humored face frowned at Daniel. "Now why didn't you come and see me if you were having trouble?"

"Simon, you have your own fields to get done."

"Now, Daniel Aaron Kirby," Simon Peter's firm voice interrupted him. "I done know ya since you was younger than this one here." Simon Peter pointed at Jacob, who was staring up at him with saucerlike eyes. "We got a good start on our planting, and Joe and Jeremiah say they can make do. Aaron, Michael, and I are set on helpin' ya plant your crops."

His sons smiled and nodded in agreement.

"And he'd be a fool to refuse your help," Mary said as she shuffled up to them. "Simon Peter, you're a sight for sore eyes." She was lost for a moment as she and Simon embraced. "How's Celia?"

"Miss Mary, it's right good to see you, too. Celia's just fine. Her sister came up a few months back, and she's staying with us." He looked past both of them and smiled and nodded. "Hello there, ma'am."

Daniel turned to see a hesitant Katherine slowly approaching. She was clutching the egg basket so tightly, he could see the whiteness of her knuckles. He quickly realized how intimidating Simon Peter must seem to someone so small and walked over to her. "It's all right," he said quietly. "This is Simon Peter Johnson. Ma and Pa hid him when Jonah was a baby. He lives just outside of Delaware with his wife, Celia."

"Will I bother him?" she asked tentatively.

Daniel smiled at her tenderhearted nature and shook his head. "Simon Peter has been a freeman for years now, Katherine. I'm sure he'll be happy to meet you. He's a large man but a gentle one." He coaxed her closer.

Mary grabbed her arm and pulled her over to stand in front of Simon Peter. "Simon, this is a dear friend of the family," Mary said, "Miss Katherine Wallace. Katherine was my neighbor down in South Carolina."

"Oh yes. The professor said you had someone staying with you." He bent down and took her tiny hand in his huge one.

"I'm very pleased to meet you, Mr. Johnson," Katherine said softly. Daniel took note of her attempt to blunt her accent.

"Ma'am, folk just call me Simon Peter," he said. "I reckon I won't answer ta nothin' else."

"I do hope I won't make you. . .uncomfortable."

A bright white smile spread across the man's face. "Oh no, ma'am, not a bit. Celia's from down there in the Carolinas. You sound a mite like her." He looked over at Daniel. "We're ready to start when you are."

Daniel looked at the men and, regretting his earlier attitude, silently thanked God for sending him help just when he really needed it. "Aunt Mary's right. I'd be a fool to refuse help now. But I intend to pay you and your sons what's fair."

Simon Peter gave him a hesitant look. "You sure?"

"I won't take no for an answer."

"Well, all right." They smiled and shook hands.

"Wow!"

Katherine jumped at the awestruck voice at her elbow. She looked down to see Jacob still standing next to her. His eyes were glued to Simon Peter, who was striding out toward the fields with his sons and Daniel. Katherine couldn't help but giggle. "I know. He's right large, isn't he?"

"He's a giant," the boy squeaked.

"Well, he's a gentle giant," Mary declared, patting Jacob on the back. "What did your ma say about working here?"

"Ma said it was fine for me to work here for as long as Mr. Kirby needed me."

Mary cocked an eyebrow at the young man. "Did she understand why?"

"Yes, ma'am." The boy winced as he reached for his backside. "She understood all right."

Katherine chuckled along with her friend, and her heart rose hopefully. She had worried the widow wouldn't allow her son within ten feet of her. Perhaps her prayers were beginning to pay off. She smiled kindly at the boy. "You'd best be off with them, don't you think?"

"Oh yes, ma'am." Jacob ran off and called out to Daniel.

He turned toward the boy and, catching sight of Katherine, smiled.

A sharp thrill rose in her chest and she smiled back.

"Thank you for lifting such a great weight from his shoulders, Father," Mary prayed aloud.

"Amen," Katherine finished softly, still smiling. Suddenly remembering herself, she shook her head. *Katherine Wallace, if you keep up this foolishness, you'll deserve every bit of what's coming to you.*

She heard Mary chuckle and turned to look at her friend. "Jacob's a funny little thing," she said.

"He is, but that's not what amuses me," the older woman replied as they walked in the house and headed toward the kitchen.

Katherine set the basket of eggs down on the worktable. "What is it then?"

"You and my nephew."

Katherine nearly dropped the eggs she and Mary were transferring from the basket to a large bowl. "What on earth do you mean?"

"You're a fool if you don't see how he looks at you."

"I...haven't noticed," she replied evasively.

"Well I have, and he has the same look on his face as Thomas did whenever he got a letter from you."

"Mary," Katherine scolded, "he does nothing of the kind." She continued to stack eggs in the bowl for another moment or two. "Even if he does, why would he?"

She heard her friend give an exasperated sigh. "Father, forgive me, but I would have liked to tell your family a thing or two."

Katherine glanced up to see a pleading look in Mary's eyes.

"Katherine, we've been over this before. When are you going to realize just how pretty you are?"

"When the mirror finally agrees with you," Katherine said gently. Before Mary could get another word in, she grabbed the bowl of eggs and took them to the root cellar out next to the house. She set the eggs on one of the many shelves and pulled down several jars of vegetables to take back in for lunch.

Sometimes Mary was too kind for her own good. Pretty is the very last word she would choose to describe herself. *Short, eyes that aren't one color or another, and a head of hair that can't decide if it's red or brown—pretty is the last thing I am,* she thought. Oh, Thomas hadn't seemed to mind her lack of beauty, but then they hadn't actually met face-to-face very often at all. And as far as Daniel was concerned, clearly Mary was only seeing what she wanted to see.

Katherine shut the door to the root cellar and leaned against it as she juggled the jars in her arms. As much as she enjoyed discussing the books she'd been reading with Daniel, it had to stop. If it didn't, she would only end up with a very broken heart. She'd realized it yesterday evening and deliberately gone to bed early.

"Hope deferred maketh the heart sick," she quoted to herself.

Chapter 11

It was easy to keep her resolve that evening. As long as the planting was going on, Simon Peter and his sons were staying at the farm during the week, sleeping in the barn. What had been going on with the Johnsons dominated the conversation in the parlor after supper.

"Are you and your family still attending the church in Africa?" Daniel asked.

The dumbfounded look on Katherine's face made Simon Peter laugh heartily. He then explained how, a year or so before the war, a group of slaves had made their way to Ohio after being freed in North Carolina. They eventually came to Westerville, a virulent antislavery community south of Delaware, and the citizens invited them to stay in some abandoned cabins north of town. They stayed and prospered, prompting one of the few proslavery farmers in the area to label the town "Africa." The new community proudly accepted the name.

Unfortunately for Katherine's plan, Simon Peter and his sons left late Saturday afternoon so they could spend Sunday with their family. Katherine once again managed to get by that evening with the excuse she was tired, but she knew she'd need to come up with something different or Mary would suspect she was getting sick.

However, making up excuses was the furthest from her mind as they went to services Sunday morning. Reverend Warren had promised to speak to the body this morning. She fought the jitters as Daniel helped her down from the carriage.

"Are you going to be okay?" he asked.

She nodded and tried not to look directly at him. He'd had to wear his uniform again this week, and seeing him in it made it hard to breathe. She grabbed on to Mary's arm.

81

The older woman found her hand and squeezed it. "Trust Him," she whispered.

They made their way to a pew and sat down. Sadly, nothing seemed very different. Most people greeted Daniel and his aunt but ignored her. She looked around and saw hardened hearts all around her. *Father, please change these hearts by the end of the service.*

May Decker came forward and played the small piano as the reverend led them all in "Just as I Am." At the conclusion of the song, he motioned them to sit and looked soberly out over the congregation of Mill Creek Church.

"It has been only a week since the passing of our dear president. He was a good man and a righteous man. Never was that made more clear to me than when I had the opportunity to read his second inaugural address in the newspaper only a month ago. 'With malice toward none; with charity for all. . .' Those words stood out very clearly in my mind as so noble, so Christlike. He had no ill feeling toward the South, in spite of the war. He said as much just days before he was taken from us. He sought not revenge or punishment, rather, as he so eloquently put it, to 'bind up the nation's wounds.'

"It is time, brothers and sisters, to begin to heal. Even while our wounds are still raw. Who of you when you have gotten cut or burned leaves the wound to itself? What would happen to such a wound? It would become angry and fetid and you would suffer the effects of such an infection. It is the same now with our country, our community, and our church. We must bind up the wounds left in our hearts and allow them to heal.

"'Whosoever doeth not righteousness is not of God, neither he that loveth not his brother.' President Lincoln clearly understood and accepted that verse. He was a true believer. If we are to be true believers, if we are to honor the memory of our president, we must love our brothers and our sisters in Christ. Be they Northern or Southern.

"'There is neither Jew nor Greek, there is neither bond nor free, there is neither male nor female: for ye are all one in Christ Jesus.' Let us treat one another without malice and let us love one another as Christ has called us."

∽

It hadn't been a long sermon, but it had made its point. At least Daniel prayed it would. He watched as the preacher stepped away from the simple wooden lectern and reached out to shake Katherine's hand.

She took his hand readily in her own and gave the reverend a gentle smile.

Giving her a somewhat sad smile in return, the man turned and nodded to May, who began a new hymn, the one usually played before communion was served.

Daniel was gratified at first by the people who came up to them after services to greet Katherine. But it was tempered by their cold manner and how few made the effort.

Frustrated, he stepped outside and walked over to the carriage.

"I did warn you, Daniel." He turned to see the reverend standing behind him.

"I had hoped for more," Daniel replied. "I would have thought your example. . ."

"It will take more than my example to change people's hearts. They need time and prayer."

Daniel sighed and changed the subject. "I didn't see Mrs. Warren this morning."

Reverend Warren looked away. "She didn't feel up to coming today."

Daniel was about to reply when he saw Katherine and Mary walking out the church door accompanied by May Decker. The younger girl was speaking very animatedly to Katherine, whose face was lit up by a broad smile.

He turned to the clergyman with a grin. "Maybe there's reason to hope after all."

"He's supposed to be returning home soon," May was saying as they approached.

"I'm so very glad for you," Katherine replied.

At that moment, William and Ruth Decker quickly walked up to them. Mr. Decker looked at his daughter sternly. "May, go wait by the wagon."

"But, Pa. . ."

"Do as your pa says, young lady," Ruth commanded. When May had gone, she turned on the reverend. "Reverend Warren, I must say this may be the last time we grace the walls of this church with our presence."

"Ruth!" Mary gasped.

"As much as this body of believers has been through, I'm surprised at you," she plowed on. "Why, poor Adele Stephens didn't even come this morning."

Daniel walked over to stand beside Katherine as she lowered her eyes. "Yes, Mrs. Decker, I noticed. But as I said—"

"Might I remind you of the punishment the good Lord meted out to Sodom and Gomorrah? The South deserves no less for all it's put us through."

"Those were unrepentant cities, Mrs. Decker," Daniel said evenly. "Miss Wallace is a sister in Christ."

"And she's always been loyal to the Union," Mary added.

"Be that as it may, the fact remains she makes more than one person uncomfortable," Ruth declared. "Why, people have a right to worship in peace."

Several other people standing nearby nodded.

"As you can see, we are not the only ones who feel this way. Perhaps it would be best if Miss Wallace stopped attending Mill Creek Church."

"Ruth, she'll do nothing of the sort," Mary retorted.

"Of course not," Daniel added.

"I'll do it," Katherine said softly. Daniel stared at her, and she returned his gaze with firm eyes. "I don't want to be any trouble."

∞

Later that afternoon, Daniel was out back in the courtyard setting up his mother's quilting frame.

Both he and Mary had begged Katherine to reconsider her decision to not return to church, but her mind was made up. She said she would sit in the parlor and read her Bible while they were at services. "I'll be able to keep a close eye on lunch," she declared. "Even have it ready and waiting when you both get home. There's nothing like a warm meal after services."

Daniel took one of the chairs he had brought from the porch and set it near the frame. Leaving it, he walked over to the garden fence and leaned against it, looking out over the poultry yard and the fields and trees beyond.

Why, Lord? he prayed. *I don't understand any of this. You want me to farm instead of teach, and now this business with the church and Katherine. . . . Why didn't You soften their hearts?* He knew the words were hard, but his ma had taught him to pray without holding anything back. "He knows what you're feeling anyway," she had once said. "So long as it's respectful, you might as well speak your mind."

He heard the screen door creak, and he turned to see Katherine walking out with a quilt top neatly folded across her arm. Mary had found it among his mother's things. Most of the blocks had already been pieced together, and it hadn't taken his aunt long to finish getting it ready for quilting. They realized it must have been meant for Jonah, based on the simple design and the fact Dorothy had mentioned it in her last letter to Daniel.

Katherine smoothed her hand over it, admiring the workmanship. "This is pieced so beautifully. Your mother was a good sewer." Seeing the look on Daniel's face, her smile faded. "It's all right, Daniel, really. Reverend Warren said it would take time." She laid the quilt top over the back of the chair and joined him at the fence.

"They've known you for a month and a half now. How much more time do they need?"

"We have to give them time," she said, raising her eyes to his. "You told me to trust God to work it out."

"And you can't be present at services for Him to do that?"

"No. It would be best if I stayed away. For now anyhow." She looked down at her hands, which were clasped tightly together as she leaned them on the fence. He knew immediately she was struggling not to touch her scar.

"Are you doing this because you feel it's the right thing to do or because you feel you deserve it?"

"Daniel, the war has been hard on everyone. What the South did—"

"Has nothing to do with you." He took her by the arms and turned her to face him. "You are not responsible for the war. Or their heartache."

She looked down. "I'm responsible for what happened to Chloe. My family owned slaves. And my brother and father fought for the South."

"That has nothing to do with it."

"But what if I *am* responsible for what happened to Adele Stephens?"

Daniel stared at her. "What do you mean?"

"Adele's husband was killed by a Confederate soldier from South Carolina. My father was a general and my brother a lieutenant colonel. What if it was a man under my father's command? Or my brother's?"

Daniel closed his eyes and took a deep breath. "Nate Stephens was one of six men who were captured by a small group of Confederates. They were all men under my command, and they had accidently crossed the lines during the confusion of battle. I managed to sneak in and free them. Nate had a leg wound and had fallen behind when Confederates realized they were gone. When I turned to look for him, they fired."

"Who—?"

"I don't know where they were from. No one did. And no one probably ever will." He let go of her and let his hands drop helplessly at his side. "If anyone is responsible for his death, it's me."

"Oh Daniel, I'm so sorry. Ruth Decker said—" She stopped and bit her lip. "I should have known better."

"It's not your fault."

"It's not yours either."

"I should have gone back for him."

"No. Then you both would have died."

The look of horror in her eyes told him just how deeply she cared for him, and the sweet realization struck him like a cannonball. Her eyes softened as he looked at her, and he slowly reached up and brushed a stray hair away from her cheek. An almost panicked look crossed her face, and she quickly walked back over to where she had laid the quilt top.

If she was worried whether or not he cared for her, she had no reason to be. Daniel just then realized he'd loved her since the first moment he'd looked into her kaleidoscope eyes.

Chapter 12

Katherine was so dizzy, she was obliged to pick up the quilt top from the back of the chair and sit down. Daniel was still looking at her, and she made a show of examining the fabric in her lap as if looking for loose strings. Had she revealed too much in answering him the way she did? She could hardly help herself. The thought of his lying dead on some Southern battlefield had torn at her heart. Why had he touched her like that?

He's grateful for what I said, that's all, she firmly told herself. *Someone like him would never—could never—think about me.*

She heard him walk over and continue to put together the quilt frame. Frantically, she searched her mind for something to say. "This is stitched so beautifully. Mrs. Kirby was a wonderful sewer," she said and immediately winced, realizing she had already said as much.

She was relieved he didn't seem to take note of that fact as he slid the long poles through the holes in the I-shaped legs. "Thank you. Ma was one of the best quilters in the township. I remember Pa setting this up for her out here, and ladies from miles away would come and quilt with her." He grabbed the other dining room chair and set it close to hers and straddled it. "Did Aunt Mary show you the quilt my grandmother made for Ma when she married Pa?"

Her eyes brightened. "Oh yes, it was lovely." She ran her hand over the frame. "Did this belong to your grandmother?"

"Pa made this for Ma when they got married. Every quilt in the house was made on this frame."

"I found some lovely pieces of fabric in your mother's rag bag." She gave him a sympathetic look. "Mary told me she was saving them for your sister."

Daniel nodded. "Ma lost more than one baby between me and Jonah.

87

She had Rebecca Ann before Toby. She died before she was even a month old."

"I'm so sorry. Do you remember her well?"

Daniel shook his head thoughtfully. "No. I was only three. I remember Ma being sad, though."

"I'll leave them be, then."

"Why? Were you going to do something with them?"

"I was thinking of making a quilt with them." She waved her hand. "I don't have to."

"No, go ahead. Ma would have loved the idea of making something beautiful with her fabric." His green eyes found hers. "I know she would have loved you, as well."

Katherine paused before answering, trying to get her pounding heart under control. "I wish I could have known her better."

"Actually you do," he replied thoughtfully. "She was a lot like Aunt Mary." He leaned forward against the back of the chair. "Just how did you meet Aunt Mary and Uncle John? We've talked quite a bit but never about that."

"No, we haven't." She looked toward the house, wishing Mary would come out. She had shooed Katherine out of the house, insisting on cleaning up the lunch dishes herself as her ankle was doing much better. But Katherine knew her friend's true motive. *Doesn't she see I haven't a chance with him?*

Realizing she couldn't avoid *all* conversation with him, she proceeded to tell Daniel about how she had met Mary and how they had corresponded while she was at school. "She became sort of a mother to me," she said softly.

"What about your aunt?"

"Oh, she was of the same opinion as my father. 'Get the drab little thing married off as quick as we can,' she'd say."

"Drab little thing? That hardly describes you."

Katherine flushed at the glint in Daniel's eyes. "Anyway, John and Mary were very good to me."

"And Thomas?"

Katherine noticed the slight tension in his voice. "We exchanged letters as well. But nothing ever happened between us."

"You told me you cared for him."

"I did. But. . ." She looked away miserably. "I managed to ruin any chance I had with him. After everything that happened with Chloe, my father made me personally break off our acquaintance. I'm afraid I was quite flippant with him." She'd had to be. Or face her father's whip.

She felt Daniel take her hand, and of their own volition, her eyes found his.

He looked at her intently. "Katherine, stop taking the blame for things completely out of your control." His eyes made her feel faint. "If I knew my cousin, he understood."

∞

On Tuesday morning, Katherine looked out the kitchen window for the hundredth time.

Mary looked up from the ironing. "Is he coming yet?"

"No, not yet."

Jacob had not shown up at the farm yesterday morning, and when he hadn't come again this morning, Daniel had decided to take the wagon and find out what was going on. It was almost lunch, and he still hadn't returned.

Katherine turned from the window to look at Mary. "It's me, isn't it?"

The older woman gave her a look of reproach. "No. Don't think that."

"I can't help but think about why she wasn't at services on Sunday."

"She could have been under the weather."

As Katherine returned to sprinkling items for Mary to iron, she couldn't help but feel a sense of loss about the whole situation with Mill Creek Church. In spite of how people had treated her, she had enjoyed worshipping there. The songs they sang were rich and faithful and sung with such feeling. And in spite of her initial misgivings, Reverend Warren was a gifted preacher. So it had been hard for her to stand her ground when both Daniel and Mary had tried to convince her to go with them Sunday. But she had promised and didn't want to cause trouble.

In fact, she was still toying with the idea of leaving altogether. It would be easier for them to move on as the reverend had asked them, wouldn't it?

Lord, I felt Your hand in my decision to come here, but now, more than ever, I can't understand why. It makes much more sense to leave these people in peace.

Dipping her hand into a bowl of water, she sprinkled one of Daniel's shirts—the white one he wore with his uniform. Her heart pounded and her hands shook as that dashing image of him rose in her mind.

She clenched her teeth in frustration. *Please, Father, I need to leave before I lose my heart even more to this man,* she begged. She sighed at the answer in her heart. There was nothing else to do but trust Him. Even if it meant having her heart broken.

As she rolled up the shirt, she began to form a new yet truthful excuse that would allow her to go to bed early that night. Happily, Simon Peter and his sons would be here. If Daniel got to talking to them first, he wouldn't notice if she slipped out early.

Mary laid her iron back on the hot cookstove and carefully folded the dress she'd been working on. "We'd best clear up in here and get lunch started," she said with a sigh. "Simon Peter and the boys will be in soon."

Katherine began to gather up the rest of the clothes when she caught movement out of the corner of her eye. She looked through the window to see Scioto tearing down the road with the wagon, Daniel leaning forward in the seat urging him on. As they swept by, her heart nearly stopped at what she thought were two bodies lying in the bed of the wagon, but it went by too fast for her to be sure.

By the time she and Mary made it to the front door, Daniel was out of the wagon, yelling for them and Simon Peter.

Katherine raced to the wagon as Daniel lowered the bed door. "Oh no!" she gasped. Adele and Jacob lay in the bed on quilts, pale and still.

Daniel climbed in and laid a hand on the young boy's forehead before swinging him up into his arms. He looked around wildly. "Where's Simon Peter?"

Before she could answer, he was there. One look and he took the boy from Daniel. Jacob looked like a rag doll in the large man's arms. Aaron and Michael ran up, and Aaron, who was built more like his father, took Adele. Katherine heard Mary tell them where to take them, but her eyes were fastened on Daniel, who watched them being taken inside.

"This is my fault," he said raggedly.

"How could it...?"

"If Nate had been here, none of this would have happened."

"Daniel, you don't know that."

"Go see what you can do. God have mercy on me if something should happen to them." He sank down against the wagon's side wall and put his head in his hands.

Katherine picked up her skirts and raced into the house and up the stairs.

The door to Jonah's room was shut, and Simon Peter and his sons filled the small hallway. She could see by the looks on their faces that they wanted to be doing something other than just standing around.

"Can you go see to Daniel?" she asked softly. "I'm afraid he's in quite a state."

Simon Peter nodded, and he and the boys immediately walked downstairs.

Opening the door to Jonah's room, she walked in to find Toby's old trundle bed had been pulled out. Mary knelt next to it tending to Jacob while Adele lay quiet and still on Jonah's bed. Katherine gasped at the sight of the boy's hand, the same one she had bandaged up only a few days ago. It was quite swollen and a violent shade of red. Worse still, the swelling was beginning to spread to his wrist.

Mary looked up. "Katherine, before you even think it, it's not your fault," she stated firmly. "He's been helping with the planting for the past couple of days. Boys being boys, it's had plenty of chances to get infected."

Katherine looked over at Adele and started. "Mary, she looks half-starved!"

"I know," the older woman replied grimly. "I loosened her stays, but there's barely anything there to cinch in."

Katherine sank down on the edge of the bed and placed a hand on Adele's forehead. "She hasn't any fever."

"No, but Jacob's burning up." The older woman rose. "Stay with them." She left, and Katherine knew she was headed for the section of the pantry that held Dorothy Kirby's collection of dried flowers and herbs.

When Mary sprained her ankle, she had instructed Katherine on how to use them to treat her injury. "My mother," she'd said, "learned a thing or two from the Indians before they were forced to move west. She passed on what she knew to Dolly and me."

But as Katherine now looked helplessly at Jacob's swollen hand and flushed face, she wondered how a few shriveled leaves could possibly help now. A prayer formed in her mind and she closed her eyes. They opened the very next instant, however, as she heard Adele mutter and stir.

"*Mein lieber, Junge!* Jacob!" Her eyes opened and she looked around blearily. "Where is he?"

"Shh, Mrs. Stephens," Katherine said softly. She hoped the woman was too delirious to know who she was. "He's here. Mary's going to take right good care of him."

To her relief, Adele seemed to calm down and slipped back into unconsciousness.

Katherine resumed her prayer and did not cease until Mary returned with a steaming mug.

"I have Daniel digging up one of Dolly's coneflowers," she said. "The roots she had were too old to use. Come here and help me sit him up."

"What's that?"

"This is tea brewed from dogwood bark. The Delaware Indians use this to control fever."

They sat Jacob up and managed to get a few sips down his throat.

"There," Mary said once they had settled the shivering boy back beneath the quilt. "I'll use the coneflower root to make a poultice. It'll help draw out the infection." She placed her hand on Katherine's and smiled. "And you've already been about the most important step, prayer."

"What about Adele?"

Mary pursed her lips slightly. "Prayer as well, along with a little food and a generous dose of common sense."

The sound of boot steps downstairs in the hall told them Daniel had finished his task. They went down and found him sitting in the parlor.

Mary nudged Katherine in his direction while she went to the kitchen.

He stood up as she stepped in the room. "Aunt Mary said it isn't as bad as it looks."

"She told me the root you dug up will help."

He nodded. "Ma used coneflower a lot." He ran a hand through his hair. The guilty look from earlier began to creep back into his face.

"This isn't your fault, Daniel," Katherine said firmly.

"Nate should be here," he snapped. "And so should Jonah. And Toby. And Ma." Katherine watched as he began to pace the room. "Why should I keep going on like this? I have what I've always wanted waiting for me at Ohio Wesleyan. Give me one good reason why I shouldn't sell out and be done with it?"

"'Trust in the Lord with all thine heart,'" she quoted tremulously, "'and lean not unto thine own understanding.'"

Daniel stopped his pacing and stared at her before walking over and pulling her into his arms. He buried his head in her small shoulder, and she found herself standing on tiptoe to return the embrace. Her fingers brushed his silky hair, and she marveled at how right it felt to be in his arms.

Don't fool yourself. He's hurting right now. Nothing more.

After a moment or two, he lifted his head but didn't release her. Instead, he looked deeply into her eyes. "Did you finish that book of Wordsworth's poems?"

She nodded, too worked up over the way he was looking at her to speak.

"Discuss it with me tonight. Don't run off so soon after dinner." He must have read the hesitancy in her face, for he pressed her further. "Please. If I can't teach, at least there's that."

She nodded and stepped away from him. "I better see if Mary needs me."

She turned and headed toward the kitchen, a hand over her wildly pounding heart. A part of her was beginning to believe what she had thought to be quite impossible.

Chapter 13

Mary and Katherine took turns seeing to Adele and her son. By the next morning, Adele was awake and lucid, and Katherine told Mary it might be best if she helped her with the simple broth they had been feeding her. *The poor woman has enough to deal with. She doesn't need the likes of me around,* she thought as she settled down with the mending in the dining room.

She was surprised when Mary came back down the stairs a moment or two after going up to see to the young widow.

"What is it? Is it Jacob?" she asked.

Mary shook her head. "No, but I need to make up a new poultice for him." She laid a gentle hand on Katherine's cheek. "Adele wants to see you."

Katherine's eyes widened, and she looked at the stairs and then back to her friend.

Mary patted her shoulder. "Go on up. She's waiting."

Leaden weights seemed to replace Katherine's feet as she walked up the stairs. She reached the door of Jonah's room and peered in.

Adele was propped up in bed, her thin hands holding the mug of broth Mary had brought her. It sat in her lap half lost in the folds of the light quilt covering her. She was staring down at her son, who lay in the little trundle bed next to her. They had managed to bring his fever down a little, but his hand was still red and swollen.

Tears pricked at Katherine's eyes as she saw the worried look on Adele's face. She slowly walked into the room, and the young widow immediately turned her head toward her. Katherine attempted a weak smile as she sank down in the chair next to her bed. "Good morning, Mrs. Stephens," she said and inwardly winced at the sound of her own voice and how much it must distress the poor woman.

"My son, how is he?" she asked, her weak voice revealing her German heritage.

"His fever is down a little. Mary is making up a new poultice." She wondered why Adele had called her up merely to ask what Mary could very well have answered.

"I tried all I knew. But he became so sick." She lifted the mug she held to her lips, but her hands shook, and Katherine immediately steadied it as she took a sip. She let Katherine take it from her and leaned back against the pillows. "How did we get here?"

"Daniel came looking for you when Jacob didn't show up." Daniel had told them the evening before how he had pounded on the door to their small shack at the edge of town. When there was no answer, he peered in a window and broke in when he had seen Adele lying in a heap on the floor. "He brought you both here."

"The infection set in so quickly," she said tearfully.

"Why didn't you send for the doctor?"

"I could not afford it." Adele looked brokenly at her son. "Mein lieber, Junge, God is punishing me."

Katherine stared wonderingly at her. "I'm afraid I don't understand, Mrs. Stephens."

Adele reached out a weak hand and laid it on Katherine's. "*Weil ich tadelte*—" She stopped herself. "Because I blamed you for Nathaniel's death," she continued softly, her accent becoming thicker as her emotion rose. "Mrs. Kirby was helping me after I lose the farm. But when you come I cannot bring myself to talk to Mary." Katherine's free hand strayed to her jaw as the poor woman continued. "We were running out of food. It is why I let Jacob come here. So he could eat. You were so kind to him, he says. He says I should not be angry." She dissolved into tears.

Katherine shakily offered her a handkerchief before calling for Mary. The older woman arrived, and Katherine left the room, unable to hold back tears of her own.

∞

By that evening, Adele was well enough to be helped downstairs into the parlor. Since her confession to Katherine earlier, she kept to herself, communicating with them through nods and short one- or two-word sentences. Jacob, while he showed some improvement, was still very sick.

Mary insisted Adele leave his side for at least an hour or so. She promised to stay with him while Katherine made dinner.

When Daniel stepped into the house, he found Adele seated on the sofa, one of his mother's quilts lying over her lap. He immediately started to leave the room.

"Daniel," she called.

He slowly stepped back in. Still weak and thin, Adele looked nothing like the woman Nate had left behind. Her blue eyes were dull and her corn silk–colored hair was thin and dry. He still couldn't believe how wasted she'd become. But she looked at him kindly and asked him to sit down next to her.

"Adele. . . ," he began and then stopped. The words he'd rehearsed over and over in his head refused to come to him. He could only look at her helplessly.

"It is good to see you again." She looked at him for a moment or two and sighed. "I am sorry. I should have written to you."

"No," he said slowly. "I never should have told you what happened the way I did."

"No, it needed to be told." She patted his hand. "I will be able to tell Jacob how brave his father was when he is older." Her face became even more drawn. "If my pride has not killed him."

"Adele, what happened?" he asked eagerly. "How did you get so sick? Why did Elijah Carr make you leave your farm?"

"I could not take care of the land. When Nathaniel died, I had to let go of the help and I could not keep up. So I gave it back to Mr. Carr."

"He said something about a debt. I thought Nate had the land paid off."

She lowered her eyes. "I borrowed money from him. So we could eat. He forgave the debt when I gave him back the land."

Daniel frowned. "Ma should have told me."

"I would not let her."

"What about your brother? Why didn't you write him?"

Adele looked at him sadly. "I tried to write him, but he never wrote back."

Daniel ran his hands through his hair. Erich had gone west not long after Adele had gotten married. He'd always written religiously. Therefore, the only explanation was that he had perished somewhere in the Western plains like so many others. "Ma should have told me. I could have sent or done something."

"Your mother did it for you," she reassured him. "She got Mr.

Henderson to let us live in his old building in Ostrander. And she would bring us baskets of food." Her own brow furrowed. "But then she got sick. I did not even know until Mr. Carr brought the last basket. He said I should stay away so we would not get sick, too." She closed her eyes and raised a hand to her face. "I came here for your mother's funeral, to speak to Mrs. O'Neal. But Miss Wallace spoke to me first, and I left. I could not come back." Adele bowed her head, shamefaced. "I did not want to see her again."

Daniel started. His mother had died almost two months ago. "Adele, how long have you been without food?"

"I stretched out what I had left from the last basket," she whispered, still looking down at her lap. "I let Jacob have most of it. But it ran out. I was too proud to say anything to those at church. So I had to come let him work for you even though I did not want him with Miss Wallace. He needed to eat." Tears welled up in her eyes. "She was so kind to my son. She bandaged his hand and gave him candy. I had treated her so poorly. Jacob said I needed to forgive. I was going to come to church last Sunday to apologize. But he got sick, and I don't remember what happened after that."

Daniel scooped her up in his arms and let her weep into his shoulder as he closed his eyes and silently worded a prayer.

∽

Two nights later, Daniel sat in the parlor as Katherine worked on some mending. He watched her delicate hands work needle and thread to repair the breast pocket of one of his work shirts. When she finished, she smoothed her hand over the pocket before setting it aside. He'd never wanted to be a piece of fabric so much in his life.

Daniel shifted in his seat and tried to focus his gaze on something else, the wall, the clock, anything other than the lovely creature who sat so near him but still seemed beyond his reach. He'd wanted to talk to her since that day at the fence. He had been certain she felt something for him, too. Had he imagined what he had seen in her eyes?

They'd had such an enjoyable discussion two nights before, and she seemed happy as they had laughed and talked. But now she was suddenly distant again. If it wasn't for Simon Peter sitting at the secretary reading the *Delaware Gazette* and Aaron and Michael playing checkers on the floor, he'd kneel down in front of her and beg her to talk to him.

He glanced at the mantel clock. Mary was upstairs with Adele and

Jacob, and if Simon Peter and his sons went out to the barn when they usually did, he might be able to speak with her before she went upstairs. Leaning back on the sofa, he opened up the book he and Katherine had been discussing. He read the first line of "Lines Composed a Few Miles above Tintern Abbey. . ." at least a dozen times before Michael finally yawned.

"It's early yet, but I'm done in." The youth looked at his younger brother. "You comin'?"

"Sure am. I'm tired of gettin' beat by you."

They put the checkers away, and Aaron looked over at their pa. "Come on, Pa. Let's get some sleep."

"I'll be along in a spell," Simon Peter said from behind the newspaper. "I just want to finish up this article they have in here 'bout them catchin' that no-good Booth."

"It's almost a mercy they brought him in dead," Daniel said as the boys headed out the door. "It spares Mrs. Lincoln the pain of a trial."

Simon Peter nodded gravely. "They talk about the president's funeral in here, too. You oughta be goin' since you served in the war and all."

"I'd like to, but I don't want to leave you shorthanded."

"We've been doin' just fine. Almost got you caught up to where you should be this time o' year."

Daniel opened his mouth to reply when Adele, aided by Mary, came into the room. Daniel immediately took her from his aunt and helped her sit next to him on the sofa.

"She heard you talking and wanted to come downstairs," Mary said. She settled down in a small rocker next to Katherine.

"Is Jacob better?" Daniel asked hopefully.

"His fever's broken," his aunt said with a smile. "And his hand is beginning to heal."

"Thank the Lord," Daniel said and embraced Adele.

"I heard what Simon Peter said as we were coming down the stairs," Mary said, and he turned his attention to her. "He's right. You should go."

"Yes, Daniel, you should go and see President Lincoln one last time," Adele said. "I wish I could go, but I do not think I am strong enough." She looked over at Katherine, and Daniel watched as the young widow gathered herself to speak to her. "Perhaps you should go with Daniel. . . Miss Wallace."

Katherine looked up, startled. "Oh, well. . ."

"I know she would like to go, Adele, but that may not be the best idea," Daniel said. Katherine had expressed a desire to say good-bye to the president a few days ago, but she knew her accent made it impossible. And there was the distinct possibility that someone would recognize her. A number of people from Ostrander would more than likely be going down. He said as much now. "I don't want to disrupt the viewing," he finished.

"He's right, ma'am," Simon Peter said. "Durin' the war down at Camp Chase, they was lettin' some Confederate prisoners of war have the run of Columbus. Them officers behaved themselves, but folk down there didn't like it one bit. Almost had a riot down there one time."

"But I remember that day in the store when we all found out. Miss Wallace, you were so sad. And Mary tells me how you have always been faithful to the Union." Adele looked imploringly at Daniel. "What if she wears my mourning clothes? I have a spoon bonnet with a veil. It would hide her face."

Mary raised her eyebrows. "If she didn't speak, it would work. And we could hem your dress. You're a bit taller than Katherine."

Adele nodded and looked at Daniel.

He glanced at Katherine.

"I'm not sure I really have any right to be there," she murmured.

"You're a citizen of this country, Katherine," Daniel said quietly. "You have as much right to be there as anyone in this room. Maybe more. You were faithful to the Union when all around others weren't."

"I have the idea President Lincoln would be very pleased to have someone from the South come pay their respects," Mary added.

Daniel watched her face as she thought it out. She finally nodded, if a bit reluctantly.

"Thank you kindly, Mrs. Stephens," she said.

Even though Katherine had tried to soften her accent, Daniel still saw a pained look flit across Adele's face. He knew she was making a concerted effort to let go of her blame and anger. It was encouraging to see the effort she now took to be kind to Katherine. But he knew she still was not comfortable with Katherine's accent. At least not yet.

To his disappointment, Katherine rose. "I'm going to bed." She looked over at Mary. "Do you want me to check on Jacob?"

"No, he's sleeping peacefully," she replied as she looked at Katherine worriedly. "Are you sure you're not coming down with something?"

"No, I'm fine." She turned to the rest of them. "Good night."

Daniel rose and followed her to the stairs. "Katherine."

She stopped and turned her head slightly. "I'm sorry, Daniel. I really am tired."

"I won't keep you then, but I want a chance to talk to you privately. Soon."

She nodded and quickly continued up the stairs. As he watched her go, he wondered if he had been wrong to think she cared for him.

∞

Katherine lay in bed a long time before she fell asleep. A certain degree of guilt had been lifted from her shoulders since Daniel had told her about how Nate had died. At least she need not feel so awful at the very sight of Adele Stephens. But leaving was becoming more and more tempting in spite of what the Lord was telling her. How could anyone around here heal if she was here?

And besides, it was very clear to her now that Daniel had feelings for the young widow. She should have seen it before.

Her hand flew to her jaw and tears pricked at her eyes. *Father, I told You this would happen. I can't stay. I have to find a way back to. . .South Carolina.* She couldn't bring herself to say "home." South Carolina would never truly be her home again. No matter where she was, her heart would always be in Ohio. She loved the crispness of the air and soft chirping of the crickets in the evening, the rush of Mill Creek and the gentle gaze of Daniel's soft green eyes.

Tears fell free and fast down her face, making her pillow damp. She'd dream about him again tonight. She'd dreamed about him almost every night since that day he'd found her crying by the creek. It had confused her at first, but it didn't take long for her to figure out it was because she loved him.

She flung her arm over her face, begging God to let her leave. Her heart went back and forth with Him for quite some time. By the time she fell asleep, she had promised Him she would do nothing. For now.

Chapter 14

Early Saturday morning, Daniel stood in the parlor waiting for Katherine to come down. He was in full dress uniform with a black band on his left arm and a fringed black sash attached to his sword hilt. According to the newspapers, all officers not on duty had been invited to participate in the proceedings, but Daniel had not been interested. He would have had to report to Tod Barracks down in Columbus at six o'clock this morning, which would have been impractical since Katherine was coming with him.

Soft movement caused him to turn and see Katherine standing in the doorway of the parlor. Normally he couldn't bear to see a woman in mourning. He hated seeing his aunt perpetually dressed in black, and he was glad Katherine, as she was not related to his family, did not have to wear the somber color in remembrance of his mother. But the darkness of Adele's dress set off Katherine's eyes and brought out the red highlights in her auburn hair.

Neither one of them said anything for a minute or two.

Finally, Daniel spoke. "I must look ridiculous in this," he half joked as he rested his hand on his sword.

"Oh no," she said quickly. "You look quite. . .military." She flushed and looked down.

Daniel had the idea she was going to say a very different word, and he wished once more that it would just be the two of them driving to Delaware. He dearly wanted to be certain of what she was feeling.

Daniel had decided to drive into Delaware to catch the train rather than getting on in Ostrander where someone might recognize Katherine. Professor Harris had very graciously offered to look after Scioto and the carriage while they were in Columbus. Jeremiah, another one of Simon Peter's sons, was in charge of the professor's stables and had come to ride with them into Delaware.

Mary came into the room just then and fussed a little with Katherine's frock. "For having so little time, Adele did a good job," she commented as she stood back to look at her.

"Yes," she replied, looking down at the hem. "I'm glad nothing had to be done to the bodice."

Daniel saw Jeremiah waiting for them in the drive. "We'd better go."

Mary handed Katherine the spoon bonnet with its heavy black veil.

Taking it, Katherine embraced her friend and looked at her worriedly. "Will you be all right without me?"

"I'll be just fine," the older woman reassured her. "Simon Peter and the boys will be back as soon as they've seen the funeral train go by." Those who couldn't make it to any of the cities where the president would lie in state were congregating by railroad crossings where his train would pass to pay their respects. Mary turned and hugged her nephew. "Take good care of her."

Daniel smiled. "You know I will."

The sun shone brightly down on the city of Columbus as long lines of people filled the sidewalk along High Street to view the body of President Abraham Lincoln, which now lay in the rotunda of the Ohio statehouse.

Daniel and Katherine were among them, quietly inching their way forward toward Capitol Square. Their train had arrived in Columbus at nine thirty, over two hours after the president's body had arrived in the capital city.

A procession had already taken him through a preplanned route around the statehouse before delivering him to lie in state inside. The doors would close, they had heard, at six o'clock that evening in order for the body to move on to Indianapolis.

The crowds were so immense Daniel had worried they might not get a chance to see him. But his army uniform caught a good deal of attention, and several people asked why he had not taken part in the procession. Each time he was asked, Daniel had nodded toward Katherine, who was holding his arm, and explained he was escorting a young lady whose only brother had died in the war. As a result, people insisted they go ahead of them. Daniel had protested at first, but most people were so vehement in their insistence, his objections fell on deaf ears. It had happened so frequently they were now approaching the statehouse far sooner than they would have been. Daniel had given up trying to stop their heartfelt gestures.

Katherine, on the other hand, despaired, hating to fool so many good people. The last time it had happened, she had given Daniel a look of dismay, hoping he would look at her long enough to make out her face through the veil.

He had pulled her close. "It's true enough, isn't it?" he asked.

"Yes, but—"

"Don't say anything. I won't have something happening to you." The look on his face made her dizzy, and she grasped his arm tightly as they walked on.

She looked around and tried to turn her attention to something else. The statehouse was now well within view, and Katherine studied it as they slowly moved along.

South Carolina had begun work on its statehouse when she was eleven, and she had seen the incomplete building in Columbia several times. It had promised to be a grand structure. But by the beginning of the war, it had been only partially complete, and over the course of the conflict, construction had ground almost to a halt. Whether it had survived the burning of Columbia she could not say.

Ohio's statehouse was similar in style, but it had a quiet elegance, which she found she preferred. Rather than a large imposing dome topped with a spire, a large drumlike cupola with windows all around sat atop the rectangular structure. The building sat on a square surrounded by a wrought iron fence with a green lawn at each corner.

Daniel had told her there were four entryways, each facing a different direction on the compass. They were drawing near the west entrance now. Black cloth was wrapped around the massive Grecian pillars in front of the doors, and black bunting graced each of the eight windows on either side.

The fence was broken by a gateway over which a sign had been hung. It read: OHIO MOURNS.

She glanced at Daniel. A weight had settled over him ever since the statehouse had come into view. As he read the sign, his face became graver.

As they moved beneath the gate, another sign had been hung directly above the pillars: WITH MALICE TOWARD NONE; WITH CHARITY

FOR ALL. Katherine recalled Reverend Warren quoting the phrase from President Lincoln's second inaugural address.

They climbed the broad limestone stairway and passed between the pillars to face one last sign, which hung directly over the heavy double doors: GOD MOVES IN A MYSTERIOUS WAY. Daniel stopped and stared at it.

A gap opened in front of them, and after another second or two, a gentleman behind them gently coughed. Katherine grasped Daniel's hand, and he looked at her as if he had just woken from a dream. Seeing the break in front of them, he quickly escorted her forward. A short hallway was before them with another small flight of steps leading up into the rotunda.

Katherine's heart pounded as she realized she would soon be looking at the face of her fallen president. She glanced down at the basket on her arm, wondering if she would be brave enough to do all she had planned. Mary had packed them food for their lunch and dinner, and at the last moment Katherine had included a small spray of violets to put on or near the president's coffin. She had been sure enough of the gesture earlier, but now she felt unaccountably shy. *Father, help me be bold.*

They climbed the last step into the rotunda. Katherine looked around her. The walls of the round room were draped in black, broken only by four arched entryways and a painting labeled "Perry's Victory on Lake Erie."

She looked up. Sunshine shone down through the pretty stained glass dome and bathed the solemn scene with light. The entire room smelled of various flowers, the scent of lilacs being the most prominent.

A black carpeted platform appeared at her feet. The line of four abreast split here as two people on each side walked up the platform to view the president. Daniel let go of her arm, and she allowed him to approach the coffin first as she reached into the basket for her spray of flowers.

They stood there for a moment, both of them taking in the still face of President Abraham Lincoln. Katherine stared at the still yet kindly face, and tears sprang to her eyes. She sent up a silent prayer for the great man's widow and children.

Daniel rubbed his right hand, and his jaw was clenched tight. He moved on a second later, and Katherine followed, but not before swiftly laying the violets at the base of the coffin. Daniel had turned to help her step off the platform and saw her gesture. He threaded his fingers through her own as they left the rotunda and followed the rest of the crowd out through the north entrance.

⌒

The line of people broke up once they exited the statehouse, and Daniel walked Katherine off to the side. The sight of his fallen leader and Katherine's sweet gesture had moved him greatly, and he hoped she wouldn't let go of his hand until he had taken a moment to collect himself.

She didn't; rather, she laid her other hand over their clasped ones. He wished he could see her face and her eyes, which he knew were probably soft with sympathy and her own unshed tears.

He squeezed her small hand. "Thank you," he whispered. Looking closely, he could just make out through the veil her small smile and a tear rolling down her cheek. While he took out his pocket watch to check the time, she wiped it away with her handkerchief. "It's nearly three and there's supposed to be an oration on the east lawn," he offered.

She nodded her approval and they made their way over.

A great number of people had already gathered, and Daniel could not get them very close to the platform, which had been erected in front of the east entrance of the statehouse. But he knew they would be well within earshot of the speakers, provided they spoke loudly enough.

People closed in around them, and he and Katherine had to stand quite close to one another. He therefore allowed himself the luxury of placing his arm around her small waist to keep her from being jostled.

He glanced down and saw he was close enough to make out her face quite clearly through the veil. Dark lashes lay against her pale cheeks, and she didn't return his gaze.

Tearing his eyes away, he watched the dignitaries step up onto the platform. He immediately recognized Major General Joseph Hooker, who had once commanded the Army of the Potomac, along with several other generals. A military band played a dirge, and a choral selection was sung before a prayer was offered up.

The state senator from Chillicothe, the Honorable Job E. Stevenson, rose and began to speak. "Ohio mourns, America mourns," he said. "The civilized world will mourn the cruel death of Abraham Lincoln, the brave, the wise, the good; bravest, wisest, best of men."

The crowd was deathly silent as State Senator Stevenson spoke. He summarized President Lincoln's life, his rise to office, his steadfast service during the war, and the forgiveness he offered the South in his last inaugural address. "But he is slain," he then declared. "Slain by slavery."

Daniel looked around as more than a few people began to murmur and nod.

"That fiend incarnate did the deed. Beaten in battle, the leaders sought to save slavery by assassination." The murmurs grew louder as State Senator Stevenson continued, and several people shouted as he declared the souls of murdered Union soldiers would rise up in judgment against the South. "Let us beware the Delilah of the South, who has so lately betrayed our strong man. Let the 'Prodigals' feed on the husks till they come in repentance, and ask to be received in their father's house— not as the equals to their faithful brethren but on a level with their former servants."

Katherine swayed, and Daniel looked down at her in alarm. Even through the veil he could see how pale she was, and he moved her through the crowd until they came to an open area of the lawn near the north exit.

She leaned heavily against him for a moment before raising her face to his. "Oh Daniel, I can't stay," she whispered tearfully.

He grasped her by the arms and pulled her close. "You *can't* go."

Chapter 15

"Why?" Katherine whispered and then caught her breath at the look on Daniel's face. As she gazed into his soft green eyes, a sharp thrill shot through her chest. In the back of her mind, something told her if it wasn't for the veil and their current surroundings. . . The thought made her dizzy, and she grasped the front of his jacket for support.

People glanced at them as they passed, and he quickly loosened his grip. "Come on," he said deeply as he slipped her hand into the crook of his arm. "We should start heading back toward the train station."

Katherine gripped his arm tightly as they moved through the busy city streets. She didn't dare put into conscious thought what she had seen in his eyes. She still wasn't quite sure she could believe it.

What about Adele? He'd seemed so attentive to the young widow the past several days. But then Katherine's thoughts swung to the way he would look at her and the way he'd held her in the parlor the day he brought Adele and Jacob to the farm. And he said he wanted to talk to her. Alone. She had assumed it would be a confession of what he was feeling for Adele, so she'd planned on making every effort to avoid him. Now she wasn't so sure.

The train ride back to Delaware was crowded, and they were both happy to get out into the fresh evening air. Jeremiah was waiting with the carriage and Scioto at the station, and they drove him back to Professor Harris's home before going on their way.

Dusk was setting in as they journeyed home. It was nearly an hour between Delaware and the farm, plenty of time to talk.

Katherine buried her hands in the folds of her dress, clenched tightly so Daniel wouldn't see how they shook. Her heart felt like a drum. It wasn't that she was afraid of Daniel—far, *far* from it—but this was a situation she had never faced in all her life. What was she supposed to do? What if she was wrong? What if she was right? The latter thought caused a thrill to run straight through to her fingertips. As her mind whirled in nervous confusion, Daniel spoke and she nearly jumped out of her skin.

"You can probably take off the bonnet now," he said.

Her heart raced so fast she began to feel ill. She glanced at him. "Don't—don't you think I should wait until after Bellepoint?"

Bellepoint was east of the farm, and Elijah Carr did a good deal of business in the town. When they had rode through that morning, Daniel told her to be sure to keep her face hidden. He now gave her a funny look and shrugged. "Most people will be turned in by the time we ride through. And I'm sure Carr is home by now. His farm isn't even within sight of the road."

"Well, best be safe than sorry," she murmured.

He gave her a slightly bemused, knowing look but said nothing in reply.

Even when they were well past Bellepoint, Katherine couldn't bring herself to even lift the bonnet's veil, much less take it off. She fussed and fidgeted, avoiding Daniel's gaze. Fortunately, he said nothing, and they rode the rest of the way home in silence.

It was dark by the time they reached the house. When Katherine attempted to get out of the carriage, the thickness of the veil nearly caused her to fall out. She felt Daniel take her by the arms and settle her safely on the ground.

His voice was filled with tender amusement as he spoke to her. "Katherine, take that silly thing off before you break your pretty little neck."

With shaking hands, she removed the pins and untied the hat, laying it aside on the carriage seat. She turned around to find him standing very close to her, and it was difficult to keep a straight thought in her head. Looking past him, she noticed the house was dark. "Oh," she breathed. "They must have turned in."

His eyes never left her. "Well, it is late."

Katherine stared at the ground. Her heart had begun its furious pounding again, and she hid her hands in the folds of her skirt.

Daniel lifted her chin with a gentle finger, and she was forced to look at him. Moonlight danced in his green eyes as his hand cupped her face. "I've been wanting to talk to you." His voice was deep and soft.

As his thumb stroked her cheek, Katherine found herself reaching out to hold on to him. Her legs had suddenly become quite weak. She felt his hand slide around her waist, pulling her closer still. "What did you want to say?" she murmured.

"Only this," he whispered as his lips brushed hers.

Katherine's hands quickly wrapped themselves around his broad shoulders, and the kiss deepened. This was what she'd been dreaming about.

Of course! This was all a dream. She'd wake up within the next few seconds like she always did and find nothing in her arms but a pillow. But instead of waking up, she found Daniel had lifted his head to look at her with such tenderness it was all she could do to not cry.

"Now do you understand why you can't go?"

She nodded. Breathless, she buried her head in his chest for a moment. "Why. . .why did you call me pretty?"

His lips brushed the top of her head. "Why shouldn't I?" he whispered.

Her voice shook as she answered. "Oh, Daniel, I'm not. I'm just this drab little. . .nothing."

"No. Don't even think that." The firmness of his voice caused her to look up and meet his gaze. "You are the most beautiful woman I've ever met, and not just here," he said, brushing his thumb across her cheek once more. "Your sweet spirit shines through everything you say and do. Especially through your incredible eyes."

"Incredible? *My* eyes?" she gasped, unable to believe what she was hearing. "You've *seen* my eyes, haven't you?"

"On more than one occasion." He smiled.

"You must have taken leave of your senses then, Daniel Kirby! My eyes are the least—" Before she could say more, he was tenderly kissing her again.

"I could lose myself in your eyes for the rest of my life," he finally murmured, making a point of gazing into them for a long while before he spoke again. "I love you, Katherine Wallace."

She stared at him. "This is one of the nicest dreams I've ever had."

"You think you're dreaming?" he asked incredulously.

"I must be. In half a minute it'll be morning, and I'll wake up to have you tell me you're really in love with Adele."

"Adele?" He laughed. "Adele is like a sister to me. What I feel for her is nothing like what I feel for you." Daniel bent his head to kiss her once more when they both caught sight of a soft light coming from the parlor window. "I guess Aunt Mary waited up after all." He placed a lingering kiss on her forehead before stepping away to lead Scioto and the carriage to the barn.

Katherine watched him, dazed, before remembering herself. Since this was all a dream, she might as well tell him how she felt. She'd woken up too soon all the other times. "Daniel!"

He was back beside her in an instant. "What?"

"Oh. . .I know I'm only dreaming. I love you."

"You're not dreaming." He smiled and reached up to stroke her cheek. "I'll prove you wrong in the morning."

"I dearly hope so."

Chapter 16

D aniel stepped out of the barn the next morning, having finished the chores and dressed for church, when he caught sight of Katherine on her way to the henhouse. She walked in before he could get her attention, and he decided to wait for her.

He leaned against the whitewashed clapboard with a pounding heart. He remembered how deeply Nate had loved Adele and the affection his parents had for one another, but he never really expected to find love himself. Instead, he had seen himself remaining a bachelor like Professor Harris. Not for lack of prospects of course. A number of girls from Ohio Wesleyan's female college had chased after him, and he had courted a couple of them. But the relationships hadn't lasted; he'd been far too interested in his studies and the young ladies too interested in catching a husband.

But Katherine was different. Daniel found in her someone who would willingly join him in his studies. She didn't sigh and look bored when he spoke of poetry or mythology. She had a passion for learning and, more importantly, a passion for the Lord.

He reached into his pocket and pulled out a small leather pouch, tipping the small gold ring it contained into his palm. Aunt Mary had given him his mother's wedding ring the day after he'd come home, and he'd carried it with him ever since. The morning sun glinted off the golden crisscrossing lines along the band, an Irish pattern. It had been in the Kirby family for generations.

Just then one of the cows lowed and he frowned. *You're a farmer now,* he thought as he returned the heirloom to his pocket. What right did he have offering her that kind of life? Oh, she seemed contented enough, but could he be satisfied knowing she would be far better suited as a professor's wife?

The henhouse door opened, and Daniel deliberately pushed the thought aside. He was eager to prove to her that his declaration last night hadn't been a dream.

Katherine set down a heavy basket of eggs, and as she turned to close the door, he grasped her hand and pulled her into his arms. Before she could say a word, he was kissing her, slowly and deeply.

"Daniel Aaron Kirby!" she gasped weakly. "Mary will see."

"Right now I don't care if the entire state of Ohio sees us or hears me telling you how much I love you." His arms tightened around her. "Still believe it's a dream?"

Her eyes softened and she bit her lip as a shy smile crept over her face. "No," she whispered.

It was all he could do to not kiss her again. Instead, he let her go and, picking up the basket of eggs, took her hand. "Come on. I'll walk you in." He relished the feel of her fingers entwined with his, and as they walked he caught her glancing at him. "What?"

"You're wearing your uniform again."

The admiring look in her eyes gave him such a rush he almost forgot to answer. "I thought it was only proper to wear this to services until the president is laid to rest later this week." He stopped, and she looked at him questioningly. "Come to church this morning."

"Daniel, I shouldn't," she replied, looking away.

"You've never really explained why you feel you have to do this," he said. "You know it's only going to take longer for them to heal and accept you."

"Is it? Seems to me the less they see of me—"

"The less they'll think about what they need to be doing, which is accepting you because you're their sister in Christ. Being Southern should have nothing to do with it." He pulled her forward and kissed her on the forehead. "Do you know what Adele told me?"

"What?"

"She said being around you is helping her let go of the pain and anger she's been feeling."

"She blamed me for Nate's death," she murmured.

"She did. But your example has shown her what she needs to do. Don't you think that's what you should do for the people at Mill Creek Church?"

She opened her mouth to answer, but Mary called to them from the kitchen door. "Will you two be joining us for breakfast?"

Inside, as they sat down at the table, Daniel noticed that Adele was wearing a dress of pale blue, the skirt being held out by numerous petticoats. Her hair was pulled neatly back in a chignon, and she looked almost like her old self. "Are you coming with Aunt Mary and me this morning, Adele?" he asked.

Adele and his aunt looked at each other. Mary was dressed in simple work clothes. "No, Daniel," Adele replied calmly. "I intend to go to church with you and Miss Wallace this morning."

He heard Katherine drop her fork and looked to see her staring wide-eyed at the young widow. "Oh, Mrs. Stephens, I've promised—"

"Katherine, this staying away from services is nonsense," Mary said firmly. "If you eat quickly, you can get yourself into something suitable before you three need to leave. I'll stay and tend to Jacob. He needs a few days more yet."

Daniel could tell by the sound of his aunt's voice she was going to brook no refusal. And from the stricken look on Katherine's little face, he knew she knew it as well.

She rose. "I'm not really hungry, I think I'll change now," she muttered, sweeping from the room.

He looked after her, frustrated he couldn't go hold her and tell her everything would be all right.

A warm hand found his, and he turned to see a sweet, knowing smile on Adele's face.

"Let me go speak with her," she said gently before rising from her seat and following Katherine.

∽

Katherine sat on her bed, still dressed in her work clothes and staring at her dresses hanging in the simple walnut wardrobe. She couldn't quite decide which dress was proper for a lamb being led to the slaughter to wear. The swish of petticoats caused her to look up and meet Adele's gentle smile.

"Such lovely dresses," Adele said as she swept over to the wardrobe door.

"Thank you," Katherine muttered. "Mary and I altered a few of hers. There's only one that's new." She and Mary had only managed to make one dress for her since their arrival. It was a pretty day dress with a rosette print and a background of deep blue.

Adele immediately reached for it. "I will tell you a secret. In spite of

113

how I felt, I always liked this on you. You must wear it, and we will be a pretty pair as we sit together this morning." She saw the terrible look on Katherine's face, and becoming more serious, the young widow sat down beside her. "This is not right. They will not come to accept you if you are not there."

"That's what Daniel said."

"He is right, you know."

"I know, it's just. . ." Katherine paused and looked back up at Adele. "Am I truly helping you to heal?"

A strained look crossed the young widow's face, and she placed her hand over Katherine's. "If you had not come here, I would have drowned in my hate. I would have grown into a bitter old woman and died far from God."

"But you've been attending church."

"Only for the sake of my son." Adele squeezed her hand. "And going to church does not make you close to Him, you know." She placed her free hand over her heart. "You must have and know Him here."

Katherine nodded. She had attended services many times with her family, but it had only been for the sake of appearances. The words of their reverend had not touched their hearts as they had hers. "But how could I have possibly been an example to you? I've hardly seen you."

"But I have seen you. You treated my son with much kindness, and I would watch you during services, and I knew how patiently you accepted how people treated you. May would tell me."

"May?" Katherine asked hopefully.

"Yes, she is a dear young lady, and she likes you very much."

"Her parents certainly don't," Katherine replied sadly.

"They are good people," Adele reassured her. "Do not think too badly of them. I hope you will come to know them as I do." She smiled. "Now you must get dressed. Your Daniel is waiting for us I am sure."

Katherine blushed, happy and shy at the same time. "Mrs. Stephens—"

"If we are to be friends, you must call me Adele."

Katherine's throat went tight. "Then, I hope you will call me Katherine."

Adele's smile broadened, and she leaned toward her. "We will go together and sit side by side. If anyone wants to say something, they will say it to me."

Whatever courage she had taken from Adele's words melted away at the first shocked look she got when the three of them walked up to the church door.

Daniel seemed to sense her discomfort and looked down at her. "It'll be all right."

Her heart flipped at the look he gave her, and she squeezed his arm tighter. She had no notion how she had managed to win the heart of such a good and handsome man. Katherine pressed her lips together at the sweet memory of his kiss this morning. No, last night hadn't been a dream.

A great deal of murmuring and pointing went on as they sat down in a pew near the front. Adele smiled calmly and greeted a few people who answered her back in stunned voices. Katherine sat down beside her and immediately reached for a hymnal. She didn't look up until the end of the opening song when she felt Daniel slide away from her. Startled, she saw none other than May Decker daintily stepping in front of him, settling herself next to her with a barely suppressed smile. Katherine began to panic. May's parents would be furious that she had not returned to sit with them after playing the opening hymn.

Adele took her hand then, and Katherine turned to see Reverend Warren step up to the lectern. A small smile was on his face, and he gave her the barest of winks as he bid them all to open to the book of Galatians.

The service slipped by more quickly than Katherine had ever remembered. May rose all too soon to play the closing hymn, and afterward the room was deathly quiet. Within a few minutes, people began to stand awkwardly yet still not saying much of anything.

Unabashed, Adele rose, pulling Katherine along with her. Linking her arm through hers, the young widow started to walk her down the aisle, Daniel and May not far behind. Katherine nearly gasped when she saw Mrs. Warren approaching them with Ruth Decker quickly coming up behind her.

"Adele," Mrs. Warren exclaimed, "how nice to see you." She glanced hesitantly at Katherine.

"Thank you, Mrs. Warren. It is good to see you as well." She smiled pleasantly. "Is it not good that Miss Wallace was able to come this morning?"

Mrs. Warren seemed to hesitate, and Ruth Decker now spoke up.

"Adele Stephens, you can't be serious. She's a secesh."

Katherine felt Daniel move behind her, and she reached back to lay a hand on his arm. His eyes were dark with anger, but he took heed of her imploring look and said nothing.

"Miss Wallace is not a secesh," Adele declared calmly. "She is a sister in Christ. I am ashamed to say I have not always seen her that way, but over the past month she has shown me that God tells us to love our enemies, not so we can heap coals upon their heads but so we might learn to love them." She looked around at the other members of the congregation who stood watching the little scene play out. "We have all lost much. Brothers, sons. . . husbands." Her voice shook on the last word, and Katherine squeezed her hand in sympathy. "But I will not allow myself to lose my faith as well. I will accept Miss Wallace as my sister in Christ."

"And so will I," May declared.

Ruth Decker seemed completely thunderstruck, but Mrs. Warren stepped toward Katherine and took both her hands in hers. Her face was awash with shame, and tears began to fall from her eyes. Reverend Warren came to stand next to his wife as she spoke. "Miss Wallace, I am so sorry. When Paul told me we needed to accept you, I couldn't. . ."

Katherine gently squeezed her hands. "Mrs. Warren, please don't give it another thought. Your husband told us about your nephew, and I am so terribly sorry."

She glanced over at Ruth Decker, who had backed off and looked very uncertain. Mr. Decker stood beside her and gave her a tentative smile. Without hesitation Katherine walked up to the woman and smiled gently. "Mrs. Decker, I never got to thank you for your kindness and hospitality when Mary and I first arrived. Thank you kindly."

Ruth Decker burst into tears and caught Katherine up in a firm embrace. "I am so ashamed of myself," she sobbed. "I can be so ridiculous at times. There's no possible excuse for how I acted."

"That's all right, Mrs. Decker. Don't worry yourself. I hope we can be friends now."

"Oh, of course," Ruth exclaimed as she released her and mopped at her eyes with a handkerchief. "I'm going to have a quilting bee very soon, and you and Mary and Adele must come."

There were other apologies after that. Not as many as Katherine would have liked but, she mused as they rode home, it was a good beginning.

Adele grasped her hand, and they smiled at each other. "I am looking forward to the quilting bee," she said.

"I am, too," Katherine replied. "Mary and I have been working on a quilt, but it won't be ready for a while yet."

A gleam appeared in Adele's eye, and she threw a quick glance at Daniel who was sitting in the seat in front of them driving. "A Double Wedding Ring pattern perhaps?" she asked in a hushed voice.

Katherine clapped a hand over her mouth to stifle her gasp. "Adele!" she hissed.

The young widow's eyes danced, but she said no more.

Katherine was glad to see her so cheerful, a stark contrast to how she must have been feeling a mere week ago. She glanced up at her new friend.

"If you had not come here, I would have drowned in my hate. . . ."

"Your example has shown her what she needs to do."

Adele's and Daniel's voices echoed in her mind, and suddenly coming here made sense. She remembered the day Mary had told her she was going to abandon her plantation and go home to Ohio. The urge to go with her was so strong she had felt sure it was God Himself guiding her.

The anxiety and worry she had felt for the past two months vanished as she now recognized her part in His plan. That God had used her as an instrument of healing gave her a sense of confidence she hadn't felt for a long while. Not since before all that had happened with Chloe.

She fingered her scar thoughtfully. *Will I ever find out what happened to her, Father?*

Daniel had written his friend as he had promised, but the man had been unable to find out anything.

Her hand dropped away from her face, and she squared her jaw resolutely. *Trust Him,* she told herself. *Don't lean on your own understanding.*

They pulled up the Kirbys' drive, and Adele immediately climbed out. Katherine knew she was eager to see how Jacob was. The boy was weak, but Mary had declared he would be fine after a few days of rest.

Adele was in the house even before Daniel had a chance to help Katherine out of the carriage. His fingers wrapped around hers as he helped her step to the ground, and her heart did a double flip as he pulled her close and placed a quick kiss on her lips. "You were wonderful this morning," he murmured.

She smiled and was about to reply when they heard the door to the house open. They turned to see Adele standing there, her face deeply distressed.

Katherine felt Daniel's arms tense. "What is it, Adele?" he asked. "Is it Jacob?"

She quickly shook her head. "Katherine has a visitor."

Katherine stared at her in surprise. "Who?"

"You must come inside," she replied stiffly before disappearing into the house.

The look on Adele's face so upset her she was up the steps and into the house before Daniel. At the door to the parlor she gasped.

A gaunt man dressed in Confederate gray stood in front of the sofa where Mary and Adele sat looking at him. He turned to Katherine, and she was shocked to hear her brother's voice come from the skeletal form. "Gather your things, Katherine. I've come to fetch you home."

Chapter 17

T he soldier in Daniel immediately reached for his Colt the instant he saw Confederate gray. He cocked the weapon as he moved to stand in front of Katherine.

The Southern officer glared at him. "You would shoot an unarmed-man, sir?"

Daniel hesitated. Glancing at the man's belt, he saw his holster was indeed empty. "No," he replied as he slowly uncocked his weapon and lowered it.

Katherine moved to go around him, but he blocked her with his arm, causing the soldier's glare to intensify. She laid a hand on his arm, and Daniel looked down at her. "It's all right," she said. "It's my brother, Charles."

Daniel reluctantly let her go by.

She started to hug her brother. When he did not return the embrace, she hastily stepped back a bit, hands clasped together. "Charles, I'm so glad to see you're alive. Aunt Ada and I found your name posted on the lists. Where have you been all this time?"

"An unfortunate clerical error. I've been a guest of the Union army for the past eight months," he replied, glaring at Daniel.

Daniel held his tongue but watched him carefully.

"The last three were at Camp Chase. I was released just yesterday. Had I not been wounded, I would have written sooner to tell you and Aunt Ada I was alive. When I finally was able to, she told me how you had abandoned her to come here."

Katherine pursed her lips slightly, but her gaze did not waver from her brother for a moment.

Mary broke the silence that had settled over the room. "You look so thin, Charles," she said gently. "Let me get you something to eat."

"No thank you, ma'am." Charles's polite words were offset by the sneer on his face. "I have only come to take my sister home." He looked piercingly at Katherine. "Her fiancé is waiting for her."

Daniel's eyes widened as Katherine gasped. "Charles, what do you mean? I was never engaged."

"You are now. Aunt Ada has it all arranged. You will finally bring prestige to our name with your marriage to Thaddeus Adams."

"Charles, you can't be serious!" Mary exclaimed. "Thaddeus Adams is nearly three times her age."

"You will kindly stay out of this." Charles snapped. "This is a family matter and no concern of yours."

"Don't talk to her that way. She's been more like family to me than you ever were, Charles."

Daniel stared at Katherine in surprise. This was a new side to her, so unlike the meek, soft-spoken woman he'd come to know. But as much as he loved her gentle ways, he was glad to see her more assertive and sure of herself. And he did not fail to notice she wasn't even reaching for her scar, as she certainly would have before. He silently cheered her on as she defiantly glared up at her older brother who was nearly as tall as he was.

Taking a deep breath and calming herself, she went on. "I'm sorry, but I won't even consider leaving here to marry Mr. Adams. Ohio is my home now."

Her brother's face grew red. "As head of our family, you are under my protection," he shot back. "You will do as I say."

"No!"

Charles's face contorted with rage as he backhanded Katherine across the jaw.

As she crumpled to the floor, Daniel sprang forward and pinned Charles Wallace against the wall, his pistol pointed directly between his eyes. Suddenly Daniel wasn't in his family's parlor but on a smoke-filled battlefield, his enemy backed up against a bullet-riddled stump. He cocked his gun.

"Daniel!"

He jumped at the warm hand on his arm and blinked as the image melted away.

Adele was standing next to him, the pressure from her hands growing as she tried to force him to lower his weapon. Mary knelt on the floor next to Katherine, who he desperately hoped was only unconscious.

He swallowed and backed away but kept his Colt trained on Charles. "Get out," he said roughly. "Get off my property and don't come back. If anyone's going to marry your sister, it'll be me."

∞

Adele and Mary made Katherine stay in bed for several days. She tried to tell them she was fine, but Mary would have none of it.

"Head injuries are nothing to be played with," she'd said sternly on the second day. "Your head hit the floor awfully hard when you fell."

Katherine remembered Charles backhanding her but little else after that save for the vague yet pleasant memory of Daniel carrying her up the stairs.

By the fourth day, she still had a large lump on the back of her head and her jaw was bruised and tender, but she felt more than ready to get out of bed. She missed Daniel terribly. Mary would not permit him to even come up the stairs, but the notes he'd been sending up had lessened the ache considerably.

The first had been a word-for-word copy of four of Shakespeare's sonnets: eighteen, twenty-nine, fifty-five, and fifty-seven. How had he known those had always been her favorites? The next evening she had blushed furiously over a copy of Byron's "She Walks in Beauty."

Now, as she sat up in bed rereading one of the sonnets, a small dark head poked its way around the corner of her door. "Jacob!" she exclaimed softly and motioned for him to come in.

She was happy to see he was up and dressed and his once-infected hand seemed back to normal. It was still wrapped snugly with clean strips of linen. Mary was taking no chances of its becoming infected again.

He sat on the edge of her bed and picked up one of the sonnets. She smiled as the child read the poem, his face becoming more confused by the second.

"What does 'bootless cries' mean?" he asked. "Is he crying 'cause he lost his boots?"

Katherine chuckled. "No, he's sad because his cries seem meaningless."

"Oh," he said, handing it back. He looked at her for a minute and frowned. "That man was mean to hit you. Who was he?"

Katherine's heart was in her throat at the thought the boy had witnessed such violence. "Oh, Jacob, I'm sorry you saw that. Why were you even down there?"

"I heard someone talk mean to Mrs. O'Neal, so I went downstairs so I could tell him to leave her alone." He smiled crookedly. "But you did that real good."

"What else did you see?" Katherine was eager to know what happened after everything went black. She had asked Adele and Mary how they had gotten Charles to leave, but they had simply urged her to rest, smiling mysteriously when they assured her he would not be back.

"Mr. Kirby, he slammed the man against the wall and pulled his gun on him."

Katherine gasped and her hands flew to her mouth. *Oh, surely Daniel didn't shoot Charles!*

Seeing the look on her face, the boy hurried on. "But Ma talked to him and he backed off and told the man to get out." A broad smile lit up the youngster's face. "And then Mr. Kirby said if—"

"Jacob." They looked up to see Adele standing in the doorway, giving her son a look of gentle reproach. "You should not be bothering Miss Wallace. She needs her rest."

"Oh Adele," Katherine said as the woman took her son's seat after shooing him out. "I feel fine."

The young widow looked at her carefully. "What did my son tell you?"

"Daniel didn't really pull his gun on Charles, did he?"

Adele nodded soberly. "I have never seen Daniel so angry. For a moment, it seemed he was someplace else. He was startled when I put my hand on his arm."

"Is he all right?"

She smiled reassuringly. "He seems fine. You can see for yourself. Mary says you may come down in a little while." Her eyes sparkled as she pulled a note from her dress pocket. "Daniel sends you this."

Katherine opened it and tears sprang to her eyes.

"Arise, my love, my fair one, and come away."
SONG OF SOLOMON 2:13

Mary came in a little later and helped Katherine get dressed. She was surprised when Mary laid out her blue dress and fussed over her nearly twenty minutes longer than necessary.

Putting her hair up in its usual style proved to be impossible; the lump on the back of her head was still so tender Mary was sure coiling braids against the nape of her neck would give her a headache. Instead, she swept Katherine's thick hair up on either side, letting the rest fall in waves down to her waist.

Katherine looked at her nervously when she'd finished. She hadn't worn her hair down since she was a young girl. "Mary, I can't go down like this."

Mary smiled gently. "It's not entirely proper, but you won't be going out in public. You look just fine. Lovely, in fact."

Katherine winced at her choice of words and, glancing into the mirror in the door of her wardrobe, started.

Mary noticed and laid a hand on her arm. "What is it, dear?" she asked.

"I'm. . .pretty," she whispered. She closed her eyes and shook her head, but nothing changed. The same attractive young lady was still staring back at her with large, expressive eyes and hair with fiery red highlights. "It must be the mirror or because my hair is down. . . ."

"Or because you've always been pretty?" Her friend pulled her into a warm hug. "Come on before Daniel wears a hole in the rug."

Mary left her at the foot of the stairs, sternly telling her she and Adele would not be very far away in the kitchen.

Katherine reached back and nervously patted her loose wavy hair once more before stepping into the parlor.

If she had somehow managed to become pretty in the course of four days, then Daniel had become twice as handsome in the same amount of time. She barely breathed as he stopped his pacing to stare at her.

Before she knew it, he was holding her tightly, like he would never let go.

∽

Daniel finally loosened his hold on Katherine and looked down at her. It was the first time he had seen her in days, and his eyes were instantly drawn to the ugly bruise Charles's blow had left on her jaw. Guilt gnawed at him as he ran his thumb over it.

Katherine's eyes softened. "It's not your fault," she said.

"I should have known better. You shouldn't have been within two feet of him."

"I'm fine," she soothed. "I've been through worse."

"And you'll never go through something like that ever again." He sealed his promise with a lingering kiss. Raising his head, he noticed her hair. "Trying to start a new fashion?" he teased, holding up a handful of it.

"No." She blushed. "I still have quite a lump on the back of my head. Mary was worried if we put it up I'd have a frightful headache." The smile faded from her face and she took him in with worried eyes. "Adele said you weren't yourself after..." Her voice trailed off.

Daniel nodded and led her over to the sofa. "The war sneaks up on me at times," he said as they sat down.

Katherine's eyes grew large with worry. "It's not like Reverend Warren's nephew?"

"No," he quickly reassured her. "Nothing like that." Loud, sudden noises had a tendency to spook him more than they used to, and Michael had once awakened him from a very ugly dream. But he didn't feel like he wasn't in control or not getting on with life. "I was just so angry when he hit you. That and your brother and I being in uniform." He grasped her hands and squeezed them. "I doubt it will happen again."

"Do you want to talk about it with me?" she offered.

"Katherine, there are things I saw and experienced no woman should ever hear about," Daniel replied gravely. "But I've spoken with Michael several times." In spite of the fact he had not fought in the war, or perhaps because of it, Simon Peter's son was a considerate and careful listener. They had also prayed together on more than one occasion.

"I'll pray for you then," Katherine whispered tenderly.

He smiled as she squeezed his hands, and he glanced down at them. "Thank you. Just your presence is soothing. Like that first day out in the courtyard."

Her eyes dropped away and her cheeks turned crimson.

He was amazed by how beautiful she was when she was embarrassed. Some of her long, silky tresses fell over her shoulder. With her hair always pulled back in coiled braids, he'd never had the opportunity to appreciate its dark, fiery depths. He gently pulled more of it over her shoulder and thought of the Byron poem he had copied for her. "'And all that's best of dark and bright; Meet in her aspect and her eyes,'" he softly quoted. Their eyes met, and he quickly found himself kissing her soft lips.

"Daniel Kirby," she reproached a moment later, "how scandalous of you to send me a poem from a man described—by his mistress no less—as 'mad, bad, and dangerous to know.'"

"Which is more scandalous, that I sent you one of his poems or that you know that about him?" They laughed, and Daniel wanted nothing more than to spend the rest of his life going back and forth with her like this.

"Katherine. . ." His voice trailed off. The words were on the edge of his lips, but he couldn't bring himself to say them. How could he? She wasn't meant for the kind of life he could offer her.

He quickly stood, and she stared at him with startled eyes. "I'm sorry. I have to do something. Tell Aunt Mary I'll be back for dinner."

Daniel was so caught up with his own thoughts he failed to notice his aunt had followed him out to the barn and down to Scioto's stable.

He turned from fetching his saddle to find her standing near the stairs with her arms crossed. Her lips were pursed slightly, and she wore a look of concern. "What happened?" she asked him.

He glanced at her and quickly returned to saddling his horse. Both Adele and Aunt Mary had expected him to propose to Katherine this evening, especially after what they had heard him tell her brother. "I couldn't do it."

"Why? Katherine loves you dearly. I never saw her this way, even with Thomas."

"No, it's not her. It's me." He took Scioto's bridle off its hook and fiddled with the straps. "She deserves better than this."

His aunt didn't pretend to not understand what he meant. "She's perfectly content here, Daniel. I can assure you of that."

"Maybe, but I'm not satisfied offering her the life of a farmer's wife." He bridled his horse and fastened the straps. "I'm going over to see if Elijah Carr's offer still stands." He turned to look at his aunt, and he was surprised by the uncertainty in her eyes. "You think I shouldn't? You were the one telling me he would give me a good price."

"Yes, I know," she slowly replied. "At first I thought you were keeping the farm because of your pa, but I've come to realize the reason is much different than that. And much more important. Are you sure you want to do this?"

"Yes," he said. He pulled himself up into the saddle and looked down at his aunt. "Don't tell Katherine. I. . .I want to surprise her." But as he rode off, he struggled to ignore the growing feeling of doubt in his heart.

Chapter 18

K atherine, did you hear what I said?"

Katherine started at Mary's question and turned away from the window. She, Adele, and Mary had been carefully piecing together quilt blocks, and they now had enough for a good-sized quilt. Some of them were laid out on the table in the dining room to see how they would look once they were all pieced together. Once the top was done, they would invite Ruth, May, and Mrs. Warren over to help quilt it. But Katherine's heart wasn't in it. She was too worried about Daniel.

Just a little while ago, for the second time in two weeks, Daniel had ridden off on Scioto with Mr. O'Conner following in his buggy. It couldn't be money related. Even during the war the farm had done well, and in spite of how it had looked when they had returned, Elijah Carr had not shirked in keeping the animals and fields well cared for.

But Daniel had been distracted and moody ever since he'd left her sitting in the parlor. At first she'd been concerned that he was having trouble with his memories of the war, but Michael had assured her he hadn't talked to him about it since her brother left.

She bit her lip and looked down at the quilt blocks on the table. Plucking one up, she looked at it absentmindedly.

"We can assume you don't like it," Mary said.

Katherine looked at her and then back down at the table. "Oh, I'm sorry, Mary," she said, replacing the block and looking at them. Mary had let her decide the pattern, and she had settled on an Irish chain. "It looks beautiful, but I wonder if we should have done it on point," she said, referring to the way they could have pieced the blocks so that the squares were sitting on one point, making them look like diamonds.

"That would have been very pretty," Adele said, looking at the squares. "But I like the way this looks just as well. Perhaps next time we will do as you suggest and we can use some appliqué. I will show you how."

When it had been decided that Adele and Jacob would continue staying at the Kirby farm, Adele brought over a quilt her grandmother had made when she had lived in Zoar. It was an orange-and-green floral appliquéd pattern on a white background, and Katherine had admired the careful workmanship.

Suddenly the wind whipped up and blew the squares on top of one another. Adele and Katherine gathered them up while Mary went to the window. "A storm's blowing in," she said, shutting the window. "I hope Daniel and Mr. O'Conner stay safe."

"Mary, just where were they going?" Katherine asked. Surely she knew something about what her nephew was up to.

"Daniel asked us not to say anything," Mary said quietly. "It's nothing to fret over."

"Then why would he tell you not to tell me?" If Katherine had been worried about Daniel before, she was twice so now. Adele and Mary looked at each other, and Katherine frowned. "What's going on?"

"Do you want some tea, dear?" Mary asked, trying to avoid her question.

But Katherine wasn't about to be put off. "Mary, I want to know what Daniel's doing."

"We should tell her, Mary," Adele said quietly.

Mary grasped Katherine's hands. "Daniel's decided to sell the farm to Elijah Carr. He's on his way to his farm now to sign the papers."

Katherine stared at them before walking out into the hall and taking her bonnet from its peg. Adele and Mary followed her and stood in the doorway. She quickly tied on her bonnet and grabbed a shawl.

"Where on earth are you going?" Mary exclaimed as she opened the door. The sky was dark and the wind was whipping the trees back and forth furiously.

"I'm going to stop him," she declared and ran out the door before they could stop her.

The rain began to fall in heavy drops by the time she reached the end of the drive, and she covered her head with the shawl. It all made sense now, his mood, the meetings with Mr. O'Conner. He was selling the land and he wasn't happy about it. And the only reason he wouldn't was if he knew he was going against the Lord's will.

The thought caused her to move faster and she began to run. But soon her skirts and petticoats were waterlogged, and she was forced to go far slower than she would have liked. Thunder shook the very air around her, and she turned to see black clouds rolling in from the west. Her heart began to pound with fear, but she hurried on, determined to keep Daniel from going against God's will.

She had just rounded a slight curve in the road when she caught sight of a horse and rider galloping toward her. It was Daniel. She was too late.

Catching sight of her, he brought Scioto to a sudden halt, and the horse danced in a small circle as he spoke. "Katherine, what are you doing here?" he yelled over the rain and thunder. "Are you crazy?"

"Daniel Aaron Kirby, how could you?" she yelled back. She was so angry she failed to notice the wind was becoming fiercer. "What do you mean by selling the farm?"

Daniel didn't answer. He took one look at the western sky and, grabbing Katherine by the wrist, hauled her up behind him in the saddle. Before she could utter a word of protest, Scioto was off like a shot and she clung to Daniel for dear life.

All at once they were back at the farm. As she slid from the saddle, she heard a low distant rumble like that of a train. Daniel heard it, too, and after jumping down, he gave his horse a solid swat on the hindquarters before grabbing Katherine's hand and running for the root cellar.

Daniel swung her inside and shut the door tight behind them. He hoped Simon Peter had been able to get his aunt, Adele, and Jacob into the secret room out in the barn. It was the safest place on the farm during a tornado. He would have taken Katherine there, too, but he could tell by the sound of the storm they wouldn't have made it there in time. Daniel fumbled for the lantern that was kept on one of the shelves and lit it. Turning around, he realized he might as well have shut himself up with an angry bobcat.

Katherine stood there with her arms crossed, soaking wet and positively livid. She had every right to be angry, of course. He was angry at himself for even considering. . .

The wind suddenly took on an awful low squeal, and although it wasn't as close as it had been before, now was not the time to discuss the matter. He pulled her down next to him against the back wall where the cellar was nestled into the side of a small hill. It would give them the best protection if the tornado hit the farm.

Katherine seemed to realize what was happening and didn't resist. Much. For a few tense seconds, Daniel wasn't sure anything would be left standing, but the low rumble seemed to go further north, and he began to relax as the winds eased a little.

"I think we're safe for now," he finally said.

"Good," Katherine declared as she jumped to her feet. "I'm not spending one more second cooped up in here with you." She started for the door, but Daniel grabbed her arm. She tried to yank it away. "Let me go!"

"No, there might be more," he snapped, and to prove his point the winds slammed into the tiny building, making it shake. "Aren't there tornados in South Carolina?"

"Yes, but the *hurricanes* there are worse," she shot back. Apparently he was just about to encounter one since she gave him a stinging slap on the arm, which hurt twice as much since his shirt was soaking wet.

"Ow! Wait, Kath—"

"How could you?" She started to lay into him again, but he grabbed her arm. "Let go!"

"Katherine, I didn't sell the farm."

She stopped struggling and stared at him. "What?"

He pulled her close. "I didn't sell the farm. I couldn't. I got all the way to Elijah Carr's drive today, but in the end, God wouldn't let me."

The last two weeks had been the worst of Daniel's life. The whole process had been difficult, as if the Lord had been giving him time to reconsider. He and Carr had been unable to decide on a price, and then business had kept Mr. O'Conner from getting the papers drawn up right away. When he had approached Dr. Harris, his old mentor had tried to talk him out of selling the farm, in spite of how eager he'd always been for Daniel to become a professor. And the distinct feeling that he was going against God's will was next to impossible to ignore.

Katherine spoke, rousing him from his thoughts. "Daniel, why ever did you consider such a thing?"

"For you," he whispered. He saw the confusion in her face and continued. "I didn't want to be a farmer when I gave you this." He pulled the ring from his pocket, laying it in her small hand. "This has been in my family since before the Kirbys came to America. My grandfather gave it to my grandmother, and Pa gave it to Ma." His heart pounded as wonder and joy softly spread over her delicate little face. "Marry me?"

She answered him with a long, slow kiss.

"I'm sorry," he said a moment later. "You deserve much better than a farmer. I—"

Katherine laid her fingers over his lips and smiled. "I *am* getting better than a farmer. Much better. I'm getting you."

∽

Katherine watched from the parlor window as Daniel strode back to the house with Simon Peter and his sons, the last bit of sunlight drifting from the evening sky. It had taken them the rest of the afternoon to round up the livestock and see what kind of damage the tornado had caused.

They had been lucky. Apparently the tornado had tracked north, skipping nearly all of their land. There was only minor damage to the barn and a couple of the outbuildings and only two fields would need to be replanted. Daniel had been grateful there had been no hail.

Everything had been accounted for. Except Scioto. Daniel's horse couldn't be found anywhere.

Stepping outside, Katherine joined Daniel as he said good-bye to Simon Peter, Michael, and Aaron.

"We'll keep our eyes open while we're riding back home," Simon said as he took up the reins. "If we find him, I'll send him on home with Michael."

"Thanks," Daniel said gloomily.

"Don't you worry," Michael said. "Jeremiah said he's never seen such a smart horse. He'll be back." The young man reached out and gave Daniel a quick hug and a slap on the back before climbing into his pa's wagon.

Katherine waved as they drove off and then turned to Daniel. "We'll find him," she said softly as he pulled her into a quick embrace. "He'll probably be standing outside the barn door come morning."

"I hope so," he said.

Stepping inside the house, they went into the parlor. Katherine immediately went over to the secretary where they kept the books they were discussing. "What shall we talk about tonight?"

"I hope it's not that Sissy man again tonight," Jacob said as he played on the floor with Toby's old lead soldier set.

Adele looked at her son from where she sat on the sofa with Mary as they sewed. "Mein *dummer*, Junge." She chuckled. "What do you mean?"

"I'm not a silly boy," Jacob said defensively. He looked at Daniel, who sat in the high-backed easy chair. "You know, Sissyroo, Sis...sis..."

"You mean Cicero?" Daniel asked and laughed when the boy nodded.

Katherine was grateful Jacob had taken Daniel's mind off his lost horse even if only for a moment.

"I think I'll just read to us from one of the Psalms tonight."

Katherine brought him his Bible, and he kissed her hand before she went to sit between Mary and Adele.

"All right, you two," Mary said reproachfully then smiled. "Well, I guess I can't be too hard on you. John and I were just as quick to steal a kiss as anyone else."

"Nathaniel was the same," Adele said softly. She was silent for a moment before smiling playfully. "But Nathaniel did not propose to me in a root cellar."

"Well, I didn't exactly plan it that way."

Katherine looked at Daniel and watched as his cheeks reddened for a change. "I think it was lovely," she declared, looking at him.

His soft green eyes glowed with gratitude

"Well, I wish I had been in the root cellar instead of the barn," Jacob said. Simon Peter had hustled everyone into the secret room Daniel had been sleeping in after making sure the livestock had been set loose. The young boy hadn't liked going down into the closed-in space in spite of the fact they'd had two lanterns.

"Better there than out in the storm," Mary said. She glanced at Katherine and Daniel. "You two were lucky you weren't blown off the face of the earth."

Daniel frowned, and Katherine knew he was thinking about Scioto again. "Where did you and Simon Peter and the boys look this afternoon?" she asked.

"We didn't have enough light to look very far," he said thoughtfully. "I wish I had seen which direction he had gone. I'm going to go looking for him after church tomorrow."

"I'll come with you," Katherine said.

"Jacob and I could use some exercise, so we will come, too." Adele smiled as her son gave a little whoop and thanked her. "Four sets of eyes are better than two. Do you want to come with us, Mary?"

"Well, I don't know about me," she replied. Her foot, while mostly healed, was still a little tender. "I think I'll stay behind and read my Bible."

Adele, Katherine, and Daniel looked at each other with knowing smiles. Mary might start out reading her Bible, but she would end up taking a Sunday afternoon nap. But she more than made up for it as she usually read every night before going to bed.

"Well, Jacob," Daniel said as he opened his Bible, "since we bored you with Cicero for the past few nights, what Psalm should I read?"

"Can we read a story instead?" the boy asked hopefully, "about Elijah and the prophets of Baal?"

As Daniel turned to First Kings, Katherine took up her sewing and caught the glint of gold on her right hand. Her heart jumped as she glanced at the ring Daniel had given her. Mary said she remembered her sister wearing the band on her right ring finger after Joseph had proposed to her, and Katherine eagerly did the same.

She glanced up at Daniel, who was now reading to a very attentive Jacob. He'd noticed what she'd done at dinner and had smiled with approval. Daniel intended that she be a fall bride. When the leaves would be just beginning to match her eyes, he'd said.

Katherine bit her lip and smiled. She hadn't been able to understand at first what was so different about her appearance when she looked in the mirror over the past couple of weeks. Then she finally understood she was seeing herself through Daniel's eyes and the love he had for her. She started in on her sewing with a contented smile.

"I will praise thee, O Lord, with my whole heart."

Chapter 19

U nfortunately, Scioto was not standing outside the barn door or any-where else about the farm by the next morning.

After services, Daniel decided the best way to look would be east of the farm. "He would have been trying to head away from the storm once I let him go," he reasoned.

After lunch he, Adele, Jacob, and Katherine set out over the fields. Daniel grasped Katherine's hand, and he showed her what fields had been planted and which fields were lying fallow for the season. But he was clearly distracted, and Katherine knew he was worried about his horse. She glanced at his belt. He'd brought his Colt with him. She just hoped if they did find the animal he wouldn't have to use it.

"Where did you get Scioto?" she eventually asked.

"He found me." Daniel stopped for a moment and scanned the horizon. The only things in view were a line of trees and Adele and Jacob walking several feet away to their left. "I'd gotten nicked in the leg by a bullet," he said as they continued walking. "I was lost in some woods, and I wasn't sure if I was behind enemy lines or not. My horse had been shot out from under me. Then I heard movement in the brush nearby, and there he was, large as life, urging me to get up. I managed to swing my-self up, and he just took off. I was back with my regiment before I knew it." He sighed and looked over the horizon once more. "As swift and sure as the Scioto River. That's how he got his name."

Katherine squeezed his hand. "We'll find him. I'm sure of it."

"Thank you, Kat." He kissed her on the forehead.

Katherine was about to ask him why he was suddenly calling her Kat when Adele called out to them. They quickly made their way over to her and Jacob.

"Mr. Kirby, I found hoofprints!" the boy said excitedly.

133

"They probably belong to our plow horses," he said as he knelt down to examine the prints. "No, these can't belong to Belle and Babe."

"Why not?" Katherine asked.

"They're too small for one, and there's only one set of them."

"Then these might belong to Scioto?" Adele asked.

"Yes," Daniel muttered and started walking in the same direction as the prints. Katherine, Adele, and Jacob followed. The tracks stopped just before the fence that marked the edge of the Kirby property and continued on the other side.

"This is Elijah Carr's property," Adele said. Her face tensed slightly. "At least it is now."

"Adele?" Katherine laid a gentle hand on her arm, and the woman clasped it.

"This land used to belong to her and Nate," Daniel said quietly. "Jacob and I could go on. Let Kat take you back to the house."

Adele looked out over the fields for a moment. "No, I will be all right."

Daniel started to climb the fence, but Katherine was hesitant, remembering how Carr had chased Jacob off his land a few weeks ago. "Do you think we should?"

"While I was out with Simon Peter, we met up with one of Carr's farmhands chasing after a stray cow. He said we could look if we needed to."

Once they were over the fence, Katherine walked on with Adele. "Our house was over that way," Adele said, pointing to the line of trees. Katherine caught sight of a slate roof.

The field they were walking over was lying fallow, and they lost the prints in the tall weeds and grass that had grown in it. They spread out, hoping to find them again, and Katherine thought it would be worth taking a peek at the farmhouse.

Brush and young trees had grown up around it, and she pushed her way through until she came to a sort of clearing. The house stood before her. It was a small frame house, and as Jacob had said, the glass windows were broken out. A pump stood nearby, and she could imagine Adele pumping water from it to get Jacob or Nate something to drink. Her heart ached for her friend's loss.

"Father," she whispered, "help Adele find happiness again." Katherine had noticed how wistfully the young widow would look at her and Daniel. She knew no one could ever replace Nate in the young widow's heart, but she believed the Lord could bless her with room for another. And then Jacob could have a pa again.

Suddenly a familiar face appeared around the corner of the house.

"Scioto," Katherine exclaimed softly.

The horse grunted as she approached, and she gathered the reins that hung broken from his bit. She led him out further into the clearing, pleased to see he seemed perfectly sound. She made certain by leading him around in a circle before bringing him to a stop. She rubbed his neck and he nuzzled her. "We've been worried sick about you, boy," she murmured.

She stiffened as she heard the click of a gun being cocked. She turned to see Charles step out of the trees.

"And I have been just as concerned for you, sister dear," he said as he leveled the gun at her.

"Charles!" she gasped.

"I'm glad to see there was no permanent damage done." He was referring to the blow he had dealt her, and she raised a hand to her face. "It's just too bad I didn't knock some sense into you."

"What are you still doing here? Where did you get the gun?"

"As I told you before, you will do as I say. We're going to leave for home right now on that horse, so lead him over."

Katherine turned, and in one swift movement slapped Scioto on the hindquarters. The horse screamed and took off running toward the fields. "Daniel!" she yelled as Charles grabbed her and threw his hand over her mouth.

"What'd you do a fool thing like that for?"

"It's a good thing she did, secesh." Elijah Carr rushed out of the trees, a shotgun in hand. "You were planning on walking out on our deal. She still has to get Kirby over here, remember?"

Charles scowled at the older man. "Well, you heard the man, sister dear," he growled as he dug his gun painfully into her ribs. "Call him again."

⌒

Daniel saw Scioto burst out of the brush at the same moment he heard Katherine calling for him. He knew instantly something was wrong. His horse came to a stop before him. Had Scioto hurt her somehow?

Adele and Jacob rushed up as Katherine called for him again. She sounded frightened, and Daniel drew his Colt.

"Daniel, what is it?" Adele asked.

"Something's wrong," he said. "Take Scioto and get help."

Without hesitation she swung herself up into the saddle, and Daniel helped Jacob climb up in front of her. As they galloped off, he jogged toward Nate's old house, slowing as he drew close.

He reached the clearing and saw Charles standing near the house with a gun pointed at Katherine's head. "Katherine!"

"Now, now, she'll be just fine as long as you do as I say."

Daniel felt the muzzle of a shotgun in his ribs, and he instantly uncocked his weapon and let go of the grip so it hung from his finger.

Elijah Carr took it and, sticking it in his belt, nudged him toward a large stump where a pen and inkpot sat. "We're just going to conduct a little business."

Daniel watched as Carr walked around him and laid the sale papers on the stump. "Where did those come from? They should still be with Mr. O'Conner."

"Mr. O'Conner had to stay with me for a while until the storm blew over." He smiled meanly. "One of my hands managed to get ahold of these for me." He nodded toward the papers. "Now sign."

Daniel looked at Katherine and then back at Carr. There was no way around it. If he didn't do what Carr asked, either he or Charles would shoot Katherine, more than likely killing her. His heart pounded, and he knelt down, picked up the pen, and dipped it in the ink.

He was about to sign his name when Katherine spoke. "Mr. Carr, all the land in the world won't bring your brother back," she said softly.

Carr stared at her. "What do you know about my brother, secesh?"

"I know he died a horrible death at the hands of foolish men. I've been praying for your nephew and your sister-in-law. And for you."

Something hit Daniel's boot. Carr's attention was diverted, and Daniel slowly looked down to see a buckeye lying at the base of the stump. He stared at it in amazement, not because it was nowhere near the season for the nuts to fall but because of the letters he saw etched in it. J. M. K. Jonah Michael Kirby. Praying that he was not imagining things, he laid the pen down and rose.

Carr looked at him then noticed the unsigned papers. "What do you think you're doing?"

"We've all been praying for you, Elijah," he replied. "Even Adele. Even me."

A look of amazement fell over Carr's face, much to Daniel's surprise.

136

He didn't know the man's face could look anything but greedy and hateful. His mother had been right. He should have been praying for the man all along.

"Mr. Carr, I—" Katherine began. She winced as Charles roughly grabbed her arm.

Daniel had to fight the urge not to do something stupid.

"My sister is obviously disturbing you, sir," he said. "So we'll be on our way."

Carr's face resumed its normal expression. "Just what makes you think you're free to leave?"

"It was part of the deal," Charles snapped.

"I don't deal with Johnny Rebs," Carr replied, turning his shotgun toward the pair.

Katherine screamed as Charles shot Elijah Carr in the chest. The man fell to the ground, and Daniel dove for his gun. He pulled it from Carr's belt, but Charles rushed up and kicked it out of his hand.

"Your turn now, Billy Yank," Charles sneered, aiming right at Daniel's head.

A shot rang out, and Charles slumped to the ground next to Carr. Daniel heard Katherine gasp as his own brother stepped from the bushes.

Jonah looked at him. "Guess it was his turn."

Chapter 20

The babble of Mill Creek filled Katherine's ears as she sank down on a rock by the water's edge. She breathed deeply and looked out over her peaceful surroundings, but her hands were still shaky and she still could not quite believe what had happened. Her brother was dead, and Elijah Carr had only survived long enough to die in his own bed.

When Charles had left the Kirby farm, he had wandered onto Elijah Carr's land and found the Stephenses' old farmhouse. According to one of Carr's farmhands, he'd been staying there for the past two weeks before being discovered the day of the storm. When Carr questioned him, he realized he could use him to get Daniel to sign the sale papers.

She began to shake as the whole episode played out in her head once more. If it hadn't been for Jonah, Daniel would be dead right now, and she would be getting dragged back to South Carolina to be forced into a loveless marriage.

She shook her head. Like everyone else, she still couldn't quite believe Daniel's older brother was alive.

Like Charles, Jonah had been reported as being killed in action. But in reality, he'd been sent to a Confederate prisoner-of-war camp, none other than the notorious Andersonville Prison. Jonah had barely survived the harsh conditions and had been forced to watch helplessly as many of his fellow prisoners died of exposure and malnutrition.

When he was finally released, the army had put him and many other prisoners from Ohio on the steamship *Sultana*. The hopelessly overcrowded riverboat trudged up the Mississippi River and was just a few miles north of Memphis, Tennessee, when it exploded. Jonah had been able to jump from the ship and swim to safety, but he became ill and had to stay in a Memphis hospital for several days before finally arriving home. He'd literally just walked up the drive when Adele had come charging up on Scioto.

Father, Your timing is perfect. Thank You for protecting us.

She heard footsteps and turned to see Daniel stepping into the shadow of the trees. He gave her a little smile. "Thought I might find you here." He walked over and sat down next to her on the rock, slipping his arm around her.

She rested her head against his shoulder. "I needed a little peace and quiet. What did the sheriff say?"

"He said Jonah only did what he had to do to defend me. When he searched Carr's papers, he found his will. The land will go to his nephew, Ben."

"Does the sheriff know how to reach him?"

Daniel nodded. "He found a number of letters from Carr's sister-in-law and from Ben. It'll take a while to reach them. They're clear out in the far western part of the Dakota Territory." He squeezed her. "What do you plan to do about your brother?"

She sighed. "I'll telegraph Aunt Ada. Most likely she'll have me bury him here. She won't want to have to tell Charleston society what happened." She brushed a tear from her eye and felt Daniel squeeze her shoulder. "I had hoped Charles would have a chance to change his heart before he died."

"I'm sorry," Daniel said.

Katherine laid her head back on his broad shoulder, and they looked out at the soothing waters of Mill Creek.

After a while, she raised her head. "How's Jonah?"

Daniel paused for a moment, and Katherine knew he, too, was finding it hard to believe his brother was alive. "Adele went with him just now to see Ma's grave." He sighed. "He's not very happy with me, though." He rose and walked up to the edge of the creek. "I'm not very happy with myself. I came very close—too close—to throwing away his inheritance. I should have trusted what the Lord was telling me."

Katherine joined him and took his hand in both of hers. "'If we confess our sins, he is faithful and just to forgive us our sins, and to cleanse us from all unrighteousness.' God will forgive you, and I know Jonah will in time."

He smiled at her tenderly, reaching up with his free hand to stroke her face. "Thank you, Kat."

She looked at him curiously. "That's the third time you've called me that today."

"It's to remind me never to get you angry." He pulled her into his arms. "You get as feisty as a wild bobcat."

"Are you sure you can love such a dangerous creature?" she teased him. She caught her breath at the look in his eyes.

He lowered his head and kissed her until everything around her spun. "Katherine Eliza Wallace, I'll love you until Mill Creek runs dry, and forever after that."

Epilogue

"Now what God hath joined together, let no man put asunder," Reverend Warren declared. He smiled at Daniel. "You may now kiss the bride."

Katherine laid her hands lightly on her new husband's chest as he tenderly kissed her.

A soft sigh of approval rose from all those assembled in the Kirby parlor. No sooner had the reverend presented them as Mr. and Mrs. Daniel Kirby than it seemed the entire crowd moved forward as one to wish them well. With embraces and handshakes, one person after another congratulated the happy pair, and Katherine thought her arms would fall off before they were through.

Jonah stepped forward and, nodding to her, soberly shook his brother's hand. "I'm happy for both of you," he said and, without so much as smiling at them, stepped away.

Katherine looked at Daniel, and he squeezed her hand in reassurance.

Mary stepped up and hugged her and her nephew.

"I pray he'll be all right," Katherine said as they parted.

Mary looked after Jonah with weary eyes. "He needs all the prayers he can get right now."

"Is he still having nightmares?" Daniel asked.

"I'm afraid so," she replied.

Jonah walked into the empty dining room and was soon followed by Adele. She laid a hand on his arm, and the hard look left his face for a moment.

"He seems a little better when she's around, though," Mary added.

Adele and Jacob were staying with the Deckers, but the young widow came out to the Kirby farm nearly every day to help Mary.

"A soothing presence," Daniel said, looking at his new bride. He

141

looked around the room before turning back and smiling at her, a spark in his green eyes. "Mary, Katherine, come here. I have a little surprise."

"Daniel Aaron Kirby, what else have you done?" Katherine asked as she lifted the full skirts of her new dress. It was made of cream-colored linen that Ruth Decker had special ordered just for Katherine. With Jonah having taken over the farm, Daniel had accepted the position as a classics professor at Ohio Wesleyan alongside Professor Harris. He'd already surprised her with their new house in Delaware and news that they would honeymoon in Maine. He also promised they would visit with his good friend General Joshua Chamberlain and his family while they were there. How could there possibly be more?

She and Mary looked at each other in confusion as Daniel led them over to where the Johnson clan stood. It had been months since they had seen Simon Peter and his sons. Jonah had taken over what was left of the planting when he came home, and they had been busy out at their own farm.

With a broad smile, Simon Peter took her hand in his. "How do, Mrs. Kirby?" he said. "Things been so busy you haven't met my wife, Celia, yet."

"I'm so glad to meet you," Celia said, clasping Katherine's hands. The woman smiled at Daniel and then looked back at her. "Mrs. Kirby, I believe you already know my sister."

Wondering what she could mean, Katherine looked to see a young woman step out from behind Simon Peter's tall form. "Katherine, I'm so very glad for you."

"Chloe!" Katherine and Mary both gasped, and they quickly embraced her.

Katherine held her at arm's length, her eyes swimming with tears. "Oh Chloe, I'm so sorry—"

"Oh no, Katherine, don't blame yourself. I never did." The two of them embraced tightly once more.

Katherine looked at Daniel. "How long have you known she was Celia's sister?"

"A while," he admitted. "I wanted to tell you right away, but Chloe wanted to surprise you."

As the guests began to slowly leave, Katherine stepped out into the courtyard for some fresh air and to breathe a quick prayer of thanks. October was starting out a bit chilly, and she shivered.

A moment later, she found herself being wrapped in something warm. Looking down, she saw her Irish Chain quilt that Mary and Adele had lovingly finished in time for her wedding day. Daniel's strong arms soon followed, and she leaned back against his chest as they watched the sun slowly dip lower over the fields.

With a sigh of contentment, she turned her head slightly to glance back at her husband, and he turned her in his arms and kissed her with a passion that rivaled the horizon's fiery glow.

"How ever did I manage it?" Katherine eventually murmured.

"Manage what?" Daniel smiled.

"How did I, of all people, manage to capture a Yankee heart?"

Wounded Heart

Dedication

After the Civil War, only men with extreme symptoms of what is now known as post-traumatic stress disorder (PTSD) were sent to soldiers' homes and asylums to recuperate. The rest worked through their war experiences as best they could with the help of family, friends, and faith, a circumstance I have tried to portray here. I wish to thank Lee Strobel for his book *The Case for Faith*, which was instrumental in creating Jonah Kirby. To my editor, Aaron McCarver, and dear friend Sally Bayless, this book is all the better for your input. Thank you. And many thanks to those men and women who suffered and died for our country from its birth up to its present conflicts. To those same men and women, this book is respectfully dedicated.

Chapter 1

Delaware, Ohio
Late March, 1866

A dele Stephens, you haven't heard a word I've said in the last five minutes!"

Adele looked up.

Her friend, Mary O'Neal, was sitting next to her in the parlor of Mary's nephew, Daniel Kirby, and her warm brown eyes held a look of reproach. The older woman set down her teacup and picked up a quilting square from the side table between them. "I asked what you thought of the quilt I'm working on."

"I am sorry, Mary," Adele said, taking the square from her. She held it up, but as her mind wandered again, she looked right through the pretty green- and brown-print squares. Suddenly the fabric disappeared, and she looked up in surprise.

Mary had taken it out of her hand and was now looking at her with genuine concern.

"What's the matter? I've never seen you so distracted," Mary said.

"Oh Mary, she barely touched her dinner." Katherine, Daniel's wife, sat on the other side of Adele. She grasped Adele's hand and squeezed it, her gentle face worried. "You aren't taking ill, are you?"

The young widow smiled at her. She had grown to love the lilt of Katherine's Southern accent. It was a perfect match to her warm and kind personality. "*Nein*," she replied in her native German. "I am sorry. I have many things on my mind."

"What sort of things?" Daniel asked lightly as he walked into the room. He stood next to his wife's chair.

Adele turned her blue eyes toward him, struggling to find the right words. She had known Daniel and his family since she was ten—he was practically a brother to her. *I must tell them.* She clenched her hands in her lap and remembered the words of the psalmist: *"Be of good courage, and he shall strengthen your heart, all ye that hope in the Lord."* She opened her mouth, but Katherine spoke first.

"Oh, of course, you're worried about where you and Jacob will live, aren't you?"

Adele and her nine-year-old son, Jacob, had been living with a family in Ostrander, eight miles from Delaware, Ohio. But the Deckers were leaving the area to live closer to their newly married daughter. Adele's parents had passed away when she was a child, and her brother, Erich Braun, had gone west several years ago.

Katherine looked at her husband. "Daniel, this house is so large. Couldn't they stay here?"

Before he and Katherine had married several months ago, Daniel had bought his bride a house in Delaware, not far from Ohio Wesleyan University, where he served as a professor. As much as she loved it, Katherine thought the house too large, too reminiscent of the plantation house in which she had been raised in South Carolina. Mary had assured her it was only half as large as that, and Katherine knew the older woman was right. Before Sherman's march rent destruction through the Carolinas and drove her to return to her home state of Ohio, Mary had been Katherine's neighbor.

Adele smiled. "Your home is not as large as you think. What if you have twins in the fall? Now that Mary is here to help, it will seem not large enough."

Katherine reddened at her friend's mention of her condition. "Adele!"

"Don't scare me, Adele." Daniel laughed. "I'm not sure Kat could handle twin boys."

"I could more than handle twin girls," his wife teased.

"Male or female, one or two, *I* pray the child will be healthy," Mary said. She leaned toward Adele and laid a hand on her knee. "I'm thankful the Deckers allowed you to stay on in their house until that bachelor cousin of theirs moves in, but he's coming this week. Do you and Jacob have a place to live?"

Adele took a deep breath. "Yes. In fact, that is where Jacob has been today."

"So you did move in with the Warrens," Daniel said. Reverend Paul Warren officiated at Mill Creek Church where Adele attended. Daniel took a sip from his cup. "I'm glad. I know you'll be comfortable with Paul and Minnie."

"We are not staying with them, Daniel." Adele turned in her seat to look him straight in the eye. "We are living with Jonah." Adele watched his eyes widen and heard Katherine gasp.

Daniel stared at her a moment before answering. "Adele, I know you've been going out to see my brother, to help him with the housework since Aunt Mary came to help Kat, but. . .well, what kind of example is that for Jacob?"

"It will be a good one. We were married yesterday, Daniel." The three stared at her, and Adele took a sip of her tea. The cup jingled slightly as she returned it to her saucer. Frowning, she carefully laid the cup aside and squared her shoulders.

After several minutes, Daniel found his voice. "Adele, you could have borrowed money from us, stayed with us until the baby came—you didn't have to do this."

She shot him a meaningful look. "That is not why we married, Daniel."

He stiffened. "Adele. You didn't."

"You cannot send Jonah to an insane asylum. It is not what he needs. I know."

"You know?" Daniel said. "You haven't heard the half of what's been going on since he's been back from the war. His mind isn't the same."

"*Ach!* Daniel, I've seen him for myself. He is angry, he is troubled, but he is not crazy."

Daniel began to pace. "I can't believe Paul Warren went along with this."

"He did not know. Jonah insisted on driving to Marysville to have a justice of the peace perform the ceremony," Adele replied. "I told him and Minnie before I came this afternoon."

"I can't say I'm surprised you didn't go to Reverend Warren," Mary said quietly. "Jonah hasn't been inside a church since he went with me right after he came home."

"So you told my brother I wanted to lock him up and throw away the key." Daniel shook his head. "He must be as angry at me as ever."

Adele looked away. Jonah *had* been angry. He'd been at odds with his younger brother since before the war, and now she had gone and made the divide wider, however good her intentions were. But she'd felt she had no other choice. "I am sorry, Daniel," she said.

He stopped his pacing to look at her. "What about Nate?"

"I have had four years to accept my husband's death, Daniel," Adele said gently. "And he would have wanted me to help Jonah."

"Like this?"

Adele gazed at him steadily. "Considering the circumstances, yes."

Daniel headed toward the door. "I have to take a walk."

Adele looked down into her teacup as the front door latched behind him. Neither Katherine nor Mary said a word, and the silence in the room quickly grew too large for Adele to bear. "Please, say something."

"Adele, I do wish you had talked to me." She looked up to see gentle reproach in Katherine's eyes. "Daniel hadn't really made any kind of decision just yet."

"I saw the letter, Katherine."

"What letter?"

"I did not mean to see it. Last week, when I went to look for a book for Jacob in the library, I saw it lying open on Daniel's desk. It was from a Dr. Peck. 'A brief stay in our facility would be in your brother's best interests,'" she quoted.

"I'm sorry you saw that, Adele," Katherine said. "Dr. Kelly communicated our concerns to Dr. Peck, a friend of his, and took the liberty of asking that the reply be sent to us. But Daniel still hadn't made any firm decision."

Adele frowned. She wished Daniel had never talked to Dr. Noah Kelly about Jonah. Daniel had met the doctor during his service as a Union officer. While Dr. Kelly was trained as a surgeon, he also "dabbled," as he put it, with problems of the human mind. "Katherine, Jonah is not crazy."

"Have you considered your and Jacob's safety, Adele?" Mary asked. Adele stared at her, and the older woman went on. "You've only seen him during the day."

"He was only having nightmares, Mary. And they are almost gone now."

"That's not what I mean," Mary said.

When Jonah had come home, Mary had lived with him for a while, taking care of the housework. When she moved to Delaware, Adele had thought it was because Katherine needed her help. Her condition was making her feel weak at times.

"Katherine's condition was not the only reason I came here. One night, a month or so ago, I heard a noise coming from the yard. I got up thinking Jonah hadn't heard it, but when I got outside, he was already there."

"He must have heard the same noise. What of it?"

"No, Adele, *he* was the noise. When he can't sleep, he walks around the farm with his gun. That evening I startled him. It was only by the grace of God he didn't shoot me. And in the daytime, he carries it with him everywhere."

"I have heard of many men doing that."

"Out West maybe, and for good reason, with outlaws and the like," Mary said. "But Ohio is not the wild frontier it used to be."

"Adele," Katherine said, "Mary says he even sleeps with it."

"He does not sleep with it," Adele said. "It lies on the floor at the foot of his bed."

"*His* bed?" Mary asked curiously. "Don't you mean *our* bed?"

"Oh! Uh...yes," Adele said carefully. "I guess I am not used to that yet."

"Of course," Katherine said with a little smile. "We understand."

No, Adele thought, *you do not understand*. It was purely by chance she had seen where Jonah kept it while he slept. They didn't share a bed. He had absolutely refused. She wanted to tell Mary and Katherine but hesitated. What would they make of it? Would it reinforce their worries about him?

She rose from her seat and walked to the window, mouth clamped shut. No, they were already worried enough over his rifle. His rifle. She hadn't realized he was so obsessed with it. She had, of course, seen it with him several times, but she had not known. Had she been too rash?

Adele looked out the parlor window and brushed back a stray strand of her bright blond hair, her eyes not seeing the fine houses neatly situated along Liberty Street. Instead, she saw Jonah as he had been before the war: tall and strong, brushing light brown hair out of his emerald eyes as a gentle smile crept over his handsome face. A stark contrast to how cold and angry he was now. *No, there was nothing else I could have done.* She couldn't have allowed one of her best friends to be hauled away against his will. *He needs an old friend now, not a doctor who barely knows him.*

Mary's voice roused Adele from her thoughts. "Dr. Kelly should be here shortly. What will you say to him?"

"I will tell him, of course," Adele replied. She noticed the slightly stricken look on Katherine's face and continued. "I have always made it clear to Noah we are friends. Nothing more."

"I know, Adele. And Daniel has tried to reinforce that over the past several months, but. . ." She looked at Mary.

"What?" Adele asked.

"He'll be done guest lecturing at the university at the end of this term," Mary said. "He's made plans to set up a practice in Ostrander. And he's made it no secret to us as to why."

Voices came from the hall, and soon Dr. Noah Kelly entered with Daniel not far behind. "Noah, you should have waited to finalize your plans."

"Don't be ridiculous, Daniel, I—Adele." Dr. Kelly smiled and stepped toward her eagerly. "I have wonderful news."

Adele stopped his progress with an outstretched hand. "Noah, I have news as well. Perhaps you should sit down."

Chapter 2

The Kirby Farm, Ostrander, Ohio

J onah Kirby quietly slipped out the kitchen door at the back of the farmhouse, his Enfield rifle in hand. He stood in the courtyard for a moment looking at the bright, full moon before walking through the small orchard and up into the trees and fields beyond. The air was cool, but it wasn't long before he felt warm from exertion.

The Kirby farm, which had belonged to his family for two generations, was set along a gentle hill that leveled off every so often as it sloped to the valley below where Mill Creek busily flowed onto toward the mighty Scioto River. The house, gardens, barn, and outbuildings sat on a wide plateau while the fields lay at the top of the incline. It was planting time, and he soon came to a field that had been plowed only yesterday. He walked along the edge of it so his boots wouldn't press down the rich brown loam.

Continuing on, he came up on the northern corner of the property, the part he had allowed to become overgrown and wild—Daniel's share of the farm. Jonah really should clear it. Plant something. The soil would be rich, and the yield from whatever crop he sowed would be well worth the effort. But his green eyes narrowed at the thought.

Before dying of a heart attack when Jonah was just a teenager, their pa, Joseph Kirby, had carefully divided up the land between his three sons. But Toby, the youngest, was dead, and Daniel was no farmer. The entire farm belonged solely to Jonah, the eldest of the Kirby brothers. He'd worked Toby's share, but Daniel's share was a different story. A few weeks after the funeral, his brother had announced he was going to go to school instead of honoring Pa's wishes. Daniel offered to sell his share to Jonah, but Jonah refused. They fought, and in the end Daniel had told him to do whatever he wanted with it. Jonah had done just that.

As he turned to go on, he caught movement out of the corner of his eye. Jonah dropped to the ground. Was that gunpowder he smelled? There hadn't been the sharp report of gunfire, but a man couldn't be too sure. Leaning into a small tree, he pointed his rifle toward a dense thicket several feet away. A man's form appeared, and Jonah began to squeeze the trigger, swearing he had seen a glimpse of Confederate gray.

The man's face materialized in the moonlight, and with a start Jonah saw it was Cyrus Morgan, laying out traps. He lowered his rifle and slunk away, acutely aware he had almost shot one of his own hired hands. He shook his head to clear the confusing thoughts. This was his own property, not a battlefield; he was a farmer again, not a sergeant in the Union Army. He'd given Cyrus permission to trap there weeks ago.

He came to an old stump at the edge of an adjacent field, sank down against it, and looked down at his rifle. Relief immediately spread through him. The percussion cap, the small mercury-filled pellet that lit the gunpowder and fired the bullet, had not been in place. He kept them in his pocket now, ever since his aunt Mary startled him one morning and he'd come so close to shooting her. But that hadn't been enough to keep her from moving out. She said it was because of Katherine's "delicate" condition, but he knew better. Jonah rested the butt of the weapon on the ground between his legs and laid his forehead against the cold steel of the barrel. He clenched his jaw and felt his fingers tighten on the gun barrel.

Being a farmer, Jonah had seen and helped butcher so many hogs that the sight of blood shouldn't have bothered him when he went to war, but it had. That and the cries of men suffering and dying, the news of old friends suddenly gone from this world, and his failure to keep himself and others from being captured had affected him more than he ever thought it could.

And then there was the realization of how futile his prayers to God were—prayers that begged for deliverance from the horrors of the notorious Andersonville prison camp. He hadn't been released until after Lee's surrender, and then it was only to be put aboard the overcrowded steamship *Sultana*, which exploded as it made its way up the Mississippi. He just barely made it to safety. When he finally got to the farm, he discovered Ma and Toby were dead. Since it had been presumed he was as well, Daniel had tried to sell the farm to a neighbor so he could marry and realize his dream of becoming a professor.

After all that, he had gone to church and had hardly been able to stand the lesson that had been taught that day: the compassionate nature of God. *God's taken too much for me to ever believe that again*, he thought as he rose and continued on his trek across his property.

He hadn't been back to church. Instead, he threw himself into running the farm. It felt good to work the soil again, feed the animals, mend equipment. After four bloody years of war, the world was beginning to make sense again. But then, from out of the blue, the nightmares came. He would wake up screaming, scaring his poor aunt half out of her wits. She had tried to get him to talk about them, but he didn't want to. He just wanted things to go back to normal.

He worked all the harder, and the nightmares faded after a while. Then, every few nights or so, he'd wake well before chore time and couldn't get back to sleep. And he couldn't think of anything better to do than to take a walk. He certainly didn't want to read his Bible as his aunt had suggested. The problem was the thought of going out at night—or anytime for that matter—without his gun made him nervous.

Jonah stopped for a moment and stared at the weapon in his hands. Well, what did he expect? That after all those years of fighting, he would be able to just lay it aside without a second thought? When he'd been caught, he'd been beside himself without it. On the way home, he'd managed to get ahold of another gun, and since then, he hadn't been parted with it."

Eventually the moon faded in the sky, and the horizon began to redden. Jonah walked a little south and soon found himself on the edge of pastureland with a full view of the house and barn. He looked over everything with a deep measure of satisfaction. Pa would have been proud. Everything was exactly as he had kept it, house and trim painted, grass kept short and tidy, the barn with a fresh coat of red paint. It looked so exactly like it had before Pa died, he half expected to hear his father calling for him.

He caught a faint scent of biscuits in the morning air, and his heart beat faster. Ma's biscuits? But the sight of Adele walking back from collecting eggs shook him back to reality. Before he realized it, he'd made a beeline for the house.

As he drew near, he could hear the pump being worked out back. His head told him to continue on to the barn, but his feet rebelled and took him along the side of the house to the brick courtyard outside the kitchen. He peered around the dormant vines on the garden trellis to see

Adele filling a bucket. His breath caught as he saw her golden hair gathered up in braids and neatly coiled together at the nape of her slender neck. He stepped back and leaned against the house. There were chores to get to, and he had no business spying on her. But he found his mind drifting back to the first time he had ever seen her.

Her hair had been the first thing he noticed. She'd been sitting under the tree in the school yard, knees pulled up to her head, on the verge of tears. She'd been Adele Braun back then, and she and her older brother, Erich, had moved to Ostrander from a German community in Zoar, Ohio, after the death of their parents. The other girls had not quite known what to think of such a tall girl with a thick accent. Jonah and Nate Stephens had been on their way to their favorite lunch spot when he saw how bright her hair was—*like corn silk*. He'd stared at her until Nate had shoved him.

"Hey!"

"Well, stop starin', Jonah! Bad enough the girls were teasing her."

She looked up, and Jonah couldn't breathe. Her eyes were so blue. It hadn't seemed right to him that they were filled with tears. He glanced at Nate then looked down. "Sorry," he mumbled. "We'll leave you be."

But Nate had edged closer and was glancing into her lunch pail. "What's that? Sausage?"

Adele nodded slowly. "*Ja.* Bratwurst. You would like some? I can share."

Nate smiled. "Sure, we'll share, too."

The other girls eventually warmed to Adele, but she remained close to him and Nate. Especially Nate. Where Jonah always seemed to trip over his own words, his best friend always knew exactly what to say. So he had won her.

Jonah looked at the ground. Nate should still be here to take care of her. But God had used the war to take him, too. *He loved her so much. How could I have married her?* His face quickly darkened. What choice had he been given? If it had been up to them, Daniel and that Dr. Kelly would have sent him to that asylum, and he could have lost the farm. Adele said if she were there all the time to take care of him, they might back down. And the only way for her to be at the farm all the time. . . *I'm so sorry, Nate. It was the only way.*

He heard the kitchen door and looked around the trellis. Adele had walked into the house with her water and come back out to look up at the sky. She closed her eyes and breathed in the crisp morning air. He marveled at how such a tall, capable woman could still look so sweet and delicate. Guilt squeezed at his heart, and he leaned back against the house. He had no business even thinking things like that. He'd made a promise, and he had to stick to it.

He straightened. There were chores to do, and besides, Adele had brought her Bible out with her. Even though they had only been married for a few days, he knew she read it every morning and night without fail. Why was beyond him. When she lost Nate, she had lost their farm as well and had to scrape by for who knows how long. How could she turn to a God who had taken so much from her? As he started to walk off, his foot tangled in the vine, causing the trellis to shake.

"Is someone there?"

Jonah winced, turned around, and walked toward where his wife sat on the porch bench.

"Oh, Jonah." She smiled as he drew close, and his heart began to pound. Her eyes flitted to his gun. "You had a good walk?"

He gave her a curt nod and turned to leave, but she laid a hand on his arm. He frowned, tightening his grip on his rifle. "I have to get to the chores before breakfast, Addie."

"Can you not sit for a moment?"

He swallowed. Her accent wasn't so thick now, but her voice was no less musical. "We need to get more fields plowed before the rain comes."

Adele looked at him with amusement as she stood. The faint smell of soap and lavender he breathed in as she brushed past made his head spin. She looked at the blue that had begun to unfold across the sky and then back at him.

"I can smell it in the air," he explained.

She smiled. "You are so much like your father. He always knew such things."

Jonah said nothing, and he saw her take a deep breath as she stepped over to him.

"I found his Bible this morning," she said. "Can I put it in your room?"

"No. Leave it in the parlor. I don't need it."

"There are notes and letters in it. I thought you might want to look—"

"No, Adele! Leave it in the parlor."

Her lovely features fell, and she nodded. He looked away, regretting his sharpness. But the suggestion had sparked his anger. He had no desire to look at those letters, and she knew it. "I need to get to the chores. Is Jake up yet?"

"Yes. Will arrived a few minutes ago, and they are milking the cows."

Jonah nodded. Their other hired hand, Will Reid, had taken Adele's son under his wing, and Jonah was glad. The boy was eager to be a farmer, like his pa had been. But he looked and acted so much like Nate—dark hair, lanky, and talkative—it unnerved Jonah.

When Cyrus arrived, he'd send him to check on them, and then he and Cyrus would set to work feeding the pigs and sheep. He much preferred the older man's company. Cyrus was hardworking and as silent as a dried-up creek bed. He had appeared in Ostrander out of the blue a few months ago and settled along the banks of the creek, relying on trapping, hunting, and what Jonah gave him in trade for his work to make a living. He had thinning hair and dark eyes and didn't associate much with anyone else.

"I'll have Will come up later to plow the kitchen garden," Jonah said. He began to walk away when Adele spoke.

"Jonah."

He stopped and turned to see her approach.

"Let me take your gun into the house." She raised her hands, and Jonah's grip tightened on his weapon.

"No."

Her lips formed a thin line. "Surely you do not need it to do the chores."

"It stays with me," he snapped and strode toward the barn.

∞

Adele watched him leave, then placed a hand to her forehead. She had not really wanted to take it, but better with her than with him out in the fields so near her son. Even if Jonah did keep the percussion caps in his pocket, she still hated the thought. *What happened to make him think it must always be with him?*

Sighing, she picked up her Bible from where it lay on the bench and took it into the parlor so she could read it after supper. Her brow wrinkled at the sight of Joseph Kirby's Bible lying on a side table. Adele knew better than to try to foist scripture on Jonah. She knew from experience it would be the last thing he wanted. But she had at least hoped he would be open to looking at the letters and notes his father had kept there.

As she walked back to the kitchen, she recalled how Jonah had looked up to his father. Joseph Kirby had been a good man, a godly man. He and Jonah had been very similar in viewpoint and temperament. Had been. Now Adele could sense anger threaded into almost everything Jonah said. An anger he refused to let go or speak of. . .even to her. Even though he had never been a very verbal man before the war, he had always been open with her.

She took the biscuits from the cast-iron oven, slamming the door shut in frustration. She couldn't stand seeing him like this. *If I could just get him to talk, I could tell him how it was for me*, she thought as she laid the biscuits in a cloth-lined basket. Sighing, she set them aside and took two eggs from the basketful she had collected. An idea sprang to mind, and a hopeful smile flitted across her face.

She took several more eggs and cracked and beat them in a large earthenware bowl. Setting them aside, she laid bacon in a skillet and set it to fry on the stove. As it cooked, she quickly chopped potatoes and onions and set them to fry as well. When the bacon was done, she chopped it and added it to the beaten eggs before pouring the mixture in with the potatoes and onions. *Bauernfrühstück*, farmer's breakfast, was a recipe she had taught Jonah's mother, Dorothy. Adele remembered Dorothy saying how much her sons had loved it, especially Jonah. Maybe making it now would remind him of better times. Times he was willing to talk about. *Thank You, Father. Surely this idea was from You.*

While she was still cooking, Will and Jacob came in with full milk pails. "Good morning," she said. "How are the cows this morning, Jacob?"

"Will says I'm getting better at milking, Ma!"

"Aye, ma'am, the lad is coming along well," Will said. He took his straw hat from his dark hair, and his blue eyes smiled at her. "I spoke with Mr. Kirby just before we came in. He and Mr. Morgan will be along in a bit. We'll just wash up at the pump."

"Will, tell me another story," Jacob said as they stepped out the door.

Adele smiled as she set the food on the table. Will had come over from Scotland just a few months ago and seemed to have an endless supply of tall tales. He lived with their neighbor, Ben Carr, east of the farm.

She placed a plate of bauernfrühstück at each place and added the biscuits, honey, and jelly, along with the strudel she had made a few days ago. She returned to the kitchen to strain a pitcher of milk, and when she returned, she was surprised to see Jonah standing at the head of the table. She swallowed a gasp at the look on his face. He shook himself as she gently set the pitcher down on the table.

"You taught Ma to make this," he said softly.

"I hope you still like it," she replied.

He looked at her, and for an instant his green eyes held no hurt or anger.

Her heart pounded, and as she opened her mouth to talk about the day she had shown his mother how to prepare the dish, his eyes darkened and he looked away.

"Need to wash up," he muttered and brushed past her.

Adele sat down. For a split second, he had been Jonah again. *The man I once knew is still there, Father. Please let me find him.* She was still praying when the men came in and sat down, and she quickly looked up to see Jacob smiling as he took the seat next to her.

"Uncle Jonah said I could say the prayer."

Adele glanced up at her husband, who would not meet her eyes. "Very well, Jacob."

Once Jacob had thanked the Lord, the men began to eat.

While Jacob, Will, and Cyrus voiced their approval for the bauernfrühstück, Adele could not help but notice that Jonah stopped after a few bites. She laid her own fork down in frustration, but when Will cleared his throat, she turned to see a question on his face. Adele gave him a small smile and nodded.

The young man looked at Jonah. "Sir, if I might be so bold to ask. . .that bit of property in the northwest corner, what might you be planning on doing with it?"

Adele watched Jonah's face stiffen before he replied. "Haven't given it much thought. Why?"

"I was wondering if I might rent it from you."

"No."

Will blinked. "Sir?"

"No, Will. That's the end of it."

Adele looked at the young man sympathetically. She had encouraged him to approach Jonah about the land, never dreaming he would refuse to rent to the young man. *He so wants to be his own man as Nathaniel had. . .*

A sudden thought leaped up in her mind. "Will, I know of some land you might rent." He looked at her hopefully, and she continued. "Mr. Carr owns a pleasant piece of land not very far from our own fields. It belonged to my late husband and me at one time." Adele could feel eyes on her and saw Jonah staring at her in incredulous reproach. She looked back at Will. "I think the house and small barn he built still stand. They will need work, but it would save you from having to build ones of your own."

"Thank you, ma'am." Will smiled broadly. "I'll speak to him this evening."

"I hear Ben Carr is selling or renting all that property his uncle left him," Cyrus said. "Going back west once everything's settled."

Adele watched her husband bristle at the mention of Elijah Carr. He and the Kirby family had never been on good terms. Before his death, Mr. Carr had owned almost all the land along Mill Creek and tried on many occasions to buy the Kirby farm. Joseph Kirby hadn't even been buried a month when Carr rode over and offered to buy the land from Jonah.

Nathaniel had been there when Jonah turned him down and told Adele about it later. He couldn't imagine Jonah being able to keep up with the farm with Daniel off at school and Toby so young. "You remember how angry Jonah was when Daniel left?" When Adele nodded, he'd continued. "He was easily twice as angry as that." A frown had creased his normally cheerful face.

"What is the matter, Nathaniel? Jonah did not strike Mr. Carr?" she'd asked.

"No!" he'd said quickly. "No, it's just I don't like seeing him so angry. It's not like him."

No, it is not *like him,* Adele thought as she looked at Jonah. How sad Nathaniel would be to see him now.

"I'm sure Ben Carr's keeping a good deal of it," Jonah said with a black look. "Wouldn't be like any of that family not to."

Adele frowned at her husband. "You are being unfair, Jonah," she said. "You should not paint him and his uncle with the same brush."

"I have always found Mr. Carr to be a very fair-minded man," Will said, not noticing the hard looks she and Jonah were exchanging. "Just the other day a lad came along—" Cyrus nudged the young man, and looking up, Will quickly decided to pay closer attention to the rest of his breakfast.

They ate in silence for a few minutes more before Jonah pushed back his chair. "Time to get to it," he said. He reached for his rifle as Jacob and the other two men filed out, but he paused in the doorway.

Adele said nothing at first and began to clear the table. But when he continued to remain silent, she stopped what she was doing and looked at him. "What is it?"

"How can you stick up for Carr?" he snapped. "His uncle all but robbed you of your land when Nate died. And how could you tell Will about it? Nate worked hard on that house for you."

"I know he did. That is why I spoke. Nathaniel would not want to see his hard work come to nothing. And as for Ben Carr, I will not stand by and watch someone be marked for who he is related to. Or where he is from." Adele felt her cheeks grow hotter as she remembered how she had once acted toward Katherine. She reached for Jonah's plate. The food had hardly been touched. "I am sorry you did not care for your breakfast."

"I wasn't hungry," he muttered and strode out the door.

Chapter 3

S top, don't go up there!"

Adele quickly rose from her bed, roused from her sleep by Jonah's yell. He was having another nightmare. Pulling on a robe, she left her room, walked across the hall, and knocked loudly on his door in order to wake him. Within a minute or two, she heard the creak of floorboards and felt certain he was awake, perhaps sitting on the edge of his bed.

"Jonah," she called.

"What!"

She jumped, his voice was so harsh and ragged. Drawing a deep breath, she sent up a quick prayer. "You are all right?"

"Fine. Go back to bed."

"I could make you some warm milk. . . ."

"Leave me alone!"

She turned and found Jacob standing in his doorway. He looked frightened and opened his mouth to say something, but Adele raised a finger to her lips and led him to her room, shutting the door behind her.

"You must be quiet, *mein Liebe*," she whispered.

"Uncle Jonah scared me," he whispered back.

"He is very troubled." Seeing the stricken look on her son's face, she grasped his hand. "What is it?"

"I don't think he likes me."

"Why do you say this? Of course he does."

"He won't show me how to do anything. Whenever I ask, he tells me to have Will show me. But he doesn't always know. And Uncle Jonah won't tell me about Pa."

She hugged her son and pressed her lips together. She had never imagined Jonah would be so cold with her son. "He does not want to talk

163

about him yet. But you can ask me."

"But you've told me all your stories. I want to hear his." He pulled back and looked up at her. "I don't like him this way. I wish he would go back to the way he was before."

"You were so very young then, mein Liebe." Jacob had only been about four when Jonah left to join up. "What do you remember?"

He shrugged. "Just how he looked, really. He smiled more. He never smiles now. Can't we ask him not to be so angry?"

Adele gave the boy a small smile. "I remember you asked that of me after your pa died. But it did not help, did it?"

The boy shook his head. Then a light came to his eyes. "But I prayed for you. And that sure worked."

"Then we will pray for Uncle Jonah now. Would you like that?"

Once they had lifted up their hearts to God, Jacob went back to his room, convinced the prayer would work wonders. But Adele found herself wondering. Was Jonah's heart already too hardened? Would she ever see him smile again or speak a kind word? Would he ever stop feeling the need for his gun?

When they had married, she had not imagined he would be this bad. Daniel had been right. She had not known the half of it. Reverend Warren had warned her that she was making herself unequally yoked, and now she frowned at her resolute answer. "His faith still lives somewhere in his heart," she'd declared. "God will help me find it for him."

Father, what else could I have done? She knew the answer. She had been so sure that Nathaniel would have wanted her to help Jonah in any way she could, but she had never inquired of the Lord. She should have gone to Him first. *I am sorry,* she prayed. *Even as You worked through the mistakes of Abraham and David, I know You can work through mine.*

But in spite of her prayers, she wrestled with her worries about Jonah far into the night. Eventually she passed into a fitful sleep.

As she went to work on the kitchen garden the next morning, she found it hard not to yawn. She looked down on the row of carrots she had just planted, kneading the small of her back. The kitchen garden was coming along well, even though it had been several years since she had planned and planted one. Jonah had been sure to give her everything she needed—a brand-new hoe, a rake, and seeds.

Thoughts of him caused her worries to reassert themselves. Adele set her jaw and tried to get her thoughts to settle elsewhere. She moved to start a new row, this time peas. *I remember when Jacob used to help me,* she thought as she reached into her pocket for seeds. Before the war, when her son was small, he would follow her and drop the seeds into the furrow. He was always very careful, as if the seeds were made of bone china. *How Nathaniel would laugh as he watched him. Jonah, too. . .*

She bit her lip as she caught herself thinking about Jonah again. *Father, help me give my worries for him to You.* As if in answer, she heard a sound behind her. Turning, she almost gasped with surprise.

A little girl stood next to one of the purple coneflowers in the adjoining flower garden. She had shoulder-length strawberry-blond hair, and her brown eyes took Adele in with wonder and a hint of fear.

Adele blinked, making sure her lack of sleep from the night before wasn't playing tricks with her eyes. She gave the child a gentle smile. "Hello, little one. Who are you?"

The girl said nothing and continued to stare at her.

Adele gently laid her hoe aside and slowly started toward her.

The fear in the girl's eyes grew, and she backed up a step.

"Oh, do not be afraid. I will not hurt you." Adele took another step forward, and the child took another step back. Suddenly Adele remembered how intimidating her tall form must be to such a little thing. She crouched down to her level and smiled. "What is your name?"

The girl looked at Adele and then the garden, a question in her eyes.

"I am planting peas," she said, reaching into her apron pocket. She held out a handful of the small tan seeds. "Do you want to see?"

Curiosity took over, and the little girl stepped forward to examine them. Adele could not help but notice that she had no shoes and her dress showed a lot of wear. She picked up a seed and plopped it into the furrow.

Adele smiled. "Yes, that is how to do it."

The girl's eyes danced, and a smile tugged at her mouth.

"If you tell me your name, perhaps you could help." But the way the little thing pressed her lips together caused Adele to reconsider. "But if you do not want to that is all right. You may still help."

The little girl helped Adele plant the entire morning. Try as she might, she could not get the little thing to utter a word, much less her name. But she was still such a sweet thing that Adele took to calling her Sweet Pea.

"Well, little Sweet Pea," she said after an hour or so of work, "I am very thirsty. Would you like a drink?"

Sweet Pea nodded and smiled, permitting Adele to take her by the hand and lead her to the water pump in the courtyard. After filling two tin cups from the kitchen, Adele watched the little girl drink, wondering where on earth she could have come from. She only looked to be about three years old. Ben Carr was a bachelor, and their other nearest neighbor, Henry Porter, had three strapping sons, all older than Jacob.

Suddenly Sweet Pea's eyes widened, and Adele looked to see Jonah come striding around the corner of the house. She turned to reassure the girl, but she was already gone, the tin cup she had been drinking from lying on the ground. They both took off after her. Adele called out to her, but she was surprisingly fast and quickly disappeared.

Jonah looked at Adele, his angry countenance momentarily replaced by surprise. "Who was that?"

She quickly explained. "I cannot imagine where she came from. But she had no shoes on, and her dress was very worn."

"Could be Southern refugees," Jonah said slowly.

"So far north?"

"It's possible. Some folk lost everything and have no place else to go." He looked in the direction Sweet Pea had gone.

"If she comes back, I'll feed her," Adele stated. "Perhaps she will tell me about her family and we can help."

Jonah shrugged. "Go ahead. But I wouldn't be too hopeful. She may not ever come back."

∞

By the time Jonah drove into town Saturday, they were still no closer to knowing who the little girl was or to whom she belonged. She had come back the next day and helped Adele with the churning but slipped away when Adele had gone into the house for something. And there had been no sign of her on Friday. Adele was worried and opted to stay home instead of making their weekly trip into town, hoping she would appear.

Jonah had grudgingly agreed to sell the butter, eggs, and maple sugar at Decker's Dry Goods. He sighed. *Just a woman's nature to fuss over something small and helpless.* But then, it was just one of the things he loved about her. He clenched his teeth and focused on the backs of Belle and Babe as they loped along, trying to push the thought out of his mind. He almost didn't hear Jacob call out to him.

"Uncle Jonah?"

Jonah started and half looked at Jacob between his and Cyrus's shoulders. The boy was sitting in the wagon bed with Will, along with the things they were selling in town that day. "What is it, Jake?"

"When we get into town, can I go see Miss Williams?"

"The schoolteacher? What for?"

Jacob glanced at Will then back at him. "I need to ask her about a book is all."

Jonah frowned. School was out for the season. He wished Adele didn't take the boy with her to Delaware when she visited his brother. Daniel was becoming a bad influence. Jacob would never be the farmer he claimed he wanted to be if he got to taking on his brother's ways.

"Thought you wanted to watch Mr. Morgan bargain with Mr. Decker."

"I do! It won't take long, just a minute. She lives right next to the school, and that's just across the tracks from the store."

Ostrander was a stop on the Cleveland, Columbus, and Cincinnati Railroad. The tracks ran right through the little town of Ostrander in front of the mercantile.

"You help us unload, then go and come straight back. No dawdling, you hear?"

"Yes, sir. Thank you!" He sat back down and smiled at Will.

Before long, Ostrander came into view, and Jacob practically fell over himself helping to unload the wagon. As Jonah watched him jump the railroad tracks and knock on the teacher's door, he wondered if he should go easier on the boy. Will told him he was a great help and was coming along well. *But at his age, even Daniel knew more than the boy does now. If Nate hadn't died. . .* Jonah scowled. Just one more way God had failed Adele and her son. He snaked his arm under the wagon seat and pulled out his gun.

"Excuse me, Mr. Kirby."

Jonah looked to see Will standing there, a hesitant look on his face. He rested the butt of his gun on the ground. "Yes, Will?"

"I was wonderin' if you would mind me getting some plate glass. Mr. Carr is allowing me to rent that land Mrs. Kirby spoke of. The house is still good and strong, but the windows are broken. I don't want any more rain to be getting on those fine wood floors."

Jonah clenched his jaw. With all the fuss over Sweet Pea, he'd almost forgotten what Adele had done the other day. He squeezed the gun barrel, wanting to say no. . . . "Fine," he muttered.

Will thanked him and strode over to the furniture goods store across the street.

Jonah stood and fumed. He knew there wasn't any real reason to be angry. What good did it do for the house to stand empty and unused and the land to grow wild? But he couldn't help it. When he thought of how Nate had saved and scraped in order to afford to give Adele a frame house with wood floors instead of a log cabin. . . He stepped up onto the boardwalk and opened the door of the mercantile just as Ben Carr was on his way out.

"Mr. Kirby, good morning." The young man offered his hand eagerly. "I'm glad we finally ran into each other."

Jonah frowned. He had managed to avoid the young man since he arrived several months ago. He didn't take his hand, and Ben quickly lowered his and cleared his throat.

"I have something I need to discuss with you if you have the time," he said.

"I don't," Jonah replied. *Something to discuss. . .he's after the farm just like his uncle.* He started to move past Ben Carr. "Excuse me."

"Well, if you can't now, when?" he asked. "It's very important to me."

"It's planting time, in case you haven't noticed. I'll let you know." *Just as soon as my hogs sprout wings and fly,* he thought as he made his way into the mercantile. Glancing back, he saw the young man walk off toward the furniture goods store and was glad that he hadn't followed him to press for a more definite time.

Two long counters lined either side of the mercantile. Cyrus was already haggling with Fred Decker at one for the price of the furs he'd brought. Fred's young clerk, Dean Perry, was helping Fanny Williams, the schoolteacher's mother, at the other.

He walked over to Mr. Decker's counter where his own items were laid out. He leaned himself and his rifle against it and closed his eyes. He'd been out walking again that morning and guessed it must have been close to three thirty in the morning when he woke up. But just as he began to doze, the bell on the mercantile door jingled, and he opened his eyes.

"I'm telling you there's a bobcat loose." Henry Porter was walking in with Earl Henderson, a dealer in purebred sheep. "You need to be keeping an eye on those sheep of yours."

"How can you be sure?" Earl asked. "There hasn't been a bobcat seen around here in ages."

"What's this about a bobcat?" Jonah asked.

"Jonah Kirby, just the man I need to see," Henry said, stepping over to him. "You seen anything strange walking around your property lately?"

Jonah started inwardly. It almost sounded like Henry knew about his early morning walks. But that couldn't be. Neither his aunt Mary nor Adele would have said anything about them, and Daniel was in Delaware. No one seemed to bother him about having his rifle with him when he came to town, but he knew folk would think it strange if they found out about those walks of his. "No tracks, if that's what you mean," he replied.

"I wish that's what I meant," Henry said. Glancing over at Mrs. Williams, he lowered his voice. "Me and Jim, my oldest boy, were down by Mill Creek near your church there hunting deer, and we came across an awful sight. A ten-point buck ripped clean open and gutted to the bone. Blood and. . .everything else was just everywhere. It was a shame to see good buckskin going to rot. It's got to be a bobcat, and a sick one, too."

"Sure sounds like a rabid animal of some sort. Wouldn't have to be a bobcat," Jonah replied.

"Didn't think about that," Henry said. "It could be a black bear."

"Black bears are gone, too," Earl pointed out.

"Not all of them," Jonah replied. "I heard of folk still seeing them south of Columbus. And I saw a bobcat down near the creek just before the war." Cyrus and Fred had stopped their haggling for the moment and were listening. "Have you noticed anything strange in your traps lately, Cy?"

"Nope."

"Be extra careful when you're out. Pa said a rabid animal is an animal with no fear of anything," Jonah said.

As Cyrus and Mr. Decker returned to business, Jonah looked out the window to see Jacob talking with a finely dressed man next to the wagon.

"Who's that?" Henry asked.

"The new doctor," Fanny Williams replied. Done with her shopping, she walked over to the men.

They nodded to her.

"Dr. Noah Kelly. He took over when Doc Sullivan retired." She looked at Jonah. "It looks like Jacob already knows him."

Jonah frowned inwardly. So this was Dr. Kelly. "Adele and Jake go into Delaware to visit Daniel and Katherine," he said. "He's good friends with my brother."

"I've heard he's a bachelor," Mrs. Williams said. "I hope he comes to church next Sunday. I'm sure Clara would like to meet him."

Jonah only half listened. He frowned as he watched the doctor hand Jacob a book and pat him on the shoulder. He started for the door. "I'll be back in a minute," he said to Earl and Henry. "You two go ahead of me."

Jacob and the doctor turned toward him as he stepped outside.

"I'm back, Uncle Jonah, just as quick as you asked," Jacob said, holding up the book. "I was just saying hello to Dr. Kelly. He's friends with Uncle Daniel."

Jonah quickly looked the doctor up and down. He wore a black frock coat with a paisley vest and a tall beaver hat. From beneath its brim, blue eyes looked at Jonah, and a friendly smile stretched out his dark Vandyke beard.

He made careful use of a wooden cane as he made his way over to where Jonah stood on the boardwalk. A black leather satchel was in the doctor's other hand, and he nodded at Jonah.

"It's good to meet you, Mr. Kirby." Dr. Kelly hesitated as he looked at Jonah's rifle. "Forgive me if I don't offer my hand."

"Dr. Kelly was a surgeon in the war," Jacob said. "A stray bullet got him in the leg. But he kept on operating and saved Uncle Daniel's captain's life."

Jonah took another look at the doctor. So he'd been an officer, like his brother.

The doctor looked down in embarrassment. "Yes, that's how we met, sir."

"He's from Pennsylvania, and he went to school in Philadelphia...," Jacob began.

"Go on inside, Jake," Jonah said. "If you want to learn anything about haggling, you'd better hurry it up. Mr. Morgan is almost done."

"Can I watch you haggle with Mr. Decker?"

"No."

Disappointment darkened the boy's eyes. "Yes, sir."

Dr. Kelly watched the boy go in and then returned his attention to Jonah. "He's a good boy." When Jonah didn't answer, the doctor cleared his throat. "I'm glad we've finally met. How have you been? Have you been sleeping well?"

Jonah stiffened, instantly on his guard. His brother told him about his walks? Of course he had. "I'm not sure that's any of your business."

The man pursed his lips in amusement. "Well, I am the town doctor."

"You're not *my* doctor."

"Oh? Who is your doctor?"

"I don't need one."

"Oh, I don't know. If you aren't sleeping well. . ."

"I never said I wasn't sleeping well. Whether I am or not, it's still none of your business." He looked hard at the doctor, who stared back.

"Jacob says Adele didn't come with you today," he said eventually. "Is she all right?"

Jonah stiffened at the sound of his wife's Christian name, and he didn't care for the look he thought he saw in the man's eyes. "*Mrs. Kirby* decided to stay at home this morning."

Dr. Kelly caught the emphasis, and his eyes darted elsewhere.

"She's concerned about a neighbor." Jonah saw no reason to tell him about Sweet Pea.

"Well, if there's anything I can do. . ."

"It's a private matter. Nothing that would concern a doctor."

Dr. Kelly looked at him with slightly narrowed eyes. "Even so, I like to help out even when it's not medically necessary."

So I noticed. "We're fine." Jonah turned and started back toward the mercantile, when the sharp sound of a train whistle sliced through the air. He whirled around, heart pounding, eyes wide and darting. He heard the faint chug of the locomotive as it approached Ostrander and started to relax, when Dr. Kelly cleared his throat.

The doctor looked at him with raised eyebrows, touched the brim of his hat, and turned away.

Chapter 4

Adele looked down at Jonah from where she sat in the buggy seat. "We will be fine, Jonah. I do not need Nathaniel's old rifle."

"I told you what Henry said...," Jonah began.

"But we are just going to church," she replied and nodded toward Will who sat in the driver's seat. "Will is with us."

"But he doesn't have his gun with him, and I don't want you going anywhere without protection," Jonah replied, scowling.

Adele bit her lip. The words, "Then come with us," hung there, waiting to be said. But she knew better. He needed to return to church willingly, not out of obligation.

"I'll take the rifle," Jacob said.

"No," Adele said, quickly taking it from Jonah. She held it awkwardly, not wanting it across her lap.

"I cleaned and loaded it last night." Jonah gave her a funny look. "I thought Erich taught you how to handle a rifle. You used to shoot as good as Nate."

She looked away. "We will be back later."

Once they were clear of the house, Adele turned to Will. "Take this," she said, handing the rifle to him. "I will drive."

"Yes, ma'am," he replied.

Adele grasped the reins as she felt her cheeks grow pink. Before the war, she would have taken the gun without a second thought. But since then, she had a hard time even looking at one without feeling anger. *How can I not when I know it was a weapon like this that killed Nathaniel?*

"Why couldn't I take Pa's rifle, Ma?" Jacob asked. She looked at him, hating that her son was in such close contact with a gun every day. When would Jonah let go of it? She especially disliked the thought that Jacob would one day learn to use one.

172

"How did things go in town yesterday?" she asked.

He looked at her for a moment. "I saw Dr. Kelly."

"He was in town?"

"He sure was. Uncle Jonah got to meet him."

Adele bit her lip. She hadn't realized Dr. Kelly would be coming to Ostrander so soon. She thought he still had another week or two of lecturing at Ohio Wesleyan. Her heart sank as she realized she had not been there to introduce Jonah to the doctor herself. "Did they seem to like one another?"

Jacob shrugged. "I don't know. Uncle Jonah told me to go inside and watch Mr. Morgan."

Adele only half listened as her son went on about how Cyrus had gotten a good price for his furs from Mr. Decker. No wonder Jonah had seemed more out of sorts than usual yesterday evening. She had put it down to being concerned about the rabid animal on the loose. What had Dr. Kelly said to him?

Fred Decker was tying up his horse when they arrived at church. "Hello." He waved as they walked up. "Jonah forgot to take these while he was in town yesterday." He handed Adele several letters.

"Thank you, Mr. Decker," she said as she looked through them. She frowned. "I cannot imagine who this is from." It was simply addressed to the Kirby Farm.

Jacob strained to see it as she showed it to Mr. Decker. "Yes," the shopkeeper said, "I wondered about that myself."

"Well, I will open it when I get home. Perhaps it was misdirected." She put it and the others in her reticule.

"If it is, just bring it into town, and I'll take care of it," he said as he opened the church doors for her.

When they stepped inside the sanctuary, Adele saw Dr. Kelly sitting with the Williamses near the front. He half stood and smiled broadly at her, and she responded with a small smile and a nod.

"Can we sit with him, Ma?" Jacob asked.

"Let us just sit here, mein Liebe," she said, indicating the third pew from the back. "Reverend Warren is ready to start."

The lesson that morning was very good, although Adele did notice Will looking at Clara Williams, the schoolteacher, several times. She was strategically seated next to Dr. Kelly, no doubt at the insistence of her mother, who sat right behind them. Adele couldn't help but give a small smile. If the right number of people sat in that particular pew, two people would have to share a hymnal. She and Nathaniel had often sat there, and Jonah had always been willing to sit with them so they could share one.

As the body of believers rose for the last song, she didn't fail to notice Clara and the doctor politely sharing a songbook. She glanced at Will, who looked none too happy. Much to his dismay, Jacob immediately dragged him over to meet Dr. Kelly once services ended. But on their way by, he was able to give Clara a nod and a smile before she was escorted out by her parents. In turn, the young lady kept looking back at the young Scot as she made her way toward the church door.

Adele watched her son and Will talk to Dr. Kelly. As he spoke, the doctor glanced over at her several times as if inviting her to join them. She sighed, wishing, for his sake, they had never met. As much as she liked him, she knew she could never have loved him. True, he was kind and handsome, and on a more practical level, his profession would mean a more stable life. But she knew their temperaments did not match, and she had always preferred life on a farm. Adele had missed it all the years she had lived in town after Nathaniel died.

Just then Minnie Warren came up to talk to her, and she was grateful to direct her attention elsewhere. "Hello, dear," she said as she embraced Adele. The older woman held her at arm's length and gazed at her with concern. "How are you and Jonah?"

Adele half smiled at her. Minnie and her husband were the only ones in Ostrander who knew the true circumstances surrounding their marriage. Adele and Jonah had allowed the rest of the town to think what they liked. Most hadn't been surprised, seeing how Jonah had been Nathaniel's best friend. That he should marry Adele seemed only natural.

"Jonah. . ." She wanted to confide in the woman, but at the same time, it wouldn't do to worry her. "Pray for him."

Understanding flowered in Minnie's eyes. "Paul and I do. Every night."

"Thank you." Adele squeezed her hands. "I have something to ask you. Do you know if there is a family in the area with a little girl about three years old?"

Minnie thought for a moment. "I can't think of any. Why?"

Adele told her about Sweet Pea. "Jonah thinks she may belong to

174

refugees from the war. I could not believe that anyone would come so far north."

"They could be on their way to Canada."

"I suppose." Adele chewed on her bottom lip. "I worry about her with this rabid animal on the loose. Did Henry Porter tell you about it?"

"Did Henry Porter tell you about what?" The two women turned to see that Dr. Kelly had joined them. He nodded to Minnie. "I don't think we've met." He glanced at Adele.

"Minnie, this is Dr. Noah Kelly. He is friends with Daniel and Katherine," Adele said. "This is Minnie Warren, Reverend Warren's wife." The two smiled and greeted each other.

"Are you married, Dr. Kelly?" Minnie asked.

Adele noticed a slight hesitation in the doctor's answer. "No. Sadly not."

"Well, as I'm sure you've noticed, we have several eligible young ladies in the congregation." Minnie smiled. "You won't lack invitations to Sunday dinner over the next several weeks."

"I'm sure I won't."

"If you'll excuse me," Minnie said, "I need to see Mrs. Perry before she leaves."

Mrs. Warren stepped out the door, and Adele turned back to Dr. Kelly. The look in his face and eyes was unmistakable. She looked around. They were the only ones left in the church. The weather was so fine that everyone else had gone outside to fellowship. Giving him a small smile, she gathered her Bible and started for the door. She paused when he called out to her.

"Let me walk you out."

She continued on more slowly to allow him to walk beside her and noticed he was leaning heavily on his cane.

"What were you and Mrs. Warren talking about?" he asked.

"Henry Porter believes there is a rabid bear or bobcat in the area."

The doctor looked at her with grave concern. "I hope you're taking every precaution."

"Jonah will take care of us," Adele replied.

He looked away.

"Your leg is hurting you today."

Dr. Kelly glanced back at her. "A little more than usual," he said. He paused for a moment. "How is the farm?"

"Fine," Adele said, giving him a sidelong glance. His voice hadn't sounded quite right. "Jonah says the planting is going very well. I did the kitchen garden this week. I had just finished planting the carrots the other day when. . ." She was going to tell him about Sweet Pea, hoping he might have heard something about refugees in the area. But just as they reached the door, he grabbed her arm and pulled her toward the corner.

"Dr. Kelly, what are you doing?"

"What are *you* doing?" He had pulled her quite close to him. Adele could see the flecks of gray in his blue eyes.

She pulled her arm free and backed away. "I am married, Noah."

"I know, but why?"

"I told you why. I could not let him be sent away."

He stared at her. "I love you, Adele," he said finally.

She shook her head.

"I was ready to marry you."

"But I was never ready to marry you." Adele looked down and said a small prayer. "Jonah is my husband now. Nothing will change that." She backed away and grasped the door handle. "And please call me Mrs. Kirby. Even in private." Opening the door, she left.

∽

Jonah walked in from the barn later on Sunday afternoon, irritated. Just after lunch, as he was making his way out to hitch Babe up to the plow, Ben Carr rode up the drive.

He dismounted and tied his horse to the fence outside the house. "Good afternoon," the young man called as he walked up to him. "Do you have some time to talk, Mr. Kirby? I was just on my way back from church in Ostrander and saw you."

He stopped short when he noticed Jonah was in work clothes. "You're working? Today?"

Jonah narrowed his eyes at him. "Yes. So I don't have time to talk to you right now. As I said before, when I'm ready to talk with you, I'll let you know." He started to move off when Ben spoke once more.

"Well, if you're set on working today, could I lend you a hand? You would get more work done and—" He stopped as Jonah swung around and glared at him.

"You'd like that, wouldn't you? Get a look at my fields and my barn to try to see how much they're worth, and then offer me next to nothing for them. You're no different than your uncle."

Ben stared at him as his eyes grew dark with anger. "And you're just like what Uncle Eli said about you. He said you and your family were a pain in the neck. Ma and I took what he said about people with a grain of salt because he tended to exaggerate. But I guess he wasn't exaggerating about you." Ben turned and left.

But his words were as irritating as a sliver of wood under the skin. A pain in the neck? Like Elijah Carr had any room to talk. He'd been constantly trying to figure out a way of buying up the Kirby farm. Neither Pa's nor his repeated refusals seemed to have any effect on him. Once, after a confrontation with the man, Jonah had vented his frustration to his mother, only to have her remind him that Elijah Carr was a hurting man and they should pray for him.

"He was brought up to believe a man's worth lies in what he can obtain," she'd said, looking up from her mending. "He needs our compassion. If we show him Christ's love, he might yet change."

But Jonah had never been able to bring himself to do that. And he knew for a fact that Carr had died just as he lived.

Shaking the thoughts from his mind, he went out to the fields and tried to get some work done. But nothing seemed to go right the rest of the afternoon. The plow stuck just about every other row he worked, and Babe was uncharacteristically antsy and shy. Jonah gave up on the field and tried working on a few things in the barn, but nothing turned out right.

Disgusted, he strode up to the house. When he went in, he was greeted by a sob coming from the parlor.

Adele stood in front of the fireplace, quickly trying to wipe her face off with a handkerchief. A letter lay on the mantel.

"What's wrong?" he asked, stepping into the room.

She looked at him and then the letter. "I have had news," she said softly. "About Erich."

Frowning, Jonah walked in and took the letter. What disaster had God brought down on them now?

Dear Sir,

My name is Silas Benton. You don't know me, but I'm writing to you about Erich Braun, the brother of Adele Stephens. He was a miner with our company near Virginia City, Nevada. I am sorry to disturb you with such sad news, but her brother died several months ago in an accident. I'm sorry to be telling you this so late, but I only recently took charge of the mine in this area, and I was not aware he had any kin back East until now. I would send his body home to her, but he's been buried for quite some time. I found several letters from Mrs. Stephens, and some had different addresses. Her most recent one was sent from this address. If she is there, could you please tell her what happened to Mr. Braun and let me know where I can send his things? And please extend our sincere condolances on the loss of her brother.

Yours truly,
Silas Benton
Silver Hills Mining Co.

Jonah stared at the letter. Erich had gone west after Nate and Adele had married, always having had a heart for wandering. He'd only stayed in Ostrander when they were younger for his sister's sake. Once she married Nate, he felt free to do as he liked.

He'd written faithfully at first, but Adele hadn't heard from him in over a year and had indeed written to her brother just after they married, hoping against hope he wasn't dead. So many went west and were never heard from again that it was a familiar scenario.

Jonah looked at her.

"I knew in my heart he was not alive," Adele said. "But I did not want to believe it."

More than anything, Jonah wanted to pull her into his arms and hold her. Instead, he grasped her elbow and settled her into the nearby high-backed chair while he took a seat on the sofa. Each tear she shed was like a knife sticking him in the back. He clenched his teeth and looked away, trying not to allow the anger inside him to burn through and show in his eyes. *How could He do this to her?*

Once he had collected himself, he glanced up. "I'm sorry, Addie."

"I will write Mr. Benton and tell him to send Erich's things here," she said softly.

"Do you want me to see if we could bring his body back? I know this Mr. Benton said otherwise, but it might be possible. Seems only proper to have him buried here."

She gave him a teary smile. "He would not have wanted me to go to so much trouble. Let him rest in peace. He is with the Lord now."

Jonah stood abruptly and strode over to the window. "He should still be here with you."

Didn't God have enough souls with Him now? Hadn't four years of war made heaven a bit too crowded?

A soft hand gently grasped his arm, and he looked to see Adele standing there close to him. Too close. "I wish he was still here, too," she said. "We could talk about him, about the good times we had while he was still with us."

Her blue eyes, while somewhat faded by her tears, almost convinced him. Would it be so bad to talk a little? It would be a comfort to Adele for him to sit with her awhile.

He clenched his teeth. No. She would somehow point the conversation in a direction he didn't want to go. So he pushed the thought and her hand away and headed for the door. There must be something he could find to do in the barn.

Chapter 5

Late July, 1866

Adele awoke to the sound of boots going downstairs. She sighed and, flinging back the sheets, rose and walked to the window. She watched as Jonah stepped out into the courtyard and looked at the moon. Then he strode into the orchard and disappeared from view. She turned from the window and slowly made her way to her bed and lay back down.

For the past four months, two or three nights a week, she had woken up every time he left. Even though Adele slept in what had been his parents' room and he just next door in his own, she still heard him. He was always very quiet, but something in her knew he was awake. She would go to the window to watch him walk away, to make sure he was all right.

Adele caught a glimpse of his face before he walked off this time. He looked as if his soul was weary of this odd ritual. As always, she prayed before going back to sleep. *Father, he has been home for over a year now. When will he have peace from this war?*

She was always given the same answer. "*If he would turn to Me, I would heal him.*"

She sat up in bed. "How, Father?" she softly asked in the darkness. "He will not listen to me. I have been patient, and I have tried to be kind and understanding, but still he will not listen."

Since the news came of Erich's death, he'd been even more close-lipped. Oh, he talked about farm matters and more mundane details, but nothing beyond that. Every night when he came into the parlor after evening chores, Adele tried to get him to open up, tried to get over the wall he had built. But she might as well be trying to scale it with sewing thread. Her every attempt was quickly and effectively snipped by a cross answer or silence. She hugged her knees and wrestled with what to do until she had to get up and start breakfast.

"Be sure you ask Fred Decker about that plow head," Jonah told her at breakfast. "You'll have to go into town by yourself today."

"Why?" Adele looked at Jonah, who was looking at her son. Jacob had become somewhat belligerent toward his stepfather over the last few weeks. Any good report Will gave Jonah about her son was shrugged off, and Jonah was forever harping about what he should know about farming at his age. She understood her son's frustration. As much as both had been praying, nothing about Jonah seemed to be changing. But even so, she would not put up with Jacob being disrespectful. She frowned. "What has happened?"

"He was shirking his chores this morning," Jonah replied.

"It wasn't like that, Ma. I was just taking a peek at a book for a second before Will and I started on the cows. . . ."

"And you'll stay home today and make up for the time you lost this morning," Jonah said.

Jacob looked at him angrily. "It wasn't more than a second."

"Jacob Nathaniel, you will not talk back," Adele said.

"But. . ." He glanced over at Will who looked away uncomfortably. The boy's shoulders slumped a little. "Yes, ma'am."

"And Will," Jonah said. "I don't pay you to work on your own property. You need to be on time."

Adele pressed her lips together as she listened to Jonah go on about the young man's tardiness. Will was working hard to make her old home livable again. From the looks he and Clara Williams shared at church, it was not hard to understand why. And it couldn't be an easy task, considering he worked at their farm from sunup until sundown. Nathaniel had worked for the Kirbys until they were married and was often late when he was building the place. As far as she knew, neither Jonah nor his mother had ever taken him to task for it. "Jonah. . ."

"No, ma'am, it's all right," Will said. "I'm sorry, sir. I'll try to be on time from now on."

Later Will brought the buggy around for Adele. She started to apologize for Jonah's behavior, but he waved it away. "No, ma'am, I'm the one who should be apologizing."

"It is very understandable why you must be late sometimes."

"No, it's not that." He looked uncomfortable. "It's Jacob, ma'am. It's my fault he's in a scrape."

Adele stared at him. "What do you mean?"

"Mrs. Kirby, Jacob was looking for a pretty piece of poetry for me to send to Miss Williams." Will was beet red with embarrassment.

Adele did her level best to hold back the smile that threatened to take over her face. "I see."

"I came to America for a new life, ma'am. And Miss Williams is just the bonniest lass. . .but I don't know how to talk to her. Jacob said Professor Kirby, your brother-in-law, used to send his wife poems before they married. He was looking for one of them. I never thought it would get him in trouble."

"That is all right, Will," Adele replied. "I will find out from Mrs. Kirby which poems he sent her, but don't you think you should try to talk to Miss Williams yourself?"

"Oh ma'am. . .I. . ."

"Will!" Jonah strode up to the buggy. He had his own rifle in one hand and Nathaniel's old one in another. "Make sure Jake is doing what he's supposed to in the barn. Cyrus and me are going out to mow hay."

Will nodded to both of them and strode off toward the barn.

Jonah handed Nathaniel's rifle to her.

"Jonah, the rabid animal is dead by now," she replied, not taking it. No one in the area had found any more mangled animals since the first part of April. "I will be fine."

He gave her a hard look. "You know as well as I do it might have infected another animal. I don't want rabid livestock."

Adele glanced at the gun then looked away. "Slide it under the seat please."

"You do know you'll have to actually touch it in order to use it?" he said as he did so.

"Nathaniel was killed with such a gun," she snapped, then looked at him instantly contrite. "Jonah, I am sorry. . ."

The hardness slid from his face. "No. I'm sorry, Addie." He ran a hand through his hair. "I was up early again."

"I know. I woke, too."

He frowned. "I didn't mean to wake you."

"You did not," she said. "Somehow I know when you wake up, and I wake as well."

He stared at her a moment. "You mean for the past four months—"

"Yes."

He looked away, but Adele saw in his face the same look he'd had when she had made bauernfrühstück for him so many months ago. He'd finally removed a brick, and the real Jonah was appearing from behind the wall he'd built.

"Jonah, talk to me. Tonight, in the parlor. I will make sure Jacob is in bed."

In an instant, the brick was replaced, and he was impenetrable once again. "You'd best get going. Make sure you speak to Mr. Decker about that plow." He retreated toward the barn, and Adele felt tears prick at the corners of her eyes.

∞

"Tell Jonah that plow head should be here in the next couple of days." Fred Decker was helping Adele pack the items she bought into the buggy. She'd bought some calico for a new dress and notions for the quilt she was making for Katherine's baby. He handed her mail to her, and Adele glanced at the envelopes. One was from Ruth Decker. "Ah, Ruth has written to me."

"She's probably asking how your sister-in-law is doing," he said. Ruth Decker was Fred Decker's cousin by marriage and a good friend of Katherine's and Adele's.

She smiled. "Yes, I imagine she is."

"How is Mrs. Kirby? I've never met her, but Ruth thinks the world of her."

"It is kind of you to ask," Adele replied. "I guess Ruth told you she is. . ."

"Yes, an October baby, I understand."

She nodded. "I saw Katherine a week ago, and she looks wonderful." Her most recent visit to her friend had gone well, in spite of Daniel's probing questions about his brother. But Mary had not been there, and Adele smiled at the reason. "I will have to tell Ruth how Mary O'Neal is doing. Dr. Harris has been taking her out driving."

"Oh, I see," Fred said with a wink. "He's that old family friend of theirs, a professor like Daniel at the university, isn't he?"

"Yes. I am very happy for her."

"Well, she deserves it, after losing her husband and son in the war." He snapped his fingers. "I just remembered." Adele watched as he went into the mercantile and came back out with a wooden packing crate. "This came on the early train yesterday addressed to you."

Adele looked at it for a moment. Her eyes softened as she realized what it was. "It is Erich's things."

Mr. Decker nodded and set it in the buggy's small bed behind the driver's seat. "I know I've already said as much, but I'm very sorry for your loss, Mrs. Kirby."

"Thank you."

"The memorial service was very nice. Too bad Jonah couldn't come."

"Yes," she said, looking down. He had gotten out of the memorial the church held by claiming one of their cows was getting ready to calf. When she and Jacob had returned and asked about the animal, he had mumbled something about a false alarm.

Fred offered her his hand so she could climb into the buggy when a voice stopped them.

"Good morning, Mrs. Kirby."

Adele turned to see Dr. Kelly standing on the boardwalk. She nodded to him. "Good morning, Doctor." It was the first time they had spoken since that disastrous day at church. Adele avoided him at services, and he never approached her when she and Jonah were in town together. He had been at Erich's memorial, but she had been careful to keep Minnie nearby to discourage him. Hoping he would see she was leaving and move on, she turned away and allowed Mr. Decker to help her into the buggy. Once she had settled herself in the seat, she smiled down at him. "Thank you very much, Mr. Decker. I will tell Jonah about the plow head."

Fred Decker smiled and made his way back into his store.

Dr. Kelly still stood on the boardwalk, and she gave him another nod as she gathered the reins. But before she could snap them, he had bridged the distance between them and covered her hands with one of his.

She looked at him in shock. "Noah!" she said, then immediately corrected herself. "Dr. Kelly."

"I'm sorry," he said, his voice rough. "Please excuse me for my boldness, but I must know how you are."

Adele saw the lost look in his eyes and glanced around. Thankfully, a train was at the station, and their side of the tracks was empty of people. "We are fine." She tried to pull her hands away, but he held on tight. "Dr. Kelly, I must get home."

"You're sure *you* are fine? You looked wretched at the memorial."

"I was saying good-bye to my brother," she said. "Now, please, I must—"

"There is something I have to tell you first."

"If you will release me, I will let you." She sighed with relief as his hands slid away.

"I've had a letter from my friend, Dr. Peck."

Adele's brow furrowed. Why would he write again?

Noah noticed her frown. "Please hear me out. This is important. I wrote to him about Jonah's walks. He's very concerned and wants to know if he's sleepwalking."

Fury made Adele shake. "*Sie hatte kein recht. . .*" she began and took a deep breath. "You had no right to speak to anyone about my husband!"

"Adele, please! If he is sleepwalking, he could hurt someone with that gun. Think of Jacob."

Her heart flipped, and fear must have crept its way across her face.

Noah laid his hand lightly on top of hers. "You *are* concerned about Jacob. You don't like him being around it."

"No, but I trust Jonah will not harm him."

"Adele, please."

"My husband is not sleepwalking," she said, brushing his hand away. "I always wake when he does this." His face fell, but she took no heed of it and continued on. "He woke this morning, and I heard him leave his room. I watched him from my window, and he was wide awake."

Dr. Kelly's brow knit together in consternation. "He left *his* room?"

"Yes," she said and, snapping the reins, drove off. She was several minutes down the road before she realized just how much her angry answer had revealed.

⁓

Jonah walked in from the fields. They had gotten the hay cut in the northeast field and were moving on to the next. It was hot work, and he was coming to the house for some switchel, hoping Adele had made some of the flavorful mix of cider, molasses, and ginger before she left for town.

He had to admit, Jacob was more than pulling his weight today. Perhaps he had been too hard on him this morning. But seeing him with that book had reminded him of the kinds of things Daniel used to pull, and he'd instantly seen red. His brother had forever been doing just enough work to get by and then taking off to the creek to read.

Jonah stopped for a moment and looked to the west. He could just make out the scrub that marked the edge of Daniel's portion of the farm. What did he think was going to happen? That his brother was suddenly going to come to his senses and show up and farm it one day? He shook his head and continued walking.

Adele was pulling up the drive as Jonah approached. He was glad the mourning period for her brother was almost over. Black made her look pale and washed out. As he drew closer to the buggy, he frowned. Adele looked tense, almost angry. Had something happened in town? He walked up to the buggy. Her brows knit together when she saw him. The tense look was gone a moment later, and he saw she mustered a smile.

"How is the mowing?" she asked—a little too lightly, he thought.

"Good." He grasped her hand and helped her down. She wobbled slightly, and he grasped her waist to steady her. Lowering her to the ground, she was partially in his arms, and for the briefest of moments, he caught a glimpse of her brilliant eyes. Shaking, he moved away and noticed the wooden box in the bed. "What's this?"

"Erich's things," she replied softly. "Will you take it into the dining room? I can manage the rest."

He took the box inside and then went to the toolshed to fetch a claw hammer. She had finished putting things away by the time he got back and was looking at the crate, which he had set on the table. He handed her the hammer, knowing his wife liked to do such things herself. "Did you make any switchel? I need to get back."

"Jacob has not been disrespectful to you again?" she asked as she pried open the crate.

"No. He's been working hard."

"I am sorry he spoke to you in that way," she said. "It will not happen again." The lid popped open, and Adele quickly pulled it off and laid it aside.

As she started to take things out, Jonah glanced at the door, eager to leave. If he stayed, she would want to reminisce with him. "Never mind about the switchel," he said and started for the door.

Her gasp stopped him. "It is a letter to me," Adele breathed. She opened it, and a bittersweet look slipped over her lovely face as she began to read. Her eyes started to shimmer, and she looked up at Jonah. "He was saving up to come home so he could help me. The last letter he got from me told him how we thought you had died. With Nathaniel gone, too, he thought he should come home and take care of me. That is why he was working for a mining company instead of wandering. The money was better."

Anger shook Jonah from head to toe. "How much longer is He going to torture you?"

Adele looked up in surprise. "Who do you mean? Erich?"

"God." Erich's Bible lay inside the crate. Jonah snatched it up and stared at it. The touch and feel of the leather-bound book made his rage keener, and he threw it down on the table. "All these promises, and for what? How can you trust Him anymore?"

"God knows what is best," Adele said quietly.

"What is best? To take your husband, your farm, and now your brother? Who will He take next, Adele? Are you ready for it to be Jacob?"

" 'For my thoughts are not your thoughts, neither are your ways my ways, saith the Lord,' " she quoted.

Jonah grasped her by the shoulders and gave her a shake. "Stop it! Don't you know what He is? How can you defend a monster that has taken everything from you?"

"God is not a monster." Adele shoved him away, so hard he stumbled. "You have no idea what I have been through. You, who are so wrapped up in your own pain, can't even take a little boy under your wing or let go of the past. You can't even walk the length of a room without that terrible gun. You let your anger fester and wound you more and more every day. You have no idea the mercy God has shown me. When I found out Nathaniel was dead, I wanted to die. I almost did die. My pride almost killed me and Jacob. And deep in my heart, I hoped it would. But God was merciful. When Jacob and I lay dying, Daniel came for us. Through him and Katherine, God saved my life and my soul."

Jonah stared at her, half angry, half thunderstruck. He opened his mouth to lash back at her, but the tears in her eyes. . . Had she really said she had wanted to die? Adele? The woman he had always seen as so strong, so steadfast? He turned and walked out of the house. He didn't have a moment's hesitation on where he needed to go, and in a little over an hour, he was walking up to the door of his brother's house in Delaware.

Chapter 6

"J onah!" Daniel stood in the doorway of his house, glasses in hand, in shirt and waistcoat.

Jonah should have expected him to be surprised. This was the first time Jonah had ever been to his brother's house. Well, that wasn't exactly true. Last fall, not long after Daniel and Katherine had married, he had taken some wheat into Delaware to sell. Curiosity had gotten the better of him, and he had made his way to the west side of town to see what kind of fancy house his brother had bought.

The sight of a large frame house, complete with bay windows, columns, and a turret rising from one corner, sitting at the top of the hill on Liberty Street hadn't surprised him in the least. But just then, a passing Ohio Wesleyan student had told him that house belonged to Professor Merrick, the president of the university.

When Jonah asked where Professor Kirby lived, he was directed across the street to a modest, two-story brick house with dormer windows surrounded by a black, wrought-iron fence. This was the house his sister-in-law had fussed about being so large? He'd driven away, positive the place was small so his brother could afford marble floors and a gold staircase.

Now, looking past Daniel through the vestibule, he saw a wood-paneled hallway with a red carpet running up stairs edged by a walnut banister. The floors were freshly polished hardwood.

Daniel stood watching him, his eyes flicking from Jonah's gun to his face. "Is everything all right?" he asked. "Nothing's happened to Adele or Jacob?"

Jonah scowled. "They're both fine. At least they are now."

"What do you mean? What happened?"

"That's what I was hoping you could tell me," Jonah replied, stepping inside.

Daniel looked at him for a moment before closing the door. "Let's go into the library. There's coffee if you want some."

Jonah left his rifle in the vestibule and followed his brother through a palm-lined parlor into the adjoining library.

A large walnut desk sat in one corner, littered with papers. Quite close was a stuffed armchair with a settee in front of it, an Irish Chain quilt neatly folded on the seat.

Daniel pulled up a more practical-looking, hard-backed chair and offered it to Jonah before pulling his own leather chair from behind the desk and sitting down. "The other chair is Katherine's," he explained. "She usually sits with me every evening and helps me plan my lessons or listens to me gripe about grading papers."

"Being a professor is not so exciting after all, huh?" Jonah asked.

Daniel gave him a slight frown. "I love being a professor as much as you love being a farmer. That doesn't mean there aren't parts of it I don't enjoy."

Jonah looked down, hating having to admit the truth of his brother's statement. He'd be very happy if he never had to shear another sheep for as long as he lived. "Where is Katherine?" he asked.

"She's upstairs asleep," he replied. "To be honest, I'm worried about her. The baby is so big already."

"I remember Ma being big with Toby."

"I do, too. It's just—" He looked toward the upstairs, then rose from his chair and walked to a side table just inside the parlor door. "I'm sorry. Let me get you some coffee."

"No maid?" Jonah asked as he took the cup his brother offered.

"Her afternoon off," Daniel said as he settled back into his chair with his own cup. "Now what did you mean when you walked in?"

"What happened to Adele and Jake before I came home?"

"What did she tell you?" Daniel asked.

"That you saved her life." He watched his brother stare into his cup for a moment before setting it aside on his desk.

"Adele wasn't herself when I came home," he said.

Jonah thought back. Just after their mother died, Daniel had been released from the Army and come home. "Can't say that I blame her. You were Nate's commanding officer. His safety was your responsibility."

"I was trying to rescue him." Daniel's eyes blazed with pain and anger. "There were so many Confederates, and the gunfire was so thick

I could have been killed. The men I had already freed would have been recaptured. Adele understood."

Jonah frowned then sighed. "What happened to her and Jake?"

"Jacob got a bad cut on his hand and it got infected." Daniel looked away. A few moments later, he continued. "When Nate died and she lost the farm, she wasn't very well off at all. Ma helped her, but then she died and. . .Jake and Adele weren't eating. If I hadn't gone looking for them, they may have died."

"You mean they were starving?" Jonah rose with blazing eyes. "How could you let that happen?"

"I didn't know." Daniel stood and returned his brother's glare. "You know how stubborn she is. She wouldn't ask for help from Aunt Mary because Katherine was with her. She hated her because she's Southern." Aunt Mary had lived in South Carolina during the war, and when she returned to Ostrander, Katherine came with her. "And her blasted pride kept her from going to anyone else."

"Even the church?"

"Especially the church."

Jonah stared at his brother. "Why?"

"She was angry, Jonah. Her faith was in shreds. She'd lost her husband, her home, you, as far as she knew." Daniel sighed and ran a hand through his hair. "If it wasn't for Katherine, she said she would have drowned in hate and anger."

"I thought you said she hated her."

"She did, at first. Everyone did." Daniel's eyes grew soft. "But as hard as it was, Katherine was beautiful about it. She never hated anyone in return. Seeing her love her enemies convicted Adele. God used Kat to bring Adele back to Him." Jonah stared at him, and Daniel laid a hand on his shoulder. "I'm sorry we never told you. But you were already going through so much, and Adele didn't want to worry you with it."

Jonah walked over to the window. God could have let her die. He had taken so many others that He should have. But He had saved her, both body and. . .soul. In spite of his feelings toward God, Jonah found he was glad for that. Adele's faith was so much a part of her. He could hardly imagine she had ever been angry at God. Like him. The thought shook him so much he reached out and grasped the window frame. He heard his brother walk up behind him.

"Are you all right?" he asked.

Jonah slowly nodded. To keep him from asking anything further, he changed the subject. "We got Erich's things today. Adele found a letter he never got to send. He was working for that mining company to earn enough money to come home and help her."

"At the memorial, Adele said she was going to leave his body there in Nevada," Daniel said. "Is she sure about that?"

Jonah nodded. "She told me Erich wouldn't have wanted her to trouble herself."

"It'll be kind of odd knowing he and Toby aren't buried here."

Jonah nodded as he thought about their youngest brother. He'd died at the battle of Cold Harbor. Daniel had intended on going down to Virginia to bring his body back, but in the end, he and Jonah had decided to leave him where he was.

"I still can't believe he ran off and left Ma to tend the farm by herself," Jonah said.

"I wish I could have gotten to him," Daniel said.

Jonah looked at him.

"I was at Cold Harbor, too. I saw him lining up with his regiment. If I could have gotten to his commanding officer, I would have made sure he was sent home."

"Who was he with?"

"A Pennsylvania unit, best I could tell."

"He went that far east to join up?" Jonah's brow furrowed. "Why?"

Daniel ran a hand through his hair. "I don't know." His eyes took on a haunted look, and he sat back down in his chair. "Cold Harbor. That's one I wish I could forget. That and Fredericksburg."

Something about the look on his brother's face made Jonah blurt out, "I was at Shiloh." For as long as he lived, he would never be able to erase from his mind the horrific carnage of that early battle of the war.

The first day had been a bloodbath. The whole Union line hadn't been prepared, plain and simple. The clear spring morning had suddenly given way to a full onslaught of Confederate fire. Incredibly, he'd found himself in a peach orchard, their blossoms falling all around him and the other men as they fought and died. Eventually darkness fell, and the cries of wounded and dying men punctuated the night, so much so he couldn't sleep. He'd taken his rifle and tried to walk away from the sound and couldn't. When he came home, he cut down every peach tree in the Kirby orchard.

Jonah raised a hand to his face and realized tears were streaming down his cheeks. He shook, and his knees buckled.

Daniel rose, caught him by the forearms, and lowered him into his own leather chair.

Through his tears, Jonah heard his brother praying for him and found himself silently doing the same. As much as he wanted to stop himself, he couldn't. *Help me—please help me,* his heart begged.

Calm slowly spread over him, and eventually Jonah looked up to find Daniel watching him, his face full of concern. Jonah took a sip of his coffee and found it was cold. Hadn't Daniel just poured it? He stared at the brown liquid, wincing at the thought that he'd lost control of his emotions in front of his brother. "I guess you're about ready to have the asylum come and fetch me," he said.

"No," Daniel replied, and Jonah looked up at him. "But I'll be honest with you. Last week when Adele was here, I almost did. I even went so far as to write out the telegram." Daniel dropped his eyes. "But that night I had a nightmare."

Jonah glared at him. "God send you a message?"

"I haven't had one since before I got married," Daniel went on, ignoring his brother's words. "I woke up screaming. Scared Kat to death."

Jonah wondered just how bad it had been. Judging from the look on his face, it must have been at least as terrifying as his own.

"I ripped up the telegram the next morning," Daniel said after a minute or two. "I'm sorry. I forgot what you were going through."

"You had nightmares?" Jonah asked.

Daniel nodded. "And loud noises used to spook me."

"How did you get it to stop?" The question spilled from Jonah's lips before he could stop it.

"I talked about what happened to me." Daniel leaned forward in his chair. "I talked to friends, and more importantly I talked to God."

Jonah looked away. He didn't want to admit God might be the key to the peace he saw in his brother's eyes. But he couldn't deny the sense of calm he felt since silently wording his desperate prayer. He didn't feel whole, and he was still angry with God, but *something* had changed. He'd talked to God, and God had answered—just not in the way Jonah had come to expect.

He glanced out the window, and the sight of the sun starting its descent in the western sky made him realize how worried Adele must be.

He had never told her where he was going.

"You, who are so wrapped up in your own pain, can't even take a little boy under your wing or let go of the past. You can't even walk the length of a room without that terrible gun."

He bit his lip as the truth of her words stung at his heart, and he rose. "I need to get home."

"Of course," Daniel said, rising with him.

They walked through the parlor and into the vestibule where Jonah picked up his rifle as Daniel opened the door for him. He paused and turned toward his brother, extending his hand.

Daniel took it, and Jonah held on a moment or two longer than needed. Their eyes met, and Daniel gave him a small smile and nodded.

Jonah turned and walked down the porch steps to his wagon in the street.

∞

Adele rebuked herself for the hundredth time since Jonah left and looked down the road for the millionth time to see if he was coming back. She was working in the kitchen garden now but earlier Cyrus had come looking for Jonah. She couldn't even remember the excuse she had given him as to why Jonah had left in the middle of a workday. But Cyrus had been satisfied with whatever it was she said and took the switchel she made back out to the fields.

Wanting to do something other than mend clothes, Adele had grabbed her hoe and started in on the kitchen garden. *How could I have said those terrible things to him?* she thought as she overattacked a weed. *What was I thinking?*

The fact was she hadn't been. Going through her brother's things, lack of sleep, her worry for Jonah, and everything that had happened in town that morning had stretched her to her breaking point. The words had spewed from her mouth before she even knew what she was saying.

But where could Jonah have gone? When would he come home? Would he even come home? *Please, Father, guide him home. Soon.*

Feeling a tug on her skirt, Adele whirled around to find Sweet Pea standing next to her. The relief she felt at the sight of the little girl was so intense she immediately set aside her worry over Jonah. Her visits to the farm had been less frequent. In fact, this was her first appearance since the end of June.

"*Kleine!*" she said. "Sweet Pea, I have missed you."

To her surprise, Sweet Pea buried herself in Adele's skirts and refused to let go.

"What is it? Are you all right?" She wasn't crying but seemed scared of something. Adele looked around and saw nothing but blue summer sky and trees waving lazily in the breeze. She gently disengaged the child from her skirts and carried her into the house.

Sitting on a small stool in the kitchen, the little girl became calmer as she munched on a molasses cookie and allowed Adele to check her for bruises or scrapes. She found neither, and since she was unlikely to get anything out of her—the little thing never spoke except for the occasional yes or no—Adele was forced to give up.

She did notice the child was still barefoot and still wore the same worn dress. It was clean, however, and still fit at the bodice but was beginning to get a little short. Fingering the hem, she noticed there was still a tuck left that she could let out, and she might even find a piece of ribbon to disguise the worn edge.

But she hesitated. If the little girl went home—wherever that was—what would her family think of her clothing being altered? *They probably will not notice. She goes off for hours at a time, and no one has ever come looking for her.* She would never have let Jacob out of her sight at such a young age.

Glancing out the window, she saw the sun was more than halfway across the sky. She needed to get supper ready. She began chopping carrots and potatoes, and as she checked on the chicken she had put in earlier, the events of the morning rushed back over her.

She wiped her hands on her apron and, sinking into a chair by the door, reached into her pocket and pulled out her brother's letter. He had been trying to come home to her. She wished she'd been able to thank him for bringing her to Ostrander and taking care of her when all the while his heart longed to move on to somewhere else. She wished she had gotten to tell him she loved him one last time. Tears formed, and as a sob rose in her throat, she heard little feet rush over to her.

Wide brown eyes looked up into her own. "Sad?" Sweet Pea's voice was sweet and clear.

Adele nodded, and the little thing leaned in and wrapped her small arms around Adele's waist. She returned the embrace, laying her cheek on her head. They stayed like that for several minutes before Adele realized she had to finish getting supper ready. She gave the little girl a kiss on the top of her head. "Thank you, little Sweet Pea."

The girl lifted her head and looked at Adele for a moment. "Anne," she said, pointing to herself.

"Your name is Anne?"

The child nodded.

Adele smiled as she wiped her face on the edge of her apron, gratified by the trust the child had placed in her. Determined to keep her from running off until she could get a decent meal into her, she led her into the parlor. Her brief examination had also shown Adele the little girl wasn't being properly fed.

The sight of Jacob's wooden toys delighted the child, and she sat down on the floor and immediately started to play. Adele prayed she wouldn't slip away as she had on previous visits. Anne played until she heard Jacob and the men walk in. Then she made for Adele like a frightened rabbit. She eventually warmed a little to Jacob, but Will and Cyrus had to sit at the end of the dining room table before she would eat. She was particularly afraid of Cyrus, who simply gave his usual shrug and paid the little girl no mind.

After supper, Anne fell asleep in Adele's lap. Adele had Will and Jacob take Toby's old trundle bed and set it up in her room, and Anne settled into it as if it were her own. Adele looked down on her with a sense of satisfaction. Someone would surely miss her if she was gone all night and would come looking for her in the morning. *Then I will tell them a thing or two,* she thought as she took the little girl's dress downstairs to the parlor to work on letting out the tuck.

Thoughts of Jonah came rushing back as she sat down with her sewing basket, and she prayed for him as she began to snip threads. *Father, please bring him home soon and safely. . . .*

Her eyelids drooped and she blinked, struggling to stay awake. The day had been so tiring. She glanced at the little clock on the mantel, determined to stay up until Jonah came home so she could apologize for her harsh words. But before she knew it, she'd laid her head back and fallen asleep.

Chapter 7

It was well into dusk when Jonah got back to the farm. The first few stars of the night had come out by the time he'd put the wagon away and tended to the horses. He saw the light shining from the parlor window and knew Adele had waited up for him.

He walked into the house and stepped into the parlor, ready to apologize for the way he left and for staying away so long. But he stopped short as he saw she had fallen asleep on the high-backed sofa. Softly, he walked over and knelt in front of her.

What should he do? She couldn't stay here all night. His palms began to sweat as he realized he would have to carry her upstairs. He shifted his weight, and a board in the floor creaked, waking her.

Her eyes flew open. "Jonah!" she exclaimed, and before he could stop her, she had wrapped her arms around his neck, hugging him.

He froze for several seconds before slowly returning the embrace. Her scent of lavender surrounded him, and her hair was soft against his neck. He closed his eyes. A lifetime of love for her rushed at him all at once, and he thought his heart might burst it pounded so hard. Had Pa felt like this for Ma? Had Nate loved her this much? Thoughts of his best friend caused him to back away and stand up. "I'm sorry I worried you," he said haltingly.

She looked up at him in surprise before she spoke. "It's all right. Are you well?"

"I'm fine." Jonah turned and, seeing the seat at the secretary across the room, made for it and sat down. It was easier to look at her now that she was farther away. "Daniel told me everything that happened after he came home."

"Oh," she said, dropping her eyes. "Then you know how horribly I behaved after Nathaniel died?"

"I'm not sure I would call it horrible," he said. "Your husband died.

How were you supposed to act?"

She paused a moment before she answered. "As a child of Christ, I should have turned toward Him instead of away."

He felt the anger rising in him. "And that's how I should have acted?"

"I did not say that."

He clenched and reclenched his fists. He looked at Adele. She was watching him with careful eyes as if he were a powder keg sitting too close to a flame. *Why not? That's how I feel. All set to explode. Like a gun ready to go off.*

He could see his gun leaning against the wall just inside the door, and the sight of it filled him with even more anger. He turned his gaze elsewhere, only to see Pa's Bible lying on the side table next to the rocker.

All right, God. Addie says You work through people. Pa always said the same. Let's see how You do. He looked at Adele with blazing eyes.

She looked back, calm, steadfast, and sure.

"Give me one good reason why I should forgive God."

The demand took Adele off guard, but only for a moment. "I cannot answer that unless I know why you are angry at Him."

His eyes narrowed. "You know why."

"Do I? When have you told me? Over the last year since you came home, when have you told me of your anger?" He didn't answer, so she continued. "If you will not tell me, then I cannot answer you."

They stared at each other. Eventually Adele started to gather her things. *Father, this is hopeless—*

"Zach."

She looked up.

Jonah was looking at her, but his eyes seemed to be in another place. Her heart began to pound. "Who is Zach?"

"He was younger than Toby, from Mount Vernon. A cannonball took his head clean off. How could God have let that happen to him?"

Adele raised her hands to her mouth. The image his words evoked silenced anything else she might have said or even thought.

After another moment, he continued on. "And they wouldn't give us water in Andersonville. There was nothing to drink from but a filthy stream. People bathed and. . .did other things in it, and we were supposed to drink from it, too. Instead, we'd lay our clothes out in the rain—when it came—to soak up the water, then wring it into shallow bowls later. And the lice never stopped eating us." His eyes filled with a cold anger. "So many people died who I wanted to live. I can't even count how many times I prayed, so many times without an answer. How am I supposed to forgive Him for that?"

Tears were streaming down Adele's face. "You think God is responsible for the sin men do?"

"He's responsible for not stopping it. Pa taught me God is supposed to be all-powerful, all-good. I'm not so sure anymore."

"But He is all those things, Jonah."

"How?"

"You are here." Adele rushed over and knelt before his chair. "You survived. You came home. Don't you know how I praised and thanked God when I saw you walking up the drive that day? Yes, many people perished, but you did not. He saved you. He brought you home to me."

"Why me? Why not Nate?"

"Oh Jonah, I do not know. I only know God is with us through our troubles. He is not the cause of them."

∞

Jonah turned her words over and over in his mind as he lay in bed that night. He thought about how many times he should have died in the war but hadn't. On at least two occasions he'd sat down at the campfire after a battle and found holes in the top of his cap—bullet holes. Once, while he'd been reloading in the middle of a battle, one had come so close to his ear he'd heard the whistle of it as it flew by, and he turned to see it had settled into the man behind him, killing him. And Andersonville. How many times should he have died there?

He sat up in bed. *The* Sultana. *I should have died then, too.* He had thought it was only by chance that he had been unable to sleep and was standing at the bow of the steamship when the boiler exploded. He had jumped in the water almost immediately. And he'd managed to help at least two other men to shore. *They never would have made it if I hadn't.* As weak as Andersonville had made him, he'd somehow found the strength to help them.

He looked up at the moon as its light streamed through the window in his room. *But why didn't You do the same for Nate? Then Adele would have a real husband and Jacob a real father.*

To his shock, he felt an answer deep in his heart. But it couldn't be right. *No. No, they're his. They were never mine, never supposed to be mine.* But the answer remained. Jonah lay back down and closed his eyes and his heart to it and fell into a fitful sleep.

∞

"Explain to me again why we have to sit clear down here?" Jonah asked the next morning. Will was crowded down at the end of the table with him, while Jacob and Adele sat at the other with Anne perched on his wife's lap. Jonah couldn't stretch out his long legs with the others sitting so close. He was glad the little girl had finally told Adele her name and had slept peacefully in her room last night, but he was still trying to grasp why she should be so afraid of men.

Adele looked at him apologetically. "I'm sorry. I'm not sure why myself. I just know she will not eat if you are near."

"If I may, ma'am, last night I think it might have had more to do with Mr. Morgan," Will said. Cyrus didn't come to breakfast on Sunday mornings. He made do in his little place near the creek. Will rose and slid his chair closer. Anne looked at him warily but continued to eat. Will smiled in triumph, and Jonah sighed with relief. His legs had been getting cramped.

He, Will, and Jacob finished up, and while the other two went out to hitch up the buggy, Jonah lingered in his seat for a moment. "She was frightened of Cyrus?" he asked.

"He is wild looking," Adele pointed out.

Jonah frowned slightly. "Cyrus Morgan is a good man. He just prefers a simpler kind of life."

"Like Erich had, I suppose," she said thoughtfully.

"I'm sorry. I didn't mean to bring up painful memories."

"No, it's all right. I need to store his things away in the attic." The crate still sat in the corner of the dining room. Adele leaned her cheek lightly against Anne's head. "Erich would have liked the memorial service. But he would have hated seeing so many people wearing black just for him. I am glad he did not see how long I wore it when Nathaniel died."

Her mention of Nate brought to mind what Jonah had felt before he went to sleep last night. He pushed away the answer that was still being offered. *She'll always be his. And I intend to keep it that way.*

Anne slid off Adele's lap, and the clunk she made when she landed broke his train of thought. His eyebrows rose. She was wearing boys' boots!

199

"Where did those come from?" he asked.

"They belonged to Jacob," Adele said with a wry smile. "I could not have her go to church with us without shoes." She took the little girl's hand and led her to the door.

Jonah followed and watched Adele tie one of her own older bonnets on Anne. It sagged and almost covered her face.

Adele tied on her own bonnet and looked hesitantly at Jonah. "You are sure you will not come with us?" she asked.

He shook his head. "I have some things to do in the fields." He saw the disappointed look in her eyes. "I'm sorry."

The disappointment faded a little, and she gave him a small smile. "It is all right."

Once they left, Jonah started to walk out of the house to head toward the barn when he saw his gun leaning just inside the door. He grabbed the door handle and tried to leave without it, but his feet suddenly felt as if they were stuck fast in thick mud. Reluctantly he grabbed it and made his way out to the shed.

There he picked up a hoe, intending to work in the cornfields, when he heard a steady drumming on the roof. He went to the door and was shocked to see it raining, heavy and hard. He stared. *It wasn't supposed to rain today.* He always knew when it would rain. Rain, frost, snow, whatever the weather was going to be, he always seemed to have a sense about it. It had made Pa amused and proud that he'd inherited his ability.

Shaking his head, Jonah put the hoe back and made a dash to the house. His clothes got soaked anyway. After he changed, he wandered around the house.

The rain did not let up, and he eventually found himself in the parlor. He sat down at the secretary with his gun. It had gotten wet during his dash indoors, and it needed to be dried and cleaned.

But he found his attention wandering to Pa's Bible. It still lay on the side table where Adele had left it four months ago—when he had told her he didn't need it. As he worked on his gun, he found himself looking up at the leather-bound book several times. Finally, he set his weapon aside and fetched it.

Returning to the secretary, he held it out in front of him, running his thumbs over the worn leather. Pa had read from this every night after supper. Jonah had to smile as he recalled how shocked Ma had been when she found he'd been writing in it. She'd thought it sacrilegious. He had explained to her he wasn't changing God's Holy Word; he simply wanted to jot down his thoughts on the scriptures as he read. Eager to see his father's handwriting, Jonah flipped it open.

"*The Lord is nigh unto them that are of a broken heart. . . .*" Jonah's eyes fell on the little note written beside the passage in Psalms: *Rebecca Ann Kirby.* His sister. Ma had given birth to her after Daniel and before Toby. She only lived a few days before passing away in the night. He hadn't been very old, only six, but he remembered how sad Ma had been. Pa as well.

When he went to flip to another page, a folded note slipped from the Bible and fell onto the floor. He picked it up. The name on it said *Dorothy,* written in his father's hand—a note from his father to his mother. Ma had used Pa's Bible after he died. She must have put it there.

He almost slipped it back, not wanting to violate their privacy, but something made him open it.

Dolly,

I'm sorry for the way I've behaved over the past two months. It seems at times I can't get little Rebecca's face from my mind. You told me I should be grateful for what the Lord has already given us, two strong and healthy sons. But I so wanted a daughter for you. And you and she looked so much alike. I know you think I've been breaking the Sabbath, working in the fields while you and the boys were at church. I must confess I did those first two Sundays, but the more I wrestled with God, the more He called me to look at scripture and meditate on its wisdom. I have wrestled long and hard with Him over why He took Rebecca Ann away, and He's finally revealed it to me, in spite of my sin and anger against Him.

I couldn't understand how God could be loving and kind and yet take away a helpless babe from devoted parents. It made me angry. Then He nudged me to open the book of Genesis, and I saw my an-swer there in the creation story. When God created mankind, He could have created beings that had to love and obey Him without question. But He didn't want that. Instead, He gave man free will. And how did His creation thank Him for that free will? By disobey-ing Him and eating the fruit of knowledge of good and evil. And in doing so, sin and death corrupted and broke the perfect world He had created. Sin is more than just man disobeying God. It's what makes it hard for me to work the soil, hard for you to be with child. Its ugliness is woven in the whole way of this world.

Nothing you or I did caused Rebecca to die, and God did not snatch her away from us. It's mankind's own fault there is sin and death in this world. We can't charge God for causing it. I wish I knew why God allowed her to die, why He did not reach down His hand and heal her. But I am not the Creator of all things. I'm just a man. As another father asked Jesus to help him with his unbelief, I must ask God to help me with my lack of understanding. And even if I never understand why, I have to trust Him. I will be with you and the boys tomorrow at church. Know that I love you most tenderly, and I will always be your devoted and godly husband.

Joseph

Jonah folded the letter and leaned back in his chair. He was shaking. Pa had questioned God, too. Had the same questions, the same anger. The way he felt about his baby daughter's death was the same kind of feelings Jonah had about the war.

He glanced at the letter again. Pa had stopped going to church for a time? He could hardly fathom the thought. Joseph Kirby was the most faithful man he knew. Then he searched his memory and suddenly remembered, vaguely, him not coming for a few weeks. Ma wouldn't say why. Now he knew.

Laying the letter aside, he opened the Bible to Genesis and read the creation story for himself. Once. Twice. He'd never thought about the story like that before and now saw the same truth in it Pa had. But something else Pa wrote niggled at the back of his mind.

"But I am not the Creator of all things. I'm just a man."

It reminded him of a passage he hadn't read in a very long time. He turned to Job, the thirty-eighth chapter, and read: "Who is this that darkeneth counsel by words without knowledge? Gird up now thy loins like a man; for I will demand of thee, and answer thou me. Where wast thou when I laid the foundations of the earth? declare, if thou hast understanding. Who hath laid the measures thereof, if thou knowest? or who hath stretched the line upon it? Whereupon are the foundations thereof fastened? or who laid the corner stone thereof; when the morning stars sang together, and all the sons of God shouted for joy?"

Jonah bowed his head, feeling foolish and scared and yet thankful. "Four years I questioned and accused You, and in Your mercy, You didn't give me what I deserved," he whispered and then fell to his knees. "I had no right to question and charge the Creator of all things. I repent of what I've said and how I've acted. Forgive me, Lord. Help me find peace and Your presence in my life again." Something loosened in his chest, and tears fell as fast and heavy as the rain outside.

Chapter 8

I thought by now I wouldn't still be doing this."

Adele looked at her husband as he cleaned his gun. They were sitting in the parlor. Will and Cyrus had gone for the day, Jacob was out in the barn, and Anne was upstairs asleep.

"Some things may take more time," she said soothingly. "You *are* trying."

Jonah slowly nodded. "I just want it all to stop." He finished with his gun and, wearily leaning it against the wall, looked over at her. Frustration clouded his green eyes.

"Give God time to work," she said.

He gave her a small smile and nodded. He started to reach for his newspaper but paused for a moment. "I never thanked you, Addie."

"Thanked me? For what?" Adele looked up from her sewing.

"For giving me what for that day."

Adele bit her lip, realizing he was talking about the day Erich's things had arrived and they had argued. She still regretted her harsh words. "Oh Jonah, no. I should have been more patient."

"No. God worked through you to finally make me listen. I've thanked Him. Now I'm thanking you."

"You are very welcome," she said softly.

He smiled and turned to his newspaper, but Adele watched him for a moment before returning her attention to her sewing.

A month and a half ago, she had returned from church to find Jonah reading his father's Bible. Since then he had slowly changed. He talked now. Their conversations, while peppered with the mundane, included spiritual matters and what exactly had happened with her faith while he was at war. There were moments when he would get angry, moments when he fumed about something he'd read or something they discussed.

But he no longer remained angry. He was beginning to let it go.

And he wasn't just talking to her. To her great surprise, he and Daniel were exchanging letters. Once, she had gently asked what they wrote about. "Things best left between soldiers," he'd explained. She understood immediately and hadn't pressed him further. After hearing the little he had told her, Adele wasn't eager to discuss the specifics of his time in the war and was glad he had his brother to discuss such things with.

His walks had diminished to about once a week, and his nightmares were all but gone. But he still felt too uncomfortable to go anywhere without his gun, a problem as he was very eager to return to church. Out of respect, he did not want to so much as carry it across the threshold of the sanctuary door.

Adele made a habit of having Reverend Warren and Minnie over for Sunday dinner. Jonah greatly appreciated this, and they were, in fact, coming tomorrow after service.

"I saw that you and Miss Williams finished that quilt for Katherine this afternoon," Jonah said.

"Yes, I am glad Clara could come over to help," Adele replied then smiled. "I think Will was, too. I know he appreciated you letting him use the buggy to take her home."

"Well, he says the house is finished." While he hadn't actually gone and helped the young man, Jonah had graciously given him more time during the week to work on it. "He's ready if he can muster up the courage to ask for her." Jonah opened the *Delaware Gazette* and laid it out across the secretary where he was sitting.

"I am sure by this time next year the school board will need to hire a new teacher," she replied. "Jacob will be sad. He always liked Clara for his teacher." She continued her sewing for a moment. "Katherine's baby is not due until next month, so I am going to enter the quilt in the fair this week." Adele snipped a thread. "I am glad we are going. Jacob is looking forward to showing his calf."

Jonah had more than made amends with her son when he began to help him with the calf he had been taking care of all summer. But he still sometimes seemed hesitant toward the boy.

Jacob looks and acts so much like Nathaniel, she thought. She noticed talk of Nathaniel seemed to bother Jonah, so she tried to avoid it. She imagined he was still having trouble coming to terms with the fact that he had survived the war while his best friend had not.

She held up the garment she was working on, a new dress for Anne. To their surprise, the little girl never left. Instead, she shadowed Adele like a ghost.

Reverend Warren had made inquiries, going up to Edinburgh, Ohio, and even as far as Millville to see if she belonged to anyone there. But his search turned up nothing. It had been agreed that she would stay with them until her family eventually claimed her, but Adele secretly hoped no one would. She had become quite attached to Anne, and she suspected Jonah had as well.

She caught him taking a glance at the little dress before he turned back to the *Delaware Gazette*. "You have won her over, you know."

"I have?" he asked, looking up in surprise. "I thought you were her favorite."

"Yes, but you have not noticed the way she looks at you. She smiles when she sees you as if you were Will or Jacob." Anne was good friends with the pair now, but she had never really taken to Cyrus. She still hid in Adele's skirts and stared at him with wide eyes whenever he was near. As Adele lowered the dress to her lap, she saw Jonah's mouth twitch. "I know you are pleased, Jonah Michael Kirby. You may as well smile."

He continued to read, but as he did so, a gentle smile spread across his face. It was the first genuine smile in so very long that Adele's heart pounded for joy. He looked like his old self again, and she paused to gaze at him.

He glanced up. Their eyes caught, and she felt a strange vibration in the air as they looked at each other. Jonah suddenly looked uncomfortable and returned to his newspaper. Adele blinked, and as she resumed her work on Anne's dress, her hands shook and she felt flushed. She shrugged off the feeling—she was simply thrilled to see him better.

Thank You again and again, Father, for working through me to heal my dear. . .friend.

Chapter 9

"A dele, you've outdone yourself again," Reverend Warren said as he leaned back in his chair.

Jonah watched his wife take the compliment with a smile and a thank-you. She really had prepared a delicious meal. "What did you say the potatoes were?" he asked.

"*Knödel*," she replied. "You call them dumplings, which I always thought was a funny word."

Jonah couldn't help but chuckle, along with the others. "Not to all these Scotch-Irish ears," he teased.

Her mouth pursed in good humor as she and Minnie rose to clear the table. "Whatever you call them, you certainly ate enough of them," she replied tartly.

Jonah found himself smiling and looking into her brilliant eyes. A strand of hair escaped the braid she wore like a crown around her head, and he wished he could smooth it back for her.

When Jacob asked the reverend a question, Jonah suddenly realized what he was doing. Rebuking himself, he looked away. Out of the corner of his eye, Jonah saw compassion and understanding sweep across his wife's face. Good. Let her think he'd had a stray thought about the war.

She turned away and helped Anne carry a plate into the kitchen.

"Well, Jonah," the reverend said, "Jacob wants to show me that calf he intends to enter in the county fair. Do you mind?"

"No, Jake's been doing real well with it," he said, and the three headed outside. They went down to the pasture where the cows were out grazing, and Jacob rounded up his Jersey calf and brought her to the fence.

"Walk her around, Jake, so we can see her," Jonah said.

The boy obeyed and looked to him for approval.

Jonah gave him a small smile and nodded.

"She's a beauty, isn't she, Reverend Warren?" Jacob asked eagerly.

"She surely is. I know you'll place well this week."

"Thank you." Jacob loosed the animal from the rope he'd gently looped around her neck and gave her a swat. She ambled off, and he climbed up on the fence in front of them. "Is it breaking the Sabbath to go fishing today?"

"Well," the reverend began, his eye sliding good-naturedly toward Jonah. "The Sabbath is supposed to be a day of rest, and I've always seen fishing as a restful kind of activity."

"May I, Uncle Jonah?"

"Yes. Let your ma know where you're going."

"Thank you!" He scrambled over the fence and made a beeline for the house.

Jonah and the reverend looked out over the cattle for a few minutes before the clergyman turned to him. "How have you been doing, Jonah?"

Jonah had known Reverend Warren all his life. The question wasn't just polite conversation. "I want to come back to church."

"I know, but I also know something's holding you back. Is it spiritual?"

"No." Jonah nodded toward his rifle, which he unfortunately hadn't failed to grab as he left the house. "I can't seem to let go of some things." He paused for a moment, not wanting to voice what he'd been thinking the past several days. "I'm beginning to wonder if I should have been sent down to the asylum in Columbus."

Reverend Warren frowned. "I wasn't going to say anything to Adele or your brother, but a lot of things could have been avoided if they had consulted me."

"What do you mean?"

"You remember my nephew, Andrew?"

Jonah nodded. The reverend's brother lived ten miles west of Ostrander and had visited with his family frequently as Jonah was growing up. Andrew Warren had been a fun-loving young man who wanted to be a minister like his uncle.

"He was very badly wounded early on in the war," the reverend continued. "They weren't sure if he would make it. His ma went down to the hospital in Washington to nurse him. They ended up discharging him from service. Physically, he was all right. But his mind. . . I visited them several times after they brought him home."

He looked Jonah in the eye. "The young man I saw wasn't Andrew. Not the one I'd once known, at any rate. He was afraid of everything and couldn't keep still. And he would go off into the woods to be by himself."

Jonah looked at Reverend Warren in alarm as his heart began to pound. He had confided in the clergyman several weeks ago about his walks.

"No, Jonah, not like you," the reverend reassured him. "He would go off for days, and half the time he didn't realize what he was doing. His pa would have to go after him and bring him back. He tried to go back to school but couldn't concentrate on anything. It finally got to be too much for them to handle. My brother eventually sent him to an asylum in Dayton." The reverend placed a hand on Jonah's shoulder and squeezed it. "You've been angry, and it can't be denied the war is having its way with you, but you never belonged down in Columbus. I truly doubted the wisdom in Adele's decision to marry you to keep Daniel from sending you there, but God has worked it out for the best."

Jonah thought back to her blunt words that had finally started him down the road to healing. No doctor would have talked to him that way. And no doctor could have related to his crisis of faith as she had. But what had she sacrificed just to help him?

"How did He work this out for the best? She should have married someone she loved." Dr. Kelly leaped into his thoughts. When they met in the spring, the man was obviously in love with her, in spite of her marriage to Jonah. Had she returned those feelings? Had she sacrificed happiness with him? Jonah couldn't imagine Adele being with someone like the doctor.

Reverend Warren interrupted his thoughts. "I think she did marry someone who loves *her* very much."

Jonah froze.

The reverend continued. "I've known you, Nate, and Adele all your lives. You may have hidden it from her, but I saw from the start how you felt about her. And how you still feel about her."

Jonah looked away. "It doesn't matter."

"Nate's gone, Jonah. She's *your* wife now."

"He loved her. And she still loves him."

"Of course she does. She probably always will. I don't know of any widow who wouldn't. But Nate's been gone for years. She's moved on. What will you do if you wake up one day and discover she's fallen in love with you?"

Jonah thought of the way her blue eyes had looked at him last night and this afternoon, and his head swam. He shook it off. "We should get back to the house. Adele was making coffee."

The reverend didn't press the issue, and they didn't speak the entire way back to the house.

Adele, Minnie, and little Anne were sitting on the parlor sofa when they came in. Adele looked at him in concern. Something caught in his chest, and he felt his face soften as he gave her a small smile of reassurance. She returned his smile and got them coffee.

Jonah leaned against the mantel while insisting the reverend sit in the high-backed chair near the sofa. The clergyman gave him a quick glance but turned his full attention to Adele and asked after Will, who had not eaten with them.

"The Williamses invited him over for dinner," she explained.

"Ah, I see. I'm glad they seemed to warm up to him."

"Well, with the wonderful things he's done with that old property of yours, I can't say I'm surprised. And Dr. Kelly never showed much interest in Clara," Minnie said. "Strange that he seems intent on being a bachelor, don't you think, Adele?"

Adele frowned, and Jonah wondered just what she felt for the doctor.

"I suppose," she said quickly. "Will showed us the ring he intends to give Miss Williams. It belonged to his grandmother. I am very glad. Clara is such a nice girl. It will be good to have her for a neighbor."

"Speaking of neighbors, I hear Ben Carr is just about done settling his uncle's property," the reverend said. "He'll be leaving to go back west after the county fair."

Jonah's conscience pricked him. He needed to speak to Ben before he left. Ironically, the young man was now avoiding him. Over the past few months, Jonah had come to realize how unfairly he treated Ben. He started to say as much, but someone knocked on the front door.

"That can't be Jake," Jonah said as he went to answer it. He frowned when he saw Dr. Kelly standing there.

"May I come in?" the doctor asked.

Jonah nodded and stiffly stood aside to allow him to enter. He led him into the parlor and saw that Adele looked at him gravely for a moment before schooling her face to a more neutral expression.

Anne did as she always did with new people—she inched closer to Adele, who put her arm around the little girl and nodded at the doctor.

"Dr. Kelly, how nice to see you," Adele said.

"Thank you, Mrs. Kirby, but I'm sad to say I'm not here on a social call." He turned to the reverend. "I'm glad you're here, Reverend Warren. Henry Porter asked me to come fetch Jonah, and I think you should come along, too."

"What is it?" Adele asked. Jonah noticed the guarded look she gave the doctor.

"Something that concerns your husband in particular," he replied quietly. She looked away, but Dr. Kelly's eyes never left her.

Jonah's face hardened. "Then let's see what it is," Jonah said. He went to the door and picked up his rifle. "If you don't mind, we'll follow the doctor in your buggy, Reverend."

The three set out and were soon at Henry Porter's farm. Eliza, Henry's wife, was standing out in front of the house. Jonah nodded to her, and she gave him a hesitant nod in return. Two of Henry's sons came and took charge of the horses and buggies.

The doctor indicated they should follow him. He led them east through the Porters' fields and north along the property line that met up with Jonah's.

Jonah's brow furrowed. What on earth was going on? Had Henry accidentally killed one of his animals? That was impossible. All his pastures were on the east end of the farm—his property and the Porters' met on the west side. The only thing on the northwest part of his property was the land that had belonged to Daniel. As they approached Henry, the metallic smell of blood hit Jonah full force. He paused for a moment.

Dr. Kelly looked back at him. "Are you all right?" he asked with raised eyebrows.

"I'm fine," he replied through gritted teeth. He took a deep breath and swept past him to where Henry stood. He offered his hand, and the older man shook it firmly.

"Thanks for coming, Jonah. I'm afraid I've got a terrible mess here."

"What on earth?" the reverend said as he pulled his handkerchief from his pocket and covered his mouth.

"It's blood," Jonah said quietly and looked at the doctor.

211

The man looked at him intently. "Unfortunately, he's right. The poor animal is this way."

Jonah stepped into the brush and saw a deer, completely gutted. As he looked at the creature's mangled body, he grasped a young tree. He was back at Kennesaw Mountain just before he was captured. Was that one of his men who he'd been sitting with around the campfire the night before? He shook his head. The deer was there again, and he turned to Henry. "Another rabid animal?"

"Hardly," Dr. Kelly said. "A rabid animal wouldn't have left so much edible meat. And there's evidence that someone used a knife on the poor creature. A human being did this. Look again."

"I'd rather not," Reverend Warren said. He had never been much of a hunter. "Let's get back into some fresh air."

They stepped out into Henry's field and walked a few paces south.

"Mr. Porter has found several animals the past few days," the doctor said.

"Deer, most of them, just like this one," Henry said.

Jonah let them talk. He was still trying to rid his mind of the horrible sight and gripped his rifle tighter, trying to get his hands to stop shaking. Reverend Warren looked at him, and he nodded, reassuring him.

"Someone destroying an animal in such a way is certainly not well," the doctor said, looking at Jonah.

Jonah stiffened, and he glared back at him. "What are you trying to say?"

"Did you take a walk this morning?"

He started toward Dr. Kelly, but Reverend Warren grabbed his arm. "Wait just a minute," the reverend said. "Just because Henry found these animals so near the property line doesn't mean Jonah did this."

"You carry a pocketknife, don't you, Mr. Kirby?" the doctor asked.

"So does every other man in the county," Henry retorted. "And how does someone with just a pocketknife do something like this? I didn't ask you to bring him here for you to accuse him."

"It's all right." Jonah looked the doctor in the eye. "I walked yesterday morning."

Dr. Kelly's eyes darted elsewhere, and he almost looked disappointed.

Jonah glanced at Mr. Porter. "When did you find this one, Henry?"

"Just this morning," Henry replied. "Anyway, I asked you here to warn you. I know you go out early and walk around your property." Jonah opened his mouth to explain, but Henry stopped him. "I've seen you from time to time. Always was an early bird. Anyway, I figured you're still trying to work out the war and all, and I haven't told anyone." He shot a look at the doctor. "Things like that should be kept private-like. I wanted you to know what's been going on so you could stay safe."

"I don't walk as often as I used to," Jonah replied. "Only been going out about once a week. But when I do, I'll keep an eye out."

"I'm glad to hear you're feeling better," the older farmer said. "With you and me keeping a good watch out, we'll get this fellow in no time."

"Now wait," Dr. Kelly said. "Whoever is doing this will not stop at simply killing animals."

Henry looked at him doubtfully. "What makes you so sure?"

"I know from experience during my education in Philadelphia."

"Well, *my* experience tells me Jonah's not doing this. Me and my boys will be keeping a good watch out. If this keeps up, we'll catch him."

"Let's just hope he doesn't take to killing a human being first." Dr. Kelly walked around the others and back toward the Porter farmhouse.

As Jonah watched him leave, he remembered something Reverend Warren had said about Andrew, that he had gone off in the woods without even realizing it. What if he was doing the same thing?

∞

"Jonah, you could not be doing this," Adele said.

The Warrens had just left, and Jonah sat at the secretary, elbows on his knees, hands clasped, and looking at the floor. He had told her everything that had happened, including the brief moment he thought he'd been back at Kennesaw Mountain.

"I would know if you left the house and were not yourself."

"How do you know? I know you wake up whenever I do, but what if I do this so quietly you don't hear me?" He leaned back in his chair and ran his hands through his hair.

Adele frowned at the worried look on his face. She wished she could smooth the lines from his brow and make all his troubles go away. Then a thought came to her. "Jonah, she would hear you." Adele was sitting on the sofa with Anne curled up beside her. The girl's head lay in her lap. She gently stroked her hair, and the girl moved slightly and opened groggy eyes. Seeing Jonah, she smiled sleepily and waved before returning to sleep. "She sleeps very lightly," Adele whispered after a moment or two.

The little smile he had given Anne faded from his face. "But would she wake you if she heard me?"

"She wakes me if she hears a tree branch against the window," Adele said with a gentle smile. Jonah looked doubtful, and she went on. "I know you. You would not do this."

"Maybe you're right," he said hesitantly.

"I know I am," she declared. "I cannot imagine what Dr. Kelly was thinking." Her voice faltered on the last words, and she looked down. Of course she knew what he was thinking. Jonah noticed the catch in her voice, and she could feel his eyes on her.

"What went on between you two before we were married?"

Adele glanced up and opened her mouth then shut it again. He frowned at her. "Any fool can see he has feelings for you."

"Yes, he does." She bit her lip at the warmth she saw rising in her husband's eyes. In spite of the fact they had not married for love, she knew Jonah felt the sanctity of their vows should be respected. "Jonah, I never returned those feelings. I have never seen him as anything more than a friend. It has been difficult for him to accept that."

She watched with relief as the heat left his face. He didn't need anything else to worry him now. As he nodded at her and rose, a thought crossed her mind. Gently moving Anne's little head from her lap to the couch, she walked over to where he stood at the parlor door. "I was thinking. You do not want to walk anymore. I am awake when you are. If you wish, I could come to your room and sit with you."

"No!" To her surprise, an almost-panicked look crossed his face.

"We could talk. We are husband and wife. It would not be improper."

"No. . .I. . .no." He went to the door and took his rifle from the corner. "I think I'll go down to the creek and see how Jake is doing."

Adele blinked in surprise. She had never wondered why Jonah had insisted they not share a bed. They were friends, and he needed time to work out his problems. It wouldn't have been right. But what harm could come for her to sit in his room with him and simply talk?

Anne wiggled and opened her brown eyes. Adele smiled at her, and she smiled back. "Ma, is Pa okay?" she asked.

The question startled her. It was the first time she had addressed either one of them in such a way. Ma and Pa? Had she really become so attached to them so quickly? If someone should come for her. . .but the little girl blinked her large brown eyes and smiled at her.

Adele's heart melted along with her questions. "Pa will be all right, little one." She scooped up the little girl and swung her in a circle.

Anne laughed and laughed and nestled herself in Adele's arms as Adele carried her into the kitchen.

Chapter 10

T he sharp, clear blue of a late September Ohio sky greeted them as Jonah drove the wagon down the creek road toward Delaware to the county fair. Anne sat between Adele and Jonah while Jacob sat in the wagon bed. Will was escorting Clara Williams, and Cyrus, ever the hermit, stayed home to look after the farm. It was the third and final day of the fair, and Jacob and Adele would find out today how their entries had fared.

"I bet you'll get the first-place premium, Ma," Jake said as they drove through the sleepy little town of Bellepoint. "There wasn't a quilt there that was better."

Adele smiled good-naturedly at her son's biased remark. "It is only a baby's quilt, my son. I saw another there, which will probably win."

"That one by Mrs. Campbell down in Liberty Township doesn't hold a candle to yours," Jonah said, glancing over at her. "The pattern you used is the same one Ma used the year she won."

"It's a good thing you two are not judging. I think I would win every category whether I entered or not," she replied. Jonah gave her a shy smile before returning his attention to the road, and Adele found her heart pounding with happiness. He was growing more like his old self every day. Well, almost.

Something in his eyes and manner told her he would never truly be the same man he had been before the war. *Scars will always remain even after the wounds are healed*, she thought. And his wounds were certainly healing. He had not walked at all this week, and more importantly, he had spent the last two days without his gun.

When they had arrived on the first day of the fair, Jonah had been asked by a fair official to leave his weapon in the wagon. He'd been surly and nervous at first, but Jacob had diverted his attention by asking to go see the livestock stalls. As he walked, he became more relaxed and, at the end of the day, seemed quite pleased to have realized he hadn't noticed its absence. And when they returned home, he'd been able to leave it by the front door while he, Will, Jacob, and Cyrus did the evening chores. He still slept with it nearby, and even now the weapon was under the seat of the wagon, but he and Adele both thought they could see the beginning of the end.

They arrived at the fairgrounds just east of the Olentangy River. Buildings holding the various produce and livestock that people had brought to show dotted the neatly fenced-in field. Two of them were brand-new. The Delaware County Agricultural Society, the organization that ran the fair, had built them to house the fruit and vegetable entries. Jonah found a space for the horses and wagon, and soon they were walking toward the hall where the needlework entries were being shown.

"Oh, but we must see how Jacob will do first," Adele said. She started to turn toward the livestock stalls when Jonah gently took her arm.

"They aren't judging that until later," he said as he guided her toward the hall.

"Then perhaps we should go see how Aunt Mary's preserves—"

"We're meeting Aunt Mary, Daniel, and Dr. Harris midday for dinner and then going over there, remember?" He looked at her curiously. "Adele, are you nervous?"

Adele's eyes widened. "No."

"You sure seem nervous, Ma," Jacob said.

"Ma okay?" Anne asked.

Adele glanced at Jonah and squared her shoulders. True, this was the first time she had ever entered anything in the county fair, and so what if the entire county was looking at the sweet little quilt she had worked on so long and hard. There was nothing at all for her to be nervous about. Not a thing. Taking Anne's hand, she gently disengaged herself from her husband's grasp and strode toward the exhibit hall.

∞

Jonah couldn't help but smile at his wife's show of bravery. He remembered, not long after they met, how he and Nate dared her to pick up a crawdad they had fished out of Mill Creek. She squared her shoulders just the same way, quickly picked up the muddy creature, and held it aloft triumphantly. When she thought they had turned their attention back to looking for more, Jonah happened to glance back and saw her shudder as she threw it back in the creek.

As he and Jacob followed Adele and Anne, he put a hand in his pocket. The percussion caps for his rifle jingled softly, and he thanked the Lord once again that he was finally beginning to feel free from his gun. Maybe on Sunday he could leave it at home and go to church with Adele. She would be thrilled.

In the hall, he watched from a few steps away as Adele knelt and helped little Anne take off her bonnet. Her light-blue skirt billowed around her, and the two smiled at each other. Looking at them, one would think they were mother and daughter. As glad as he was that the two had bonded, Jonah seriously worried someone might still come and claim her. He knew he wouldn't be able to stand to see the heartbreak it would bring to Adele. And, he realized, he didn't want to lose the little girl himself. He remembered holding her tiny hand yesterday and how she had giggled as he lifted her down from the wagon a few minutes ago. His heart twisted. *Lord, allow her to stay with us always.*

"What will you do if you wake up one day and discover she's fallen in love with you?"

Over the past several days, Jonah couldn't seem to get the reverend's words from his mind. What *would* he do? Nate had been gone for almost four years now, and on the occasions Adele did speak about him, there was a bittersweet sadness to her voice but no real grief. Love as well, but no longing. No indication she still pined for him. The reverend was right. She *had* moved on.

Adele, Jacob, and Anne all stood together, and the image of himself standing with them as a family so filled his mind that he walked over and stood next to her. Their eyes met, and everything else but her faded away. Was it at all possible she might come to feel the same as he did? His hand began to reach for hers when the moment was broken by Jacob's excited gasp.

"Ma, look! I told you."

They both turned to see the judges place the first-place ribbon on Adele's quilt. Jonah shot her a smile, and her hand went to her chest as the judges congratulated her. The second-place premium went to Libby Campbell, and Adele approached her.

"I must compliment you. Your quilt is so very beautiful," she said with a smile. "I have to wonder if the judges made a mistake."

Mrs. Campbell smiled in return as she smoothed back a strand of her rich brown hair. "Thank you, but yours is much better than mine. However did you do those appliqués?"

As the two talked, Jonah introduced himself to her husband, Isaiah Campbell. The Campbells owned a fruit orchard down near Powell, and they had three children, Andrew and Ginny, who were close to Jacob's age, and Abby, who was the same age as Anne. They all walked around together for a while and eventually stopped over at the fruit hall to see the apples and pears Isaiah had entered. One placed first and the other second.

Jonah asked him how he had managed to raise such fine fruit. His own small apple orchard was healthy, but he had always wondered about growing pears. *And I really should replace those peach trees with something,* he thought soberly.

Destroying them had been foolish. He'd done it because he knew the sight of them in blossom would dredge up painful memories of the battle at Shiloh. But Jonah hadn't counted on the apple trees, with their similar-colored petals, having the same effect on him. He'd been tempted to cut them down as well, but he couldn't bring himself to destroy the whole orchard. Jonah prayed he could learn to live with it. It saddened him. He'd grown up climbing the trees in that orchard. He set the thought aside as he heard Isaiah answer his question.

"Oh, pears are pretty easy," Isaiah was saying. "They take a little longer to mature, but once they do, you just need to watch out for fire blight. Had a spell of that just this past summer. The leaves on some of the branches will suddenly whither. You have to cut the whole branch off right then and burn it."

"I'd be interested in buying some saplings from you come spring," Jonah said.

"Bartlett is a good variety, very popular. Come on down just before the thaw, and I'll set you up," Isaiah said. The two shook hands. "Sorry, we have to be getting on down to the track. My brother has a horse entered in the race later."

"I wonder how much of a future horse racing will have at the fair," Jonah commented. "The society is very determined that it stays centered on agriculture." He was an active member of the society, and much of the last meeting had focused on the subject.

"Oh, I agree, but there are still a good number of people raising horses in the county," Isaiah said. "They should have a chance to show them off as well."

"Time will tell, I guess."

They parted company with the Campbells and made their way back to the wagon to get the basket of food Adele had prepared for their lunch.

"Jonah, does the society plan to build better places for people to eat?" she asked. There were makeshift stalls dotted all over the fairgrounds for people to eat in, but they were far from permanent structures.

"We should be eating in something better than the livestock," he agreed. He made a mental note to bring it up at the next meeting. Maybe something could be done about it by next year's fair. He looked out over the crowds and soon saw Daniel's beaver skin hat bobbing through the crowd. He stood and waved. "Hey there."

"Hello," his brother said as he approached with Dr. Harris.

"Where's Mary?" Adele asked.

"Katherine wasn't feeling very well this morning," Daniel replied. "We gave our maid the day off to attend the fair, so Aunt Mary stayed with her."

Jonah noticed the worry in his brother's eyes. "Is Katherine all right?"

"Aunt Mary says she's fine. The doctor has her in bed for the next month."

"We will pray for her before we thank the Lord for our food," Adele said. They all sat down on the thick blanket Adele had spread out, and Jonah asked God's hand to be on Katherine and thanked Him for their food. Everyone ate heartily.

Daniel smiled when Adele pulled out her famous apple strudel. "If it was anything but your strudel, I would say I couldn't eat another bite," he declared.

Adele chuckled as she handed him a piece on a cloth napkin. She handed one to Anne.

Jonah watched his brother flash the little girl his most charming smile. "You must be Anne."

Her eyes widened. She had nestled close to Adele when Daniel and Dr. Harris first arrived but seemed to forget their presence while they ate. After staring at him a moment or two, she cocked her head and gave him a shy little smile. Jonah was glad to see she was getting better at meeting new people.

"Daniel said you can't seem to locate her family," Dr. Harris said. "I know a lawyer here in Delaware who could make inquiries."

"That is very kind, but Reverend Warren has already looked very carefully and could discover nothing. I cannot imagine her wandering over to our farm all the way from Delaware." Adele looked down at the girl, and Jonah could tell Dr. Harris's offer bothered her as she stroked the girl's strawberry-blond hair.

Later he, Daniel, Dr. Harris, and Jacob walked around while Adele stayed with Anne. The little girl had fallen asleep as she tended to do in the afternoon.

Dr. Harris strolled over to Jonah while they looked over the purebred sheep. "I hope I didn't upset Adele," he said.

"She's become very attached to Anne over the past couple of months," Jonah said. "For her sake, I pray we'll be able to keep her."

"I understand." The professor looked thoughtful for a moment. "I wonder, Jonah, if I might have a word with you and your brother."

Daniel came up just in time to hear what his old mentor had said, and he smiled knowingly. "You have our full attention."

The older man looked down and stroked his graying beard. "Well..." he said. "Well, I've been calling on Mary—I mean, Mrs. O'Neal—for several months now, and I thought it only proper, since you both are her closest male relatives, to ask you for her hand in marriage."

Jacob came up just then. "What's going on?"

"The professor here is asking to marry your aunt Mary," Jonah said. He laid a hand on the boy's shoulder. "Should Uncle Daniel and I give him permission?"

Jacob gave the professor a long look. "How do you plan on supporting her?" The sudden burst of laughter from the three men caused the boy to jump.

"Where did you hear that?" Jonah asked. He drew a deep breath and let it out again. He laughed so hard there were tears in his eyes. It had been years since he had found something so funny.

"Will told me Miss Williams's pa asked him that," Jacob replied. Will had asked for Clara's hand last Sunday and had clearly regaled Jacob with the whole tale. "Isn't that what you're supposed to ask?"

"Not in this case," Jonah chuckled. Like Daniel, Dr. Harris was a professor at Ohio Wesleyan, so there was certainly no concern that he could not support a wife. He turned to the professor and shook his hand. "You have our blessing."

As Daniel gave the older man a warm embrace, Jonah saw Ben Carr not far off at the horse stalls. He nudged his brother and nodded toward the young man. They exchanged glances. In his last letter to his brother, Jonah had mentioned his run-in with Ben Carr, and the two agreed they both needed to talk to the young man. Telling Jacob to stay with Dr. Harris, the brothers made their way over.

Ben saw them approach and frowned. "Mr. Kirby, Dr. Kirby," he said coldly and started to step away. His frown deepened when Jonah laid his hand on his arm.

"Please, Mr. Carr," he said. "I've come to apologize."

The young man pursed his lips but stopped and looked at them.

"First of all, I'm sorry for misjudging you. I had no right to say the things I did. Will Reid is one of my hired hands, and he says you're one of the most fair-minded men he's ever met." Jonah looked down. "Secondly, I should have treated your uncle better. I was taught to love my enemies, but I guess I didn't learn that lesson very well. Looking back now, I guess I was kind of a pain in the neck."

"No more than my uncle must have been," Ben said. "I'm well aware of what his faults were. My ma says that's why we left for the Kansas Territory. My pa couldn't stand to watch Uncle Eli's greed eat him alive."

"Mr. Carr," Daniel said, "I feel I should apologize as well. I thought the same way about your uncle." Jonah noticed his brother glanced at him before continuing. "I shouldn't have offered to sell him the Kirby farm and then backed out at the last minute."

"No need, Dr. Kirby. As I said, I know how bad Uncle Eli behaved."

"That still doesn't excuse how we acted," Jonah said.

Ben nodded. "I suppose." He offered them his hand. "Why don't we put this all behind us and start fresh?"

"That sounds like a good idea," Jonah said as he, Daniel, and Ben shook hands. "But I hear you're leaving soon. Headed back to the Dakota Territory?"

"Yes," the young man replied. "I've got most of my uncle's land sold or rented." Ben paused for a moment. "The fields adjacent to your farm are the only ones I still hold. I would like to give them to you."

Jonah blinked in surprise. "What for?"

"I really feel I should make amends for what my uncle did."

"You weren't responsible for his actions. And I have more than enough land of my own."

"No, I insist," Ben said.

Jonah hesitated. He didn't really need more land. What would he do with it? An idea suddenly came to mind, and he smiled. "Fine, I accept. My lawyer's name is O'Conner, Edward O'Conner." Out of the corner of his eye, he saw his brother's eyebrows rise. "He has an office here in Delaware."

"Thank you," Ben replied as they shook on the deal. "I'll be sure to see him before I leave."

"When will that be?" Daniel asked.

"Sometime next week. With the money I'm getting from the land here, I can finally start my own business." Ben looked down for a moment, a half smile on his face. "And I hope to marry and start a family."

"We'll pray everything goes well for you," Jonah said. "Be sure to write us. We'd like to know how things go for you."

"What on earth are you going to do with more land?" Daniel asked as they watched the young man walk away.

"These fields border the land Will is renting," he replied with a smile. "A couple of those acres will be a perfect wedding present for him and Miss Williams. I'll rent out the rest of it to someone who needs it." Jonah raised his eyebrows at the frown on his brother's face. "What's wrong? I think it's a good idea."

"No, it is a good idea," Daniel said. He looked away, but Jonah caught the guilty look in his eyes. "I never really apologized to you for trying to sell the farm. I'm sorry."

Jonah reached out and squeezed his shoulder. "Don't worry about that. You did think I was dead."

"But still. . ."

"Oh, come on." Jonah slapped him on the back. "They're judging Jacob's calf soon. Why don't you and Dr. Harris take him over to the livestock stalls while I go fetch Adele and Anne?"

"Sure," Daniel said, and Jonah was glad to see the guilt leave his face.

As he made his way through the crowds, Jonah hoped Anne would still be asleep. Ben's talk of marriage and family had him eager to talk to Adele alone, even if only for a few minutes.

Chapter 11

Adele had brought some mending along, anticipating that Anne would sleep after dinner. She found her thoughts turning to Jonah as she worked. She wondered at the look he had given her just before she won first place for her quilt. It was not one that worried her. It just seemed as if the way he was looking at her—especially over the past week—had changed. It reminded her of how Nathaniel would gaze at her when they were courting.

Her needle slipped and jabbed her thumb. Sucking the blood away, she dismissed the silly thought. *How ridiculous! He is just grateful for the way I helped him.* The thought lingered, even though she stubbornly continued to brush it away, trying her best to think on something else. She almost cried out with relief when she heard her name being called.

"Adele Kirby." She looked to see Fred Decker's cousin, Ruth, walking up with her newly married daughter, May Hamilton, behind her.

Adele rose and hugged them both. She had not seen either of them since her marriage to Jonah. "Ruth, May, it is so good to see you. I miss seeing you both when I go to town." She invited them to sit down. She noticed Ruth looking at Anne, who was still sleeping peacefully in a little ball.

"Now, who do we have here?" the woman asked. "Is she a relative of yours?"

By the time Adele explained how Anne had come to them, the little girl woke and decided to pick some of the clover growing in little white clusters across the field.

"Why, the poor thing," Ruth said. "May, you haven't heard of a child missing lately, have you?"

"No," May said as she went to help Anne pick clover. "But we live so far from Ostrander, I can't see how she could be from all the way up in Radnor."

"I suppose not." Ruth's face brightened "Why, here comes Jonah."

To her surprise, Adele's heart suddenly began to pound as her husband came into view. She took a deep breath and schooled it back to a normal rhythm.

Anne caught sight of Jonah and ran up to him. He smiled and knelt down to hug her.

Adele glanced at Ruth, who was smiling at the pair.

"Jonah Kirby, if you don't mind me saying so, you look like a new man," she said.

"I don't mind at all. Thank you, Mrs. Decker. The Lord has been working on me," he said, picking up the little girl.

"There. You even sound more like yourself," the older woman said with a broad smile.

Noticing Jonah was not sitting down, Adele looked up at him. "Is it almost time for them to judge Jacob's calf?"

He nodded.

"We'll help you with all this," May said.

While Adele gathered her mending and put it and the dinner leftovers in the basket, Ruth and May folded the blanket. She took it from them and handed the basket to Jonah. Their hands brushed, and Adele jumped.

"Are you all right?" he asked.

"Yes, I. . .must have caught my thumb on the basket. I pricked it while I was mending."

Jonah set the basket down and reached for her hand. "Let me see."

"No. It is nothing. It will be fine." She busied herself arranging the blanket over her arm and wondered what on earth was the matter with her.

"I am sorry we had such a short visit," Adele said to Ruth and May.

"Oh, don't worry about it," Ruth said as she embraced her. "We don't want to keep you."

May hugged Adele as well and then laid a gentle hand on Jonah's arm. "I hope you don't mind me saying, but I think it's just wonderful the way you are taking care of Adele for Nate. I always admired your friendship with him. It reminded me of Jonathan and David in the Bible. How loyal you both were to each other. Well, we have some place to be, too! I hope Jacob does well."

Adele watched the two of them disappear into the crowds with a smile. She would have to write to the young woman and thank her for her kind words. She turned to say so to Jonah but stopped at the pensive look on his face. "What is wrong?"

"Nothing," he said quickly. "We should get over to the cattle stall."

☙

Guilt was nearly strangling him as they stood in the cattle stall along with Daniel and Dr. Harris. What had he been thinking? How could he have thought even for a moment that Adele could be completely his? He glanced at her then quickly looked away. *No. I've already half broken the promise I made to Nate. I won't break it all the way.*

Since the moment Nate and Adele had become engaged, it had been a struggle for Jonah to hide how he felt. But when he refused to read the thirteenth chapter of First Corinthians at the wedding, Nate had wanted to know why. He pushed and prodded until Jonah finally admitted he was in love with Adele. Nate had been so hurt and angry that Jonah promised then and there never to tell her how he felt.

Jonah looked up to see the judges moving toward the calves. Anne gave a little sigh and laid her head on his shoulder. *All this belongs to Nate. Not me.* But when the judges awarded the first-place premium to Jacob, he could not help but feel pride for the boy.

With a dumbfounded smile, Jacob walked over to them and gave the money he'd won to his mother. "Save it for me, Ma."

Jonah looked at him curiously. "What are you saving money for?"

"School," he replied, looking at Daniel.

"School." Jonah glared at his brother. Through their letters the past few weeks, he'd become closer to him than ever. While the farm had not been their chief topic of conversation, Jonah thought Daniel would know that he didn't want Jacob lured to Ohio Wesleyan or any other school. "He's not going off to school like you did."

"It's not like that, Jonah," Daniel said raising his hands. "Let me explain—"

"Professor Kirby." They turned to see a young man pushing his way through the crowds.

"Isn't that one of your students?" Dr. Harris asked.

Out of breath, the young man stopped in front of Daniel. "Sir, it's your wife. Mrs. O'Neal sent me to come get you."

Any anger Jonah felt toward his brother vanished as he watched his face whiten. "The baby?"

"She says it's coming."

"But it's too soon," Daniel said as he took off, his student and Dr. Harris not far behind.

Adele gripped Jonah's arm, and his chest tightened at the fear he saw in her eyes. "Jonah, I might be able to help. Please take me to Katherine."

∞

"You're going to wear a hole in the floor."

"I don't care."

Jonah watched his brother pace the length of the parlor. The pocket doors leading to the library were shut. Anne was in there asleep, curled up on Katherine's chair, and Dr. Harris had taken Jacob to his home next door. Jonah and Adele had arrived at the same time as the doctor, and he had taken Adele upstairs with him immediately.

That had been several hours ago. Night had fallen, and twice Jonah had restrained Daniel from going to his wife when they had heard her cry out. It had been quiet for almost half an hour now.

Jonah rose from his chair and took his brother's arm. "Let's pray."

Daniel ran a hand through his hair and nodded.

They sat, and Jonah cleared his throat. "Lord, we come before You again to ask that Your hand be with Katherine and the life she is about to bring into this world. Guide the hands of those helping her, and in all things, may Your will be done. Amen."

"Boys?" They looked up to see a very tired Aunt Mary standing in the doorway.

Daniel practically flew out of his chair. "How is Katherine? The baby?"

Their aunt raised her hands and smiled. "Katherine is tired, but the doctor says she'll be fine."

Jonah grinned and gave his brother a slap on the back.

Daniel looked at him with relief. "And the baby?"

Aunt Mary's smile deepened. "Perfectly healthy."

"Is it a boy or a girl?" Jonah asked.

Her eyes slid from him to Daniel. "Stay down here. I'll let you see for yourself."

As she walked up the stairs, Jonah gave Daniel a bear hug. "Congratulations!"

They stepped into the parlor, and Daniel flopped back down in his chair. He bowed his head and closed his eyes. "Thank You, Lord."

"Yes. Thank You," Jonah prayed. He sat down next to him, and Daniel squeezed his arm.

"And thank you for staying with me even though you must be furious with me about Jacob," he said.

Jonah frowned as he remembered what Jake had said at the fairgrounds about going to school. "I'm not furious, but I do want an explanation."

"The school Jake wants to go to is the Ohio Agricultural and Mechanical College."

"There's no such place."

"If things go the way I think they will, there will be. A bill was passed in the Ohio Senate just this past spring to grant its establishment."

"He wants to go to an agricultural college," Jonah said slowly. He had to admit the choice made sense for Jacob. Going to such a school would widen his knowledge and make him a better farmer. He was always going on about new gadgets and had even convinced Jonah to consider using mechanical threshers this year along with some of the other farmers around Mill Creek. Jacob said it would save a lot of time and help them get the grain to market sooner.

Daniel interrupted his thoughts. "He's a farmer at heart, just like his pa and just like you. But like me, he's also a thinker, and he wants to learn about the newest and best ways to farm." He paused. "If he goes and does well, the farm would be left in good hands."

Jonah chewed the edge of his lip, choosing his words carefully. While he and his brother had mended many fences in the past month, Jonah still felt as if Daniel had betrayed their pa. "Pa left that land to me, you, and Toby."

"I know. But I'm not a farmer, Jonah. Oh, I know the fundamentals, and I hope I did a good job taking care of the farm all those months before you came home. But it's not in me the way it's in you." Daniel looked at his hands. "When we were growing up, I sometimes wished it was. I know Pa loved me, but he never really understood me. He always understood you and Toby."

Jonah was silent for a moment. It hadn't occurred to him that Daniel had felt left out. As much as he loved his younger brother, he had always seen him as an annoying smart aleck. He was sorry now he had ever entertained such thoughts. Taking a deep breath, he looked at Daniel. "Pa is with the Lord now, and the Bible says when we're with Him our understanding is complete. He understands you now. And you did a fine job with the farm. I wouldn't admit it at first, but now I can honestly tell you so. I'm proud of you. For how you ran the farm and for the life you've chosen now."

Daniel gave him a crooked smile. Rising from his seat, he walked over to the bay window and looked out, wiping at his eyes.

"Daniel. . ." Aunt Mary was coming down the stairs with a tiny bundle in her arms, and to Jonah's surprise, Adele followed with yet another.

"You have a son *and* a daughter," Adele said with tear-filled eyes.

Thunderstruck, Daniel took his son from his aunt's arms, and his gaze went from him to the baby girl in Adele's.

Jonah chuckled at seeing his brother speechless for a change.

"Katherine is pleased that you can use both the names you picked," Mary said.

"What names?" Jonah asked.

Daniel, Adele, and Aunt Mary smiled at each other before his brother answered. "Joseph Tobias and Rebecca Ann."

Jonah smiled. "Ma and Pa would have loved that."

"Daniel, the doctor said you can come see Kathcrine," Mary said and, taking little Rebecca from Adele, followed her nephew upstairs.

Adele turned to Jonah and wrapped her arms around him. He allowed himself to return the embrace for only a moment before gently pulling away. Wisps of hair hung in her face. She looked worn out, but he had never seen her more beautiful.

He glanced down. "I'm glad Katherine is all right."

Adele's brows knit together, and she clasped her hands. "She will be fine, eventually. Dr. Barnes said she will not be able to have any more children."

Jonah sighed. "Well, at least they have the twins. We should thank the Lord for that."

"I have." She paused as she tried to smooth back stray hairs. "Jonah, can you manage out at the farm without me? Katherine is very weak still, and she and Mary will need my help."

"Of course. Will is always saying he's not too bad in the kitchen. I'll see if he can cook for a week or two."

"Thank you. And do not worry about Anne. She can stay here with me." Adele laid a hand on his arm and gave him a wistful smile. "I will miss you."

He froze for a second, wondering what he should say. If she was beginning to have feelings for him, he had no business encouraging her. He gave her a little smile and lightly patted her hand before walking over to the door. "Jake and I will leave in the morning. Dr. Harris took him to his house awhile ago. Told me to come over when I knew anything, no matter what the time. I'll probably stay over with them."

He turned away from the small frown on her face and opened the door. "Good night," he called over his shoulder.

Chapter 12

I did not know twins could look so different," Adele said. She walked a fussy Rebecca over to her mother, who was nearly drowning in the pillows propping her up in bed.

Katherine smiled as she took her daughter. "Or act so different. Just look at him over there." She nodded at her son, sound asleep in his bassinet near the bay window.

Adele chuckled as she sat on the edge of the bed. It could honestly be said the Kirby twins were as different as night and day. Both children had been born with a beautiful swath of hair but with vastly different colors. Rebecca seemed to have inherited her father's sandy-blond locks while Joseph had his mother's fiery auburn hair. And while Joseph seemed reasonably content most of the time, Rebecca fussed for everyone except her mother. Even though she had only been in Katherine's arms for a few seconds, she had calmed and begun to fall asleep.

Katherine reached over with her free hand and took hold of Adele's. "Thank you so much for staying."

"You do not have to thank me. I am glad to do anything for you." Adele squeezed her hand. "And I am happy you will be all right."

It had been a week since the twins' births, and Mary and Adele were still fussing over them and Katherine. The new mother had tried to tell them she felt strong enough to manage a few things on her own, but both insisted she remain in bed for at least another week. Dr. Barnes and Daniel had been quick to agree.

Adele had helped with births before, but she had to admit Katherine's had been her first truly alarming one. Even after a full week of rest in bed, the young mother still looked pale and fragile.

"I wish it could be different." Katherine's face grew wistful, and she looked down at her daughter. Adele knew she was thinking about the

231

news Dr. Barnes had told her just this morning. It had been kept from her initially due to her delicate condition. Rebecca stirred slightly and sighed, stretching out the fingers of one tiny hand. "But I have learned to trust God and not my own understanding. He was very gracious to bless us with two all at once."

Just then, Mary came in followed by Anne. The little girl carried Adele's prize-winning quilt folded up neatly in her arms. "Hi, Aunt Kitty!"

Katherine greeted her as Adele relieved her of the quilt with a smile. Anne had come up with "Aunt Kitty" after hearing Daniel refer to Katherine as "Kat" all week. She had tried to correct the little girl at first, but Katherine insisted she was delighted by it and pointed out how much easier it was for the little girl to say.

"Mrs. Campbell stopped by with that just a few minutes ago," Mary said. "Such a nice young woman."

"Yes, it was very kind of her to take care of this after the fair," Adele replied as she spread the quilt out on the bed next to her friend.

"Oh Adele, it's lovely," Katherine exclaimed. She fingered the appliqué with her free hand. "No wonder you won the first-place premium."

"I am glad you like it," Adele said, smiling at Mary. "I will be sure to make another just like it so both your children may have one."

"Mercy, this can't be for me."

"Of course. Babies must be kept warm."

Katherine's eyes glistened with tears. "Thank you, so very kindly."

"It's time you got some sleep while this one doesn't need you," Mary said, as she gently took Rebecca and walked her over to the bassinet.

Anne followed her and watched as she laid the babe next to her brother. The little girl looked at Adele. "Dolly go night-night?"

Mary quietly chuckled. "She isn't a doll, dear. Here. . ." The older woman lifted the little girl so she could see Rebecca and Joseph sleeping. "Look at the little babies."

"Ooooh," she breathed. "So pretty."

Katherine smiled as she allowed Adele to remove some of the pillows from behind her. "She's such a dear little thing."

"She is not as timid as she used to be," Adele said as she arranged the covers over her. "She has taken to Mary and your maid very well."

Mary put down the little girl, who trotted over and lifted her arms. Adele picked her up, and Anne hugged her. "Ma. Babies sleeping."

"You're still her favorite," Mary said. She gave the bedcovers a final twitch before drawing the shades over the bay window. "Now Katherine, as long as they sleep, you sleep."

"Night-night, Aunt Kitty," Anne said softly as they left the room.

The three walked downstairs. Adele and Mary settled themselves in Katherine's elegant parlor, and Anne made off to the kitchen to have a snack and tell Polly, the Kirbys' maid and cook, all about the "pretty babies."

As Mary watered Katherine's numerous houseplants, Adele wandered over to the fireplace mantel. Next to the clock sat a framed photograph of Daniel and Katherine on their wedding day. Mary and Jonah were also in the picture, and Adele's eyes settled on her husband. She had taken to looking at the picture every chance she got over the past week, in spite of the fact that he wore a cold, rigid expression on his face. It had been taken only a few short months after he had come home. *He does not look like that now,* she thought, smiling.

"Jonah looks so surly in that photograph. I can't imagine why you like looking at it so much," Mary said. She set the slender, tin watering can down on a side table and joined Adele.

"It reminds me how much the Lord has worked on his heart." Adele reached up and ran her fingers across his image. "I am glad he has been restored to me."

"So I see," Mary replied.

A knock came at the door.

"That must be another well-wisher," Mary said with a chuckle as she went to answer it. Adele heard the low murmur of a young man's voice and assumed it was another of Daniel's students coming to leave a calling card and offer congratulations. Although Adele knew he would never admit it, Daniel was one of the more popular professors at the university. Before her condition made it too difficult for her to attend, Katherine had sat on several committees connected to Ohio Wesleyan's Female College, and many young ladies had stopped by as well.

Adele heard the door close, and to her surprise, Mary returned to the parlor not with a student but with Will Reid and Jacob. Adele's heart froze at the terrible look on her son's face.

"Ma," he said as he threw himself into her arms.

"Jacob, what is it? Why are you here?" She looked over at Will.

"Mrs. Kirby, I'm so sorry to have to come for you like this," he said, twisting his black felt cap in his hands.

Adele's heart went to her throat. "What has happened? Is Jonah hurt?"

"No, ma'am. It's Mr. Porter. He was found dead this very morning."

"They're saying Uncle Jonah did it!" Jacob said. He lifted his head to look at his mother. "Ma, I'm scared. They came and took him away."

"Who, Jacob?" Mary asked.

"Dr. Kelly and the county sheriff."

"We were just sitting down to dinner when they came," Will explained. "Ma'am, there's something else. Mr. Morgan's gone missing. He hasn't been seen these past two days. We thought he might have moved on—him being a drifter and all—but Dr. Kelly seemed determined to think Mr. Kirby had something to do with it."

Adele's mind whirled as she tried to take it all in. Noah knew better. He had to know better. Surely he wasn't allowing his feelings for her. . . She clenched her fists and looked at Mary. "I must go. Jacob, you stay here while Will and I go to Ostrander. I must make the sheriff see Jonah cannot have done this." She started for the hall tree where her bonnet and wrap hung, when the sound of Anne giggling drifted in from the kitchen, causing her to stop and turn anxious eyes toward Mary.

"I can manage her. Just go before she wanders in." The older woman thrust Adele's bonnet into her hand.

"What will you tell Katherine? She cannot become troubled over this."

"Let me worry about that." The older woman embraced her. "I'm already praying for both of you."

The trip from Delaware to Ostrander was only about an hour, but as far as Adele was concerned, the buggy wheels might as well have been coated with molasses. All she could think of was Jonah. What would this do to his faith? The thought of that old anger once more rising in his beautiful green eyes almost caused her to tear the reins from Will's hands and urge the horse on faster. Instead, she prayed. *Please bring him comfort, Father. Help him to be strong.*

As the church came into view, she felt a measure of comfort. Surely Reverend Warren was with Jonah. But as they approached the Warrens' house, which was just down the road from the church, she saw the clergyman outside tending his rosebushes. Adele urged Will to stop and quickly climbed from the buggy. "Reverend," she called as she strode over to him.

"Adele, what a nice surprise." He stopped at the look on her face. "What's the matter?"

"Why are you not in town with Jonah?"

"Why should I be?"

Minnie came and joined them as Adele explained what had happened. "I would have thought Mr. Henderson and the others would have come for you."

"No, I didn't even know the sheriff had been sent for," Reverend Warren said as he stroked his long, gray-flecked sideburns. "I'm always included in these decisions."

The county had not yet recognized Ostrander as a village. Even though they had a post office, they still had no jail or lawman. The town's businessmen along with members of the clergy made important decisions, such as calling in the sheriff in rare moments such as these.

"Let me fetch my hat and coat and come with you," the reverend said. "We'll soon get to the bottom of this."

When they arrived, they found the town's businessmen congregated outside the mercantile. Fred Decker was there, along with Earl Henderson; Charles Franklin, the owner of the Ostrander Hotel; and James Fry, who owned Fry's Furniture Notions.

Adele quickly climbed from the buggy and walked over to them. "Where is Jonah?" she asked.

Earl Henderson looked at her with a frown. "He's at Dr. Kelly's office. The doctor just took the sheriff over there a few minutes ago." He opened his mouth to say more, but Reverend Warren interrupted.

"Why wasn't I told about all this?" he asked as he and Will approached. "And where is Reverend Dean?" Reverend Michael Dean ministered to the souls of the church in town, just two streets over from where they were now.

"He's out visiting someone at the moment," Mr. Franklin said. "And I was just about to come to your house and get you. Dr. Kelly jumped the gun a bit and sent for the sheriff without telling any of us."

"After hearing everything that's been going on, I'm not sure that was such a bad idea," Earl said. James Fry nodded in agreement.

"What do you mean?" Adele said as dread grew in her heart. What had Dr. Kelly told them?

"I mean him carrying his rifle with him everywhere he goes. Getting up in the middle of the night to walk around his property armed like something's going to attack him." Earl's frown deepened. "And you and him getting married so his brother wouldn't send him to the asylum down in Columbus."

Adele's face grew hot with anger and embarrassment. "Dr. Kelly had no right to tell you such things."

"Are they true?"

"Yes, but please let me explain. . . ."

"I don't think that will be necessary." To her horror, Earl and all but Fred Decker began to leave.

"Stop!" They all looked at her. "You've known Jonah Kirby all your lives. You owe it to him to hear what I have to say."

"She's right, Earl," Reverend Warren said quietly. The men looked at each other and walked back over to stand in front of her.

As Adele explained everything that had been going on for the past six months—Jonah's anger over the war, his struggles with his faith, and his efforts to go without his gun—their attitudes softened.

"I'm glad he's getting better, Mrs. Kirby. I am," Earl said. "But this doesn't look good for him."

"What do you mean?" Reverend Warren asked.

"Henry was shot. Several times." Mr. Fry looked at Adele hesitantly.

"Please go on," she said, squaring her shoulders.

"He was stabbed, too."

Adele paled. "Like the deer?"

"If you mean those deer that Henry was finding at the edge of his property and yours, then yes," Earl said. From the look on his face, it was clear he wasn't entirely convinced of Jonah's innocence.

"Earl, Jonah and Henry were on very good terms," Reverend Warren said. "Why would Jonah want to hurt him?"

"The doctor said he's been sleepwalking, too," Earl replied. "That he might be going around doing things he wasn't aware of."

"He is not sleepwalking," Adele replied firmly. "You have my word on that."

"And while Jonah has been suffering from the effects of the war, he hasn't done anything to cause me any concern," Reverend Warren said. "After my experiences with my nephew, I'm sure you know what I mean."

"It makes sense to me, Earl," Mr. Franklin said. Although Charles

Franklin hadn't served with Jonah, he, too, had served in the war. "I saw a lot of men whose heads weren't right after a battle. And I can't honestly say Jonah's been acting like that."

"And Daniel now regrets even considering he be sent down to Columbus," Adele said.

Earl slowly nodded. "I'm sorry we doubted him."

"Speak for yourself," Fred Decker said. He had said nothing during the entire course of the conversation, and Adele had almost forgotten he was present. "I never doubted Jonah for a second."

"Then why didn't you say so?" Mr. Fry asked.

"Because I knew you'd come to see sense eventually," he replied.

Earl waved a self-conscious hand in his direction. "You're right, Fred. But unfortunately, the one who really needs convincing is the sheriff. He heard the same story we did."

Adele squared her shoulders. "Then I will go over to the doctor's now and see if he will speak to me."

"I'll come with you," Reverend Warren said.

"Now wait. What about Cyrus Morgan?" Mr. Fry asked. "Dr. Kelly said he hasn't been seen the past two days."

"I'm sure Mr. Morgan has simply decided to move on," Adele said.

Will nodded in agreement. "Aye. He's that sort of a fellow, you know."

"His coming here was sudden to begin with," Mr. Decker said. "Anybody think to ask if *he* had something to do with Henry's death? Doesn't he trap near Jonah and Henry's property line?"

"Did anyone search his place?" Earl asked.

"I don't think so."

"I know where it is," Will said. "I'll go there myself and check it out."

"I'll come with you," Mr. Franklin said. "We'll take my team. I'll just go get my gun." He turned to Adele. "Mrs. Kirby, I hope you won't need it, but I'll tell Lydia to make sure there's a room ready for you if you need to stay in town tonight."

"Thank you, Mr. Franklin." She looked in the direction of the doctor's office. "Excuse me. I must go see what is happening."

Adele said nothing to the reverend as they walked. She was too busy wording a silent prayer. The doctor's office was at the north edge of town, and the street it sat on faced the woods, which ran along the edge of Little Mill Creek. As they drew near, they saw Dr. Kelly and a burly man wearing a badge standing outside the doctor's office near the gate. He was clearly the county sheriff, and Adele wondered if he had talked to Jonah yet.

Reverend Warren walked up to him. "Sheriff, my name is Reverend Paul Warren. I'm Jonah Kirby's minister." They shook hands, and the reverend nodded at Adele. "This is Mrs. Adele Kirby, his wife."

"Reverend, I'm glad you're here. I'm Sheriff Cal Wade." He had white hair and round spectacles. He looked grandfatherly, but there was an air of authority about him. He took Adele's hand gently in his. "Ma'am."

"Sheriff, my husband could not have done this. . . ."

"I understand you feeling that way, but I do need to speak to him myself and look at the evidence," he said gently.

"Evidence?" she asked.

"Yes, the bullets Dr. Kelly took from Mr. Porter. I have to see if they could have been fired from your husband's gun."

"I would like to see Mr. Kirby, if I could," Reverend Warren said. "Perhaps you would allow me to be present while you speak with him? This has all been very sudden." He shot the doctor a frown.

"Considering the circumstances, I'll permit it," Sheriff Wade said after a moment's thought. "But only while I'm examining his rifle. I'll need to question him alone. Why don't we step inside?" The reverend gave Adele's elbow a squeeze, and the two men stepped into the doctor's office. Once the door had closed, she turned to Dr. Kelly.

"Adele, I'm so sorry. . . ."

White-hot fury coursed through her, and she slapped him across the face before he could say anything else.

"*Lügner!*" she said. "Liar! How could you, Noah?"

"I didn't lie," he said.

"You told them Jonah was crazy. And you know that is not true."

"It's entirely possible he is. You can't possibly know everything that he does every moment of the day." He gave her a pointed look. "Especially at night."

Adele's palm itched to slap him once more, but she restrained herself. "That does not matter. I *know* he is not sleepwalking. I *know* he did not kill Henry."

"His mind could have snapped while you were in Delaware this week." She turned away from him, but he grabbed her arm and swung

238

her around to face him. He laid his hands on her shoulders, but she immediately shrugged them away. "Adele, listen to me. I know you are upset right now, and that's clouding your judgment. . . ."

"You are one to talk," she snapped back. "Do you think this would make me care for you?"

"No. I'm only trying to protect you."

"I do not need your protection. I do not need protection from the man I love." Adele's eyes widened, and her heart began to pound as she took in her own words. The man she loved? She took a few steps back and laid her hand on her heart.

When had it happened? At the fair when their hands had brushed or the first time he had looked at her with the anger washed from his eyes? As the last year and a half swept over her like the Scioto River, her breath caught. It had been the day he came home, walking up the drive, thin and gaunt and barely looking like the man who had left four years earlier, but alive. Tears flew to her eyes as she realized that was why she had married him and had been so determined that she be the one to help God heal his wounded heart. She loved him.

Remembering Dr. Kelly, she looked up.

He was standing there staring at her with bloodshot eyes.

"Oh, Noah. . . ," she murmured.

He slowly turned and, like an old man, hobbled his way over to the door of his office. Adele followed. He opened the door for her, his eyes averted, and she walked in. Jonah and Reverend Warren sat facing each other, and the sight of her husband sent her heart racing at such a speed she thought she might faint.

"Addie," Jonah said.

"Is something wrong?" the reverend asked.

Just then, the sheriff walked in from the examination room with Jonah's rifle. "What's going on?"

Dr. Kelly had stepped in behind Adele. He hung up his coat and hat, limped over to his desk, and sat down, his back to them.

"I'm sorry to disturb you, Sheriff Wade, but I have come to conclude that I may very well have been wrong about Mr. Kirby."

The four looked at each other, then back at the doctor. The sheriff spoke. "You're sure about that?"

Dr. Kelly nodded.

"I see." Sheriff Wade looked at Adele. "Are there any other guns at your house, Mrs. Kirby?"

"Only one. Another rifle," she replied.

"And your hired hands?"

"Will has a rifle at his house, and so does Cyrus," Jonah said.

"Well, the bullets that killed Mr. Porter came from a revolver." He looked at Jonah. "And to be honest, I had my doubts to begin with. You're free to go, Mr. Kirby."

Adele sighed with relief and looked at Noah. But his face was turned away from all of them.

Jonah rose from his seat, and he and the sheriff shook hands.

"I'm sorry for keeping you, Mr. Kirby."

"That's all right, sir," Jonah replied. "You've been very fair-minded, and I appreciate it."

"I'm mighty glad that bullet couldn't have come from your gun," the sheriff said. "I would have hated having to detain a man who fought to preserve our country."

Jonah nodded then looked at Adele. The whole room suddenly seemed brighter. "It's time we headed home."

"Yes." The word seemed to stick in her throat, and she cleared it as she turned to the sheriff to shake his hand. "Thank you. When will you return to Delaware?"

"Not until this is cleared up," he said. "I'll be at the hotel until then. I don't think I need to tell you two to be careful around your farm until we get to the bottom of this."

"We'll get through the chores quickly and lock up tight," Jonah replied. He turned to Reverend Warren. "Thank you."

"Thank Adele. She was quite passionate back in town." He gave Jonah a knowing look she didn't quite understand. "Earl and the others had their doubts about you."

Jonah's eyes darkened, and he looked toward the doctor. He hadn't moved since he sat down.

Adele quickly sent up a silent prayer before taking Jonah's hand. "We should go," she said softly.

He nodded, and they stepped out the door. They walked along for a few minutes before Jonah looked at her. Dusk was beginning to settle over the town, and his green eyes seemed to glow in the dim light. "Did Will come for you?" he asked.

"Yes, he and Jacob," she replied.

He frowned. "I told him not to. Katherine needs you."

"You needed me more," she said, and their eyes locked for a step or two before Jonah looked away. Adele's stomach flip-flopped, and she took a deep breath before going on. "Mary will manage. There have been so many young ladies from the Female College offering their services that I do not think she will have trouble finding help."

"Where are Anne and Jacob?"

"With Mary. Will and Charles Franklin went out to look at Mr. Morgan's place, so I will help you do the chores." She wondered at the look on his face. "What's wrong?"

"Maybe you should stay here in town tonight. To be safe."

"Don't be silly. You cannot do all of those chores by yourself. 'Two are better than one; because they have a good reward for their labour.'"

He nodded and dropped her hand.

She looked at him. What did he feel for her? She could only wonder as the last few months flew through her mind. Since he had begun to heal, their friendship had redeveloped and even grown. Yet he had kept a certain distance from her. Until the day of the fair. He had acted as if he wanted something more. She thought of that long look he had given her right before they had judged her quilt. He had always broken off such looks before.

But then after the babies were born, he had left her so quickly. He almost pushed her away. Had Jonah come to decide that friendship was all he would ever feel for her? She desperately hoped he hadn't.

Suddenly Nathaniel's face filled her mind. What would he think of her feelings for Jonah? She had been sure he would have wanted her to help Jonah in any way she could, even to the point of marrying him. But this was different. *Father, is it wrong for me to feel as I do for Jonah? Would Nathaniel object? I will always love him, but I love Jonah, too.* The answer the Lord placed on her heart thrilled her to the very core.

Fred greeted them at the mercantile, very glad to hear Jonah had been cleared. They asked about Will, but he and Charles had not yet returned.

Jonah told Mr. Decker to have Will stay in the hotel and he would pay for any expense. "I don't want him walking home in the dark," he said.

By the time they got home and finished the chores, they were exhausted. So it surprised Adele to be awakened a few hours later by the sound of Jonah moving around in his room. She quickly pulled on the dress she had worn earlier over her thin nightdress and, lighting a lamp, took it with her to the door.

Jonah was leaning in the doorway of his room, staring at the stairway. He didn't have his gun, and she could just make it out at the foot of his bed by the light of the moon that shone through his window.

She set the lamp down on the hall table. "Jonah?" she said softly.

He started slightly and looked at her, his eyes widening.

She raised a suspicious hand to her hair and sighed. It had loosed itself from its braid again. Every night she worked her hair into a long braid, and every night it managed to free itself from its tie and unravel. She gave him a little smile, embarrassed. "I am sorry," she said. "My hair likes to do whatever it wishes. I must look terrible."

"No," Jonah said quickly. His eyes held hers, and she felt almost mesmerized. "You look—" He stopped and looked down.

Adele found herself grasping the door frame to steady herself. What was he going to say? That she looked beautiful? Taking a few moments to still her heart, she spoke again. "What are you doing?"

"I can't sleep." He glanced back at his gun in his room. "I don't want to go out and take that with me, but with everything that's happened, I can't go without it." He glanced in her direction but didn't quite look at her. "Don't worry about me, Addie. Go back to bed."

Squaring her shoulders, Adele pushed herself away from her door and approached him. She couldn't bear it anymore. She had to know what he felt. "But I am already dressed." She drew a shaky breath and reached out and turned his face to hers. "There is a chair in your room. We could talk."

The look in his eyes made him handsomer than she ever remembered. He pushed himself away from the door frame, and her hand fell away from his face as he stepped closer to her. He brushed back a strand of her hair, and his eyes drifted to her lips. Her eyelids drooped, and she tilted her head slightly. Just as she thought their lips would touch, he pulled away.

The shock and dismay she felt was almost physical. What was it? Was it her?

"I can't," he said roughly as he walked to the stairs.

"Why?" He must have heard the tears in her voice, because he stopped cold and clenched his fists.

242

"You belong to Nate. You're his. You always have been." He took a step forward. "You always will be."

Tears fell freely down Adele's face as the truth finally dawned on her. "No, Jonah. The dead cannot keep the living. I belong to you." He turned and stared her full in the face, an incredulous question in his green eyes. "I love you with my whole heart."

In less than a second, Jonah bridged the distance between them, and his lips found hers. His hands buried themselves in her long, thick hair, and she clung to his broad shoulders for support. It wasn't a light or hesitant kiss, but deep and slow with an intensity that shocked her into the realization that his love for her had been held in check for years, not months or weeks.

She wanted to speak, but when they parted, all her questions died on her lips as she took in the passion in his eyes. Questions could wait. Taking only a moment or two to bask in the glow of his green eyes, she returned his kiss with equal passion and pulled him toward her door.

He stopped as they crossed the threshold and looked at the room. For a split second she feared he would leave. Instead, he shut the door behind them.

Chapter 13

The next morning, Jonah had a good start on the chores when Will arrived from town. He was about halfway through milking when the young man walked into the barn.

"I'm sorry I'm late, Mr. Kirby," he said as he grabbed a stool and bucket.

"That's all right, Will," Jonah replied. "I'm sorry we left you in town last night."

"Oh, don't trouble yourself over me, sir. Mr. and Mrs. Franklin run a very comfortable hotel."

"What did you and Charles find out at Cyrus's place? Did it look like he packed up and left?"

Will didn't answer right away, and Jonah rose from his stool and stood in the doorway of the stall where he was working. The young man had a frown on his face. "It was the strangest thing, Mr. Kirby," he said. "All his things are there except a few traps. Like he just went out to check his lines and never came back."

Jonah frowned. He knew Charles and Will had gone out there thinking Cyrus might have had something to do with Henry's death. Jonah had disagreed. Having worked with the man for several months, he just couldn't see Cyrus harming anyone. He'd honestly thought Cyrus had his fill of Ostrander and moved on. This was unexpected. "You told the sheriff what you found?"

"Yes, sir. He said he would go take a look at Mr. Morgan's place himself and might stop by the farm in a few days. When I told him about the missing traps, he wanted to know where he laid his lines." Will pushed his hat back on his head and looked up from his milking. "About yesterday, sir, I know you told me not to go after Mrs. Kirby, but it just didn't feel right not to."

Jonah smiled and patted him on the back. "No, it's all right. Thank you."

"You're very welcome. Say now, I had myself breakfast at the hotel. Why don't you let me finish all this? You and Mrs. Kirby can eat without the wee ones about."

"Thank you, Will," he said quietly. "There is something Mrs. Kirby and I need to talk about." He walked out of the barn and stopped for a moment to look at the house.

He could see smoke rising from the chimney of the summer kitchen. Even though the weather had cooled a little, Adele liked to use the little structure behind the house as long as possible. She enjoyed cooking out in the fresh air.

Slowly, he walked around to the back and saw her pumping water to fill a wooden bucket. Her hair was up in its usual braided bun, but the memory of it falling softly to her waist, loose and free, filled his sight. He shook his head. If he kept thinking like that, he would never be able to say what needed to be said.

She started to reach for the bucket when he walked forward and grabbed it. "Let me get that for you," he murmured.

Her brilliant blue eyes caught his. "Good morning," she said, smiling.

"Good morning," he said and looked down at the bucket. "Where do you need this?"

She cocked her head. "In the washtub, on the stove."

As he headed toward the door of the summer kitchen, he heard her following him.

"I will move the trundle bed out of our room later. Anne can sleep in your room now."

He stopped short of the kitchen door and took a breath. "I wouldn't do that, Addie."

"It is not very heavy. I am sure I can do it myself."

"That's not what I mean." He looked out at the kitchen garden, glad he wasn't looking at her. "Things need to stay the way they are."

"Why?" Her voice was soft with confusion and hurt.

He laid a hand on the kitchen door frame to steady himself. "Because of Nate."

"Nathaniel is gone, Jonah," she said.

He looked at her and immediately felt like kicking himself for making her look so sad.

Adele took his hand. "I love you."

Her words made him drop the bucket and gather her into his arms. "And I love you."

"I know. You have for a very long time, haven't you?"

He pulled away, hands on her forearms as he stared at her.

She smiled. "How long?"

He was so surprised that the words flew out of his mouth before he could stop them. "Since the day we first met. How did you know?"

She ran her thumb across his cheek. "That first kiss," she said. "It said more than you know."

He grabbed her hand and gently lowered it, and then he stepped back and ran both hands through his hair. "I shouldn't have told you. This is all such a mess."

"Why? I will always love Nathaniel, but he is with the Lord now. I love you. Now."

"It's not that. I promised Nate this would never happen." He walked over to the pump and laid his hand on the cool, wet spout. "The night before you married him, he found out how I felt about you. He got angry, and I told him I'd never tell you how I felt." He turned to go into the house. "Just leave the trundle bed where it is."

"No." Her answer stopped Jonah in his tracks, and he swung around to face her. The calm, yet resolute look in her eyes made them bluer than ever. "Last night, before we came home, I wondered what Nathaniel would think of my feelings for you," Adele said. She took a deep breath and continued. "I asked the Lord if what I felt was wrong." She walked up to him and stood very close. "He said no."

Jonah stared at her. *Lord, I promised.* God placed the same answer on his heart as He had months before. Yet even with His blessing, Jonah still felt a sense of betrayal. "He was my best friend," he murmured.

Adele took his hand. "Nathaniel was a godly man, Jonah. He would have wanted what God wanted."

Tears sprang to Jonah's eyes. The simple truth of her answer dissolved any other objection he might make, as easily as snow melted in the spring sunshine.

He pulled Adele into his arms, and as they embraced, he knew Nathaniel was smiling down on them from where he sat in heaven.

∞

"They should be back anytime now, Addie," Jonah said with a smile as he watched his wife look toward the road yet again. He and Adele were working in the kitchen garden while Will drove into Delaware and fetched Anne and Jacob.

"Do you think she spent the night well?" she asked as she reluctantly turned her gaze to him.

He stood and laid a few more carrots in the basket she held. "I'm sure Annie slept fine."

"You had better remember not to call her that when she gets here," his wife said with a reproachful smile.

"I know. I'll get 'the look.'"

Jonah's habit of changing or shortening people's names didn't sit well with the little girl. Every time he tried to call her anything but Anne, her little face scrunched up and her bottom lip pouched out to the side. Jonah chuckled. She looked so adorable, he was tempted to call her Annie as soon as she arrived.

He knelt down and started to pull more carrots while Adele got another basket. But the sound of a wagon caused her to drop it and smile at him before quickly making off in the direction of the drive. He followed, and soon both of them were getting hugs from two very delighted children.

"Ma!" Anne squealed as she clung to Adele.

Jonah was gratified by the strong hug Jacob gave him. "I'm glad you're home, Uncle Jonah," he said.

Will jumped down from the wagon, and Adele turned to him as she picked up Anne and wrapped her son in a one-armed hug. "How is Mrs. Kirby?"

"Mrs. O'Neal told me to assure you she and the wee ones are right as rain." He smiled and turned to Jonah. "Dr. Kirby was all ready to send his lawyer, Mr. O'Conner, back with me, but I told him it wasn't necessary, seeing how the sheriff let you go."

Jonah nodded. "I hope he can catch whoever this is soon. In the meantime, we need to keep a sharp eye out while we're in the fields." He looked down at Jacob. "I think it might be best if you stayed close to the house today."

"But we're getting ready to bring in the wheat," the boy said.

"I know, but your ma needs a good strong boy out in the kitchen garden." He gave his shoulder a squeeze. "I'm not trying to coddle you, Jake. I just want you to be safe."

The boy nodded, although he was clearly disappointed. "Okay."

"Go on into the garden. Your ma will be out in a minute."

Jacob walked over to the garden, and Jonah went into the house with Adele and Anne. Jonah's old room was now done up for the little girl, and they both wanted to show it to her. Adele had even found a few of her old playthings. Jonah leaned against the door and watched the two walk in. Anne looked at the room and bed with wide eyes and looked up at Adele. "Little bed?"

"No more little bed," Adele said with a smile. "That big bed is for you." She looked questioningly at her. "Ma and Pa will be right next door."

Anne looked from her to Jonah and then smiled. "Okay." She climbed up and looked at the playthings on the bed.

Adele sat down on the edge. "Those are for you, Kleine. They used to be mine."

The little girl picked up each toy and looked under it, her eyes growing sad. "Dolly?" she asked.

Adele looked over at Jonah, and he walked over to the pair.

"Where's Dolly?" she asked him, taking one of his fingers in her little hand.

He looked at Adele.

"I am sorry, Anne," she said gently. "I could not find my old one."

Anne's little face crumpled. She lay down on the bed.

"No Dolly," she said tearfully, looking up at them.

Frowning, Jonah looked at his wife, who looked just as distressed if not more.

Anne lifted up her arms, and Adele immediately picked her up. The little girl let out a sob and buried her face in her neck. Jonah laid his hand on her back and rubbed it. He could just make out her words through her tears. "No Dolly."

Adele bit her lip and rocked her until she fell asleep. After laying her in her new bed, they walked out to the hall, closing the door behind them. Adele looked at Jonah, close to tears herself.

He took her hand. "She must have had a doll she had to leave behind," he said soothingly. "When she saw those toys, she must have thought you found it for her."

Adele nodded, and Jonah pulled her into his arms. After a moment or two, she pulled back and looked at him. "She is ours now." It was half a question and half a statement.

Jonah gave her a gentle smile and smoothed back a stray strand of her hair. "She is from where she stands. But we should wait a little longer before we do anything official. I hate to say this, but someone may still be looking for her."

"But Jonah, it has been months. Surely someone would have come by now."

A wave of tenderness swept over him. He wanted little Anne to be theirs as much as she did, but one of them had to be realistic. "Adele, you shouldn't get too attached to her. If someone does come, imagine how heartbroken you'll be."

She looked him in the eye, and inwardly he groaned. She had that stubborn look in her eye. "I will go to town tomorrow and buy her a doll," Adele said.

Jonah sighed. He knew better than to argue. "Of course. Fred has one."

She looked at him for a moment. "How do you know that?" A sly smile crept across her face. "Jonah Michael Kirby! You were going to buy her one before this. You, who just said I should not get too attached."

He felt his face redden. "I saw it there last week."

She kissed him on the cheek. "I love you."

She started to move away, but he held her fast, wanting one moment more with her in private. The fact that she was truly his still felt like a dream.

Her bright blue eyes glowed as she smiled at him. "Why do you look at me like that, Jonah Kirby?"

"I still can't believe you're mine," he replied softly.

She responded with a long, lingering kiss.

Chapter 14

Next Sunday, Adele invited Reverend Warren and Minnie to dinner to celebrate. For the first time in almost a year, Jonah had gone to church with them that morning. He finally felt reasonably comfortable without his gun, although circumstances demanded it ride with them under the seat.

"We'd like to come," the reverend said after services. "But we ended up walking this morning. Our mare is a little lame."

"Ride with us. We have enough room," Jonah replied. "I'll take you back later and have a look at her if you want."

"Oh, I couldn't have you do that on the Sabbath, Jonah."

" 'The sabbath was made for man, and not man for the sabbath,' " Adele quoted.

Reverend Warren laughed in agreement.

After dinner they settled into the parlor for coffee. Jacob had been excused to go outside, but Anne sat between Minnie and Adele on the sofa.

"It's good to have you back," the reverend said.

Jonah was standing next to him at the fireplace mantel, but he only half heard him. He was too busy looking at his wife. She and Minnie were fussing over Anne. Reverend Warren chuckled, and Jonah started. "I'm sorry, Reverend. What did you say?"

"I was saying how glad I am you've come back to church," he said. "But I see your mind was elsewhere. I'm glad you finally saw the sense in what I said a few weeks before."

Jonah smiled and felt his face redden a bit. "It's good to be back." He sobered a little. "I won't ever go back to the way I was before, will I?"

"I can't imagine you will."

Jonah nodded. He suddenly knew how the apostle Paul felt when he spoke of the thorn in his flesh. But unlike Paul, Jonah couldn't understand its purpose. He sent up a silent prayer, and the Lord reminded him of the correspondence between him and his brother. Daniel's letters had been a balm to him in a way no one else's could have been since they had both served in the war. He thought of Charles Franklin and other men he knew who had served. Perhaps he could reach out to them.

"Have you heard anything about Cyrus?" The reverend's question broke through his thoughts.

Jonah looked at him. "No. The sheriff was here yesterday afternoon. All we found were his missing traps. The sheriff is going to come again tomorrow, and we're going to go further into the northwest corner."

"I hope you find something, for Mrs. Porter's sake."

Jonah nodded. Henry Porter's funeral had taken place several days ago. After the service, Jonah and Adele had asked Henry's widow, Eliza, if there was anything they could do. She thanked them but said she and her boys were doing fine for now. Jonah promised himself to check back with her soon. Henry's oldest son was just a little younger than he had been when his pa had passed. He knew very well what the young man must be going through.

"Anne, I have something for you."

Jonah looked and saw Adele hand the little girl a pasteboard box with a scrap of ribbon tied around it. He smiled as he anticipated her reaction to their gift. The china doll they had bought in town yesterday had hand-painted brown hair with a green-print dress and white apron. Mrs. Warren had seen them buy it and had praised their choice. He was glad she would have the opportunity to share this moment with them. Over the course of the last few months, she and the reverend had become more like family again, as they had been while Jonah's ma and pa were still living.

Anne lifted off the lid and gasped. "Dolly!" she squealed as she took it out of the box. But as she took a closer look, her face fell. Tears welled in her eyes as she looked at Adele's startled face. "Not Dolly." She handed the doll to Minnie and climbed into Adele's arms. "I want Dolly."

"Well, my goodness," Minnie said softly.

"I thought she would like it," Adele said. She bit her lip and hugged the crying child closer.

"Give her some time," Jonah said. He walked over and rubbed his wife's back. "She might come to like it."

"I should take her upstairs," Adele replied. She looked over at Minnie and Reverend Warren. "I am so sorry."

"Now, don't you worry yourself," Minnie said. "We understand perfectly."

"We should be getting back anyway," the reverend said. Minnie nodded and gathered her reticule and Bible.

"I shouldn't be too long," Jonah told Adele. He patted the little girl on the back. As he drove the Warrens home, her little voice crying, "Not Dolly," echoed in his ears.

∽

It didn't take long for Adele to get Anne to go to sleep. Her tears had made her sleepy. As Adele gently shut the door to the child's room and made her way downstairs, she tried to fathom why the little girl had obviously lost her doll. Had someone taken it from her, or was it, as Jonah had guessed, that she had been forced to leave it behind?

Walking into the parlor, she picked up the doll from where it lay on the sofa and looked at it. She should put it away, but it was so pretty she decided to prop it up on a side table against one of the painted kerosene lamps. She hoped Jonah was right. Perhaps with time Anne would grow to like it.

Minnie had helped her clean up after dinner, so she took a basket and made her way out to the flower garden. It had not frosted yet, but since Jonah said it would soon, Adele started picking any flowers that were still blooming. She could put some of them in that lovely vase that had belonged to Jonah's mother.

She had been at it for a while when the sound of whistling caused her to look up and see her son sitting in one of the apple trees in the orchard. She set her basket aside and walked over to the tree he was sitting in.

"Hello, mein Liebe."

"Ma," Jacob said as he scrambled down the tree and jumped down in front of her. "Can't you call Anne that now?"

She chuckled as she ruffled his dark brown hair, then sighed as he tried to duck away from her hand. "You are getting too old for that, I suppose." She saw a thoughtful look on his face. "Is something wrong?"

He cocked an eye at her. "Can I ask you something?"

"Of course."

"Do you love Uncle Jonah?"

"Why do you ask?"

"I saw how you were at the fair and how you've been looking at each other."

She took a deep breath and said a quick prayer asking the Lord to give her the answers her son needed. "Yes, Jacob, I do."

"Like you did Pa?"

"Yes."

He stopped, and she did, too. "So you don't love Pa anymore?"

She gently grasped her son by the shoulders. "I will always love your pa, Jacob. Always. But I love Uncle Jonah, too."

Jacob looked down for a minute. "So you love them both?"

"Yes, it is just one is here, and the other is not. Do you understand?"

"I think so. But I miss Pa."

"I do, too. So does Uncle Jonah. They were best friends."

"Do you think Pa would have liked Uncle Jonah taking care of us?"

Adele smiled and nodded. "Yes."

"Since Uncle Jonah's better now, do you think it would be okay if I ask him about Pa?"

"I think he would like that now, mein Liebe— Oh, I am sorry."

"It's okay this one time, Ma," he said with a crooked smile and gave Adele a long hug.

Jacob decided to go visit his calf, and Adele went to fetch her basket. She stayed in the garden for a while longer before going in to check on Anne. Glancing at the clock in the parlor, she realized she should probably wake the little girl or she would not sleep later that night.

As she walked up the stairs, she thought back to what Jonah had said about waiting to officially adopt her and sighed. She had been going to press the issue with him, but she knew he was right. They should wait awhile longer. When she reached the top of the stairs, she saw the little girl's door was open. A frown came over her face when she walked in and saw that Anne was not in her bed.

"Kleine?" she called and rushed over to look under the bed. She wasn't there. Adele went across the hall and opened the door to both Jacob's room and her and Jonah's. Anne was nowhere to be found.

Adele fought to stay calm as she checked the kitchen and the courtyard. Then she saw something white near the gate leading out to the orchard and ran over to it. It was the store-bought china doll. "Anne?"

she called, her eyes scouring the orchard. *Oh please, Father, let her be hiding behind one of the trees.* When she didn't appear, she called out again, louder. "Anne!"

"Ma, what is it?" Jacob called as he ran over from the barn.

"I cannot find Anne. Help me look in the orchard."

They searched and called, but except for the doll, they could find no sign of her. Adele started for the barn for a horse. She had to get Jonah. Just as she reached the drive, she saw him pulling in. Will was with him. Jonah waved, and Adele went running toward him.

"Will was on his way home from the Williamses," he said as he came to a stop. "I offered him a ride—" He took one look at her face and jumped down from the wagon. "What's wrong?"

"We cannot find Anne." She held the doll out toward him. "I found this near the gate to the orchard. Why would she leave?"

Before Jonah could reply, she heard Jacob's voice. "Ma! I see her!" The boy had climbed one of the tallest apple trees at the edge of the orchard.

"Are you sure it's her?" Jonah called up as they ran over.

"Yes. I can see her dress. She's headed toward the northwest corner." He scrambled down. "She disappeared just over the crest of the hill."

Chapter 15

Jonah ran over to Will, who handed him his gun from where he had stowed it under the seat. They shared a worried look. It was clear Cyrus had gone missing while laying his traps in the northwest corner. And as they rode home, he and Will had discussed the distinct possibility he was no longer alive. Even if he'd had an accident, he would have made it back by now. "Go for the sheriff," he told Will.

The young man nodded and climbed up into the wagon.

"You think she is in danger?" Adele asked as he hurried past her.

"Tell Sheriff Wade where I went when he gets here." He didn't want to tell her about Cyrus or where Henry had been found. Not until he had brought Anne back safe.

"I will have Jacob tell him."

"Why Jacob?" he asked.

"I am coming with you."

"No." He grabbed her by the arm. "Stay here. I'll find her. I promise."

He released her, but she grabbed his hand. "Jonah, be careful. I cannot lose you the way—"

Her blue eyes started to fill, and he wrapped his free arm around her, pulling her close. "We'll both come back. I promise," he whispered into her hair. He gave her a quick kiss on the forehead before taking off up the hill.

When he reached the top, Daniel's share of the farm spread out before him. The front part was full of young trees, low bushes, and patches of tall grass, but as it continued back, larger trees and more mature plants grew as part of a natural windbreak that ran all along the north part of the Kirby property line. To the far right was a cornfield that Jonah had decided to allow to lie fallow for the season. He looked out across it hopefully. He could see all the way to the property line, but there was no sign of the little girl. He returned his gaze to the left and looked at the wild piece of land. *Guide me, Lord. Where is she?*

He walked west along the edge, making for the little path he had made during his walks for the past few months. He felt his body tense. The sheriff had been able to describe exactly where they had found Henry. It wasn't too far off the path he was now on. The body had been taken away, of course, but he hoped Anne wouldn't stumble upon anything that might have been left. Or worse. He stopped the thought and tightened the grip on his gun.

He walked along the path for a minute or two and tried calling her. "Anne!" he called. A gleam came to his eye, and with a small smile he tried again. "Annie!" But the only answer was the wind blowing through the trees.

He kept on, scanning in front and around him. As he approached the tree line, he saw something to his far right fluttering in the breeze. Tromping through the brush and saplings, he came to a wild blackberry patch. A small scrap of pale-blue fabric was stuck in its thorns. It was of the same pattern as Anne's dress. Kneeling down, he could tell something about her size had made its way through.

He followed her trail for several minutes. The trees became larger and stood closer together. This was the thickest part of the tree line—a small forest almost that neither he nor Henry nor Bill Walker, his neighbor to the north, had ever bothered with. The biggest part of it was on Kirby property since Jonah had refused to farm this part of his land. He was amazed at how overgrown it had become. He came to a fallen tree. It had been down for some time; flat yellow mushrooms grew on its side, and it was almost green with moss. He stepped over it and around a few trees and came to a clearing. He gasped at the sight before him.

His mind felt as if it had been jerked back in time. In the small clearing before him, a white canvas tent was set up. Toward the center of the space were the remains of a small campfire with an old log set in front of it. And between two young trees to his right was a clothesline. The uniform of a Union army soldier hung on it. Jonah broke out in a cold sweat. Where was he? Ohio or back down in Georgia near Kennesaw Mountain?

As he stood staring, Anne popped out of the tent with a china doll in her hands. Seeing Jonah, she gasped softly and ran over to him.

The sight of the little girl shook him back to reality, and he knelt down and hugged her.

"Pa!" she said, wriggling free. She held the doll out to him. "See? Dolly."

Laying down his rifle, he took the doll and saw it was very similar to the store-bought one except the painted hair was darker and the doll's head had been broken and clumsily repaired. No wonder she had reacted like she did to the new doll. Jonah handed it back, and she smiled at him as she hugged it. He looked her over. Her dress was torn from walking through the brambles, and she had a long scratch on her forehead. Other than that, she seemed fine. "Anne, who else is here?" he asked.

Her eyes grew sad. "Ma."

"Where?" Adele was here? How was that possible?

"There." She pointed past the clothesline toward some bushes. "Sleeping."

Jonah darted over and pushed back the brush. His heart stopped. A woman was lying there, curled into a ball. At least what had once been a woman. Dry, brittle hair still clung to her skull, and a plaid shirt and plain brown skirt covered the rest of the body. Insects and the elements made her face almost inhuman. And the smell. . . . He stumbled back into the clearing. It certainly wasn't Adele. From the looks of the poor woman, she had been dead almost two months now.

The faces of dead men suddenly filled his vision, men he had watched die and later helped bury. He rubbed his eyes with the heel of his hands, and when he looked again, they were gone.

Anne was right where he left her. He ran over and picked her up. They had to get out of here—and now. The sheriff needed to see this. Whoever killed that woman had almost certainly killed Henry and prob-ably Cyrus. Holding her in one arm, he grabbed his rifle and stood up.

"Ma sleeping?" she asked sadly.

"Yes, sweetie," he replied as she wrapped her arms around his neck. "She's sleeping." He hadn't so much as taken one step when he heard a cough behind him.

Chapter 16

Adele shaded her eyes with her hand and looked toward the crest of the hill again. Where were they? Had something happened? Wringing her hands, she walked back and forth in front of the pump. The sensible thing would be to find something to do in the house or out in the garden. But she couldn't still the growing sense of dread in her heart. *Father, please bring them back safe.*

She looked around for her son and saw him perched in the same tree he had climbed earlier. After Jonah left, Jacob had climbed back up. She walked to the base of the tree and looked up. "Jacob, do you see anything?" she asked.

"No." He looked down, and his eyes told her he was no less worried than she. "Should it be taking Uncle Jonah this long?"

"I did not think it would," she said. "Keep looking, mein Liebe. Tell me as soon as you see anything." She resumed her pacing under the tree.

Why had Jonah sent for the sheriff? Surely he didn't think. . . She stopped. The animals Henry had found were close to their property line. Adele looked up the hill with a sinking heart. "Near the northwest corner," she whispered. She closed her eyes and covered her mouth with her hand.

Suddenly Jacob gave a shout and scrambled down out of the tree. "They're back!" he called as he flew toward a figure making his way down the hill. Relief flooded her heart as she saw Anne. But who was carrying her? It wasn't Jonah. As they approached, she saw and heard the little girl crying. Cyrus Morgan was carrying her. She rushed up to them. "Mr. Morgan! What has happened?" she said as she took Anne from the man.

He was out of breath and had to pause for a moment before

answering. His clothes were dirty and torn in several places, and his face was bruised as if someone had beaten him.

"He's crazy, ma'am. Plum gone 'round the bend."

"Who?" Her face whitened. "Not Jonah?"

"No, ma'am. There's a man been livin' back in the woods at the tree line. I was out laying my traps, and he came up behind me and knocked me out cold. When I woke up, I couldn't talk sense to him. He thinks he's still at war. He tied me up and said I was a prisoner. Said General Sherman would come see about me. Then he left. Then Mr. Kirby comes along and unties me, and next thing I know, this feller comes back and goes after him. I scooped up the little girl and ran like he told me to."

Peeling Anne away from her, Adele thrust her into Jacob's arms and ran as fast as she could up the hill, ignoring the little girl's wails and the sound of voices behind her telling her to stop and wait. When she reached the crest of the hill, she saw the path Cyrus had made in the tall grass. She followed it, unmindful of the brambles that tore at her dress and scraped her hands as she pushed them away.

Before long, she came to the clearing. The sight of the camp made little impression on her. All that filled her vision was the sight of Jonah tied to a slender tree. He was sitting on the ground, slumped over, and she raced over to him. "Jonah!" she said, lifting his head in both her hands. His face was bloody from a gash near his eye, and as her fingers brushed his neck, she gasped in relief as she felt his pulse racing.

Suddenly he started, and his eyes widened at the sight of her. "Adele! Get out of here before he comes back," he said.

"No, we will both leave," she said as she knelt down behind him to untie the ropes.

"Adele, he thinks we're still fighting the war. He's armed, and I don't know what he'll do if he sees you."

"I am not leaving you."

"Adele."

Ignoring his pleas, she went to work on the knots. They were so tight she could not get them loose. She was about to look around for a knife when the wildest-looking man she had ever seen came marching out of the woods next to her.

He had a long, unkempt beard and was thinner than even Jonah had been when he returned from the war. He carried a revolver in one hand,

and a bowie knife hung sheathed on his belt. Looking back at the woods, he gave a nod and a smart salute. "Yes, sir," he said to the empty air. "I'll keep him until we hear from the general." He turned to her and started. "Deborah!" His eyes narrowed. "What are you doing?" He grabbed her by the arm and pulled her to her feet. "The general is coming. You need to fix something special." He pushed her away and knelt to check Jonah's bonds.

Adele looked at Jonah. He nudged his head in the direction of the farm, and she shook her head. She wasn't about to leave him. If she played along, perhaps she could take him by surprise. "What shall I cook?" she asked.

The man stopped and looked at her. "What happened to your voice?"

"I—" Her accent! "I have a cold." He was still staring at her, and she tried to distract him by asking another question. "What does the general like to eat?"

"Just make it good. He always likes what you make."

Adele looked around. There didn't seem to be anything she could use to make any kind of meal. Her eyes went toward the campfire. Seeing it needed to be restarted, she walked toward the clothesline and started to gather sticks. As she edged toward the bushes, Jonah coughed. Glancing back, she saw the warning look in his eyes. She stood up too quickly and had to take a step back into the brush. Looking back to get her footing, she saw the edge of a woman's skirt. Gasping, she dropped her small load of firewood.

"What?" the man asked. He was sitting on the log whetting his knife.

"Nothing," Adele said. She began to pick the wood up as quickly as her cold hands would allow. "A. . .spider."

The man stared at her a moment then blinked. "Get away from there," he said. His voice was strange, almost sad. "Who are you?"

"I am Deborah," Adele said. She walked to the campfire and started to stack the wood. After a moment or two, he came and stood over her. She paused then continued with her task.

The next instant he hauled her to her feet, and she felt the cold edge of a knife against her neck. "You ain't Deborah," he said. "Where is she? Who are you?"

"Please let me go." Adele struggled to keep her voice calm. "Perhaps I can help you find her."

But the knife pressed harder against her throat.

"I know where Deborah is." Adele's heart raced as Jonah spoke. What was he doing?

The man turned and stared at him.

Adele looked at him with pleading eyes, but his focus was trained on her captor.

"Where is she?" the man asked.

Jonah nodded toward the bushes near the clothesline. "Over there."

Never lowering his knife, the man dragged Adele along with him, tromped through the brush, and moved it aside with one foot. Adele averted her eyes, and the man swayed for a moment. She felt his grip on her arm loosen for a second, but it tightened before she could pull free. The man let out a throaty growl and pushed her away as he strode over to Jonah.

She stumbled to the ground.

"That's not her!" he roared. "Where is she? What have you Rebs done with my Deborah?"

Adele screamed as Jonah stopped the deranged man from burying his knife in his chest. Having somehow freed his hands, he now wrestled with him for control of the knife. But the man was surprisingly strong.

Adele scrambled to her feet, looking for something, anything to help her husband. Seeing Jonah's gun lying on the ground, she grabbed it just as the man managed to pin Jonah with his knees. Cocking the weapon, she took aim and squeezed the trigger.

Nothing happened, and her heart stopped as she watched the man raise his knife. Suddenly a shot rang out. The knife flew away, and the man grasped his hand in pain.

Jonah immediately pushed him off and pinned him to the ground. "Thank you, doctor," he said, looking past Adele.

Whirling around, Adele saw Will, the sheriff, and several others from town coming through the trees. Behind them stood Noah, breathless and leaning on his cane, a smoking revolver in his free hand.

∞

"You almost dislocated your shoulder getting your hands free," Dr. Kelly said. "The arm will need to stay in a sling until the muscles heal."

Jonah looked up at the doctor, who kept his gaze focused on wrapping his left shoulder. They were in the dining room. Adele was upstairs settling a distressed Anne into her bed while Will and the sheriff were going through the wild man's camp.

The doctor had quickly wrapped up the man's hand and given him something to calm him so that he and Sheriff Wade could safely transport him to Delaware. Dr. Kelly finished with Jonah's shoulder and was helping him put his shirt back on when Adele walked into the room.

"Is Anne all right?" Jonah asked.

"Yes, she is finally asleep," she replied, sinking down onto the seat next to him. The doctor stepped away, and she finished buttoning his shirt. Then she looked at him, and as she gently ran her fingers near the gash the doctor had stitched up, her brow furrowed with concern.

He smiled reassuringly and took her hand and kissed it. "I'm all right."

"I'll see to a sling in a moment," Noah said quietly. "Your shoulder wasn't the only thing you injured." He carefully examined Jonah's left hand, which had gotten badly scraped when he pulled it free of the rope. "It's nothing too bad. I'll bandage it up."

Jonah watched as Adele looked up at him. "Thank you."

He paused then turned to his bag, which sat open on the table.

She opened her mouth to say something else when Will and the sheriff came in the door.

"What did you find?" Jonah asked as they sat down at the table.

"More than I thought we would," Sheriff Wade said. He pulled a picture and a folded piece of paper from his pocket. He opened the paper. "According to this, his name is Robert Wells and he's from Butler County."

"That is close to Cincinnati, is it not?" Adele asked.

Jonah nodded as he took the paper from the sheriff. The large half circle of text reading, *"To all whom it may concern,"* surrounding an eagle, was very familiar to him. He'd received a similar document when he'd been mustered out after his release from Andersonville. A wave of compassion swept over him. The paper stated Robert Wells had been a farmer. The reason for his discharge in 1863 was vague. It only stated that his *"services were no longer required."*

"Here's why he thought he recognized Mrs. Kirby," the sheriff said, handing him the picture.

Adele gasped when she looked at it, and Jonah almost did himself. The woman in the picture could almost have been her twin. Taking it from him, she flipped it over. The only thing it said on the back was "*Deborah, 1861.*" "Do you think this was his wife?" she asked.

"We found a wedding ring with that woman's remains," the sheriff replied.

"And Anne called her Ma," Jonah said.

"But why would he kill her?" Adele turned the picture back over and looked at it.

"My best guess is his mind snapped." They all turned to Dr. Kelly, who had finished with Jonah. Having bandaged his hand and settled his arm in a sling, the doctor was slowly putting things back in his case. "He thought himself still at war and took his poor wife and child along with him, thinking they were fellow soldiers marching to battle. She probably tried to get her child away from his madness, and he ended up killing her."

"No wonder little Anne took to you so easily, Mrs. Kirby, and all the while fearful of us," Will said.

"What should we do about her, Cal?" Jonah asked. "Adele and I would like to keep her."

"I'd say that's the best thing for her for now," he replied. "But I'll have to talk to the authorities down in Butler County. She might have relatives looking for her."

Adele nodded and looked at Jonah with hopeful eyes. He squeezed her hand.

The sheriff rose from his seat. "Well, I need to be getting back. I'd like to get Mr. Wells over to Delaware before dark." He shook Jonah's hand, and nodding to Adele, he took his hat from the table and looked at the doctor. "I'll be waiting out near your buggy."

"I'll see to everything the rest of the day, Mr. Kirby," Will said, rising from the table.

"Did Cyrus go home?" Jonah asked.

Will shook his head. "He insisted he was just fine. Wouldn't even let the doctor look at him."

"I'll go out to his place later," Dr. Kelly said.

Will reached for the doctor's bag. "Shall I carry that out for you?"

He handed it to the young man and took hold of his cane. "Yes, Will. Thank you."

He started for the door, but Jonah rose and blocked his way. He looked at Will. "Carry his bag out to the buggy. The doctor will be along in a minute." The young man left, and Jonah looked at Dr. Kelly, who avoided his gaze. Jonah offered him his hand. "Thank you."

The doctor didn't take it. "I don't know anyone who deserves to be thanked less," he said quietly.

"You saved my life," Jonah replied.

"I almost ruined your life," Dr. Kelly said, finally looking at him.

Jonah lowered his hand.

"I tried to have you committed. Then I coveted your wife and allowed my feelings for her to lead me to accuse you of a very heinous crime. I behaved in the most un-Christian manner imaginable, and I do not deserve your thanks or your forgiveness."

"The Lord commands me to forgive my brother seventy times seven times," Jonah said. He gave him a half smile. "Let's just say you have a ways to go." He offered his hand again.

This time the doctor took it. "I don't want to keep the sheriff waiting. And I have some packing to do." He moved past them and took his hat from the hall tree.

"What do you mean?" Adele asked.

"I can't stay here," he said. "After I help the sheriff take Mr. Wells down to Dr. Peck in Columbus, I'm going to leave. I think I might head back to Philadelphia." He struggled with his coat, and Adele went and helped him put it on.

"Please feel free to write and tell us how you are," she said, stepping back.

Dr. Kelly looked at both of them for a long moment. "I might in time. Good-bye."

He walked out of the house, and Adele stepped to the window to watch him drive away. She turned back to Jonah with sad eyes. "He was a good friend before all this. I wish you both could have met differently."

"I hope he writes," Jonah said quietly. "Maybe we could start over." Adele smiled, and he suddenly couldn't stand being away from her any longer. He wrapped his free hand around her waist and pulled her to him, acutely aware of how close he had come to losing her. "That was a reckless thing you did today," he said. "Coming after me like that and then refusing to leave."

She looked up at him. "You were in trouble. I could not help myself this afternoon any more than I could so many months ago when I asked you to marry me."

"It doesn't seem fair, you asking me."

"So ask me."

Jonah looked down at her, wondering at the impish gleam in her brilliant blue eyes. "Adele, will you marry me?"

"No," she said, smiling at the surprise in his eyes. "I already did."

He answered her refusal with a kiss.

Epilogue

December 24, 1866

I still say the *Weihnachtsbaum* is too tall," Adele said as she and Jonah sat in the parlor. She sat on the high-backed sofa sewing while Jonah sat beside her reading the *Delaware Gazette*.

He lowered the newspaper and looked at the fir tree that stood in the corner next to the fireplace. "I cut three feet off it before I brought it in," he said.

"And then you had to take it back out and cut off another two feet more." She glanced over at him and caught the sheepish look on his face just as the newspaper hid his face from view.

Adele smiled. When she had first suggested they have a Weihnachtsbaum, or Christmas tree, Jonah had been all for it. As she was growing up, she and Erich had always had one, and when the Kirby boys had seen it, they begged their parents to start the tradition. Unfortunately, while not being critical of the Brauns' custom, Jonah's parents had not felt the need for one and had gently but firmly adhered to their own custom of putting up stockings on the fireplace mantel.

"When do we light the candles?" Jonah asked. He had finished his newspaper and gotten up to take a closer look at the tree.

Adele rose and joined him. "Erich and I always lit them on Christmas Day in the evening. Then we sang carols."

"Erich sang?" he asked with raised eyebrows. Erich Braun had not been known in the township as the best singer. In church he was often relegated to the end of whatever pew he happened to sit in.

"Yes, but I helped," Adele giggled. She looked back at the tree and pursed her lips as she looked at all the presents he had stacked under it. "I knew you cut off those branches at the bottom for a reason. Jonah Michael Kirby, you will spoil that little girl."

"But it's Anne's first Christmas with us," he said, smiling as he wrapped his arm around her waist. "You want it to be as special as I do."

She had to admit he was right.

Two months ago, Sheriff Wade had personally come to tell them that no relatives could be found for the little girl. The Butler County sheriff talked to neighbors who confirmed the Wells family had disappeared at the end of last year. They also told him that Robert and Deborah had moved to the county just a few years before the war and that they had no idea where they had originally come from or if they had any living relatives. So Adele and Jonah had adopted the child, signing the papers only yesterday that officially made her Anne Kirby.

But even so, Adele still didn't think it was cause for overdoing it. She turned her head to give her husband a reproachful look. "There are other ways to make the day special besides presents."

"Not all of these are from me," he pointed out. "The little wooden ark is from Will and Clara, and Jake whittled the animals to go with it. Daniel and Katherine sent her the books, and Aunt Mary and Professor Harris—"

"Uncle James," Adele corrected. Mary and the professor had married just before Thanksgiving.

"They sent her the new dress, and Cyrus gave her the little fur muff." Anne had finally warmed to Cyrus, and he decided to make his stay in Ostrander permanent by renting some of the land Ben Carr had given to Jonah.

Adele pointed under the tree. "And that?"

"That's my present," he said with satisfaction.

"Why does a three-year-old girl need a crib big enough for a real baby?"

"Well, she does have two dolls."

Adele couldn't hold back any longer and laughed along with her husband. She turned in his arms and hugged him tightly. Raising her head, she looked in his green eyes, which were as dark and beautiful as the fir tree beside them.

Sometimes as they talked or while they ate dinner, he would wander back to a dark memory and grow a little distant. And while he no longer walked or took his gun everywhere with him, he did clean it nearly every night and kept it handy by the front door. He would never be exactly as he was before the war, but what he was now was more than enough for her.

A gentle smile drifted across his lips, and he tucked back a stray strand of her hair before kissing her with a passion that left her dizzy.

Almost too dizzy. She laid her head on his shoulder.

"Are you all right?" he asked, rubbing her back.

"I am tired. I should sit down."

He led her over to the sofa and looked at her as she resumed her sewing. "You've been tired quite a bit lately."

She glanced at him. She had wanted to wait until tomorrow to tell him. "I have been working on a present for you."

"For me?" he asked with raised eyebrows.

"Yes. But I cannot give it to you tomorrow."

"Why?"

Adele looked at him and bit her lip before answering. "It will not be here for another six months."

He stared at her a full minute before a smile crept onto his face and his eyes started to glow. He gently hugged her. "I love you."

"And I love you. Merry Christmas."

Restored Heart

Dedication

Thanks to everyone who has been praying for me, and a big thanks to Max Lucado. Your books and UpWords helped me through this book in so many ways. This book is dedicated to Brian Arthur Carmen, my dear brother in Christ, fellow alumni of The Ohio State University, and *i*-dotter for the OSU marching band. I look forward to heaven, when your presence will finally be restored to me.

Chapter 1

Pittsburgh, Pennsylvania
May, 1884

I can assure you, Peter, I'm just as surprised as you."

Peter McCord stared at his uncle. Two months ago, he was the most eligible bachelor in Pittsburgh society and the apple of his grandfather's eye. One month ago found him keeping vigil at the old man's bedside. A week ago, he watched as Granddad was laid to rest, and less than a minute ago the words he'd just heard uttered left him speechless.

"There must be some mistake," he said, finally finding his voice. "Let me see the will."

Randall McCord rose from his seat behind the heavy walnut desk and handed the document to him. Peter took it and, rising from one of the leather chairs, crossed his grandfather's wood-paneled study to the window. He felt the blood leave his face as he took in Granddad's final words. He'd been left nothing, absolutely nothing. Peter's brow furrowed. "I don't understand," he muttered.

"I realize after my misunderstanding with my father you imagined he would leave everything to you—"

"Misunderstanding?" Peter locked eyes with his uncle. "I would hardly call nearly ruining everything Granddad worked for a 'misunderstanding'!" His uncle's eyes narrowed, and Peter knew he'd struck a nerve. Uncle Randall's heavy-handed ways had almost run McCord Steel and Ironworks into the ground. The mill had lost a great deal of money and the workers had come close to rioting. Granddad had been beside himself with anger; so much so, he cut off his only son. "In light of that fact," Peter continued, "I'm the most logical choice as heir in spite of the fact that my interests lay elsewhere."

271

"Oh yes, your *interests*," his cousin Edward drawled, leaning against the bookcase behind his father. "Horse racing and chasing after every attractive young lady in the city."

"At least I have them to chase," Peter shot back. With his strong, handsome face, chocolate-brown hair, and—as Granddad used to say— eyes greener than a spring meadow, Pittsburgh's eligible young ladies were more than willing quarry. Of course, being Hiram McCord's heir didn't hurt either. "Tell me, how are your marriage prospects?"

A slow, smug smile grew over his cousin's face. "Much improved now that *I'm* heir of McCord Steel and you're—"

"That's enough." Uncle Randall glanced sharply at his son. "Peter, what exactly did you expect? Considering your disastrous time at Princeton—"

"I did graduate," Peter snapped, rereading the will carefully.

"Barely. You spent more time at the racetracks than attending to your studies. I'm sure my father realized you couldn't possibly oversee his fortune."

"Granddad knew I wouldn't run the mill like he did. He knew I had every intention of hiring the best possible man to oversee its operation."

"While you exhaust the McCord fortune on horses, I suppose."

"Granddad approved of my interest in horses. It was his idea to buy the farm in Ligonier—"

"Then why didn't he leave you even the smallest stipend to keep the farm running?"

Ignoring the question, Peter strode over to his uncle. "Granddad couldn't have left everything to you. He wouldn't have." He shook the document. "This can't possibly be the correct will. It must be an older version."

"It's the correct one, Peter," Edward said. "Didn't you check the date?"

Peter looked at the will again. It had been signed a little over a year ago. He put his hand over his eyes. What could he have done over the past year to cause his grandfather to do this? Why hadn't he at least warned him? Peter stiffened. That last night, before Granddad slipped away in his sleep, the old man had begged for his understanding when the will was read. Peter had thought it was the laudanum talking. He felt a hand on his shoulder. His uncle had risen from his seat and now stood next to him.

"It was my father's last wish that you be taken care of, and it is one I intend to honor," he said, his hand turning viselike.

Peter shook free, handed the will to his uncle, and walked to the door. "I'll take care of myself, thank you, Uncle Randall."

"And how will you manage to do that, may I ask?"

Peter turned. His uncle resumed his seat behind the desk.

"You've been left with nothing. Not even the smallest sum of money." Peter remained silent and he continued. "As I said, I am willing to support you, but there will be a few conditions."

"And those would be?"

"It's high time you used that education my father paid for. I assume you learned *something* in spite of your horrendous marks." His uncle's eyes narrowed keenly. "You will come to work for me at the mill and earn your keep for a change."

Peter smiled humorlessly and shook his head.

"My thanks for the offer, Uncle, but I have a very promising colt that will be ready to race soon. I think I'll take my chances with him. In the meantime, I'm sure Henry won't mind me staying with him." Peter knew he and his horse trainer would think of something to keep the farm running. Sell off a few mares perhaps— His uncle's voice stopped him in midthought.

"You could, if the farm still belonged to you."

Peter felt the blood leave his face. "What do you mean?"

"Despite the fact he bought it for you, it seems the farm is still in my father's name. Not yours. Therefore, it now belongs to me. I intend on dismissing Henry Farley and selling off the animals as quickly as possible."

Peter tried to digest what he'd just heard as his uncle moved swiftly on. "The other condition concerns Miss Leticia Jamison."

He looked at his uncle blankly. Leticia—Letty—was the daughter of his grandfather's lawyer, Simon Jamison. "What about her?"

"A month or so ago, you and she were invited to the club as guests of Mr. and Mrs. Braddock, were you not?"

"Yes." Nearly every young person of his acquaintance had been invited. Hazel Braddock had recently become engaged, and her parents arranged a sort of extended engagement party at the hunting and fishing club on Lake Conemaugh. Even as sick as he was, Granddad had insisted he go, eager for his grandson to make a match. Peter had been delighted to mingle with some fine young ladies from Harrisburg there, and even now, he couldn't help but smile at the memory of their charms. They had all but fallen over themselves, vying for his attention. How could they not? Uncle Randall cleared his throat and Peter blinked. "I'm sorry, did you say something?"

"I said, what exactly happened between you and Miss Jamison?" Uncle Randall asked.

"Nothing. If I hadn't rescued her, I doubt I would have talked to her very much the whole trip."

Letty was a sweet enough girl. Pretty, too, but not really Peter's type. Far too bookish for his tastes, she wasn't part of his circle of friends. She'd gone to school with Hazel, the only reason she'd been invited in the first place.

"Oh yes." His uncle shot his son a look. "You two took a walk and got lost, I believe?"

"Miss Jamison got lost," Peter corrected. "She'd never been to the lake before and wandered off by herself. We all went out looking for her, and I found her." And he'd been considered quite the hero by the rest of the young ladies as a result.

"I also heard she was hysterical when you brought her back."

"Well, of course—she was out in the elements by herself for over an hour." Peter wished his uncle would get to the point. He needed to go to his room and figure out what he was going to do. If he could just get a few minutes to himself. . .but his uncle's next words jarred any other thought from his head.

"Her dress was ripped, almost beyond repair."

Peter frowned. "What are you implying?"

"Father's not implying anything," Edward said. "Letty says you took advantage of her."

"What? No!" That was a line he was always careful to not so much as approach—much less cross—no matter how tempting. The price, a wedding ring, was far too high. "She said she fell before I found her. She told everyone as much."

"To avoid any embarrassment, I'm sure," his cousin replied. "But she won't be able to explain the state she'll be in within a few months. Not without being married."

A sick feeling rose in Peter's gut as he realized he had a bigger problem than simply being penniless. He looked from his uncle to his cousin.

"That can't be true. Nothing happened," he said.

"Her doctor has assured me that it is true."

"I'm *not* marrying Letty Jamison."

"Then you may leave this house at once. I'm sure my father would understand my refusing to abide by his last request considering the circumstances." A gleam appeared in Uncle Randall's eyes. "And if you think you have friends around here that will take you in, think again. One word of this will close every door in Pittsburgh. Considering your reputation, no one will doubt it for a moment."

Peter felt all control of his world slipping away. It must have shown on his face, judging by his uncle's next words.

"Your aunt will help her with the arrangements. Since we are in mourning, the wedding will happen quietly in the parlor in a month's time. I think you'll agree we shouldn't wait any longer—for Miss Jamison's sake."

∽

One month later, Peter shrugged reluctantly into a linen shirt and buttoned it, while his valet sorted through his cuff links.

"The mother-of-pearl set will do fine, Jimmy."

Though surprised, he did as he was told. A knock at the door interrupted them. Setting the links aside, Jimmy walked over to answer it. Peter scowled as he heard him speak a few murmured words. What on earth did Uncle Randall want from him now?

Jimmy returned, a velvet box in his hand and an uneasy look in his eyes. "Your uncle sent this up. He says it's a gift. . .for her."

Peter opened it. A pearl necklace lay inside, and not just any piece of jewelry.

"This belonged to my mother." He clenched his jaw. His uncle had taken charge of it when he had Peter's things moved from his spacious room on the floor below to this small, cramped, forgotten room in the garret. "And he expects me to give it to Letty?" He snapped the box shut. "He can go straight to the devil!"

Peter slapped the box down on his desk and snatched up his cuff links. He fumbled with them, trying to put them on. Jimmy quickly came to his aid. Poor Jimmy. He was valet to Edward now, but Peter had insisted the young man be permitted to help him dress one last time. He needed a friend close by on the day he would lose what little freedom still remained to him.

"Thank you, Jimmy. I'm sorry I sounded short."

"It's all right, sir," the young man said as he handed Peter his tie.

"I'm sorry, too, for all this. My cousin can't be very pleasant to work for." Peter couldn't help but smirk as he fashioned a perfect four-in-hand knot. "Although, I have to admit I am pleased every time I see one of your sad knots hanging around his neck."

Jimmy gave him a self-conscious smile. Tying cravats and ties was the young man's only failing as a valet, but Peter had never minded.

"And he thought you were the master behind my perfectly formed ties," he said.

"Yes, sir, thank you for keeping that secret for so long." He helped Peter into his frock coat and brushed imaginary dust from the shoulders. As Peter made some final adjustments, Jimmy picked up the velvet case. "May I, sir?"

Peter nodded and watched him open the case and look admiringly at the necklace inside. It was the only thing of his mother's Peter owned. Granddad had given it to him several years ago, and he remembered that moment as the sole time his grandfather ever mentioned her. Even then, it was only to say that she had been a lovely young woman. The sadness in his face and eyes had kept Peter from pressing him for more. Sarah McCord's death had been tragic; a carriage accident had taken the life of Granddad's only daughter. Peter's father divorced and abandoned his mother before his birth, which was why he bore the name McCord.

"If you'll pardon the cheek, sir, it's not right for Miss Jamison to have this." He set it back on the desk then walked to the window and peered out.

Jimmy had been the only one to believe his assertion that nothing had happened between him and Letty. He'd been as outraged at her claim as Peter had, if not more. Peter smiled humorlessly. "Don't apologize; you're right. But as much as I agree with you, I don't think I have much choice in the matter."

He joined him at the window. A starling flitted from one bush to another in the gardens that lay directly below them. He envied the bird's freedom. Peter's every move had been closely monitored for the past month. He felt as if he were being kept in a deep hole, only to be taken out when needed. Almost sick with anger, he turned away from the window and ran frustrated hands through his hair. Spying the velvet case, he opened it and carefully removed the pearls. They shimmered gently in his hands, and the ornate clasp glittered. Bile rose in his throat as he imagined them around Letty's neck. He glanced at Jimmy.

"Who brought the necklace up here? Jenkins?" His uncle had fired Martin, their old butler, when he and his family came to live at the McCord mansion, and elevated one of the older footmen to his position. Albert Jenkins, a sharp-eyed man, reported Peter's every move to his uncle.

"No, sir, it was one of the maids. Jenkins is sick as I understand it."

Opportunity whispered in Peter's ear. Laying the necklace on the desk, he sat down and pinched the bridge of his nose. "Would you mind getting me something to drink?"

"Of course, sir. Anything in particular?"

"Something that will get me through the rest of the day." He looked at him with raised eyebrows, and Jimmy smiled and nodded before leaving the room.

With one fluid motion, Peter pulled out pen and paper, scribbled a note to the valet, and then placed the envelope where only Jimmy would find it. Glancing at himself in the mirror, he traded the frock coat for his sack suit jacket and quickly dispensed with his tie and collar. That was better. He looked a little more working class now. There was only one thing to be done, only one way out, and he intended to take it. He went to the door, down the back stairs, out the servant's door, and on his way to the section of Pittsburgh that boasted the most pawnshops.

Chapter 2

A nne Kirby pulled her trunk from the corner where it sat over to her bed and raised the lid. She stared at it for a long moment and then bit her lip, trying to set her mind on preparing for her trip. But her wandering thoughts tumbled like jagged rocks in her mind, and a headache began to prick behind her brown eyes. Closing them, she sat on the edge of her bed, not hearing her mother come in.

"Are you all right?"

The lilt of her mother's German accent and the gentle pressure of her hand on her shoulder startled Anne. She looked up, a smile flickering across her face as she rose. "I'm fine, Ma. I was just...thinking."

"Why is your trunk out?"

"I thought I might pack a few things." She walked over to her wardrobe and began taking her things out and laying them on the bed. She felt her mother's eyes on her as she knelt in front of the trunk. "I'll need some paper."

"Anne, you do not leave for a week yet." She held out her hand to her daughter. "Sit with me for a moment."

Anne paused then took her hand. They sat on the bed, and her mother brushed a thumb across her cheek.

"I do not like to see you hurt."

Anne nodded, her gaze directed at her lap. Her mother grasped both her hands and squeezed them.

"I'm sorry Sam McAllister treated you as he did. He shouldn't have courted you if he had feelings for another. Your pa was ready to go up there and give him a piece of his mind."

Anne glanced up. "He was? Does he still have a mind to do that?"

"No, Kleine, I convinced him not to go. He promised me he wouldn't."

"Good. I would just as soon forget the whole thing." Her heart pounded with relief. She wished she could forget those months she had taught school in the northern part of the county. Everything had looked so promising at first. She brushed a strand of ginger-colored hair from her eyes before changing the subject. "Ma, don't you think I'm a little old for you to still call me 'Kleine'?"

Her ma smiled and gently touched her chin. "Don't you know no matter how old you are, you will always be my 'little one'?"

Anne grinned lopsidedly. It was still appropriate, she supposed. She was the shortest one in the family. Even her younger sister, Millie, was an inch or so taller than she.

Her mother cupped her face. "Besides, calling you Kleine always reminds me of that special day."

"The day you found me," Anne said.

Her ma nodded and wrapped her arms around her. Barely three at the time, Anne remembered only snatches of what had happened, like the purple flowers she'd hidden behind, and the kindness in Ma's blue eyes as she coaxed her to come closer. And seeds. Ma had been planting the kitchen garden and convinced her to help. But the gentle memory contrasted sharply with the hard truth. She formed her next words carefully.

"I wish I knew exactly when my birthday is and how old I really am." Anne pulled away and scrutinized her mother's face. The barest hint of apprehension slipped across the older woman's face before a gentle smile settled there.

"I know, Kleine. But your parents were already gone when we found you." She rose and looked from her daughter to the clothes on her bed. "I suppose we can pack some of your winter things. It will save time later. I'll get some newspaper."

While she was gone, Anne carefully folded her skirts and waists. She'd always known she was adopted—everyone in Ostrander knew—but she hadn't known there was more to it until recently.

Your parents were already gone. . . .

She winced at the half-truth. For a moment, her clothes faded from sight and clear, precise handwriting flashed before her eyes, words never meant for her to see. Her brows angled, V-shaped, above her eyes, and she squeezed her eyes shut, swallowing her desire to tell Ma what she knew. What good would it do to say something now? Telling her parents she knew the truth would only hurt them and most certainly keep her from carrying out her plans. After all, it was only after Anne made certain concessions that they agreed to let her leave. She wondered if she still wanted to go through with it. *No, this has to be done.* At least, no one else in Ostrander appeared to know. And if things went as she hoped, they never would. Her thoughts gave her hands urgency, and she reached for the quilt at the end of her bed and folded it. Her mother returned to the room.

"Ah, you're taking your quilt." Ma stood beside her. "I remember when I made this for you. You helped me—do you remember?"

"Yes, I remember pricking my fingers so many times I left a drop of blood on it." She smiled as she lifted a corner of the quilt to reveal the tiny brown dot that never fully washed out.

Her mother carefully laid it over the heavier items already packed in the bottom of the trunk. "We'll miss your help around here."

Anne chuckled ruefully. "I'm not that useful. That's why I became a teacher, remember?"

If her parents hadn't told her she was adopted, she would have figured it out on her own. Pa and her brother, Jacob, could sow crops in seawater and they would grow. Her ma ran the farmhouse with an efficiency that, according to Pa, would be the envy of any army drill sergeant. And Millie's needlework had won more first place premiums at the county fair than Anne could count. She, on the other hand, couldn't sew and burned water, and the last time she had charge of the kitchen garden, everything nearly died.

"You will still be missed, Anne." Adele, her hands on her hips, looked at her. "Although, I still don't see why you must leave or why you're going to work in the library at The Ohio State University. You are a teacher."

"I wanted a change. And there were no positions available for me in Columbus, at least, not right now." Anne avoided her gaze and laid a waist into the trunk. "The young lady I'm filling in for is supposed to return in a few months. Maybe by that time—"

"Anne." Her mother squeezed her arm. "I know what happened with Sam was hard, but why can't you stay?"

Anne looked down at the things in her chest, the real reason nearly flying from her lips. "Ma, I—" She took a breath. "I need to do this." She looked up at her mother with pleading eyes.

Her ma wrapped her arms around her. "We will pray for you, kleine, that God will heal your heart to love again."

"Thank you," Anne murmured then gently pulled away and walked over to the wardrobe. She made a play of looking for any forgotten items while attempting to swallow the lump in her throat. Her parents had never pushed her to get married, but she sensed they were eager for her to find a match soon. At twenty-one, most young women her age had been married for a few years. It wasn't that she didn't want to marry or that she lacked beaus—she'd simply never found someone she felt she could walk alongside for the rest of her life. She had always trusted God would lead her to that person when the time came and, until a few weeks ago, she thought that person had been Sam McAllister. Now she had to wonder if there really was anyone for her to call her own. Composing herself, she picked up a forgotten shawl.

"I am glad you will not be on your own down in Columbus," her ma said as she approached. "Your uncle will take good care of you."

"Yes." Anne folded the garment. When she first told her ma and pa of her plan to work at the university's library, they had given her their consent, but only if she lived with Uncle Daniel, a professor at the institution. They simply wouldn't hear of her living at one of the boardinghouses near the school, even if they did cater exclusively to the female students. At first she thought it would be a problem, but then she realized she would not have to pay for her room and board. That would make saving her money for passage west all the easier. She laid the shawl in the trunk. "That's all my winter clothing."

"We can pack the rest later." Ma closed the lid. "Let's go see how Millie is doing with dinner."

They made their way out behind the house to the summer kitchen. Although Anne didn't cook, she managed to help out by fetching and carrying various things her mother and sister needed.

"I'm rolling out the dough now, Ma," Millie said as they came in.

"The dough for what?" Anne inhaled the fragrant chicken boiling in a large pot on the black cast-iron stove. "Oh Ma, you shouldn't be going to such trouble."

"Yes, I should. I couldn't have you leave without making your favorite dishes."

"Tonight we're having chicken pie, green beans, fresh bread, and Ma's strudel for dessert." Millie smiled broadly and brushed a strand of her bright blond hair from her face.

Tears caused Anne's sight to swim for a moment. Blinking them away, she took a basket from the worktable. "I'll go pick the green beans."

"I've already done it."

"Is there anything for me to do just now?" Anne asked hopefully.

Ma looked at her and then sighed. "No. You can go on out to the barn."

She smiled. "Thank you, Ma."

Anne stepped inside the barn and breathed in the familiar, earthy odor of weathered wood, hay, and straw. It was one of her most favorite places. She missed the days of her childhood when she would follow Pa from the haymow above to the milking stalls down below, helping him and the hired hands tend the livestock. But as she grew older, Pa told her she shouldn't be hanging around the barn so much. Learning to take care of a home, not animals, was more important, he'd said. She found it a little ironic that the one thing she felt gifted to do on the farm was the one thing that wasn't proper for her to do. At least Pa had allowed her a little leeway lately. A soft nicker greeted her approach to the horse stalls. A dark head with a graying muzzle appeared, and Anne smiled, drawing from her pocket the carrot she had snitched from one of the feed bins.

"Hello, Scioto," she said, dropping it into his feed trough, glad that the horse would be coming with her.

Scioto belonged to Uncle Daniel. He leased a house on university grounds, and Pa had been boarding him while the university built a stable on the property. The horse finished the carrot and looked to her for more. She smiled as she scratched his withers, a favorite spot.

"That's enough for now, boy." Pa had left his care to her since she came home, and she had become attached to the horse over the past few months. The bay Morgan nuzzled her, and she stroked his neck.

"I hear you started packing your trunk. I don't suppose Ma was able to talk you out of leaving."

Anne turned to see Pa approach. She smiled apologetically, shaking her head. He sighed and wrapped his arms around her, bending his tall form as he did so.

"How's my Annie?"

"I'll be all right."

She felt his arms tighten and knew he still struggled not to go confront Sam. A mixture of panic and guilt surged through her. What if he did? He would certainly find out that Sam had not led her on as she had allowed her parents to believe. *No, he promised Ma,* she told herself. *And he never breaks his promises, especially to her.* While the thought eased the panic, it did little to assuage her guilt, and the urge to blurt out the truth once again enveloped her. She bit her lip and clung to Pa. How she would miss his hugs and the way he called her "Annie." He was the only person in the whole world allowed to call her that. Scioto snuffed at them, demanding attention, and Anne's throat loosened as she laughed softly.

"This horse sure has become attached to you." Pa released her to face the animal. "I hope he eats for whoever Danny hired."

"So it won't be me?" It was silly of her to ask, she knew, but she had hoped, since she'd been allowed to take care of him here—Pa laid a gentle hand on her shoulder.

"I only let you take care of him when you came home because it seemed to make you feel better, but it won't be fitting for you to see to him down there. You let the stable boy see to him."

"Yes, Pa." She stroked the horse's neck. If she didn't take care of him, who would she talk to? Scioto had become her sole confidant. Well, she could still go visit him—in the evenings, maybe.

"Besides, all those young men down there won't want you smelling like horse," he added.

Anne said nothing and fussed with Scioto until Pa took her by the chin, forcing her to look up at him.

"I know it's hard, but trust God with your heart and your future."

Anne swallowed the words impossibly stuck in her throat. It wasn't about trust. Not really. She trusted that God knew what He was doing. She just couldn't understand why. With Pa's gentle eyes still watching her, she tried to form a reply. The gentle low of a cow told her it was time to do the milking.

"The cows are waiting," she said.

"I'd best go let them in," Pa said slowly. "Think on what I said." She nodded, and he gave her a quick hug then turned to leave.

Once he was gone, Anne fetched a brush and stepped into Scioto's stall to groom him. The swish of the brush as it smoothed his coat usually had a soothing effect on her. But packing her trunk today had nudged her plans into motion, like the wheels of a train pulling from the station. She leaned against the horse's shoulder, and he gently snuffed and nuzzled her. She shed a few tears into his mane then dashed them away when Pa came in to do the milking.

∽

It was the ache in his head that woke Peter more than the fact he was comfortable for the first time in months. He raised his hand to his head then opened his eyes when it came in contact with a bandage. The images around him were blurry at first, and he blinked to clear his vision. It was dark outside, and the low lamplight glowed softly over the room. He was in a bed with clean sheets and, judging from the feel of the cloth against his skin, clean clothes as well. Raising himself up on one elbow, he tried to look beyond the edge of the soft pools of light. The room was small but nicely furnished. So much so, he wondered if he was back in Pittsburgh. As his eyes adjusted, he could just make out a man's form in a chair near the foot of the bed. His heart started and he spoke without thinking. "Granddad?"

The man chuckled. "No, I'm not quite that old."

"I'm sorry," Peter said.

"Don't be; I'm sure to be called that someday, just not quite yet." He leaned into the light. Round spectacles sat on a slender face, which the lines of age were clearly beginning to march across. His dark blond Van Dyke beard and mustache were shot with a generous amount of gray, as was his hair, which was swept back and to the side. He had a reassuring smile on his face. "I'm Professor Daniel Kirby. Who might you be?"

"Peter," he replied then looked down at the bedclothes. "Peter. . .Ward." He'd dispensed with his real name long ago, but it still felt strange saying the new one aloud. Ward had been his father's last name. The way Peter saw things, it was time the man who sired him contributed something to his life, seeing how he'd never wanted anything to do with him while he was growing up.

The professor was silent for a moment. "I see. We'll let that be for now. What do you remember?"

Peter closed his eyes against the onslaught of memories the question evoked. One foolish decision had made him utterly homeless, and he'd been tramping his way around three different states in as many months. He'd gained a few friends as he eked out an existence, but it was still a lonely and often dangerous way of life. He remembered hopping a boxcar in Cincinnati and drifting off to sleep. The next thing he knew, he heard yelling and felt hands taking hold of him. "I remember being pulled off the train by a group of boys. They forced me to run between two rows of them while they tried to hit me with sticks." He could feel the lump on his head through the bandage. "I guess I didn't do too well."

Professor Kirby nodded. "It's called a 'timber lesson,' an education young boys and—I'm sad to say—some grown men like to give tramps." He shook his head. "It all comes from too much freedom in the home. Boys raised like that seldom end well." Peter winced slightly, and the professor, his face full of concern, asked, "Are you in pain?"

"No, not really." The truth of those words had stung, though. In the past months, he'd been forced to look his own lack of guidance square in the eye.

"The Lord was surely looking after you today. It had to have been His hand that guided my colleague, Professor Townshend, and me to pass that alley when we did. We put a stop to it, but not before you took quite a blow to the head." The professor stood and gently forced Peter to lay back. "Professor Townshend also happens to be a medical doctor. He says you should stay in bed for a few days."

"Then, I suppose, you'll send me off to the poorhouse." Sighing, he laid his arm over his eyes. He'd spent one night in a poorhouse and swore never to do so again. He'd been shocked to see people placed in such deplorable conditions just because they were poor.

"No."

The professor's decisive tone surprised Peter, and he lifted his arm to look at him. His face was just as firm as his voice had been.

"I'm curious about your clothes." Professor Kirby nodded to where they lay, across the back of a chair next to the bed.

Peter's heart began to pound. They were worn and dirty, but not nearly enough for someone not to see their quality.

"The sack suit jacket seems appropriate enough. But where does a man like you get such finely made shirt and pants?"

Peter swallowed and looked away. He already liked this man and didn't want to lie to him. But how could he tell him the truth? Meeting his eyes, he settled for partial truth. "I didn't steal them."

There was a pause, then Professor Kirby nodded. "I believe you." His gaze dropped and Peter just made out what he said next. "Looking at you, how can I not?" With a slight shake, he roused himself, raised his eyes, and smiled slightly. "We'll leave the other mysteries about you for later. It's late, and you should rest."

"Sir?"

The professor looked back as he opened the door.

"Where am I?"

"You're in my home. On the grounds of The Ohio State University in Columbus, Ohio. Try to sleep now." The door closed quietly behind him.

But Peter lay awake. How would he explain the mysteries about himself to this man who had so kindly taken him in, at least for the moment?

"Too much freedom in the home."

The words echoed in the walls of his heart, their truth tearing at him. Being forced to beg for food and shelter had humbled him considerably. He'd come to see how spoiled he was. Earning your food was much different from having it set in front of you by a servant every night. No wonder Granddad had been angrier about Uncle Randall's cuts in the workers' wages than about the money McCord Steel had lost under his uncle's care. He'd seen more than his share of youngsters homeless because their families couldn't afford to feed them. Saddest of all were those who couldn't hold a job because something was wrong with them—their mind or body had been injured and work wasn't possible.

As Hiram McCord's grandson, he'd always thought himself too good to have to earn his keep. He didn't think that way now. His uncle had been right, at least on that score: high time he earned his way in the world. The irony of it all was now that he wanted to work, he couldn't find a job—one look at him and no one wanted to hire him. The professor was the first person in a long time to see the man, not the tramp.

"The Lord was surely looking after you today."

Professor Kirby was clearly a man of faith. He said those words as if he'd been speaking of a friend. If anyone would be willing to help him find an honest job, it was him. He just hoped he wouldn't have to tell the professor any more about his past than necessary. At least he'd believed him when Peter said he hadn't stolen the clothes.

He found the man's faith curious. Peter had never met someone who actually followed what the Bible commanded. He certainly hadn't done so, nor had anyone else in his acquaintance. For appearance's sake, Granddad had made him go to church every week without fail, and as a result, he'd taken to seeing God as nothing more than someone he had to listen to once a week. As sleep finally began to melt over him, he wondered if there might be more to God than just that.

Chapter 3

"You've decided to keep the beard."

Peter looked up from his breakfast to find Dr. Kirby scrutinizing him. It had been a week and a half since he'd been brought to the professor's home. He was up and about now, and although he'd made some changes to himself, the beard hadn't been one of them.

"Mrs. Werner tried to get me to shave it again this morning, but I told her I've decided to keep it." He smiled, remembering the housekeeper's less than enthusiastic reaction.

"I'm a little. . .surprised," the professor replied. "I never liked having a beard when I was your age."

Peter thought he sounded disappointed. In all honesty, he'd have rather been clean shaven, but the thought that his uncle might be looking for him was enough to decide otherwise.

"At least I look a little more presentable now. I can't imagine why you bothered with me, looking as I did." He'd been shocked to see himself in the mirror a few days ago when Mrs. Werner gave him a trim. His hair and beard had grown considerably in the three months he'd been on the road. "I must've looked like a wild man."

"You were still a man, Peter. And in God's eyes, you were worth the bother. Don't you remember our discussion about Zacchaeus, yesterday?"

Peter nodded. That, and many other discussions, had been born out of his attempt to keep all conversation away from himself. Professor Kirby had been only too happy to talk about God, but Peter sensed he saw through his ploy. While that, indeed, may have been his plan at first, by his second or third day in bed, Peter began to feel a hunger for God he hadn't known before. The professor's kindness tapped something in his heart, and he drank up all the professor told him and eagerly read the Bible he'd loaned him.

"It doesn't matter who you are in man's eyes. God looks at the heart." Dr. Kirby's expression grew wistful. "That was one of my wife's favorite verses. First Samuel 16:7: 'For man looketh on the outward appearance, but the Lord looketh on the heart.'"

Peter watched him, concerned. While he'd managed to reveal little about himself, Dr. Kirby shared much about himself and his family. He still felt keenly his wife's death over a year ago. "Professor? Are you all right?"

"I was blessed to have my Katherine for the years I did." Dr. Kirby roused himself. "She's with God now, celebrating the decision you made a few days ago."

Peter smiled. His second day out of bed had been fine, and he and the professor went for a walk. Dr. Kirby led them alongside a spring until they came to what the student body called simply the Lake, nestled in a tree-lined vale. On its shores, their conversation turned quite serious. And Peter decided to clothe himself with Christ.

But his excitement of feeling right with God was dampened because he couldn't bring himself to tell Dr. Kirby his whole story. He couldn't bear the thought of the disappointment in the doctor's eyes when he told him about the ugly person he had once been. He could hardly think of it himself. Maybe it would be best if he moved on as quickly as possible. But how? He didn't have a job. He didn't even own the clothes he now wore. He looked at the professor.

"Thank you for giving me these clothes, sir. I'll return them to you when my own are clean."

"Keep them. I insist."

Peter bit his lip. However much had been spent on him, he was determined to pay back.

They finished their breakfast, or rather, Peter did. Professor Kirby had been eating until he mentioned his wife. After that he'd allowed the rest to grow cold, between reading the *Columbus Dispatch* and staring out the window. He revived somewhat when he discovered Peter intended to spend time reading his Bible and invited him into the library.

"Classes will begin soon, and I have lecture notes and lessons to review. It will be nice to have company for a change."

The library connected to the parlor through a set of sliding doors, which were open. While the professor settled behind his desk, Peter found himself drawn to the pictures on the oak mantel.

"Are these of your family, sir?"

"Yes," Dr. Kirby replied. "Please, feel free to look at them."

The first was a photograph of two young people, only a few years younger than he. "Are these your children?"

"Yes. Rebecca and Joseph. She's married and lives in Cincinnati. My son is in college—in Maine."

Noting the slight pause, Peter looked closely at Joseph. Was his relationship with the professor strained? He thought better of asking, especially after noticing the pensive look that crossed the professor's face before he turned his attention to the papers before him.

The next pictured a lovely dark-haired woman sitting on a chair, the professor standing behind her. It was, without a doubt, a picture of him and his wife, taken several years ago. They both looked so young. Peter now understood, if only a little, Professor Kirby's pain. The look of kind serenity on Katherine Kirby's face was enough to assume she must have been a gentle and gracious woman. In some hazy way, she reminded him of his own mother. He had vague memories of her having that same sweet look on her face, and dark hair as well. Peter moved to the next picture, and his eyes widened at the vision.

It would be nothing short of an insult to call the young woman merely pretty, at least to Peter's way of thinking. As far as he was concerned, she was the most beautiful thing he had ever seen. The black and white photograph made it impossible to tell exactly the color of her hair, but her ringlets shone smooth, and her large eyes were lively above a small, straight nose and pert mouth. The more he looked at her, the more fascinated he became, and he immediately began to plan how to win her over. Every girl was different. Some required gifts, others responded to effusive compliments. He'd even attended a temperance meeting in order to win one young lady's affections. Some girls were hard to crack, and some were ridiculously easy, but one way or another, they always laid their hearts at his feet. Certainly, she would be no different.

"That's my niece, Anne."

He started but covered it by quickly turning his head toward the professor. "Your brother's daughter?" He hoped he spoke loudly enough to drown out the pounding of his heart.

"Yes, that's him in the next picture over."

Peter turned to see the professor's wedding picture. Two other men were in the photograph besides Dr. Kirby. One smiled jovially, the other looked angry and surly. Just as he was hoping the pleasant man was the young lady's father, the professor spoke again. "I'm sorry he looks so cross. Jonah didn't feel himself that day."

Peter's heart now pounded twice as hard. He took another look at Jonah Kirby, feeling sure the man somehow knew what he'd been thinking about his daughter. He looked down at the stonework on the fireplace, guilt bearing down on him like a steel beam. How could he think that way about the professor's niece, or any young lady for that matter? Hadn't his near miss with Letty taught him anything? And on the road, how many times had he watched men charm young women into committing deplorable things for them? His thoughts added more weight to the guilt he already felt. He should be ashamed of the way he'd treated the fairer sex. Letty included.

"They'll be arriving next week." Peter almost didn't hear the words. He looked up as they fully registered.

"They will?"

"My niece is coming here to live with me. She'll work in the university library." He rose and joined him at the mantel. "Their arrival brings me to something I wanted to discuss with you." Apprehension must have shown on Peter's face because Dr. Kirby smiled and patted him on the shoulder. "Don't look so alarmed; I have no intention of putting you out. Quite the opposite." He took his arm. "Let me show you something."

Peter followed the professor through the dining room and kitchen, and out the back door. They walked to the northwest corner of the fenced lot, where a brand-new stable had been erected.

"My brother has been taking care of my horse, Scioto, while the university had this built." Dr. Kirby opened the door, and they walked in. As Peter breathed in the smell of fresh wood, straw, and feed, a host of other memories assailed his thoughts. A deep longing for his own stables rose in his heart. But he quickly dashed it against the hard fact that his love of horses had cost him dearly. *"Remember the racing park in Pittsburgh? You wouldn't be homeless now if you hadn't placed all your money on that 'sure thing.'"*

"Jonah will bring Scioto with him when he brings my niece," the professor said. "I'd like for you to stay and take care of him. I don't know what your background with horses is, but I was brought up on a farm, and I'm more than willing to teach you all I know."

Peter took in the hopeful look on the professor's face and then looked around the stable. The offer was the chance he'd been hoping for; a job that would pay wages, giving him the ability to earn his keep. But, considering his past, could he trust himself to take it?

∞

Anne was worried about her uncle.

As they sat at the breakfast table, she couldn't help noticing that, once again, he'd ignored the food Mrs. Werner prepared. Oatmeal, eggs on toast, and the remainder of her mother's strudel remained untouched. The oatmeal's presence meant Mrs. Werner worried about him as well. She had to have gotten up quite early to make it. Coffee was all he'd consumed between reviewing notes for his first class and reading the *Dispatch*. She eyed the strudel, truly surprised he hadn't taken even a bite. It was one of his favorites. Ma had sent it with her, having made it specifically for him. But in the few days since she arrived, Anne had eaten most of it.

Since her aunt's death, he hadn't been the same, but she didn't recall him behaving quite like this. She used to see her uncle more often, when he lived just east of the farm in Delaware and taught at Ohio Wesleyan. Since starting at The Ohio State University, contact between him and her family was limited to weekly letters and holiday visits, and he'd always seemed reasonably cheerful. Over his shoulder, she caught a glimpse of Mrs. Werner opening the kitchen door a crack. Anne shook her head, and the housekeeper, pressing her lips together, returned to the kitchen. Anne rose from her seat and took up her dishes.

"Can I get you more coffee, Uncle Daniel?"

He looked up from his notes and smiled. "No, thank you, Anne. You can take my dishes. I'm finished."

She looked at him reprovingly. "Uncle Daniel, you haven't eaten anything."

"I'm not very hungry this morning."

Anne sighed and set all the dishes on the tray Mrs. Werner had left on the side table. She lifted it and carefully backed her way through the swinging door leading to the kitchen.

"He will waste away to nothing if he keeps eating so." Mrs. Werner took the tray from Anne. " 'Tis true he never ate much since I came to work for him, just after Mrs. Kirby died, God rest her soul, but since young Mr. Ward left—"

"Mr. Ward? Who's he?"

"Ah, I thought he had told you about him. A week before you arrived, Dr. Kirby went into town with Professor Townshend. They happened upon this young man being beaten in an alley and brought him back here." She washed the dishes, and Anne dried them with a dishcloth.

"Why was he being beaten?"

"He was a tramp. Some young boys thought it was good sport."

"How barbaric! Was he badly hurt?"

"No, although Dr. Townshend did have him stay in bed for about a week. Dr. Kirby took a shine to him though. Spoke to him about the good Lord, and young Peter took it to heart." Mrs. Werner handed Anne the last plate and wiped her wet hands on her apron. "He offered him a job looking after his horse, but Peter turned him down. Ever since he left, Dr. Kirby's been distracted and melancholy."

Anne's brow furrowed as she put the dried dish in the cupboard. "That's odd. Did my uncle say why he turned the offer down?"

"No, but he had the coloring of your cousin, Joseph." She gave Anne a knowing look.

It made sense now. Her cousin was one of the reasons Uncle Daniel decided to teach at the university. Joseph had decided to attend the university, but just a few months before he was to start, Aunt Kitty passed away. He'd abruptly decided to switch schools and instead left Ohio to attend Bowdoin College in Maine. Her uncle missed his son dearly.

Anne sighed. "Well, Mrs. Werner, let's give him some time. Maybe my being here will help."

The housekeeper nodded. "I surely hope so." She handed Anne a cloth-covered basket. "You'll be eating lunch with him, I expect. See what you can do about getting him to eat."

Anne smiled. "I'll do my best." She set the basket on the counter. "I think I'll have a better chance if I add the strudel." She carefully wrapped the pastry with a piece of paper left over from packing their basket. "So what are you going to do with your morning off, Mrs. Werner?"

"I intend to visit my sister-in-law down in the south part of the city."

"That's a long walk; I hope you'll be careful."

"Oh, me old legs couldn't stand walking that far. I'll take the streetcar."

Anne glanced up, her interest piqued. "Columbus has streetcars?"

"Aye, horse-drawn, they are. They run along High Street, from

Dodridge to the north to well past Broad Street. The last stop is near City Park, right where I'll be getting off."

Anne smiled. "Well that's good to know." *Yes*, she thought, *that* is *good to know.*

"It's not fast, mind you, and it smells something awful if your seat's in the wrong spot, but it's certainly better than walking."

"Anne?" Uncle Daniel poked his head in. "Are you ready? Neither of us should be late on the first day." He smiled at Mrs. Werner. "Thank you for breakfast this morning."

Mrs. Werner opened her mouth to say something just as his head disappeared. "That man!"

Anne laughed. "I'll make him eat something at lunch, I promise."

Basket in hand, Anne walked to the front hall where her uncle waited for her. She eyed the hall clock. "I thought you said we were late."

"If we're to take a trip out to the stable first, we'll need extra time."

"I should have known," she said, taking his arm.

"I'd ask you if you mind, but I know better," Daniel said as they walked. "You didn't think your Pa wouldn't tell me the regard you have for my horse, now, did you?"

"Of course not." Anne sighed. "He told you to keep me out of the stable, didn't he?"

He stopped and looked at her. "He told me some other things as well. I'm very sorry, Anne."

She felt him squeeze her hand where it sat in the crook of his arm. "Pa's hoping I'll make a match down here and forget about what happened."

"Is that what you want?"

Yes nearly escaped her lips. "I don't know if I'll ever really forget."

"I can understand that. Pain can leave a lasting and bitter aftertaste." His eyes sobered, then he smiled gently. "I know my brother. He wants what's best for you. And so does God. Trust them."

Anne tugged on his arm, trying to maintain a peaceful countenance. They walked on in silence for several moments.

"If you don't mind my asking," Uncle Daniel said, "all other matters aside, did you enjoy teaching?"

Anne smiled. When she decided to get a teaching certificate, her uncle had been delighted and given her every encouragement. Taking a breath, she tried to soften how she really felt as best she could. "I don't know. It wasn't awful. But I didn't enjoy it as much as I enjoyed working with our animals when I was younger. I can't remember liking anything better than that." She looked at him in wide-eyed apology. "I'm sorry."

He chuckled and patted her hand. "Don't be, but I can't imagine you'll enjoy the library much better."

"I know." Her uncle's house sat close to High Street, and she caught a glimpse of a streetcar going past. Her true reason for taking the library job twisted her heart so much it was hard to form her next words. "But it's only for a few months."

"True, I had forgotten Miss Fuller hopes to return from her convalescence just before the spring term starts." He squeezed her hand again, and she turned back to him. "You're always welcome to visit Scioto. I'll be praying for you."

When they reached the stable, Uncle Daniel opened the door for her, and she immediately saw Scioto at his stall door. He grunted as they walked over to him. Daniel stroked his horse's neck, reminding Anne of how her uncle used to be before Aunt Kat died. She scratched the horse's withers, noticing he hadn't yet been groomed. She looked in Scioto's feed bin to see if he had finished eating. It certainly appeared he had; so why wasn't Ben brushing him down? She'd always groomed him just after he ate. She was about to say something to her uncle when the young stable hand appeared.

"Good morning, Professor Kirby, Miss Kirby," he said with a smile.

Anne nodded, and her uncle quickly turned to him. "How has he been spending the night?"

"Very well, sir, I hardly ever hear him."

"Is he behaving better for you now?"

"Yes, sir. He's a little less fractious now that we've gotten to know each other a little."

Uncle Daniel chuckled. "I'm afraid he's always been like that. With the exception of my niece here and. . .my late wife, he's never taken well to new people."

"I was just getting ready to let him out in the paddock awhile."

"If you don't mind, I'll lead him out," Uncle Daniel said eagerly. He took the lead from Ben and snapped it onto Scioto's halter.

Anne laid her hand on Ben's arm before he could follow Scioto and her uncle. "Ben, I was wondering something about Scioto—"

"Don't worry, Miss Kirby," he said quickly. "I'll take real good care of him."

Remembering how Pa had told her to stay out of Ben's way, she nodded. "Of course you will."

She watched him join her uncle. She truly hoped Ben would take care of Scioto, considering how attached her uncle was to his horse. But Ben was young—seventeen—and a little too eager to please and prove himself. She shook her head. Scioto's daily care wasn't her responsibility any longer. People had different ways of doing things. Perhaps Ben didn't see the point in grooming him until after Scioto had been exercised. She hoped he would remember. Scioto trotted around the perimeter of the paddock before loping over to Uncle Daniel. He smiled and gave him a final pat.

"I'll be back, old boy." He shook Ben's hand then joined Anne. She watched his face lengthen a little, and she mustered a cheerful smile as she took his arm.

"We can come back this evening and spend more time with him," she suggested as they made their way back to the front of the house.

He shook his head. "We won't have time, I'm afraid. If you recall, Dr. Townshend invited us to his home tonight. He's sending a carriage for us." He glanced back at his horse. "I'd have Scioto take us, but he's still getting used to it here, and I haven't gotten a new buggy yet."

"Then we'll visit him tomorrow morning."

He nodded slowly, and Anne decided she would make sure Ben took proper care of her uncle's horse. Promise or no, she couldn't stand to think of the melancholy Uncle Daniel would sink into should something happen to Scioto.

Chapter 4

"I thought four o'clock would never get here!"

Anne smiled at Emma's exclamation as the young assistant librarian closed the door. It had been an exhausting first day. Never had she imagined that working at the library would be so similar to teaching, at least regarding discipline. She'd spent a great deal of the day attempting to keep the students quiet and the young men from propping their feet up on the windowsills and tables. At one point, when a young lady had fetched them to help get some reference material, several young men had situated their feet on the shelves such that it was impossible to access the tome she required. Some had actually removed books from the shelves and set them aside to make room for their feet. They hadn't bothered to replace them. Anne and Emma now took up the numerous volumes sitting about and began to reshelve them.

Anne looked around as they worked. She couldn't help but admire the library's new home on the third floor of the Main Building. She'd been told the room used to belong to the botanical department. They had moved upon the completion of their own building, opening up this space. It was a large room with elegant wooden columns running down the middle. The smell of fresh wood still hung in the air from the newly built shelves, and broad tables for students to work at stood in neat rows. Anne sighed as she looked at all the books stacked on them now. The library seemed to have so many volumes already, and yet Emma had told her the university intended to acquire more!

She looked at the sunshine dancing in from one of the windows, longing to step outside. There hadn't been one opportunity to do so all day, not even at lunchtime, since Uncle Daniel's office was just down the hall. When she had been teaching, she'd always made it a habit to step outside for at least a few minutes during the day.

Emma set down a stack of books at the sound of a knock at the door. "I'll bet that's that engineering student, begging to be let back in for just one more peek at a book." Her huff poofed up her brown fringe of curly bangs. "I'll shoo him back to his dormitory."

Anne chuckled as she took an armful of books to where they belonged. She heard Emma open the door, but judging from the tone of her voice, it must not have been him. The door closed, and a moment or two later when she returned to the study tables for more books, Emma was there.

"Mike Dixon, the university janitor, sent his assistant over to check the gas pipes before cold weather sets in," she said, taking up a stack of books. "He won't be but a few minutes."

Anne nodded and took up a particularly large book. She walked over to its shelf only to find that she was too short to put it back where it belonged. She grimaced in disgust, wishing yet again she were a respectable height. "Emma, do we have a step stool?"

"It's back in the corner, near the science shelf. Sorry it's tucked away, but I hardly ever use it."

Anne sighed. Of course Emma didn't use it. She was at least four inches taller than Anne. She walked over to the corner and spied the stool. She was so intent on fetching it and getting back to work, she didn't notice the janitor's assistant working close by. She knelt down and grasped it, barely moving it an inch before she shrieked. A spider scurried out and sat on the wooden floor, all too close to the hem of her skirt. Anne froze in fear. The vile thing was the size of a large walnut and just as black. The sound of Emma calling her name began to register in her mind as a brown boot came out of nowhere, crushing the spider. She gasped and looked up into a pair of emerald eyes. Their owner offered his hand. "Are you all right?"

She reached out a shaky hand and felt his fingers fold over her own. Somehow their warmth helped steady her racing heart as he helped her to her feet. Emma popped out from between the shelves and hurried over. "Anne, are you all right? What happened?"

"A spider gave her a fright." The quiet manner in which the man said it gratified Anne. Most thought her fear of spiders silly. He lifted his boot and gently squeezed her hand as she looked away in revulsion.

Emma's face registered disgust as well, and she shuddered.

"I'll clean this up, Miss Long," he said, handing Anne off to Emma.

She found herself releasing his hand reluctantly and couldn't help but look back at him as Emma gently grasped her by the elbow. His voice sounded young, but his full beard and mustache made her wonder if he was much older. He knelt down, took out a handkerchief, and wiped up the remains of the spider. "Thank you," she said, hoping to catch sight of his green eyes once more. But they remained focused on his task, and he simply nodded.

∞

Peter's heart raced. She wouldn't have been hurt, of course; wolf spiders weren't poisonous, but the sight of them was anything but pleasant. What set his heart at such a pace was his first sight of Anne Kirby.

He'd known when he'd taken the job working for Mr. Dixon he might cross paths with Professor Kirby's niece. He just hadn't expected it to happen so soon or in such a way. Normally he would have caught the spider and let it go, but the look of fright on her face compelled him to crush the thing.

And he certainly hadn't expected her to be even more beautiful in person. Her small build, porcelain skin, and ginger-red hair made her look just like one of the china dolls he'd seen in the shops back in Pittsburgh.

Stop it, he told himself sharply. She wasn't a toy for him to play with, but a person. He tried to reinforce that thought in his mind by remembering the fear in her brown doe eyes and how shaky her hand had been as he helped her to her feet. Peter shook his head. Thinking of her like that didn't help either.

He wadded up his handkerchief and, not seeing a trash can handy, placed it in his pocket. He'd shake it out and wash it later. He finished his work, placed the tools Mr. Dixon had given him in their bag, and slipped out the door. He struggled to push thoughts of Miss Kirby from his mind as he made his way over the gravel walkway to the new botany building.

Setting his jaw, he tried to go over the list of things Mr. Dixon wanted him to check, but all he heard was her soft voice, thanking him, making it hard to concentrate. Why had he helped her to her feet? He still felt the gentle pressure of her fingers on his. Peter was so focused on his thoughts, he bumped into someone as he walked.

"Hey, watch where you're going!"

"Sorry," he said. He began to move on when someone grabbed his arm. Frowning, Peter turned to see a dark-haired man a few years older than him. Another man stood beside him, thumbs in his suspenders.

"Who are you? What do you think you're doing with that bag?"

His superior tone sparked Peter's temper, but he managed to answer civilly. "I'm Peter Ward, the janitor's assistant. Mr. Dixon gave me this bag this morning."

"No, I know all the fellas Mike uses as assistants," he said. "I've never seen you before."

Peter noticed the man with the suspenders looked at him with a glimmer of recognition in his eyes and was instantly on his guard. Had he been sent by his uncle? He quickly decided to be on his way.

"Well, I'm new. Now if you two gentlemen will excuse me—"

The first man grabbed his arm. "Whoa! How about this guy? Us 'two gentlemen'? Pretty fancy talk for a janitor."

Suspenders gave him a hard look. "Mike said he was going to hire me for fall term. Why'd he hire you, fancy-pants?"

Peter narrowed his eyes, sorely tempted to give them the fight they sought, but held back. He needed this job and the anonymity it provided. Gently but firmly, he freed his arm. "I have to go. Mr. Dixon has things for me to do."

Scowls crossed their faces, and Peter steeled himself for a fight just as Mike Dixon walked up.

"There you are, Pete. I've been looking for you." He caught sight of the men. "Hello there, Frank. What are you and Harvey up to?"

"I brought Harvey by like you said." Frank pointed to the man with the suspenders.

"What's with this guy?" Harvey jabbed his finger toward Peter.

Peter worked his jaw but kept his mouth shut.

Mike sighed and stepped up to him. "I'm sorry, Harvey. Pete really needed a job. He's been out of work for a while."

"Then why doesn't Mr. Cope know about him? We just saw him a few minutes ago, and he didn't think you'd hired anyone yet."

"He will. I'm going to tell the board at their next meeting."

"You never did that before," Frank said. "You always told them before you hired anyone."

"There wasn't time. This came up at the last minute." Peter looked at him. Mike sounded like he'd hired him only yesterday. He'd been working a couple of weeks now.

Harvey glared at him. "I need a job, Mike."

"I'm sorry, but I don't have the funds for you."

"Yes you do," Frank said. "The university always gives you enough for two extra men fall term."

"Well, not this year."

Frank frowned and shook his head at Harvey. His face scrunched up like that of a sulky schoolboy, and Peter choked back a laugh. "You just don't want to hire me do you?"

"To be honest, I can't say I've ever heard good things about you," Mike said. "I'm sorry."

Both men glared at Mike for one long, tense moment. Peter hoped it wouldn't come to blows but was ready to help if his boss needed him.

"Fine." Harvey said finally. "Let's go, Frank." The two veered off the gravel path, stomping through the newly cut grass.

Mike shook his head. "Jack will need to rake that now," he said, referring to the groundskeeper.

"Who's Mr. Cope?" Peter asked.

"The secretary to the board of trustees," he replied. "Don't worry. I've worked here since '78. I'm sure they won't mind me hiring someone without their approval. They've never refused anyone before, even someone like Harvey Pryce." He pointed his thumb in the direction the men had gone. "Come on, let's finish up in the botany building and get dinner."

An hour or so later, Peter and Mike sat down to eat in Mike's log cabin, which stood on university grounds. It had been there since before the university's founding, and when the state bought up the land, the cabin had been deeded over to the institution. Mike said it hadn't been used until the university offered it to him just a few years ago. He'd installed a potbellied stove, which Peter now stood over, frying up some ham for them both.

"You sure took to the cooking real quick," Mike said as Peter slid meat onto his plate. "It's kind of hard to believe you'd never done it before."

"Well, not over a stove. I learned to cook a lot of things over an open fire." Peter put another slab of ham in the cast-iron skillet.

"So you really were a tramp, huh?"

"Not by choice," he replied with a half smile.

"If you don't mind me asking, just where are you originally from?"

Peter looked at his boss a moment before answering, then laughed at himself for hesitating. Mike Dixon, a kind and simple man, was by no means stupid but hardly a Pinkerton agent working undercover. "Pittsburgh."

Mike nodded. "Never been there; heard about it though. Those steel mills sure put out a lot of smoke, I hear."

Peter bent to tend to the fire in the stove, hiding a small smile as he did so. "Yeah, they sure do."

He carried the skillet to the table and slid his meat onto his plate then returned it to the stove. He sat down next to Mike. The older man worded a small prayer before they started on their meal.

"Did you get to the pipes in the Main Building?" Mike asked as they ate.

"Yes I did, Mr. Dixon."

The man rolled his eyes. "Son, do me a favor. *Please* call me Mike. Even the students call me that."

Peter smiled. "All right."

It would be odd, though. Mr. Dixon—Mike—was several years older than he. Granddad may have given him free rein in most areas, but he'd insisted Peter respect his elders.

"Everything in the Main Building seemed fine," he said.

"You checked the new library, too?" Peter nodded, and Mike smiled in approval. "Good. It won't do for students to catch cold while they're studying, not to mention those young ladies who work so hard keeping that place looking nice." He shot Peter a grin. "Did you get a chance to meet them? They're just about your age."

"Ah—yes. Miss Long introduced herself. I didn't get the other young lady's name." It was true. He'd been too busy cleaning up that spider.

"She's Professor Kirby's niece, I hear. They're pretty girls, too."

Peter smiled at the look the man gave him. "I've got too much to do right now to think about things like that."

Mike's eyebrows shot up. "Well that's a surprise. But I suppose I understand. Never did decide to get married myself. A lot of fuss, women.

Not that I don't appreciate them. Just seems easier to be on your own, you know?"

"Yeah," Peter said thoughtfully. All those days of chasing Pittsburgh's eligible young ladies came back to him. He'd never been serious about any of them. For one reason or another, none of them seemed right—too tall, too short, too something. Or had that been just an excuse? He pushed the ham around on his plate with his fork. Not all of them had been like that. He could have fallen in love with at least one or two if he'd allowed himself. Well, those days were over now. He'd told the truth a moment ago. He was too busy to be thinking about courting someone. He didn't intend to try ever again. But even as he made that vow, doe-like eyes and a sweet face filled his vision.

He sighed inwardly as he picked up his plate and took it over to the washtub. The whole reason he'd turned down the job with Professor Kirby was so he wouldn't be tempted to return to his old habits. And he would have if he'd stayed. Look at the way he had behaved today, acting like some sort of knight-errant. He shouldn't have allowed the professor to help him get this job with Mike, but after seeing how his refusal to work for him had disappointed the man, he hadn't had the heart. Well, at least Anne Kirby worked in the library. The chances of him seeing her again were quite slim.

Peter helped Mike clean up the dinner plates and then settled down at the table with his Bible while his boss sat and whittled. Dr. Kirby had insisted Peter keep it when he left. At the time, he'd felt bad that he couldn't pay him for the book, but at the moment he was glad. With Anne Kirby's beauty running rampant in his head, he flipped back and forth through its pages, looking for a verse on self-control. As he still wasn't familiar with it, he quickly came up empty.

Frustrated, he stopped. The pages fell open to the book of Psalms. As he idly skimmed them, the twenty-third caught his attention:

The Lord is my shepherd; I shall not want. He maketh me to lie down in green pastures: he leadeth me beside the still waters. He restoreth my soul: he leadeth me in the paths of righteousness for his name's sake.

He sat back, staring out the cabin's narrow window. It was a heartening verse and gave him hope. The idea of the Lord leading him in his new life, looking out for pitfalls along the way, made him feel more at ease. *Lord, lead me in the right path; show me where You want me to go,* he prayed. *I know with Your guidance I can throw away my past and begin again.* He was a new creation now, and that meant he should desire a whole new life, one without horses or chasing young ladies.

Chapter 5

Anne entered her room with a frown creasing her lovely features. When she and Uncle Daniel returned to the house, he'd urged her to get ready quickly, as Dr. Townshend's carriage was coming for them in less than an hour. But she hadn't been able to resist slipping out to the barn to check on Scioto. To her consternation, while the horse seemed content enough, he was wild and shaggy looking, as if he hadn't been near a brush and currycomb all day. And Ben was nowhere to be found.

Though not nearly as thorough as she would have liked, she quickly brushed him. What could Ben have been thinking? Scioto wasn't a plow horse. Uncle Daniel intended to ride him every so often and use him to convey the two of them back and forth to church. He may be an older horse, but he was still a strong animal. Professor Townshend had even brought a couple of his mares up to the farm this summer to breed with him. Anne opened the door of her room and found Mrs. Werner waiting for her.

"There you are," she exclaimed. "Dr. Kirby fetched me almost fifteen minutes ago to help you get dressed." The housekeeper frowned and crinkled her nose. "You went out in the stable, didn't you?"

"Oh no! I smell like horse, don't I?" She unbuttoned her bodice. "Maybe it's just my clothes."

Happily that was the case, and soon she stood in front of her oval mirror in her best dress. It was dark green with three-quarter sleeves. Anne smiled, remembering Pa's frown when she, Ma, and Millie had shown it to him. He hadn't quite approved of the square neckline. But Ma had been careful to make sure it was more than proper. It was actually shallower than the one on the dress she and Millie had copied from *Godey's Lady's Book*. Tears pricked her eyes as she thought how hard they'd worked, making this just for her to wear for best. She fingered the ruffles at the end of her sleeve and resolved to take special care of it. It would be a reminder of them once she was far from Ohio. Mrs. Werner began to fuss with her hair, and Anne glanced at the clock on her bed table.

"I'm not sure there's time, Mrs. Werner."

"Now, now, I'm just going to re-pin a few of these ringlets. You fluff those curly bangs of yours."

Anne did as she was told just as her uncle's voice came from behind her door. "Anne, are you ready? Dr. Townshend's carriage is here."

She escaped from the housekeeper's hands and rushed to the wardrobe to get her shoes. A small spider scrambled out as she did so, and she gasped then crushed it with one shoe.

"What is it, lass?" Mrs. Werner joined her by the wardrobe.

Anne stood with one hand across her chest, trying to still the quick leaps her heart was making. "Just a spider," she murmured.

"A spider?" Mrs. Werner smiled. "I thought you'd seen worse than that."

Anne's face reddened slightly as she slipped on her shoes. Her fear of spiders was so silly. She'd grown up on a farm, for heaven's sake. But she couldn't remember a time when she hadn't been afraid of them. A small one like that didn't affect her badly, but if it was a large one like the wolf spider she encountered in the library, fear refused to allow her to move an inch. She shuddered to think where that spider might have crawled if the janitor's assistant hadn't killed it. Her heart quickened once more as she thought of the man's green eyes and the gentle firmness of his fingers squeezing hers. He'd been so kind and gallant. *Stop that. None of that for you, remember?*

"Anne?" Her uncle's voice came from the bottom of the stairs this time, and she quickly took her wrap and reticule from Mrs. Werner. She had every intention of explaining why she was late as her uncle hurried her out the door, when she saw a young man she didn't recognize sitting in the carriage. She'd have to wait to talk to her uncle about Ben.

"Good evening, Patrick," Uncle Daniel said as he helped Anne climb up. "I'm sorry we're a little late."

Anne settled into the rear seat and took in the young man who sat opposite her. He was handsome with blond hair and a mustache, and he wore a sack suit and bowler hat. Uncle Daniel settled in next to her. She looked at him expectantly.

"Ah yes, I forgot you two aren't yet acquainted," he said as the carriage lurched forward. "Mr. Howard, this is my niece, Miss Anne Kirby. Anne, Mr. Patrick Howard, one of Dr. Townshend's students."

"I'm pleased to meet you, Mr. Howard."

He tipped his hat and shot her a charming smile. "The pleasure is mine, Miss Kirby. I hope you'll enjoy yourself tonight. The rest of us are looking forward to meeting you."

Curious, Anne glanced at her uncle.

"Oh yes," he said. "I forgot to mention there would be a few upperclassmen there as well." His eyebrows rose along with the right corner of his mouth.

Anne bit the inside of her lip. Uncle Daniel had led her to believe the other dinner guests were limited to the faculty and their wives. Clearly, Pa had gotten him to promise more than just limiting her time in the stable. Her eyes slid back to Mr. Howard, and taking a deep breath, she smiled politely. "Are you a farmer, Mr. Howard?"

"My family owns a dairy farm near Lodi. I hope to become a veterinary surgeon."

"Mr. Howard is a senior this year, Anne," her uncle said. "He'll be graduating at the top of his class."

"Well, I hope to," the young man replied humbly. "I understand your family lives in Ostrander, Miss Kirby."

The three of them chatted the rest of the way to Professor Townshend's home at the edge of the university's grounds. As they pulled up, Anne looked at the cozy home with no small amount of trepidation. The evening would be difficult for her if the rest of the young men at the party were as nice as Patrick Howard. She thought coming to the university to work would be easier than this. She had only been here a week and she seemed to be surrounded by eligible men. If only she were an eligible young woman. As Mr. Howard helped her alight, he held the same hand the janitor's assistant had grasped. The memory of his green eyes and gallant actions caused her to sigh.

"Are you all right, Miss Kirby?" Mr. Howard asked.

"Yes, of course." She accepted the arm he offered.

At least there, she was safe. She couldn't possibly see much of him in the future. Besides, he had to be much older than her, and married with about a dozen children. She couldn't help but envy his wife. If he was half so gallant at home, she was a blessed woman.

It was an animated dinner. There were Dr. and Mrs. Townshend and their two daughters, Alice and Harriet; Professors Lazenby, Tuttle, and Orton, and their wives; and five male students, including Mr. Howard. It came as no small surprise when she found herself surrounded by them after dinner when the party retired to the parlor after they ate.

"So what do you think of The OSU?" one of them asked her. He had been introduced as George Smart, a philosophy major and editor-in-chief of *The Lantern*, the university paper.

"*The* OSU?" she asked with a smile.

"Surely your uncle told you we are *The* Ohio State University."

"Yes, but I'm not sure why."

"The board of trustees decided that our original name, the Ohio Agricultural and Mechanical College, wasn't a broad enough name for our institution. After all, more is taught here than agriculture and mechanical engineering. Calling us 'The Ohio State University' fulfills that idea and sets us apart from the other colleges in Ohio."

"Be careful, Mr. Smart. Pride goeth before destruction. . . ," Anne warned.

"You think there's something wrong in being proud of one's university, Miss Kirby?" another young man asked. Anne couldn't quite remember his name but recalled he was an arts major.

"No, but it doesn't seem very Christian to look down on the other fine institutions Ohio has to offer," she replied.

"You misunderstand me, Miss Kirby." Mr. Smart smiled. "None of us look down on any of the other colleges here in Ohio or anywhere else." The other students murmured in assent. "We just want The OSU to be one of the best educational institutions in the country. Mark my words, one day we will be."

"I've heard the library is certainly getting us off on the right foot," Mr. Howard said. "I understand the new location in the Main Building is much larger."

"I didn't have the opportunity to see the library in the old room, but the new one is quite impressive," Anne replied.

"I'm sure your presence and hard work make it even more so." Mr. Howard smiled broadly. "I'll have to visit sometime very soon."

"Yes, Pat, with the start of the new term, I'm sure we'll all make time to visit—and often," George added.

The men nodded, and it wasn't lost on Anne that their library visits would be more than just educational in nature. She politely returned their smiles, all the while clenching her teeth, determined to politely rebuff them when the time came. She hated to have to do it. They were all very nice young men, but she wasn't what they were looking for in a wife.

Anne excused herself and joined her uncle, who was talking with Professor Townshend. "I'm glad those two mares seem to be working out," he said as she approached.

"Yes, they should foal next summer," Dr. Townshend replied. He smiled broadly at her approach. "Well, Anne, how nice to see you."

"Hello, Dr. Townshend." The professor had been with the university since its inception and a great help to her brother when he had been one of its first agricultural students.

"How is your brother?" he asked.

"Jacob is doing very well. He speaks of you often."

"I'm glad he and your father were able to attend the free lecture we gave last year."

"They went on about it for days after they returned," Anne replied. "If you'll excuse me, but were you and my uncle talking about the two mares you brought to the farm to breed with Scioto a few months ago?"

"Yes, we were," Uncle Daniel replied. He gave her a warning look, but she ignored it in her enthusiasm to find out about the mares' condition.

"I would love to see them foal when the time comes," she said eagerly.

"Really?" Anne turned to see Patrick Howard standing behind her, his eyebrows raised. "That can be a rather distressing sight, Miss Kirby."

Seeing a way of getting rid of at least one potential suitor, she went on. "I don't think I'd find it distressing in the least, Mr. Howard."

"Oh, you don't?"

Relief shot through her as the puzzled look on the young man's face told her she had hit her mark. But it evaporated when her uncle looked reprovingly at her. Dr. Townshend quickly changed the subject and began to discuss the hopes he and Professor Lazenby had for the relatively new agricultural experiment station.

Later it wasn't surprising when Patrick Howard excused himself from accompanying on their short trip home. Her uncle remained quiet as they rode, and Anne didn't pretend to not know why. She had no desire to talk about it. But the silence was stifling. Eventually she spoke just to clear it.

"I wonder if it will rain tonight," she said.

"You didn't ruin your chances with just him, you know." It was hard to see his expression in the dark, but his quiet tone painted a clear picture. "Those other four young men room in the same boardinghouse."

"I'm. . .I'm sorry, Uncle Daniel. It's just—" Tears edged her voice. She regretted what she had done, but what else could she do?

Her uncle misread her sadness and took her hand. "I'm sorry, Anne. I ambushed you tonight. But your ma and pa and I, we want to see you settled. You must at least try."

Anne dabbed at her eyes and turned the conversation around. She didn't want to make a promise she couldn't keep. "What about you, Uncle Daniel?"

"What about me?"

"You've been sad, too. Mrs. Werner told me about Mr. Ward." He still held her hand, and she squeezed it. "I'm sorry. I know you miss Joseph."

For several minutes, he said nothing, and only the crunch and hiss of the gravel under the carriage wheels and the clop of the horse's feet echoed in the background.

"I had hoped he would stay," Uncle Daniel said finally, his voice soft and distant. "It seemed like he wanted to. I don't understand why he didn't. It was like having him back again."

Anne felt tears beginning to reassert themselves and quickly swallowed them. "But Joseph will be back for Christmas, won't he? And Rebecca will be here with her husband?"

"What? Oh yes, I got a letter from each of them a few days ago. They'll be home for Christmas."

"There then, you'll have them both back for a few days at least. That's something we can both take comfort in and look forward to."

Her uncle nodded. "Yes, you're right. I guess it was a little foolish of me to pine away for the past." He sounded a little more like himself. "We both must be about 'forgetting those things which are behind, and reaching forth unto those things which are before.'"

She swallowed, her smile fading. "I'll try."

"As for me, having Scioto here now is a blessing and a comfort."

The house and stable came into view. She didn't like having to tell him about Ben now, but in light of what he just said, he needed to know. "I'm sorry I was late coming down. But I just had to slip out to see Scioto before I got dressed."

Her uncle listened quietly as she told him about his horse's condition, how she'd quickly brushed him down, and her concerns about Ben. By the time she finished, they stood on the front porch. From the light of the oil lamp shining through the parlor window, she could make out his stern expression.

"I promised your pa I would keep you from doing anything more than visiting Scioto," he said quietly. "You promised him the same. How do you know Ben wasn't out fetching something he needed? He could also have been out having his dinner."

Anne lowered her gaze. Neither of those things had occurred to her. "I'm sorry, Uncle Daniel."

"Let Ben take care of Scioto," he said gently.

∞

October, 1884

Peter walked toward the lecture room where chapel was held. The short faculty-led devotional took place every day in the Main Building at this time and was mandatory for every student. Ever since Mike had given him the task of sweeping up the room afterward, he managed to time the rest of his duties so he would arrive to catch all if not most of the service. He stood outside the door, of course. Although no one had ever discouraged him from doing so, he didn't feel right sitting in on the services.

He could hear the student choir singing as he approached, indicating that they had only just started. Taking his usual spot next to the room's double doors, he leaned himself and his broom against the wall, wondering which of the faculty would speak today. Whoever it was, he hoped they would read a passage from scripture. Many times one of the professors simply read from the writings of a renowned theologian, and once, a passage from Emerson had been read. But when a passage of the Bible was chosen, the comments afterward were always enlightening. There were still portions of the Bible that left Peter completely lost, and this was the only opportunity he had to have scripture explained to him. Mike kept close to the university on Sundays, and the day usually entailed them singing a hymn or two and reading from one of the Gospels.

The choir began another song, and Peter's mind wandered to the other tasks Mike had assigned to him today. His boss was very pleased with how well he had taken to his job. Peter seemed to have a knack for fixing things. It would appear that God had answered his prayers about His path for his life. *Then why aren't I happy about it?* He found himself still yearning to be around horses. A great number of his duties were around or near the university farm buildings. Every time he saw the horses stabled there, he felt a pang of longing and envied the students assigned to care for them.

Then there was Anne Kirby. Try as he might—pray as he might—her face was never too far from his thoughts, and he always seemed to see her somewhere, in the halls of the Main Building or walking home in the afternoon with her uncle. Even more troublesome was the sense of sadness about her. It made the urge to charm a smile back on her face even more difficult to control. Thank goodness there had never been an opportunity to speak to her again. *I'm trying to do what's right, Lord. I'm trying to walk away from my past, but I feel like a horse on the end of a lunge line, going in one big circle.* He winced. Couldn't he even pray without images of his old life crowding in?

From inside the chapel a voice began to speak, and Peter's heart gave a start as he recognized it.

" 'The Lord is my shepherd; I shall not want.' " Dr. Kirby read. "'He maketh me to lie down in green pastures: he leadeth me beside the still waters. He restoreth my soul: he leadeth me in the paths of righteousness for his name's sake. Yea, though I walk through the valley of the shadow of death, I will fear no evil: for thou art with me; thy rod and thy staff, they comfort me. Thou preparest a table before me in the presence of mine enemies: thou anointest my head with oil; my cup runneth over. Surely goodness and mercy shall follow me all the days of my life: and I will dwell in the house of the Lord forever.' "

If there was more, Peter didn't hear it. He was too much in awe of how God had just used the voice of Professor Kirby to speak to him. How could he have forgotten the promises of the Twenty-Third Psalm? *Thank You for reminding me You're still guiding me.* He was still praying when the double door opened and students began to stream from the room. Peter shook himself, and after the last of the students had exited, he entered, all eyes on the podium, upon which sat a Bible. It still lay open to Psalm 23. He was rereading the words when he heard voices.

"I had hoped the reading today would bring you comfort."

Peter turned. Professor Kirby and his niece stood near the window. Neither of them had seen him; the professor's back was to him, and Anne's eyes were lowered. She said nothing in response to her uncle, and Peter heard him let out an exasperated sigh.

"Jonah never should have allowed Sam McAllister to get away with leading you on in such a way. If I were him, I would have beat the living daylights—"

Peter quickly cleared his throat, and they both turned to him. "I'm sorry," he said. "I thought the room was empty."

Anne looked away, and a smile quickly replaced the startled look on the professor's face. He walked over to Peter and shook his hand. "Not at all. It's very good to see you."

"I didn't hear much—"

"Don't give it another thought. We should be having this conversation in a more private place. Please, allow me to introduce my niece, Anne Kirby." With reluctant steps, she joined them on the podium. "Anne, this is Peter Ward."

"Actually, we've met already," Peter said. "Sort of." Her cheeks reddened, making her look so beautiful that he forgot himself, his charm overriding all else. "Please let me know if you find any more spiders. My boot is at your service."

The professor looked at Anne with raised eyebrows. "I encountered a spider my first day at the library, Uncle Daniel," she said. "Mr. Ward was kind enough to kill it for me." His heart swelled at the little smile she bestowed on him. "Thank you again."

"Not at all," he replied. Their eyes locked for a moment, and he swore he saw something other than melancholy color in them, but it quickly vanished. He carefully closed the Bible on the podium and handed it to her.

"If I'm not mistaken, this goes with you." Their fingers brushed, and he thought he could power the whole university with the surge that the brief contact triggered. He thrust his hands in his pockets.

"If you will excuse me," Anne said. "I really should get back to the library."

"Of course," Dr. Kirby said. A gentle sort of sternness colored his voice. "We'll talk later."

She nodded and, with a final glance at Peter, left the room. He didn't realize he was still looking at the door until the professor grasped his shoulder. Words of apology sat on his tongue, but he didn't need them.

"Thank you," the professor said.

"Sir?"

"That's the first smile I've seen from her in a week. I guess you can surmise what happened to her from what you overheard."

Peter nodded. "I'll pray for her, sir." He almost regretted making that promise, but he didn't like the weariness that suddenly lined the professor's face. God would just have to help him handle whatever feelings praying for Anne evoked. He rubbed the back of his neck. "But I am sorry that I overheard your conversation. I had no idea you both were standing there."

"Don't be. Probably best that you know how shamefully she was treated so you can be clear in your prayers." The professor pulled out his pocket watch then snapped it shut. "I should go. My next class is waiting for me." He shook Peter's hand and left.

Peter retrieved his broom from the hall, and as he swept the lecture hall, he wished he could sweep away his guilt as easily. He'd never seen the other side of his actions before, never seen the condition of the hearts he'd left broken. Seeing the sadness in Miss Kirby's eyes gave him an excruciatingly clear picture. *Lord, please allow her heart to be healed of its hurts. And forgive me for ever doing to anyone what was done to her.* The words of the psalm returned to his mind. *Restore her soul.*

Chapter 6

nne climbed the stairs to the library with shaky steps. She hadn't imagined that the janitor's assistant was the same young man her uncle had helped over a month ago. Since that was clearly the case, then he certainly wasn't married. It had been easier to keep thoughts of him far from her mind when she'd imagined him with a wife and children. She stopped on the landing between the second and third floors. *It will still be easy once I go into town tomorrow.* Tomorrow was Saturday, and her uncle had a faculty meeting for a large portion of the day. If she could get by Mrs. Werner, she intended to take the streetcar into the city. She couldn't wait any longer. The prospect made her feet turn to water as she continued.

"There you are," Emma said as Anne walked back into the library. She took the Bible from her. "Are you all right?"

"Fine," Anne replied. "Those stairs can be quite a chore."

"Yes, it's taking me some time getting used to running up and down them myself."

Anne looked around the library. Shelves blocked some of her view of the room, but from what she could see and hear, it seemed empty. "I guess we better shelve some books while we have the chance." A mysterious smile formed on Emma's lips. "What?"

"Nothing," she said a little too brightly. She took the Bible from Anne. "I'll start with this. I think there are some books lying on a shelf on the far side of the room."

Anne walked between two shelves to the open area where the study tables sat. Patrick Howard sat at one of them with a mythology book lying open before him. She knew studying was not his motivation for his visit. She sighed. This was the third time in as many weeks that he'd come to the library specifically to visit her. What she had said at Dr.

Townshend's party hadn't deterred him for long. He'd clearly seen the advantage in the possibility of a wife who had no trouble seeing animals born.

She stepped back and leaned against the shelf. With the exception of Mr. Howard, she may have put off the other young men from the party, but there were certainly more where they came from. Several eligible young men had approached her since the term started. With few exceptions, the majority of them were nice, and Anne truly hated discouraging them. Each time she did so, it was a reminder that her chance to become someone's wife and helpmeet was no longer possible, the reason she'd become sad and moody over the past month. She peeked out at where Mr. Howard sat. She might as well get this one over with.

She stepped out from between the shelves, and he looked up and smiled at her.

"Good afternoon, Miss Kirby."

Anne pasted on a polite smile. "How are you today, Mr. Howard?"

"Very fine, thank you. I enjoyed your uncle's reading during chapel. It's nice hearing the Twenty-Third Psalm recited with such meaning. It was as if he were trying to give someone a bit of comfort."

Anne's smile flattened a little. "Is *Bullfinch's Mythology* required reading now for a degree in agriculture?"

Mr. Howard's face reddened. "No, it was just sitting here when I came in." He stood and walked over to her. "The weather has been very fine, lately, and I wanted to ask if you would be interested in accompanying me and some other students to Goodale Park tomorrow. I understand from your uncle you have no plans."

His invitation caused Anne to pause. Goodale Park, according to her uncle, was close to the city. Accepting might be to her advantage.

"Oh, but I'm not a student, Mr. Howard. Would the others want me along?" If she accepted too quickly, he and Uncle Daniel—who was clearly in on this—might suspect something.

"It's all upperclassmen, Miss Kirby. Seniors, mostly." Hope shone in his eyes. "Please come, we'd love to have you."

"Very well, Mr. Howard, you can count me in."

If Mr. Howard was pleased with her response, her uncle was even more so when she told him as they walked home that evening.

"I'm glad, Anne. Patrick Howard is a fine young man." He smiled down at her. "I guess that psalm helped more than either of us thought."

Anne looked away as she remembered listening to the Twenty-Third Psalm in chapel that day. She knew Uncle Daniel had meant well, but she wished he hadn't read it. Hearing what had once been such a source of comfort for her was now almost akin to torture. The words "*He restoreth my soul*" echoed mockingly in her ears. How was that possible now? Tears toyed with the edges of her vision. She stumbled a little and firmly grasped her uncle's arm. He, in turn, slowed to steady her. "Careful now, it won't do for you to twist your ankle."

"No, it won't." She looked out over the darkening university grounds. "Will you have a chance to visit Scioto when we get home?"

Her uncle paused for a moment then sighed heavily. "No, I'm afraid, not again tonight. Too many papers to grade." He hefted the leather satchel. "You know, when I told you a month ago to let Ben take care of him, I never meant that you should stop visiting him altogether. He misses you."

"Does he?"

"Of course, horses are social by nature. He's wondering where the main member of his herd has gone."

She could just make out his wink in the dusk and had to chuckle. "Uncle Daniel, are you trying to tell me I resemble a horse?"

Her uncle laughed. "Hardly, but I really should see about getting a stable mate for him. Since you seem less interested in visiting him—"

"It's not that I don't want to see him," she said softly. Nothing could be further from the truth. "I'm just trying to stay out of trouble."

In her mind, her departure approached far too quickly. Only yesterday Emma had mentioned that Clara Fuller, the young woman Anne was filling in for, was doing well and might return as early as the first of the year. Anne had realized it would probably be easier on both her and Scioto if she visited infrequently. After her uncle rebuked her for brushing him down, she'd gone to see him a few times, but over the past couple of weeks, she hadn't been out to the stable at all.

"Ben's doing fine with him," Uncle Daniel said. Anne hoped that was true. Now that the term was in full swing, her uncle rarely had time to go see him, and when he did, it was in the evening. It was hard to tell just how well a horse looked in lamplight. "You'll see for yourself tomorrow. I intend to ride him over to the faculty meeting."

The next morning, something about Scioto didn't seem quite right when her uncle led him out of the stable. Was it that his coat wasn't gleaming as brightly as she remembered? Or that he seemed to hold his head slightly lower than he had when she cared for him at home? Mr. Howard, who had arrived for their outing, seemed not to notice anything amiss.

"He's a fine animal, Dr. Kirby," he said. "He looks good for his age, too. A Morgan, isn't he?"

"Yes," Uncle Daniel replied. "I found him during the war, after my own horse was shot out from under me. A year or two after the war ended, I was able to find out who he originally belonged to and pay them. He was quite valuable. You should see his bloodline."

"No wonder Dr. Townshend was eager to breed him. He is sure to be pleased when those foals come this summer," Mr. Howard replied.

Anne watched her uncle mount, still not quite satisfied by the way Scioto looked. Her uncle smiled, and prodding his horse into a slow trot, guided him down the path that led to the main road. She bit her lip. He seemed to be moving well enough. Maybe she was imagining things. She turned to find Ben leaning against the stable door.

"Is he eating well?" she asked.

Mr. Howard interrupted before the young man could answer. "Miss Kirby, of course he is. I would think even you could see that."

She arched an eyebrow at him. "Even me?"

"Not to be mean, but you're a librarian."

"But I was raised on a farm. I can tell when a horse looks ill."

"But *I* will eventually be a veterinarian. And I can tell you for certain that horse is as healthy as a horse his age can be." He pulled out his watch and glanced at it. "Are you ready? We really should be going. The streetcar will be coming by soon."

Anne looked in the direction her uncle had ridden. She didn't appreciate Mr. Howard's condescending attitude, but she had to admit he might be right. After all, she hadn't been out to see Scioto for quite a while.

"Yes, let's go." She took his arm. As they walked down to the main road, Mr. Howard squinted against the morning sun toward High Street, the road that led directly into the city of Columbus.

"Come on," he said and began to walk faster. "The rest of our party is already at the streetcar stop, and I think I see it coming. We'll have to be quick to catch it."

It wasn't far, but Mr. Howard walked faster than Anne was used to and she stumbled.

"Oooh!" She stopped, and letting go of his arm, knelt down to grasp her ankle.

"Miss Kirby, are you all right? I'm so sorry!"

"I'll be fine, but I don't think I'll be able to come with you today." She rose and tried to put her weight on it then winced. "Ooh! No, I'm sorry."

"Then I won't go either."

"No, Mr. Howard, please don't give up your day on my account." She grabbed his arm. "Why don't you take me back to my house? It's only a few steps, and I'll get Mrs. Werner to come to the door. She'll look after me."

It took a little convincing, but she managed to get him to leave her at the front door. He waved as he ran to catch the streetcar and, as soon as he and the others were on it, Anne quietly opened the door. Once inside she peered down the front hall. She didn't see Mrs. Werner. The faint sound of an Irish tune being sung reached her ears. The housekeeper was busy in the kitchen, it seemed. Anne quietly made her way upstairs, her foot perfectly sound, and returned with a dark cloak and an old bonnet of her mother's. Bonnets were out of fashion, but it was the only way she knew to hide her face. Better to be out of fashion than be recognized. It would also make her seem a bit older.

She quietly let herself out and looked toward the street. Taking a deep breath, she walked down to High Street. Her heart pounding, she stepped onto the next car that stopped and settled herself down for the ride into Columbus.

Chapter 7

A yell and the throaty whinny of a horse caused Peter to stop his work and walk to the other side of Professor Tuttle's residence. Next door, outside Professor Kirby's stable, stood a bay horse, shaking his head and prancing. Dr. Kirby sat on the ground holding his arm, and Dr. Townshend knelt beside him. Peter immediately noticed the way the horse moved, favoring his front right hoof. Instinct took over, and Peter jogged closer, slowing as he drew near.

"Are you all right, Professor Kirby?" he asked in a low voice.

"I'm fine. Peter, you'd best stay back. He can be fractious with people he doesn't know well."

But Peter slowly and calmly walked toward the horse. Speaking soothing words, he scratched him on his withers before reaching out and taking the reins. The horse calmed, although he bobbed his head and angled it several times toward his right hoof. Peter looked around. Didn't the professor have a stable hand? "Where is your man, sir?"

Both professors were staring at him. "I'm not sure where Ben is," Professor Kirby said slowly. "But you certainly have a way with him. He doesn't take to strangers well. Does he, Norton?"

Dr. Townshend shook his head. "It took a full week for him to get used to me the short time I was around him this past summer."

Peter looked away as he realized what he had just done. When he'd turned down Dr. Kirby's offer a month ago, he'd allowed the professor to believe it was because he knew next to nothing about horses, which certainly wasn't the case. Henry Farley was one of the best trainers in the business, and he'd agreed to leave a good-paying job in Philadelphia to work for Peter on one condition: that Peter learn to care for the horses he intended to own and race. As a result, he could handle any horse in any situation. Henry said he had "the touch." But it was a talent that he'd thought best to abandon, considering what it had cost him. Scioto shook his head again, and Peter automatically laid a steadying hand on his nose.

Dr. Kirby nodded toward them. "I'll be fine, Norton. Go help Peter."

The agriculture professor walked over and arched a questioning eyebrow at him. Peter avoided his eye, and Dr. Townshend ran his hands along Scioto's shoulder and down his leg, coaxing the animal to raise his foot. It didn't take much effort. Peter's brow furrowed as he caught a look at the back of the horse's lower leg. It was quite swollen.

"A sprained tendon," he blurted.

Professor Townshend looked at him and then at Dr. Kirby.

"He's right. He sprained a tendon, Daniel."

Dr. Kirby's face darkened. "I shouldn't have ridden him so hard. No wonder he threw me."

"I have a poultice that should help." Dr. Townshend gently lowered the foot as he described the treatment.

Peter nodded. It was the same one Henry had always used, and he knew it would produce good results. Dr. Kirby struggled to rise, and Peter handed Scioto off to Dr. Townshend to help him to his feet. Holding his injured arm to his chest, he slowly walked up to his horse.

"I'm sorry, old boy." He rubbed his neck with his good hand.

Peter spoke without thinking. "Don't worry sir, I know that poultice. It will work." Once again they both stared at him. "I—used to work in a barn. Once."

Dr. Townshend's eyebrows arched. "Young man, if I didn't already have more than enough students working at the university farm, I'd hire you on the spot."

"You know quite a bit for someone who has simply worked in a barn once," Professor Kirby remarked.

Peter's eyes darted anywhere, trying not to take in Dr. Kirby's intense and curious stare. "I'd better get back to work," he said, backing away. "Mr. Dixon will be looking for me."

He could feel their stares on his back as he walked away. What on earth was the matter with him? He had tried so carefully to avoid horses and young ladies, and in the past two days he'd been in close contact with both. *Why are You leading me this direction, Lord? Don't You know me? Lead me away from this. Lead me in paths of righteousness.* When his feet hit gravel, he looked up in surprise. He'd been so intent on his prayer, he took no note of where he was going and realized that he'd made his way to the road that ran in front of Dr. Kirby's house. He still needed to go to Dr. Tuttle's and finish the work he'd started. Wheels in need of some oil made him look up. A horse-drawn streetcar stopped on the opposite side of High Street. Several people got out, including a woman in a dark cloak and bonnet. A bonnet? He hadn't seen anyone wear a bonnet since he was a child. Once she crossed the street, the woman pulled off the hat, and to his surprise, it was Anne Kirby. She walked toward the house with lowered eyes, her face more melancholy than usual. Curious, he waited for her to approach.

"Miss Kirby?" She looked up, and the astonishment in her eyes was tempered by the redness of recent tears. "Are you all right? You're not hurt are you?"

"Mr. Ward." She paused, glancing away before looking at him again. "I'm fine. What are you doing here?"

Peter blinked. "I was working next door at Dr. Tuttle's house when I heard a commotion. Your uncle's horse threw him—"

"What?" She raised her hand to her chest.

"Your uncle's all right. But I think he might have hurt his arm somehow."

"What about Scioto?"

Peter stared at her for a moment. "I'm afraid it looks like he sprained a tendon. Dr. Townshend is here, too. He's already suggested a poultice."

She rushed past him and flew up the steps to the house. "Thank you, Mr. Ward," she called back.

"You're welcome." But she was inside before he finished speaking the words. He shook his head and turned toward the Tuttle residence to retrieve his tools. What was she doing, getting off the streetcar alone and dressed in a cloak and bonnet? According to Mike, the streetcar went into Columbus. Well, maybe she hadn't gone far, perhaps only a few blocks to visit a friend. But that didn't make sense. Why pay streetcar fare when she could walk? And if she had been visiting a friend, why would she return close to tears?

Peter quickly finished the minor repair to Professor Tuttle's home and gathered his tools. As he walked to the Main Building, an uneasy thought crossed his mind. Just how disgraceful had this Sam McAllister's conduct been toward Miss Kirby? Surely she wasn't in the same state as Letty Jamison. But her sadness and her behavior today offered no other explanation. He strangled the handle of his tool bag and curled his other hand into an iron-like fist. No wonder the professor had wanted to beat the living daylights out of the man. But wait. If that were the case, certainly her pa would have already forced the young man to marry her. Recalling the face of Jonah Kirby in the professor's wedding picture, he could tell he was hardly a man to be crossed. Then it hit him. *They don't know.* It all made sense—her tears, the cloak and bonnet. She'd been in town to visit a doctor.

The weight of that thought stopped him cold. He ran his free hand through his hair as another question seared its way through his head. Had she given up her virtue willingly or had it been stolen from her? His gut told him it had to be the latter. A woman could not possess such innocent eyes and be some sort of siren. It made sense, too. She hadn't said anything to avoid embarrassment and was now finding herself in an even worse situation. The blame for that sort of thing always seemed to fall on the woman, which Peter had always found to be monstrously unfair. During his time on the road and in the finest homes in Pittsburgh, he knew from experience that was not always the case.

He started on his way again and found himself wondering if that might have been the case with Letty. But why had she said he was responsible? He shook his head. It didn't really matter now. After all this time, her father would have either sent her somewhere out of state or found someone else to marry her. In spite of her dishonesty, he found himself praying everything would turn out for the best. At least her prospects were more hopeful than Anne Kirby's. If he were right about her, he felt he needed to find some way to help.

In the distance, Peter saw Mike coming from the boiler house behind the Main Building, and he waved to him. As he drew closer, he saw someone approach his boss. He frowned. It was Harvey Pryce.

"Mr. Cope asked me to give these to you," Peter heard him say as he approached. "Couldn't help but notice some of those bills are past due."

Mike took the bundle of papers and gave him a look. "These papers are between me and the board."

Harvey shrugged. "He also happened to ask me if I was working for you this term. I told you already had someone." Noticing Peter, he gave him a nasty smile. "I knew I recognized you before. I guess our 'lesson' didn't mess you up too bad."

Peter stared at him for a second as his full meaning sunk in. Then he dropped his bag and lunged at Harvey. He was stopped by Mike's arm across his shoulders.

"Whoa, Pete! What's going on?"

"He was with those boys who beat me," he said. He'd told Mike about his timber lesson when he hired him. "I wasn't hurting anyone. Why'd you pick on me?"

"It was my job, keeping tramps like you from hitching free rides," Harvey replied. "Handing out timber lessons was working until you showed up. My boss found out and fired me."

"I ought to have you arrested," Mike said.

Peter opened his mouth to agree but stopped himself. If he had to testify against Harvey, it might draw unwanted attention. What if his uncle was still looking for him? Peter didn't put it past him for a second that he might want to find him out of sheer spite. His departure had most assuredly caused his uncle a great deal of embarrassment.

"No." Peter said. "I'd rather put that behind me."

Mike stared at him. "You sure?"

"Yes."

Mike lowered his arm and looked at Harvey. "I think it's time you left."

Pryce's face turned smug. "Yeah it is, now that you mention it. I have to pack. Finally got me a job." He walked off.

Peter hoped it would be a long time before he saw Harvey Pryce again.

∽

Anne watched as Uncle Daniel paced in front of the parlor mantel after listening carefully to the news Patrick Howard had given him concerning Scioto. It had been a full day since Scioto's injury, and Professor Townshend had sent the young man over to see how the poultice was doing. He had not given them good news.

"Why isn't it working?" her uncle asked.

"Sir, your man hasn't been applying it," Mr. Howard replied.

Uncle Daniel stopped and stared at him.

"Why not?" Anne asked.

"He told me it wouldn't work. He said all the horse needs is rest and a little liniment." Mr. Howard scowled. "But I can't find any evidence that he's even been applying that."

Anne watched her uncle's knuckles turn snow white as he clenched his fist and tapped it against his leg. His other arm was in a sling. It was fortunate that her uncle had only severely sprained his shoulder when Scioto threw him. And at the moment, fortunate for Ben, too. Her uncle looked like he wanted to throttle him.

"Please be so kind as to ask Ben to come inside, Patrick," he said after taking one more turn in front of the fireplace.

Mr. Howard left, and Anne watched her uncle resume his pacing. She was as worried about Scioto as he was—perhaps even more—but she couldn't help but feel glad that all the fuss had kept Mr. Howard from asking about her "injured" foot. The questions it would raise would inevitably lead to her uncle finding out where she'd gone yesterday. She squirmed as she thought of how she had deceived both of them, but she hadn't seen any other way around it. *I'm sorry, Lord. Please forgive me. I'll tell Uncle Daniel what I did eventually. Just not yet.*

A few minutes later, a frightened-looking Ben stood before all three of them, twisting what might have been a hat in both hands. He looked so wretched that Anne couldn't help feeling sorry for him. Her uncle must have, as well, for his voice held only a slight edge.

"Would you care to explain why my horse is still suffering almost a day after his injury?"

Ben refused to look at any of them. "I can't really get near him, sir."

Her uncle looked at her then back at Ben. "But you've been caring for him for almost a month and a half now. You told me weeks ago he was behaving for you."

"I know, sir. I'm sorry; I really am. I just wanted this job so bad."

"You should have said something," Anne said. Tears rose in her eyes as she thought about how neglected Scioto must have felt. If only she hadn't avoided seeing him for so long.

"If you can't go near him, then how was it he looked so well yesterday?" Mr. Howard asked.

"I got up real early. It took me till first light to get him ready and saddled."

Her uncle drew in a long breath. "I'm afraid I'll have to let you go, Ben."

The young man's shoulders slumped and his hands fell to his sides. "Yes, sir, I'll go clear my things." He turned to go, but Uncle Daniel spoke again.

"Your family isn't from Columbus, are they?"

"No, sir, we're from Celina."

"If you decide you want to go back home instead of finding work here, please come see me. I'll see that you get home."

The news appeared to lighten Ben's load a little. "Thank you, sir."

"We need to apply the poultice immediately," Patrick said after Ben left. "I wonder if you could help me."

"Of course," Anne replied, rising from her seat.

Patrick raised his eyebrows. "Thank you, Miss Kirby, but I was speaking to your uncle." He turned to him. "Scioto wasn't very happy with me either, sir. I know it might be difficult with your arm—"

"He should be fine if I'm holding on to his halter." Uncle Daniel gave Anne a sympathetic glance. "Ask Mrs. Werner to heat up some water."

"Not to boiling though," Patrick said.

"I'm familiar with the poultice Dr. Townshend recommended, Mr. Howard," Anne said, frowning slightly. "If you'll excuse me, I'll go speak with her now."

∽

A few hours later, she and her uncle stood outside Scioto's stall as Anne tried not to fume over the slow, careful way Patrick had explained to her how to continue with the poultice. He'd left for his boardinghouse moments ago. Anne must have had a sour look on her face because her uncle chuckled.

"You're sure you got all that now?" he mimicked. Anne gave him such a withering look that he held his free hand up as if to forestall a blow. "I must admit he went a little overboard."

Scioto lowered his head toward Anne, and she laid her hand across his nose. "I should never have stopped visiting him."

"And I should have made more time to do so." Uncle Daniel rubbed the horse's neck. "We'll let him rest for the time being."

Anne nodded. She needed to go in and heat more water to keep the poultice warm. "Who will take care of him now?" she asked as they walked to the house.

"Mr. Howard said he'd make enquiries, but he wasn't very hopeful," her uncle replied. "He said he'd do it himself, but his studies won't allow him the time."

"We can't move him," she said carefully. "With your arm and teaching schedule, you doing the job is out of the question, and Mrs. Werner is not particularly fond of horses." She looked up hopefully at her uncle.

A deep frown creased his face. "I don't like it, Anne. I promised your pa."

"I know, but considering the circumstances, I don't think he'd object." Anne waited through a long pause. She was eventually rewarded for her patience.

"I don't see how we have much choice." He looked over his glasses at her. "I know you'll take good care of him, but it will only be until I can hire someone." His gaze turned thoughtful. "In fact, I may not have to look far."

Anne didn't let his last few words spoil her delight. She squeezed his good arm. "I understand. Thank you, Uncle Daniel."

Chapter 8

Late November, 1884

T his is all my fault." Peter sat on his cot and watched his boss pack his things.

"Don't blame yourself, Pete," Mike said as he worked. "I don't."

"But you never would have lost your job if you hadn't hired me. You said the board wasn't happy about it."

Mike stopped packing and rubbed the back of his neck. "That's not it, exactly." He sat down on the cot next to Peter. "I kind of got myself in this mess."

"What do you mean?"

"Those bills Harvey gave me a few weeks ago were supposed to be paid by me. Then the board was to reimburse me." He paused, looking more than a little embarrassed. "I sorta forgot about them. And this hasn't been the first time. The bills went past due and got sent to the board. Again."

"Ah, Mike." Peter said sadly. "I wish you had told me. I could have helped you remember."

"Well, that's not all. Before you came, I told the board how much money I needed for this term, and they gave me enough for two assistants." He looked at Peter. "When Dr. Kirby spoke to me about you, I felt real sorry for you. So I paid you salary for two men."

Peter ran a hand through his hair. He'd always wondered if his pay was too high, but since he'd never worked for someone before, he'd never questioned Mike about it. Now he wished he had. A knock sounded at the door and they looked at each other.

"I still don't believe they hired him," Peter said.

"I tried to tell them." Mike rose wearily to answer the door.

Harvey Pryce walked in with his friend Frank. Both men were

loaded down with wooden crates. "Humph," Harvey said as he took in the one-room cabin. "Not much, but it'll do."

"It keeps the rain off your head." Mike continued with his packing.

"I guess." Harvey set down his crate and looked at Peter. "What are you still doing here?"

"Don't worry, I'll be gone by the morning," Peter said.

"I wanted to try and convince you to keep him on," Mike said as he stuffed the last of his things in an old carpetbag. "He knows how things work around here."

"I'm pretty sure I can handle it," Harvey said.

Peter couldn't stop the chuckle that escaped his lips. Harvey glared at him.

"I would've had this job sooner if me and the boys had given you a better lesson."

Peter stood, his fists clenched tight. "Maybe it's time I give *you* a lesson."

"Pete," Mike warned. "Don't do it."

"Ah, come on, Pete," Pryce taunted. "Let's have at it."

Common sense quickly prevailing, he turned away from Harvey. "No. It's not worth it."

Harvey sneered at him then nudged Frank, who had also set down his crate. "Let's go get something to drink. We'll bring the rest of my stuff over tomorrow."

"You start tomorrow," Mike retorted. "How are you going to move in and do what needs done around here?"

"That's my business," Harvey said as he and Frank walked out the door.

Peter shook his head. "He really has no idea what he's getting into."

Mike nodded in agreement and set the carpetbag near the door, along with the rest of his things. "I guess that's it for me." He held out his hand and Peter shook it. "I'm sorry they don't need you over at the shop."

"That's all right. I'll find something." As Peter spoke, a wagon pulled up outside.

"That'd be the fellas for me," Mike said.

Peter followed him over to the door, picked up some of his things, and followed him outside. A couple of Mike's friends had driven over to help him move to a boardinghouse near Columbus Machine Company, where he'd found a job. They jumped down and Mike introduced them. "This is Geoff Evans and Steve Brock."

"Sorry to hear about your job." Steve shook Peter's hand. "I think there might be an opening where I work. I can check and come by and get you tomorrow if you like. It'd be around lunchtime. Think you'll be here?"

Mike smirked. "Harvey wants him gone by the time he comes back tomorrow. But he and Frank went out drinking. Pete will be here."

They laughed and soon had all of Mike's things in the back of the wagon. "I'll see if there's a room at the boardinghouse," Mike said as he climbed up. "I know the fella Steve works for. More than likely, you'll have a job come tomorrow."

Peter shook his hand. "Thanks, Mike. For everything."

As the wagon rolled off, Peter stood outside, looking at the fading sky. A new job in the city would be an answer to prayer. He needed to leave the university. Dr. Kirby had been forced to fire his stable boy and had offered the job to Peter. As much as he wanted to accept it, he knew he shouldn't. Then there was Anne Kirby. As much as he wanted to help her, there just didn't seem to be a proper way to go about it. It also didn't help that the few times he'd seen her in the last month she hadn't seemed any better, at least in unguarded moments. She seemed normal enough when she was with her uncle, but on the few occasions he'd checked the pipes in the library, he'd caught glimpses of her dabbing her eyes. *Lord, You know all things and You know this situation she's in. Lead her to someone that can help her. Restore her soul.*

A brisk gust sent him back into the house, and he put more wood in the stove. The weather had been unpredictable. The days had been pleasant enough, but the nights had been getting quite cold, at least to Peter's way of thinking. He'd never liked being cold. He put another piece in for good measure then set about packing up what few things he had and making sure the log house was more or less in order. Lately Peter had been reading a passage in Romans about enemies. If being nice to Harvey Pryce meant that "coals of fire" would be heaped on his head, so much the better. He only wished he could do a few nice things for Uncle Randall and his cousin Edward.

He pushed the wood box closer to the stove. What about his grandfather? Did he desire the same thing for him? As much as he thought the answer should be yes, his heart didn't agree. In the end, Granddad's cutting him off had been a good thing. He was a better man now. The thought made him shake his head at himself. Was he really? He'd just wished the worst for three different people. When Dr. Kirby first pointed out that passage to him after Peter had been injured, he'd been quick to say it wasn't about revenge. It was about forgiveness. *That's something You'll have to help me with, Lord. Forgiving them just isn't on my heart right yet.* He set the last few things in order and fell into bed, not bothering to remove his clothes. The one blanket he had wasn't exactly the warmest.

It was the heat that woke Peter later. Heat and the light from the raging fire that flickered up the wall opposite his bed. It had begun to spread to a good portion of the roof as well. He ran out the door, yelling for help. Several figures were running toward him from the direction of the student boardinghouse, some carrying buckets.

"Come on," one of them shouted. "We'll form a bucket brigade from the lake to here."

"What about the fire department?" Peter yelled as they started for it.

"They'll be here soon. We already sent someone to the signal box." The student stopped and looked around in alarm. "Where's Mike?"

"He's not here." Peter pulled on his arm. "Come on!"

But their buckets might as well have been thimbles. By the time they formed the line, flames engulfed the whole building. All they could do was make sure the fire didn't spread. It was only after the fire department arrived with its steam-powered pumper that they finally took a break. Peter slumped on the ground, head in his hands, coughing from the smoke. How on earth had this happened?

"Where is he? He's got to be here somewhere."

Peter looked up. Harvey Pryce strode up to the scene, a police officer on his heels. He spotted Peter and immediately made his way over. "There he is. Arrest him!"

Peter jumped to his feet. "What?"

"Now Mr. Pryce, let's just wait a minute," the officer said. "We don't even know if this was an accident or what."

"It's no accident," Harvey said. "This guy has a grudge against me because I got his boss's job. He took a swing at me earlier tonight, gave me a sore jaw. Now he's burned down my house out of spite."

"That's not what happened!" Peter yelled.

The students that had formed the bucket brigade wandered over to watch.

"I have a witness," Harvey declared. "My friend Frank Morris saw the whole thing."

"I—" Peter began. The policeman took hold of his arm. "Wait, I didn't do anything."

"I've heard enough to know that this needs to go before the court." The officer slapped handcuffs on him. "You're going down to the city prison for the time being."

∞

Peter soon found himself confined to a small cell with several other men. Since it was the middle of the night, most of them were asleep or, judging from the smell, passed out from too much liquor. One or two woke up when he was let in, but he quietly made his way to the back of the cell and ignored their insults and veiled threats. A low stone ledge ran beneath the window, and he climbed up on it. He couldn't even contemplate the idea of sitting on the floor.

He moved into the corner and, leaning back, drew his knees up. Scrunching his eyes shut, he tried to wake himself up from the nightmare he found himself in. But the stench of the cell and the smoke that hung heavily to his clothes and beard told him he was wide awake. Not to mention the cold breeze that blew in from the window. Bars were the only thing that covered the square slit near the top of the cell. When he rested his head against the wall, he could see a bare sliver of the night sky. He stared at it, not quite sure what to think or even what to pray.

After about a quarter of an hour, he closed his eyes. *I'm sorry I let Harvey provoke me, Lord. I shouldn't have said anything.* He wondered what the judge would say. According to the jailer who had led him to the cell, he'd go to court sometime tomorrow. How was he going to get out of this? The only person who knew that Harvey was lying was Mike, and he had no way of getting ahold of him. And what if they decided he started the fire? *But I didn't do it. I didn't do anything to start that fire.* He wondered if Harvey had started it on purpose. He couldn't imagine why. He hadn't even liked the place. Was he worried that he would still try to arrest him for having him beaten? Peter shook his head. Whatever the reason, it certainly didn't matter now.

A commotion drew his attention to the cell door, where a man was forced inside. He fell on top of a rough-looking fellow who'd been leaning against the bars, sleeping. He cursed and kicked him off. The man tumbled to the ground, and Peter jumped up to help him.

"Hey, are you all right?" he whispered. He squinted at the man's face in the dim light. "Uncle Billy?"

"Petey!" the man exclaimed. A couple of men cursed and shushed them, and Peter immediately hauled his friend to his spot at the back of the cell.

"Hey now, Lieutenant," Uncle Billy said. "You watch yourself there. I'm your superior officer, remember?"

Peter smiled inwardly. How could he have forgotten Billy's. . .eccentricities? He stood up straight and gave him a quick salute. "Sorry, sir. What are you doing here?"

"Them Rebs got me." He shook his head. "They tried to take the general away from me."

"Is he all right, sir?"

Uncle Billy grinned as he reached his hand into the pocket of his threadbare Union jacket. When he pulled it out, there in his hand was a small brown field mouse. "Them Rebs won't get General Grant that easy."

Peter nodded and smiled. Uncle Billy had kept him company many times during his tramping days. Or rather, Peter had kept Uncle Billy company. He'd first met him in Circleville, a little town south of Columbus, and he wasn't popular with the other transients. His ramblings about the War between the States and his unshakable belief that he was General William T. Sherman made them uncomfortable. Then there was the mouse he carried around in his pocket, which he insisted was General Ulysses S. Grant. Peter had felt sorry for him and befriended him. The war still rested heavily on his mind, but all in all, he was a kindhearted soul. The only time he became violent was when anyone tried to go after his mouse. "I'm glad their latest attempt to capture General Grant was unsuccessful," he said, patting Billy on the back.

The man raised the mouse up to his face. "He's worried about the next campaign. See how he's pacing?" He looked at Peter. "You know anything that'd soothe the general?"

Peter smiled. "Yes, sir." He knew just the thing. God had placed it on his heart to memorize over a month ago. He helped Uncle Billy up on the ledge and hopped up next to him.

"'The Lord is my shepherd; I shall not want,'" he quoted softly. "'He maketh me to lie down in green pastures: he leadeth me beside the still waters. He restoreth my soul. . . .'"

Chapter 9

"Thank you for letting me eat with you and Anne today, Dr. Kirby," Emma said.

Uncle Daniel smiled at her from behind his office desk as she and Anne laid cloths out on it and unpacked their lunch baskets. "We're glad to have you join us, Miss Long. Although, I have to wonder who is taking care of the library right now. I thought you two took turns keeping an eye on things during lunch."

"Normally we do," Anne replied with a smile. "But there are so few people who come into the library at this hour, we decided we could probably get away with leaving a note on the door explaining where we are."

"I hope no one comes looking for us," Emma said, laying out her ham sandwich. "Or we'll be in for a short lunch."

"Oh, it can't be that someone will need both of us. I'll go if someone comes." Anne handed her uncle a boiled egg, along with a small paper packet of salt.

"Thank you, Anne." Emma brought a couple of chairs forward for them to sit in. "I'm going to miss you come January."

"So you've heard from Miss Fuller?" Uncle Daniel asked.

"Yes, Clara says she'll be back at the start of winter term."

"Then that means you'll have to find a new position, Anne." Her uncle smiled at her. "Have you started looking yet?"

Anne nodded. "Yes, I've written a few letters." She took a bite of her sandwich so she wouldn't have to elaborate. She'd sent several letters, all to districts out West. A small school district outside Topeka, Kansas, had recently replied, offering her a job. Their letter requested her to start at her earliest convenience. All she needed to do was make the arrangements, but that would take another trip into Columbus. She laid her sandwich down—the thought had made it suddenly taste like shoe leather. But it had to be done. She glanced at her uncle, trying to remember when he'd said his next faculty meeting would take place. Hopefully it would be soon.

"I heard you found a new stable man," Emma said between bites of her sandwich.

"Yes," Uncle Daniel answered, his glance sliding toward Anne. "A very well-trained individual, but it's only temporary, I'm afraid."

Anne looked down, concentrating on peeling her hardboiled egg. She'd been so glad to take charge of Scioto again. It had been hard not talking to anyone about her troubles over the past month, but opening up to him hadn't been the same as it had been at home. Instead of feeling better, she felt worse. She couldn't understand it. She felt God nudging her to talk to Him. *Why, Father? What more is there to say?*

Someone knocked on the door, and Emma groaned.

"I'll see who it is," Anne said. Instead of the student she'd anticipated seeing, Mike Dixon stood before her. Uncle Daniel caught sight of him and rose from his seat.

"Hello, Mike." Her uncle joined her at the door. "We were so sorry to hear you'd been let go."

"Yes, we'll miss you, Mike," Anne said, and Emma, leaning back to catch a glimpse of the janitor, echoed the sentiment.

Mike nodded. "Thank you. Dr. Kirby, I was wondering if I might speak to you in private."

Anne looked at her uncle. "Do you want Emma and me to leave for a moment?"

"No, of course not. We'll just step out into the hall." He smiled and shut the door behind him.

"I wonder what that's about," Emma wondered aloud.

"Maybe he wants to use my uncle as a reference." Anne sat back down.

"That can't be; I've heard he has a job." She wiped her hands on a cloth napkin and folded up the paper from her sandwich. "Did you hear the bells from the fire engine last night?"

"Yes! They went right past our house," she replied. The janitor's house burning down last night had been the talk of the students all morning.

"A few of the fellows from George Smart's boardinghouse ran out to help."

Anne's eyebrows rose. "How do you know?"

"George stopped by the library this morning just to tell me." She blushed.

"I'm glad for you. He seems like a nice young man. Although I'm surprised he didn't go, too."

"He would have, but he was away visiting family." She cocked her head at Anne. "Patrick Howard is a pretty nice fellow, too."

Anne frowned. "I know."

"I still don't understand why you chased him away." Emma looked at her reprovingly. "You couldn't ask for a better man."

Anne was saved from replying by the sudden reappearance of her uncle. "I'm afraid there's an emergency that needs my attention." He shrugged into his suit jacket and handed Anne a key. "Lock up my office and place a sign on my door. I'll have to cancel my afternoon classes."

"What's wrong?" she asked. The look of concern on his face alarmed her. "It's not Scioto, is it?"

"No, my dear, he's fine. I'll explain later. Hopefully I'll be home by dinner."

☙

Throughout the long night, Peter silently repeated Psalm 23 to himself. He spent the morning keeping Uncle Billy out of trouble with their cell mates. Not long after lunch, they were all ushered to a closed police wagon to be taken to the courthouse. The psalm had kept Peter's heart at ease until he asked the police officer who rode with them about the judge they were soon to face.

"The mayor is the police and judge," he said gruffly.

"What's he like?"

"He won't go easy on you if he thinks you're guilty. Now be quiet."

Uncle Billy glared at the officer. "You watch yourself! That's my lieutenant you're talking to."

"And who are you supposed to be?"

"I'm General William Tecumseh Sherman." The officer and the other prisoners laughed. "Don't believe me? General Grant will confirm it." The old man reached into his pocket, but Peter quickly stopped him.

"The general needs his rest, sir."

Uncle Billy didn't look pleased but left the mouse in his pocket, much to Peter's relief.

His heart pounded as they were marched into the courtroom. Mayor Walcutt was a gruff-looking man with a long goatee, a mustache, and a stern eye. But as he worked through the cases brought before him, Peter saw that he was a fair-minded man, only fining or imprisoning those who truly deserved it. The man right before him had beaten his wife in a drunken stupor. The woman came before the judge to plead on her husband's behalf, but Mayor Walcutt wasn't swayed. His eyes turned to black coals as he stared down at the man, saying, "I only wish it were within my power to sentence you to the same beating you gave this woman who came to intercede for you."

Peter's case was called, and as he walked up to stand before the mayor, he glanced out over the gallery. Harvey Pryce was there, along with Frank Morris, but Mike Dixon's and Professor Kirby's presence surprised Peter. He felt both relieved and mortified. Mike would certainly tell the judge the truth, but Peter wanted to hide in shame from Dr. Kirby. What must the professor think of him?

"Mr. Peter Ward?"

Peter looked up at the judge's stern face. "Yes, sir."

"You've been accused of assault and burning down a log house belonging to The Ohio State University." The mayor's eyebrows drew together. "How do you plead?"

"Not guilty, sir."

The mayor looked down at the papers before him. "Mr. Harvey Pryce, please step forward."

Harvey did as he was told. "Yes, Your Honor?"

"Tell me exactly what happened."

"Well, I've recently been hired as janitor up at the university. Frank and I were moving my things into the janitor's cabin when Ward here starts getting nasty and hits me."

The mayor took a long look at him. "Is that how you got the bruise on your jaw?"

"Yes, hurts like the devil, too."

"And you have a witness who can verify this?"

Harvey motioned to Frank. "Yes, sir." He looked back at his friend, who hadn't moved, and said, "Come on, tell the judge what happened."

But Frank looked from Harvey to Peter then to the mayor and got up and walked out of the courtroom. Someone cleared his throat, and Peter turned. Both Mike and Dr. Kirby had risen from their seats. "If you will forgive me, Mayor Walcutt, Mr. Dixon and I would like to speak on Mr. Ward's behalf."

Frowning at Harvey, the mayor nodded. "I think that would be very helpful, Mr.—?"

"I am Dr. Daniel Kirby, a professor at The Ohio State University. This is Michael Dixon, who, until recently, was the janitor for the university."

The mayor listened carefully as Mike described exactly what happened the night before and what Harvey had said and done to provoke Peter. "I won't lie and say Pete didn't want to let him have it, but he never touched Harvey."

"Then how did Mr. Pryce get his bruised jaw?" Mayor Walcutt asked.

"Him and Frank decided to go drinking last night, Your Honor. We both heard him suggest it to Frank before they left the cabin."

"I see." The mayor looked at Harvey, who was looking anywhere but up at him. "Very well, I'm satisfied that Mr. Ward did not hit Mr. Pryce. But there is the burning of the log house to consider."

"I can vouch for this young man's character in that regard," Dr. Kirby said firmly. "He has been a guest in my home, and I am convinced he would not do such a thing."

"Oh no," Peter blurted out. He'd replayed over and over in his mind everything he'd done last night and suddenly realized what happened. He felt the blood leave his face. "I think I started the fire."

Dr. Kirby looked at him, incredulously. "What do you mean?"

Peter locked eyes with Mike. "It was so stupid of me. After you left, I got cold. I put a couple of logs on the fire, and while I was straightening up, I—I think I moved the wood box too close to the stove. Then I fell asleep." How could he have been so stupid? Mike had warned him about putting anything flammable too close to the stove, in case it overheated. He looked up at the judge. "It was an accident."

The mayor looked carefully at him. "I believe you, son. But I will need to hear what the fire captain says." He looked at Professor Kirby. "I will release him to you, Dr. Kirby."

"Thank you, sir," he replied. "I am confident you will find everything just as Mr. Ward described."

Peter's hands shook with relief as the bailiff removed the handcuffs. He looked up to thank the mayor but found the gentleman looking at Harvey.

"Mr. Pryce," the mayor said. "I should have you arrested for what Mr. Dixon just told me about you giving Mr. Ward a timber lesson."

Harvey looked up at the judge, his dark eyes wide.

"Sir, please," Peter said. "I'm fine now. Let Mr. Pryce go."

"This man should be brought to justice, Peter," Dr. Kirby said.

"I know, sir." But it wasn't the desire to remain anonymous that moved Peter now. He felt God nudging him to show Harvey the same mercy as the professor had shown him. "I haven't always been the man I am now. I was given a second chance, sir. Harvey deserves one as well."

"Admirable, young man, admirable," the mayor said. "Consider yourself lucky, Mr. Pryce."

Harvey looked so angry, Peter thought he might burst into flame. But he only glared at him, saying nothing, as he rose and stalked out of the courtroom. Dr. Kirby, Mike, and Peter started to leave when Uncle Billy's name was called.

Peter stopped short of the courtroom door and looked back. His friend shuffled up in front of the judge and pulled off his worn forage cap.

"Is Uncle Billy your real name?" the mayor asked.

"Well, no sir," Billy said. "That's what the men call me. My name is William Tecumseh Sherman."

Peter quickly strode forward but not in time to stop his friend from pulling out "General Grant." Mayor Walcutt's eyes grew large, and a woman in the gallery screeched.

"Sir, please, I don't know what the charges are against him—" Peter began.

"He bit me," said a voice from the gallery. A man with a bandaged hand stood up. "He brought that vermin into my saloon, waving him around, asking people to buy a cigar and a drink for 'General Grant' there."

"That Reb tried to capture the general!" Uncle Billy exclaimed.

Peter shook his head. He'd done that again? "Sir, please, he doesn't really know what he's doing."

"That much is clear," the mayor said. "Do you know his real name?"

"Give me just a moment, sir." Peter gave Uncle Billy a salute. "General, do you have your papers on you?" Peter had thought he'd seen Uncle Billy with official-looking documents on more than one occasion but had never gotten a good look at them. He prayed he still had them.

Uncle Billy looked doubtfully at him. "Why do you need my papers, Lieutenant?"

"I don't, sir, but this gentleman does." Uncle Billy's frown deepened, and Peter grasped for an explanation. "It's. . .official business, sir. Spies have been seen in the area."

Slowly, the old man pulled a worn set of papers from inside his shirt. He handed them to Peter, who handed them to the bailiff. Mayor Walcutt took them and read the name he found written there.

"Harold Albert Cooper, sergeant for the Union Army, discharged June 1865."

The words had a dramatic effect on Billy. He began to shake uncontrollably and raised his hand to his forehead. His eyes swam, and he looked miserable and confused. Peter's heart tightened, and he laid his hand on his friend's back. Dr. Kirby walked forward.

"Mayor, under the circumstances, I don't think a normal sentence is called for." The professor's face was even graver than his voice.

"You're right, Professor," Mayor Walcutt replied. "Anything else would be an insult to the men I commanded in the war." The mayor looked up at the man Billy had assaulted, who nodded agreement, but Peter didn't care for the fear and distrust in the man's face. It wasn't as if Uncle Billy could help what was wrong with him.

"I'll send word to Dr. Finch and see what can be done." The mayor nodded to the bailiff, who gently took Uncle Billy out a side door.

Dr. Kirby, his hand on Peter's arm, guided him to the door. "Who is Dr. Finch, sir?" Peter asked. "He's not the poorhouse doctor, is he?"

"No," the professor replied, his eyes thoughtful. "Dr. Finch is the superintendent of the Columbus Asylum for the Insane. You can be sure your friend is in good hands." He took a deep breath and then looked at Peter. "Now, young man, we have a great deal to discuss."

Chapter 10

Good afternoon, Miss Kirby. How is Scioto doing?"
Anne looked toward the voice. Patrick Howard stood at the bottom of the steps of the Main Building.

Sighing inwardly, she made her way down to join him. "He's doing very well, Mr. Howard."

"It's fortunate your uncle found someone to care for him so quickly. But he didn't mention who it was."

Anne bit the inside of her lip before answering. "Oh—it's someone who came down from Ostrander a few months ago." She held her breath, hoping he wouldn't ask more. To spare Anne's reputation, Uncle Daniel hadn't wanted it known that she was performing a man's job.

"A family friend, then?"

"Yes," she answered brightly.

He nodded and looked behind her toward the door. "Where is your uncle this afternoon? Don't you usually walk home together?"

"Yes, we do. He was called away around lunchtime. Some sort of emergency, but he didn't say what it was."

"I hope it wasn't anything serious," Mr. Howard said. "Do you think it had something to do with the fire at the janitor's house last night?"

Anne blinked. "I wouldn't think so. But—"

"But what?"

"Well, Mike Dixon came to speak to him just before he left."

Patrick Howard nodded. "Then it must be about the fire."

"Why do you say that?"

"Because I heard they arrested the janitor's assistant for it," he explained. "Didn't your uncle help him get the job?"

"Yes, he did." Anne's brows furrowed. Why on earth would Mr. Ward burn down the janitor's house? She knew he'd lost his job when

Mike lost his, but she had never imagined him capable of something so violent. She shrugged. "I'll find out when I get home. He's sure to be back by now."

"Would you like me to escort you? I can make sure the new man is treating Scioto properly."

Anne gritted her teeth as she reminded herself that Mr. Howard had no idea who the "new man" was. "No, thank you. It's not a very long walk, and I can assure you that Scioto is just fine."

Mr. Howard looked resigned. "I see," he said. Stiffly, he tipped his bowler hat. "Please give your uncle my regards."

Anne watched Mr. Howard walk south toward his boardinghouse. One more young man finally chased away. Tears pricked at her eyes as she wondered if she shouldn't reconsider everything. Was spinsterhood her only option? Memories of last month's visit to Columbus sharply asserted themselves. No, for everyone's sake, this had to be done. Besides, how could she court, or especially marry, someone without telling him the truth about herself? *You tried that with Sam, remember? See how that turned out!*

Dusk began to fall as she walked into the house. She poked her head into the kitchen, and Mrs. Werner told her Uncle Daniel was out back with "that horse of his." Chuckling, Anne went to change, eager to make her way to the stable. Even though her conversations with Scioto weren't as helpful as they used to be, working in the stable was still something of a balm.

Uncle Daniel was standing outside Scioto's stall when she came in. "Good afternoon, my dear."

"Hello," she said, giving him a hug. "Now, what was all the fuss about today?" She checked Scioto's feed bin. It was empty, and she looked inquiringly at her uncle.

"He's already been fed," he replied with a slight smile.

Anne walked to the tack room and returned with the grooming kit.

"I was called away to the courthouse."

"The courthouse?" Anne let herself in the stall. Scioto gently nudged her in greeting. She slid his halter on and secured the lead. "Why? Did it have to do with the fire at the janitor's house?"

"As a matter of fact, it did."

She was about to ask what happened when she ran her hand over Scioto's coat. Turning, she looked at her uncle in consternation. "Don't tell me you groomed him as well? I thought your arm was still a little stiff."

"It is."

"Then who groomed him?"

"I did."

Anne stepped out of the stall. A handsome young man came down the stairs that led to the stable man's chambers above. He was wiping his freshly shaven face with a towel, and his chocolate-brown hair looked as if it had been recently trimmed. He flung the towel over his shoulder, his green eyes taking hold of hers. She stared at him, struggling to figure out just where she'd seen those eyes before.

"Anne," her uncle said. "Surely you remember Mr. Ward."

"Mr. Ward?" she breathed. No, it couldn't be. Could it? Was it possible that all that hair had covered up such a handsome face?

He smiled, and Anne thought her heart would stop from sheer exhaustion. "At your service, Miss Kirby; as you can see, I do more than kill spiders."

His meaning quickly shot through her addled thoughts and brought them to order. She frowned. Handsome or not, why was *he* doing *her* job? And him a criminal! She crossed her arms. "I thought you also swept rooms and fixed gas pipes, not to mention burning down houses."

Her uncle frowned. "Anne."

"Patrick Howard told me they arrested him last night for burning down Mike's house!"

"The charges were dropped," Uncle Daniel replied sternly. "Mike came to get me today because he knew Mr. Ward was innocent and wanted me to speak with him on Mr. Ward's behalf."

"Then how did it burn down?"

"It was an accident," Mr. Ward replied. "I'm afraid I left the wood box too close to the stove. I fell asleep, and the stove overheated." He looked at her uncle with sincere eyes. "I can assure you that won't happen here, sir."

Uncle Daniel smiled and patted him on the shoulder. "Of course not; I know you'll take good care of Scioto."

"But he's a janitor, Uncle Daniel," Anne countered.

"Actually, Mr. Ward is a man of many talents," her uncle said. "Ones that will no longer go untapped." Anne saw the look he and Mr. Ward exchanged.

"Yes, sir." Mr. Ward smiled slightly. He turned his green gaze to her once more. "I have to compliment you, Miss Kirby. You've done a good job."

"Yes, Anne was very thorough," her uncle said. "I'm sure she'll be relieved to have the responsibility taken out of her hands." Anne swung around to look at him. "You do remember agreeing you'd do the job only until a replacement could be found."

"Yes, but—"

"Now, I believe Mrs. Werner is nearly finished with dinner and I'm famished," her uncle said before she could protest further. "It's been along day."

Anne, watching Mr. Ward walk into Scioto's stall and pick up the grooming bucket, felt a slight sense of betrayal as the horse nudged him just as he'd done to her a few minutes earlier. He smiled, and she saw the regard he already held for the animal as he gently stroked Scioto's neck. He put the grooming kit away then held the door open for her and her uncle and followed them out.

She was surprised and more than curious that her uncle insisted Mr. Ward eat with them. Don had always eaten with Mrs. Werner in the kitchen—when he'd been around. She also noticed the way her uncle looked at the young man every now and then. Seeing him now, clean shaven, she didn't see how he'd reminded her uncle of her cousin.

"Where are you from, Mr. Ward?" she asked as they ate.

"Pittsburgh."

"And you worked in a stable or a livery there?"

His gaze met her uncle's. Mr. Ward looked down and leaned back in his chair. "No, I learned everything I know about horses from a man named Henry Farley. He trained racehorses."

Anne furrowed her brow. "Then you *did* work in a stable?"

"My family owned the stable."

Anne's eyes widened. She looked at her uncle.

"Mr. Ward is the poor relation of a rather wealthy family," her uncle explained.

"Oh," she said. "I see."

Mr. Ward glanced at her then returned to his dinner.

Anne frowned. He had to be hiding something. If he was trained to work with horses, why hadn't he found a job in a livery or a stable? Why tramp around—for who knows how many months—then become a janitor? Just because the charges for the fire had been dropped didn't mean he wasn't a wanted man elsewhere. She glanced at him, wondering if her uncle was letting his fatherly feelings for this young man lead him astray. His handsome face and charming manners might be hiding a more vicious nature than they imagined.

This thought drove Anne out to the stable the next morning. All sorts of scenarios had run through her head the night before—from Mr. Ward harming Scioto to out-and-out making off with him. She was relieved to see the horse's familiar face greet her when she came into the stable. He nudged and snuffed at her, clearly looking for food. Anne looked at his feed bin. It was empty. He hadn't been fed yet? Furious, she filled a bucket with oats and was about to open his stall door to pour it in when a sharp voice brought her to a halt.

"Stop!"

Anne whirled around to find Mr. Ward walking in the door with an old, banged-up pot, steam rising from its contents.

"If you don't mind," he said, looking from her to the stall door.

Anne opened it, and he poured the pot's contents into Scioto's bin. The horse sniffed it then began to eat with relish. Mr. Ward smiled and patted the horse on the neck.

"There you are, old man," he said. "Sorry, it took a little longer than I thought." He looked at Anne. "And I'm sorry if I sounded a bit rough. This is better for him than that."

Anne frowned. "Since when are oats poor feed for horses, Mr. Ward?"

"Oats are excellent for horses, but they're even better when they've been cooked."

"You cooked porridge for my uncle's horse?"

"Mrs. Werner gave me the same look." He laughed. "The German military cook their horses' feed. It helps them digest it."

"I've lived on a farm all my life, Mr. Ward. I've never heard of anything so outlandish."

"I assure you it works. My friend Henry Farley swears by it. I'll ease him onto it, of course, but he certainly seems to like it."

Anne frowned as she glanced at Scioto who, she had to admit, was enjoying his breakfast more than he usually did. The horse nudged Mr. Ward's arm. "You should feel honored. He doesn't take to new people so easily."

Mr. Ward's eyes locked onto hers. "I know. I guess he knows I'm someone he can trust."

Anne felt her face grow warm, and she looked down.

"I have a deep regard for your uncle, Miss Kirby. He helped lead me to my faith in God. I can see how much Scioto means to him. And to you. I would never do anything to hurt him."

Anne reached over and stroked the horse's neck. The fact of the matter was, she really wanted to find something wrong with Peter Ward so she could still take care of Scioto. But her uncle had always been a good judge of character, and she couldn't ignore the sincerity in Mr. Ward's voice and face. *I'll be leaving soon. Maybe it's for the best.* Feeling a hand on her arm, she jumped. Mr. Ward was looking at her curiously.

"Are you all right, Miss Kirby?"

"Yes, of course," she replied with a smile she knew had to looked forced. "He's finished eating. He likes to be groomed now."

Mr. Ward raised a brow at her but walked over to the tack room to fetch the grooming bucket. "I have to admit I'm almost sorry to be taking your job away from you," he said when he returned. "You did an excellent job."

Admiration shone in his green eyes, and her heart jumped in her chest. He was not quite as tall as her uncle, but he was close. Less than a head shorter, she estimated. And undeniably handsome. She decided he was indeed a dangerous man. Just not in the way she originally thought. "Thank you, but if you'll excuse me, I don't want to be late for work."

"You can come and visit him whenever you like."

She paused but didn't look back. "Thank you, Mr. Ward."

Peter stopped the buggy outside the stable and opened the wide door to the carriage stall. He turned. Dr. Kirby had already climbed down and now stood at Scioto's head, ready to lead him in.

"Here, sir, let me do that. It's what you pay me for," Peter said.

"Yes, so I do." Dr. Kirby chuckled as he moved to let Peter take him.

"Thank you for letting me come along with you to Professor Townshend's home for Thanksgiving dinner," he said, unhitching the horse. "I've never had a better one."

"Mrs. Townshend and her cook did themselves proud, didn't they?"

he said. Peter released Scioto's harness from the shafts, and Dr. Kirby took hold of his bridle. "Here, allow me."

Peter pulled the buggy into its place then took Scioto and began unbuckling the harness. Scioto shook his head.

"You're ready for a rubdown, aren't you, old man?" He smiled as the horse raised his head higher and pricked his ears forward.

Dr. Kirby laughed. "You're doing a fine job with him, Peter."

"Thank you, sir."

"Come in as soon as you're done. With Mrs. Werner visiting her family today, I'm afraid it will be up to me to make us some coffee."

Before long, Peter sat next to the professor in the parlor with a cup of the brew in his hands. It had turned quite chilly, and between the coffee and the fire dancing in the hearth, Peter soon felt quite warm.

"I'm surprised you didn't go with your niece to Ostrander, sir. I'm sure your family would have liked to see you."

"I'll see them at Christmas," Dr. Kirby said. "They're all coming down to visit with me then, and this big house will feel livelier for a change. The university originally built this for a professor with a much larger family, but he decided to teach elsewhere." He looked at Peter. "Will you be going back to Pittsburgh over Christmas?"

Peter squirmed. The professor was fishing for information again. For the past week, he'd been dropping hints and asking leading questions, attempting to encourage Peter to tell him more about his past. After leaving the courthouse, the professor had brought him here and demanded to know how he knew so much about horses. Peter told him about working with Henry and then told him he was a rich family's "poor relation." He'd hoped that would be enough to satisfy his curiosity, but the professor seemed determined to know more detail. Peter was at a loss to understand why. He chose his words carefully. "My family would probably rather I stay away."

"Oh?" The professor's eyes gleamed curiously.

"I didn't leave under the best of circumstances."

"I see." Expectant silence ruled for more than several moments. The professor finally broke it. "You're not going to tell me more, are you?"

"No, sir." He knew he should be able to trust Dr. Kirby with his past, but he still couldn't bring himself to tell him everything. Peter saw a frown form on his face, and he settled for a portion of the truth. "We had something of a falling out."

The professor studied him. "Does it have something to do with what you said in the courtroom? 'I haven't always been the man I am now.' I believe that's how you phrased it."

Peter stared into his coffee cup. "There are things in my past I'm not proud of, sir. I'd rather just leave it at that."

"I wish you would tell me, Peter."

"And I wish you would tell me why you were so adamant I work for you instead of helping me find a job at a stable in Columbus. Or why you insisted I shave my beard." He bit his lip, ashamed at himself for being so sharp. The fire snapped and crackled in the hearth. Peter looked up. But instead of a frown, the professor wore a strange kind of smile.

"You remind me of someone." He leaned back in his chair. "Has my niece been trying to help you in the stable?"

"No, sir, she hasn't," he replied, surprised, yet relieved at the abrupt change in subject. "As a matter of fact, I only see her on mornings you both come to visit Scioto." That fact was a great relief to Peter. The knowledge that Anne Kirby was a very capable horsewoman made her even more attractive. The care she'd given Scioto had been excellent. She was like the jewel of great worth he'd read about in the Bible a few nights ago. A man would do just about anything to possess someone like her. *Stop it*, he told himself. *She's been hurt enough without the likes of me toying with her heart.*

"She wasn't happy to have you come along and replace her," the professor said thoughtfully. "But I promised her pa to keep her out of the stable. He and her ma want her to settle down and find someone to marry. She can't do that, doing men's work."

Peter sighed inwardly at the irony of the situation. The one person who wouldn't mind having a wife capable and willing to do man's work was the one person who didn't deserve her. *I'll only end up hurting her like all the others. Something about her will make me abandon her, and I just won't do that again, especially to her.* "I'll make sure she only comes to the stable to give Scioto the occasional sugar cube, sir," he said firmly.

But the morning after Anne's return, Peter came down to the stable to find that Scioto had been groomed. His brow furrowed as he ran his hand over the horse's gleaming coat. There was no doubt she had done it, but *when*? Peter rose early to cook Scioto's feed before Mrs. Werner needed the stove for breakfast. Was it possible Miss Kirby had risen even earlier than that? He watched her carefully as they sat down to breakfast. She didn't appear tired. But something told him the cheerful face she put on was forced.

"Did you and Mr. Ward enjoy yourselves at Dr. Townshend's, Uncle?" she asked.

"Yes, our feast was very good. I don't have to ask about yours. Your ma is one of the finest cooks in all of Delaware County," he replied. "How is everyone? How is Millie getting on with that young man she's been seeing?"

Peter swore he saw all color leave Miss Kirby's face. The professor was taking a bite of his eggs and didn't notice. By the time he looked up again, she had pasted a smile on her face.

"Andrew Campbell proposed to Millie," she said, a little too brightly. "They want to get married in the spring."

"That's wonderful news!" the professor said. "I'll have to write to Jonah and congratulate them."

"Congratulations, Miss Kirby," Peter said. "I'm happy for your sister."

Anne nodded and picked up her plate as she rose from her place. "I am, too. Thank you, Mr. Ward."

He watched her walk into the kitchen, wondering just how happy she was. As it turned out, he didn't have to wait long to find out. After finding Scioto groomed for the next two mornings, he decided to confront her about it. He'd be breaking his promise to the professor if he didn't. He went to bed early and managed to wake up while it was still quite dark. He dressed quietly and saw a light as he crept downstairs from his room. She was standing in Scioto's stall, brushing him down. Something glinted on her face in the lamplight. He frowned. Was she crying?

"I love Millie, but I can't help but envy her happiness."

She spoke softly to the horse, but the tightness in her voice told him everything. He walked to the stall. The door stood open. He moved in behind her and gently laid his hand on her shoulder. Without thinking, he used her Christian name. "Anne?"

Her head dropped. "I'm sorry, Uncle Daniel."

Peter cleared his throat uncomfortably.

She turned to look at him. Her eyes widened.

"Mr. Ward!"

She thrust the brush she held into his hand and left the stall. Scioto started and pawed his straw, forcing Peter to lay a comforting hand on his neck and speak a few soothing words to him. By the time he'd calmed the horse, she was gone.

Chapter 11

Two days later, Anne stepped onto the streetcar, paid the fare, and settled into a seat near the rear of the car. She'd watched Mrs. Werner leave on an earlier car, and her uncle had left on Scioto an hour or so ago. He'd told her he didn't expect to be back until dinner. The only other person to evade was Mr. Ward, and that had been easy enough to accomplish since he spent most of his time in the stable.

Heat rose in her cheeks as if she'd sat in front of the fire too long. She closed her eyes. It had been a foolish thing to do; sneaking out to the stable so early to be with Scioto. She should never have snuck out to groom him. Then Mr. Ward wouldn't have suspected anything. How much had he heard the other morning? Worse, would he tell her uncle? It hadn't appeared he had yet, but that didn't mean he wouldn't. If he did, she'd come up with some sort of explanation. The harder thing to face was that she certainly couldn't risk sneaking out again.

The car left the area around the university and soon approached the rail yards. The road sloped downward and entered a short tunnel. Many trains had to cross High Street to get to Union Station, making the tunnel a necessary evil. The filth created by the streetcar horses made the odor within quite strong, even for Anne's farm-raised nose. She raised a handkerchief to her face, and she and the other passengers took a great gulp of fresh air when the car resurfaced.

She kept track of the streets as they rolled by so she wouldn't miss her stop. Spring Street, Long Street, Gay Street, and then finally, Broad Street. Broad and High bustled with activity, even on a Saturday. She got off and stood on the northwest corner of the intersection, admiring the tall three- and five-story buildings. Her favorite was a castle-like building directly across Broad Street. It was the Huntington Bank, where her uncle did business. He said Mr. Huntington, the owner, was one of the friendliest men who ever lived. She was smiling over what Uncle Daniel had told her about the banker greeting customers as he sat whittling on the steps of his bank, when the Broad Street streetcar stopped in front of her. Sharply reminded of her errand, the smile slipped away, and she got on, once again taking a seat near the back.

She carefully adjusted her bonnet, making sure it hid her face as much as possible, and wrapped her cloak closer. She was glad they were so worn that no one would wonder too much that they were out of fashion. Most would merely assume they were all she had to wear to keep out the chill.

Within fifteen minutes, a wide, well-kept lawn came into view. The streetcar stopped, and she alighted with shaky hands. Rubbery legs took her up a long path to an imposing Gothic brick building. It had a mansard roof with two large square towers on both ends. An arched cupola rose from the center. Many simpler brick buildings spread out behind it on either side. She'd heard it was one of the better institutions; that its founder had been good friends of social reformer Dorothea Dix, and its patients were well treated. But that hardly made her visit to the Columbus Asylum for the Insane pleasant.

As Anne stepped through the doors, the visitors' attendant greeted her.

"Good morning, miss," the young man said. "I see you've come for another visit."

"If he's up to it," Anne said quietly.

"Why don't you sign in, and we'll find out."

Anne did as she was asked, taking care to sign in under the name of Wells, and sat down on a bench to wait. Before long her name was called, and she was led to the institution's conservatory. She'd been told on her visit last month that it was a recent addition to the asylum. A donor had left a certain sum of money with the wish that it be used for the benefit of the patients. Plants from all around the country had been purchased, some even donated by the National Conservatory in Washington.

But their lush beauty was lost on Anne as she was led to a wrought-iron bench where a man sat, stone-faced, with hair as ginger red as her own. He was comfortably dressed and his hair and beard neatly trimmed. A large male attendant stood just a few feet away, and she nodded to him as she knelt down in front of the man. She swallowed in an effort to free the words that were sticking in her throat.

"Hello, Pa. I'm back to see you."

He said nothing. His brown eyes stared right through her, just as they had before. According to his doctor, whom Anne spoke with on her first visit, he hadn't always been completely motionless. In the years following the incident that led the Kirbys to adopt her, he had spoken wildly and at times had to be restrained. But over the last few months, he had slipped into this state. His attendant could move him in any position, and he remained that way. He either couldn't or wouldn't speak. Neither could he walk. His attendant had to carry him. Anne slowly sat next to him on the bench. She removed her bonnet and reached out to take one of his hands, which rested on his knees. It was cold and waxy, and his fingers refused to curl around hers.

She sat with him for some time, looking at him occasionally, willing him to return her gaze. He never did. Her emotions swung erratically, and she couldn't figure out which to lock on to—anger at what he had done or pity over what had happened to him. A great surge of shame and grief welled up inside her, threatening to burst forth like a flash flood during a spring thunderstorm. She managed to swallow most of it, but a stray tear escaped and splashed onto her free hand. Someone knelt at her feet and offered her a handkerchief. She looked up to find herself gazing into green eyes that were as filled with compassion as much as her own were filled with tears.

Anne took the handkerchief and used it to cover her face. She heard her father's attendant move forward.

"I should take him back to his room now, Miss Wells," he said.

She felt her father's hand slip from hers as his attendant picked him up to take him back to his room. As the footsteps faded away, Mr. Ward took the place beside her. He didn't speak, but Anne could feel the questions he wanted to ask. Who was that man? Why was she here? Why had the attendant called her Miss Wells? She took a shaky breath.

"That man's name is Robert Wells. He's my father. He lost his senses fighting the war. . .that's why the Kirbys adopted me. They never told me." She tried to go on, but months of pent-up emotion suddenly spilled out and she found herself leaning against Mr. Ward's shoulder sobbing uncontrollably. She was dimly aware of his arm coming around her shoulders and pulling her close.

How long they sat there that way she didn't know. Her tears lessened, and he pulled her to her feet. He handed her the bonnet, and with wooden fingers, she put it on. He took her gently by the elbow and walked her out to the streetcar. Before she knew it, they were home. Mr. Ward walked her up to the door, and she looked at him, apprehensively. What would he do now? Would he tell her uncle where she'd been?

"Get some rest, Miss Kirby," he said. "We'll talk later."

She went up to her room and lay down on her bed, but rest was the last thing on her mind. Just what was Peter Ward planning to do?

∽

Peter ran his hand down Scioto's leg. It still looked sound, and he smiled at the professor. "He's fine. It's healed nicely."

The professor smiled. "Good, then I must have been imagining things. I swore he started to limp a little."

They were outside the stable, the professor having just returned. Miss Kirby had joined them and looked on. Peter handed the bridle to her.

"Would you mind walking him around for me? I want to be sure he's sound."

He saw the questioning look in her eyes but didn't react to it. Pursing her lips, she took the reins from him and did as he'd asked. Peter watched them both as she walked Scioto back and forth. He'd hoped she would get some rest, but looking at her now, she still seemed troubled. When he had gone to the asylum today to visit Uncle Billy, he'd never dreamed he'd find her there. He was relieved that her problem was not what he'd originally imagined, but that didn't make it any less delicate. It was clear she was shouldering this burden by herself. As much as he was trying to keep her at a distance, she clearly needed to talk to someone, a person and not a horse. A thought occurred to him just as the professor's voice invaded his thoughts.

"Peter?"

He blinked. "Yes, sir?"

"I said he seems fine to me."

"Yes, sir, he is." He smiled apologetically as he took Scioto from Miss Kirby. "I'm sorry. I was a little lost in thought."

"What about?"

"Your niece." They both stared at him, and he quickly rephrased his answer. "I meant I was wondering if I might trouble your niece to help me with something."

Miss Kirby arched an eyebrow at him then looked at her uncle. "What can I do for you, Mr. Ward?"

"As you know, I like to cook Scioto's feed in the morning and evening. But that takes time. Would it be possible for you to cook it and bring it out to me?"

She pursed her lips. "I would if I could cook, Mr. Ward."

The professor chuckled at Peter's surprised look. "Sad to say, it's true, in spite of my sister-in-law's best efforts."

"Well, I'm willing to give it *my* best effort." Peter smiled at Miss Kirby's doubtful look. "It's not hard, I promise. I'll be happy to show you after dinner if, of course, this is agreeable to you, Dr. Kirby."

"I don't see the harm in it." The professor smiled at his niece, who still seemed hesitant. "Go on and try. It can't hurt."

A few hours later, the two of them stood over the stove in Mrs. Werner's sparkling kitchen. Dr. Kirby, wishing them well, went into the library to grade papers. Miss Kirby looked around her with pursed lips. "I hope you're prepared to scrub this place down once we're finished, Mr. Ward."

Peter gave her a droll look and peeked into his worn cook pot. "We're just boiling water right now, Miss Kirby."

She shook her head. "You haven't seen me in action."

"Here," he said, bringing forth a bucket of oats. "Put about two scoops of this into the water." She did so, and he handed her a flat wooden paddle. "Keep stirring it so it won't scorch."

"Is this all we put in?"

"We need to add equal parts of wheat bran and salt, but not quite yet."

While she did spill some of the bran and the result was slightly scorched, Scioto didn't seem to notice. He munched away unconcerned, and a small smile graced Miss Kirby's face.

"You seem to be feeling better now."

The smile disappeared, and he instantly regretted his words. Her face was so much more beautiful when she smiled. "I hope we can forget about what happened earlier today, Mr. Ward. Thank you for your kindness in seeing me home, but it's really no longer your concern."

"I'm afraid I can't do that, Miss Kirby."

"Why?" Her brown eyes grew dark.

"No one should have to carry such a burden alone."

"I'm not carrying it alone," she retorted. She reached out and stroked Scioto's neck.

"As much regard as I have for Scioto, he's not going to answer you, and he's not going to help you solve anything."

"I don't need him to solve anything. I just need him to listen."

"That doesn't seem to be working out very well." He grasped her elbow, forcing her to face him. Her eyes were dark pools, glimmering in the lamplight. "It isn't, is it?"

"No," she whispered, and lowered her head against his chest.

Peter couldn't help but allow himself to wrap his arms around her. When he had asked God to send her someone who could help her, he hadn't imagined that He intended on sending him. *I don't want to hurt her, Lord. I don't trust myself not to.*

"Then trust Me."

Steeling himself, he gently pulled her away and led her over to a small bench across from Scioto's stall, near the harness room. He offered her his handkerchief. She took it with a small, humorless laugh.

"I still have your other one."

"It's all right. I have plenty." He patiently waited for her to dry her face before speaking again. "Tell me about him."

Chapter 12

A nne looked at him for a long moment. He returned her gaze, his eyes filled with the same compassion he'd shown her as she sat beside her father at the asylum. Where was the fear, the revulsion? *He doesn't know all of it yet.* No, he didn't know everything. He might understand her natural father losing his senses, but he'd never understand the rest. She'd just have to be careful.

"I only found out about him a few months ago," she said. "The Kirbys had always told me I was adopted but never told me about him."

"To protect you," he stated.

Anne nodded.

"How did you find out?"

She shut her eyes against the memory. It had been a warm spring day, and Pa had sent her to find a letter from Uncle Daniel.

"Pa asked me to fetch a letter from the desk in the parlor. I thought I found it, and when I opened it to be certain, I found a letter from. . .the asylum." The words she'd read still haunted her. "*Mr. Wells's condition has not improved. . . . He still has no knowledge that you and your wife adopted his daughter, Anne.*" How she managed to find the right letter and give it to Pa with any measure of composure, she didn't know. "The asylum sends yearly updates to Pa through my uncle. I found most of them." Afterward, she'd slipped downstairs every night, piecing together the whole story.

"What about your natural mother? Did you find out what happenedto her?"

Anne looked down, lest something in her expression tell him more than she wanted. "She died."

"Have you been praying about this?"

"I did at first. But the more I prayed, the more I realized—" She stopped, acutely aware that she'd almost revealed too much.

"Anne?" At the sound of her uncle's approach, relief seared through her, until she saw the expression on Mr. Ward's face. "Please don't tell him."

"He should know."

"No, please. He'll tell my parents, and I don't want them to get hurt."

He hesitated then nodded reluctantly. "But you know you can't keep this from them forever."

"I know, and I won't; I promise." It was the truth. She'd always intended to tell her family, but only after she and her father were safely out West—when what he was and what he'd done couldn't threaten their reputation any longer.

∞

A clear, cold December day had given way to a fiery purple dusk as Anne made her way to the stable with Scioto's feed. She'd been fixing it for two weeks now, and when she delivered it in the evenings, she always lingered in the stable, watching Scioto eat and afterward talking with Peter as he groomed him. She smiled as she knocked her foot against the door. When had they started calling each other by their Christian names? She couldn't be sure, but she knew that because of their talks, her heart felt lighter than it had in months. It didn't make her departure any easier, but it didn't hang over her head like it had been. The door to the stable opened, and she came face-to-face with Peter's devilish grin.

"What took you so long?"

Anne smiled reprovingly as she walked in. "I'm right on time as always."

"Of course you are." He shut the door. "I could set my watch by you." He lifted the latch that secured the top half of the stable door and pushed it open, as always. It made the stable a little chilly, but at least no one could accuse them of impropriety. Mrs. Werner had a clear view of them from the kitchen window.

"Here, let me take that from you." He poured the feed into Scioto's tub and set the pot down near the door for Anne to take with her when she went back inside. He leaned against the stable door next to her as they watched Scioto eat. "How's life in the library?"

Anne rolled her eyes. "Suffocating, literally."

"What do you mean?"

"When the Main Building isn't one big block of ice, it stinks of sulfur fumes. Our new janitor can't seem to get the gas to work right."

Peter shook his head. "Mike tried to warn the board Mr. Pryce wasn't the man for the job."

"Well, it goes without saying that everyone misses you and Mike. I wish someone would help the poor man."

"Maybe I should go see him tomorrow after I have Scioto settled."

"Are you sure you should do that?" Peter had told her about his run-ins with the man. She didn't like the idea of him possibly being goaded into a fight.

"I might be able to help him. It's the right thing to do." Scioto finished eating, and Peter fetched the grooming kit from the tack room. Anne watched him in silence for a few minutes.

"Peter, what happened that made you become a tramp?"

His back was to her, but she could tell the question bothered him as his brushstrokes slowed. In all their conversations, he'd never really brought up his past. He'd told her a few stories about working with Mr. Farley, but never anything about his childhood or who had raised him.

"Necessity," he replied.

"Did your family fire you? Or sell the stable?"

"The stable was sold."

"Then why didn't you get a job at another stable? I don't understand why your family would let you go homeless."

Peter turned and came over to the stall door. He looked gravely into her eyes. "Anne, my family and I had a falling out. I wasn't the best of men before I came here, and there are things in my past I'm not proud of. But I'm different now—a new creation, thanks to God—and I just want to leave all that behind me."

Anne nodded. She certainly understood what he meant about being ashamed of things in his past. Her eyes flicked to the stable floor. Her natural father had certainly given her nothing to be proud of. Peter ducked his head, catching her eye. She raised her eyes, and he cocked his head at her. "Are you all right?"

She smiled slightly. "Yes, I'm fine."

He studied her face. "You're sure?"

She nodded.

"All right." He squeezed her hand then turned to continue grooming Scioto.

Anne was glad his back was to her again, so he wouldn't see the effect his touch had on her. Heat flew to her cheeks and a delicious thrill flowed from her head to her toes. She bit her lip as she tried to tamp it down. She had no business letting herself feel something for this man— this handsome, wonderful, faithful man who sometimes let her groom Scioto when there was time before dinner, and who seemed to actually admire her ability with horses. He was everything she'd ever wanted in a man and more. She screwed her eyes shut. *Stop it.*

She would be gone in a few weeks. The school outside Topeka expected her, and the Topeka Insane Asylum had written to tell her they had room for her father. The letters were tucked in the waist of her skirt, beneath her bodice. She patted them to make sure they were still there. The only thing she had yet to do was speak to her father's doctor in Columbus. She wondered if Peter planned to go back to the asylum to visit the friend he'd told her about. The question was on the tip of her tongue when he spoke first.

"I enjoyed Reverend Aylsworth's lesson, yesterday." He smiled at her over the top of Scioto's back. Reverend Aylsworth was their pastor at Central Christian Church in Columbus.

"He preached on your favorite passage, didn't he? The Twenty-Third Psalm." As hard as it had been to hear the sermon, she was glad Peter enjoyed it.

"It helped me keep my head together before I faced Mayor Walcutt." He finished grooming Scioto, unhooked the lead, and took off his halter. The horse nuzzled him, and he rubbed Scioto's nose in return. He stepped out of the stall and paused in front of her. "I've been praying that for you."

"What?" She wished he'd tell her as he took the grooming bucket back to the tack room. It would be so much easier to breathe.

"That God would restore your soul. You still seem sad sometimes, like you were a minute ago."

"I'm fine, Peter."

"Are you praying again?"

She nodded. She had started to pray again. Sort of. She prayed God would take away these feelings she had for him. If He didn't, leaving in a few weeks would be sheer torture.

"I'm glad." He didn't move, and Anne found herself getting lost in the green of his eyes. Mesmerized, she took a step closer to him. Just then, a nicker and a dark head appeared between them, and she all but cried out in relief.

"We should get inside. I'm sure Mrs. Werner has dinner ready," she said.

Peter shook himself, looking almost as relieved as she, and as she watched him walk to the tack room to put away the grooming bucket, she couldn't help wondering why. Was it because he also felt something? Or because he didn't?

∞

"I still don't believe I did it," Anne said. "I actually fried an egg!"

"And I actually ate it," Dr. Kirby remarked, grinning. "And I'm still breathing."

Peter grinned at the semi-withering look she sent her uncle as the three of them walked toward the Main Building. Since he'd wanted to help Harvey with the heat today, he'd gotten up extra early and beaten Anne to the kitchen. Once he fed and watered Scioto, he came in to find her disappointed that the chore was already done. To make up for it, he taught her how to fry an egg.

"I told you it wasn't that hard," he said. "If I can do it, anyone can."

"If *you* can?" Dr. Kirby mused.

Peter looked over Anne to the professor, expecting to see that curious look of his. Instead, he was greeted by a knowing smile. Uncertain what to make of it, Peter gave him a half grin and looked out at the new coat of snow.

"Looks like Christmas will be white if the weather holds," Peter said.

"Yes," Anne replied softly. He glanced down at her. She had that sad, wistful look on her face again, the same one he'd tried hard not to kiss away in the stable yesterday.

He returned his gaze to the snow-covered campus. *Thank You for letting Scioto interrupt, Lord.* A few seconds more and she'd have been in his arms. *You sent me to help her, not break her heart. I'll try to be more self-controlled.* But even as he prayed, he felt a disappointment he didn't quite understand. He pushed it away as they approached the Main Building.

"Well, Peter," the professor said. "I sincerely hope your time with Mr. Pryce will be fruitful."

"Thank you, sir. I hope your day goes well, too."

"Oh, it will, my boy, it will." He looked almost gleeful.

Anne noticed it as well and gave him a quizzical look as he kissed her cheek. "Are you feeling all right, Uncle Daniel?"

"The difficulties with the heat have given me the beginnings of a cold, I'm afraid," he replied. Peter couldn't help but grin at the look of consternation on Anne's face. That hadn't been the answer she was looking for. Dr. Kirby either didn't notice or pretended not to as he went on. "Are you coming up with me?"

"I think I'll wait for Emma. She should be along any moment," she replied slowly.

"Tell her I said 'hello' then," Dr. Kirby said. Nodding to Peter, he turned and walked up the stairs and went inside.

"I'm glad to see him so happy," Anne said as she and Peter looked after him. "I just can't imagine why he is."

"He's up to something," he said.

"How do you know?"

"My granddad used to get the same look in his eye. It always meant—" He stopped himself as he realized what he'd just said. He hazarded a look at Anne. Despite that they weren't related by blood, Peter couldn't help noticing she and Dr. Kirby had similar expressions of curiosity.

He sighed. "All right, you caught me. My grandfather raised me after my mother died when I was a toddler."

"Oh Peter, I'm so sorry. What happened to your father?"

"He abandoned my mother before I was born. I've never met him."

He was glad they were standing outside with students walking here and there on their way to class. The look of sympathy on her face was so endearing, he struggled not to embrace her.

"I haven't seen my uncle look that happy since before Aunt Kitty died," she said.

"Aunt Kitty? You mean his wife, Katherine?"

"Yes. That was my own special name for her. My brother and sister called her Aunt Katherine, but to me, she was always Aunt Kitty." The corners of her mouth curled thoughtfully. "It's because I always heard Uncle Daniel calling her Kat."

"I saw her picture on the mantel in the parlor," Peter said. "She seemed like a very kind and gracious lady."

"Oh, she was." Anne's smile grew as she recalled her aunt. "I loved listening to her talk. She was from South Carolina."

"Really? Did your uncle meet her during the war?" Peter asked. He recalled the professor telling him he'd been a major in the Union army.

"No, she came north after the war ended. A lot of people didn't like that she was Southern, but Uncle Daniel didn't care. In spite of everything, he loved her anyway. . ." The sad look returned to her eyes.

Peter frowned. *She deserves to be happy*, he thought. *And I'd like nothing better than to spend the rest of my life making her that way.* His heart nearly stopped in shock. He stared at Anne, looking at her in a way he'd never looked at another woman. He plumbed the brown depths of her eyes, and Anne's cheeks, already crimson from the cold, became even more so, and she looked away.

"Good morning."

They both started. Emma Long stood before them.

"Good morning," Anne said, her voice breathless with relief. "Emma, do you remember Mr. Ward? He used to work for Mike."

Emma's eyes widened. "I thought I recognized you. You certainly look different without that beard!"

Peter tore his eyes away from Anne long enough to tip his hat. "Thank you, Miss Long." He looked back at Anne, who still avoided his gaze.

Emma locked arms with Anne, her eyes dancing. "We should get inside; it's nearly nine o'clock."

"Yes, of course." Anne quickly glanced at him as she turned to leave. "Take care today. I'll see you later."

Peter nodded and watched as she and Miss Long walked up the steps of the Main Building. His mind still whirled. He couldn't quite believe it. For the first time in his life, he found himself truly and deeply in love.

Chapter 13

"You've come to gloat, haven't you?"

Harvey Pryce stood outside the boiler house, his arms crossed. Peter had stood what seemed like forever outside the building, waiting for him to show up. Pryce looked anything but happy to see him.

"Who sent you? Mr. Cope?"

"No one sent me. I heard about your problem and wanted to help."

"I don't need your help!"

"Harvey, we both know the buildings aren't being heated properly," Peter said. "Just tell me what's wrong."

The man still scowled at him. "It's the coal. It's not good quality."

"What happened? Did you stop buying from Lyonsdale Coal Company?"

"It's just bad coal is all."

"Let me come in and see what's going on."

"Why? You want your job back?"

"No, I have a new job now."

Harvey's expression softened. A little. "Oh yeah, thought I heard that. You work for Professor Kirby, don't you?" Peter nodded and a little more of the hardness fell from his face. "He's one of the few professors who's been decent to me about all this."

"He's a good man," Peter said.

"Was it him who's getting you to do this?"

"No, but it's his good example. He's the one who took me in after you gave me that timber lesson."

Harvey's shoulders dropped and his arms fell to his sides. "Why didn't you let Mayor Walcutt charge me?"

"'Therefore if thine enemy hunger, feed him,'" Peter quoted. "'If he thirst, give him drink.'"

"'For in so doing thou shalt heap coals of fire on his head.'" Harvey finished the quote. "Don't look so surprised. My ma taught me that when I was young. Guess I kinda forgot a lot of things she taught me. If she could see me now, she'd sure heap coals of fire on my head."

Peter smiled and slapped him on the shoulder. "How about I help you heap coals of fire so the university stays warm? I'll show you how it's done."

"Would you mind an awful lot helping me out today? Frank's sick."

"Sure."

It was nearly dark by the time they finished; but in the end, Peter had helped him get caught up in a number of things and made sure Harvey knew how to properly maintain the heat. Most important of all, Harvey promised he'd come to church. Peter offered to lend him his Bible, but the man declined, saying he had his mother's old one tucked away.

Judging from the sky, he knew Anne and Dr. Kirby had already headed for home and, more than likely, were already there. Despite how busy he'd been, Anne hadn't been far from his thoughts all day. He still marveled over how he felt about her. Shaking his head, he smiled. A Pittsburgh society matron, whose daughter he'd courted then dropped, once said the three rivers would turn purple before Peter McCord fell in love. The Monongahela, the Allegheny, and the Ohio rivers must be positively violet by now, because that day had finally come.

If he'd thought her beautiful the first time he'd seen her picture, she was more than twice that now. All the qualities a young lady needed to start a home—she didn't possess. By her own admission, she couldn't sew, could barely cook, and would rather spend her time in a stable than a parlor. By society's standards, she was a failure. But she was perfect as far as he was concerned—perfect for him.

Now he had to convince her it was possible for him to love her. The way she'd spoken about her aunt and uncle suggested she didn't feel worthy of someone's love. He smiled roguishly. No worries there. He had plenty of experience in that department. Best of all, he would mean every charming word he intended to utter. And for the rest of his life, every gallant deed would be exclusively reserved for Anne Kirby. He lifted his head to the dusky sky. *Thank You, Lord. I see now the path You want me to follow. Thank You for these green pastures and still waters.*

He was thankful when he arrived at the path between Professor

Tuttle's and Professor Kirby's. It hadn't been a long walk, but it'd certainly been a cold one. In the failing light, he could just make out the stable. He frowned. The door gaped open. He began to jog until he heard a voice cry out. Certain that it was Anne's, he broke into a run, covering the distance in seconds. He skidded to a stop in the stable doorway. His heart dropped at the sight before him. Scioto lay thrashing on the floor of his stall. Anne, halter in hand, stood just inside the door, dodging his flailing hooves to reach his head.

∞

Scioto grunted and let out a short squeal. As soon as she'd seen him down, Anne's only thought had been to get him back on his feet. Again, she attempted to get around his hooves, but a strong arm wrapped around her waist and yanked her back.

"No," she cried out. "He'll hurt himself."

As she was pulled out of the stall, she twisted herself around and came face-to-face with Peter. Silently, he took the halter from her and entered the stall. She started after him but found herself pulled backward into her uncle's arms.

Scioto squealed, and Anne gasped as his hoof flew dangerously close to Peter's head. Peter dodged it and moved nearer the horse's head. He slipped on the halter, and after several dreadful minutes, pulling and shouting, Peter managed to get Scioto on his feet. He immediately led the horse out of the stall before he could lie down again.

"I need to walk him," he said, his broad chest heaving like a bellows as the two left the stable. "Get the box stall ready."

Anne grabbed a pitchfork and began spreading straw. The box stall was larger than the other two stalls. Should Scioto begin to thrash again, he'd have more room to move. She winced at the thought. She turned. Her uncle had entered, sleeves rolled up and tie hanging loose around his neck. They finished quickly, and he looked at her. "What happened?"

"I came out to light the lamp and get feed to cook for him." Her voice shaking, Anne took a deep breath, trying to steady it. "When I didn't see him at the stall door, I looked in—" She couldn't go on, and her uncle pulled her close.

"Let's pray it's just a mild case of colic," he said.

Anne nodded against his chest. They both looked up as Peter returned with Scioto. Grabbing their pitchforks, they quickly moved out of the way as Peter led the horse into the stall. Anne's hand flew to her mouth in horror as she watched Scioto kick at his belly and roll his eyes, drenched in his own sweat. She'd seen colic in one of Pa's plow horses. But this was much, much worse. Peter struggled to keep him from lying down again. He glanced at her uncle.

"He needs a veterinarian, sir. This is beyond me."

Uncle Daniel nodded. "By God's grace, one just happens to be staying with Dr. Townshend." He grabbed his coat from where he'd thrown it on the stable floor. "I'll be back with him as soon as I can."

Anne gripped the post next to the door. Peter looked exhausted, his brown hair dampened with sweat despite the cool air. "Let me come in and help you."

"No! He's in too much pain, and I won't have him hurting you." Scioto brushed against the wall. "I don't understand this. I checked on him at noon and he was fine."

"Colic can come on quick."

"But what caused it? We've been so careful about his feed and water."

Anne swallowed the lump in her throat. They'd been very careful with Scioto's care, but they both knew the reason for the condition could be something neither could help nor foresee. It was a fact that Anne felt Peter, at least for the moment, refused to accept.

"I need to walk him again," he said, pulling the poor horse through the door and outside once more.

Anne followed, hoping the movement would bring Scioto relief as was usual in a case of colic. But the more he moved, the more the agony increased, and Peter soon walked him back inside. Scioto shivered and slowly lowered himself to the stable floor. Peter sank down on his knees near Scioto's head.

"Let him rest," he said as Anne cautiously entered the stall. "He's exhausted, and so am I."

She knelt down and laid her hand on Scioto's neck. He didn't respond to her touch. He simply lay there, his breathing labored. She turned her attention to Peter, who looked at the horse miserably, his eyes dark, the green in them barely showing.

"What did I do wrong?"

She took his hand, forgetting herself at the sight of the wretched look on his face.

"You didn't do anything wrong. You know this might be something neither of us could have stopped."

He groaned and pulled her closer, laying his head on her shoulder. Her heart beat furiously, but there was no way she could pull away, he was hurting too badly. Instead, her traitorous hand stroked the damp ends of his hair. Scioto began to thrash, and Peter quickly hauled her up and outside the stall. He calmed again and lay still. Anne looked down at her fingers, entwined with Peter's. And they stood there that way, watching Scioto until her uncle returned. Professor Townshend accompanied him, along with another man. The man, with white hair, a long beard to match, and round spectacles, introduced himself as Dr. Henry Detmers. His German accent, while slightly thicker than Anne's mother's, sounded comforting and familiar. He immediately entered the stall, and Peter followed him.

"Did walking him help?" Dr. Detmers knelt down beside Scioto.

Peter shook his head. "It seemed to make him worse."

The doctor frowned and felt the horse's legs and ears. "Cold," he muttered, and Anne saw Peter's face harden, his mouth forming a thin line as the doctor's fingers pressed on Scioto's throatlatch, taking his pulse.

"It's red colic, isn't it?" Peter asked quietly.

"Enteritis, yes, I'm afraid so." Dr. Detmers opened his black satchel. "I won't attempt to check his belly. I can tell now it will only pain him. We'll need to administer linseed tea and laudanum." He looked up at Dr. Townshend, standing next to Anne. "Unfortunately, I don't have as much of either with me as I would like."

"I have more at my home," Dr. Townshend replied.

"And I'll make the tea—as much as you need—" Anne offered.

Dr. Detmers continued treating Scioto far into the night, assisted by Peter. The medicine seemed to calm him, but in the end, they could only wait. Mrs. Werner made coffee, which Anne tirelessly took to the men several times over the course of the night. When she came out with yet another serving, Peter looked at her wearily.

"You should go to bed," he said as she set the tray down on a small table they'd brought down from Peter's room.

"I want to stay," she replied as she poured a cup.

Uncle Daniel joined them at the table. "Anne, it would be best if you went inside."

She shook her head and, handing him the cup, found he already held something in his hand. His Colt, the one he'd used during the war. She dropped the cup and grabbed his arm.

"Uncle Daniel, no; he might get better." She felt Peter gently grip her shoulders.

"Anne," he said close to her ear. "It's been hours now. There's no change and he's suffering."

Tears sprang to her eyes as she laid her hand over her mouth, allowing the truth of his words to sink into her heart. *Oh Lord, is there truly nothing else to be done?* She bowed her head at the answer. Her uncle took her hand and squeezed it. He looked wretched, having spent most of the night pacing back and forth outside the stall. Disheveled hair and bloodshot eyes, he had the look of a man who'd been keeping vigil, as he had the horrible night Aunt Kitty slipped away. As much as it hurt, she knew it was best for Scioto.

He flicked his eyes from hers to Peter's. "Take her inside."

"Sir," he said, his voice rough. "This is my fault, I should—"

"No, Peter. You're not for one second to believe that. You've taken better care of this horse than even I did when he first came to me. This happened for reasons known only to God. I've accepted that."

As he spoke, Scioto groaned. They approached the stall, and Anne watched as he struggled for a few moments then lay very still. Dr. Detmers felt for his pulse and shook his head. Scioto was gone.

Anne buried her face in her hands. Peter wrapped his arm around her waist, pulling her close, and she felt the warmth from his brow resting on the back of her head. Quiet filled the stable; the only sound was that of Dr. Detmers putting away his instruments. Taking a deep breath, Anne lifted her head. Peter released her as Dr. Townshend offered his handkerchief. Taking it, she gave him a watery smile. "Thank you for staying, Dr. Townshend."

"You're very welcome, my dear." He looked at Uncle Daniel. "Some students and I will come and get him tomorrow."

"Thank you, Norton." He offered his hand to Dr. Detmers. "Thank you for coming on such short notice."

Dr. Detmers shook it. "You're welcome, Dr. Kirby." His eyes swept over to Peter. "You were a great help to me tonight, young man. You should consider becoming a veterinary surgeon yourself."

Peter smiled thinly. "I'm afraid I never was much for book learning, sir, but thank you."

Even as tired as she was, his comment piqued Anne's curiosity. Was this yet another clue to Peter's past? She chastised herself. *It doesn't matter now. You'll be going away soon.* She realized, startled, that Peter actually would go away before her. With Scioto gone, he had no job and no reason to stay. The thought should've brought her relief. Instead, it hurt her so keenly she reached out her hand to steady herself. Her uncle grasped it and her elbow, and she leaned against him.

"It's time you went to bed," he said firmly.

"And sleep yourself out," Dr. Townshend said. "Make sure she stays home tomorrow, Daniel."

"I can't. Emma needs me at the library," Anne protested. But everything finally began to take its toll on her, and she found she could no longer keep her eyes open. Before she knew what happened, her uncle helped her inside and Mrs. Werner tucked her into bed.

Chapter 14

P eter began straightening up the stable. He'd slept all day yesterday, only waking when Dr. Townshend and some students came to haul away Scioto's body. After that, he slept fitfully and came down early this morning to work. He mucked out the stalls and then laid down fresh straw in each one. He checked the harnesses and bridles, oiled Dr. Kirby's saddle, and looked over the buggy three times. When he finished, he stepped back, frowning. Why on earth was he doing all this—for a horse that was no longer here?

As he worked, he'd gone over everything he'd done those last hours of Scioto's life. Nothing had been amiss, *nothing*. The horse had been right as rain when he fed and watered him that morning. And when he'd come home at noon, Scioto had pranced around the paddock without a care in the world. He looked at the rag in his hand and threw it on the ground. *What was it, Lord? What did I do to kill him?*

"It wasn't your fault, Peter."

He turned. Dr. Kirby stood in the door of the stable. He closed it behind him, walked over, and laid a fatherly hand on his back. "There was nothing you could have done."

"There had to be *something*!"

He squeezed his shoulder. "No, Peter. Dr. Detmers and Dr. Townshend performed a necropsy this morning. He twisted his intestine somehow. It had nothing to do with your care of him. Not even your friend Henry Farley could have prevented it." Peter looked at him. The professor's face was sad but firm. "I won't have you beating yourself up over this. Let him go."

He nodded, weighing Dr. Kirby's words. How many times had Henry told him about the possibility of something like this happening to a horse? And burying himself with guilt wouldn't help anyone.

372

"Yes, sir," he said finally.

"We must be 'forgetting those things which are behind, and reaching forth unto those things which are before.'" He looked over at Scioto's empty stall. "Not that any of us will be forgetting him anytime soon."

"No, sir," Peter replied. It would be a long time before he forgot Scioto, if ever. He took a deep breath. "I guess I better pack my things."

Dr. Kirby looked at him sharply. "What are you talking about?"

"What would you have me do, sir? I can't stay here and do nothing all day."

"I'll find something for you to do," the professor snapped.

Peter's eyes widened. He hadn't meant to make him angry. Dr. Kirby's brow smoothed, and he patted him on the back.

"Please, stay. I'll get a new horse in time. And you must stay for Christmas. The rest of the family is eager to meet you."

"All right," he said slowly. "Although, I can't imagine why you would tell your family anything about me."

"Why shouldn't I?" he asked. "Anne's brother, Jacob, is eager to speak with you. He's been thinking of raising Percherons for profit."

Peter didn't hear the rest of what Dr. Kirby said. His mention of Anne had drowned out all else. "Sir, if you don't mind my asking, how is your niece?"

The professor regarded him carefully, and Peter looked away. In spite of everything that occurred that night, Dr. Kirby clearly noticed the way he had embraced Anne after Scioto passed. But he didn't mention it when he spoke.

"She slept late into the day yesterday," he said. "And claims to have slept fine last night." The concern in his eyes told Peter she hadn't looked it. "She's very insistent that we allow her to go to the library today."

"You should let her, sir. It will take her mind off everything."

"You're probably right." A small smile spread over the professor's face. "You two are getting along very well."

Peter felt his face redden and, looking down, rubbed the back of his neck.

"Anne's adopted, you know."

He looked up, surprised. "Yes, sir, I know. She told me."

Dr. Kirby's smile broadened like that of a Cheshire cat's. "Did she? I'm glad." Before Peter could say anything else, he went on. "It's time for us to leave. Mrs. Werner mentioned some repairs you might do around the house." He gave Peter a final pat on the back and left.

He would've put more thought into what Dr. Kirby said if he hadn't missed Anne so much all that day. She was never far from his thoughts, and he sent many prayers up for her as he helped Mrs. Werner around the house. The professor's family would be arriving in a week, on Christmas Eve, and he helped her lift things down from closets and made minor repairs here and there. They finished not long before Anne and Dr. Kirby were due home, and Peter went out to the stable. He changed into clean clothes then walked downstairs. There was Anne, standing in front of Scioto's stable.

She heard him and turned. His heart nearly broke at the sight of her face. Her eyes looked dull and dark. Circles stained the fair skin beneath them. She certainly hadn't slept well last night. Even her fiery, ginger hair seemed less brilliant. He walked closer. His arms ached to hold her. Instead, he gripped the stall door while she directed her gaze to the lonely bed of straw within.

"I still can't believe he's gone," she said.

"Neither can I."

"He was the first horse I ever rode," she whispered. "I was five. I was visiting Uncle Daniel and Aunt Kitty. Uncle Daniel had ridden Scioto to a meeting, and when I saw them trotting up, I ran out to meet them. He asked me if I wanted to ride Scioto. He was such a big horse that I was a little frightened. But Uncle Daniel said Scioto would take care of me." She looked at him, her eyes bright, filling with tears. "And he did. He knew—as soon as Uncle Daniel put me in the saddle—he went so slow, so steady."

Her voice broke on the last word, and Peter couldn't stand it any longer. He pulled her into his arms and allowed the waves of her grief to break against him, rubbing her back as she shook with sobs. When her tears were finally spent, she lifted her head but didn't look up at him.

"I've spoiled your shirt," she said, vainly wiping at it with her hand.

"I have another," he said, lifting her chin. Her eyes wandered hesitantly over his face. A few tears still shone on her cheeks, and he gently wiped them away with his thumb and forefinger. She swallowed, and her eyes darted away, but he continued looking at her until they once again locked onto his. He leaned in and gently brushed her forehead with his lips, her curled bangs brushing his skin like a feather. He longed to kiss her but knew this wasn't the time for it. He wouldn't take advantage of her grief. She stepped back, and he released her.

"It's time we went in for dinner." Her voice was soft and shaky, and she wouldn't look at him.

"I'll be there in a minute."

She nodded and slipped out the door.

Chapter 15

The next week slipped away quickly, and Anne's grief at losing Scioto eased. A bittersweet pang rose in her heart whenever she thought about him, but she comforted herself with the knowledge that his passing had not gone unnoticed by God.

"'And one of them shall not fall on the ground without your Father,'" she whispered as she and Uncle Daniel walked home from the Main Building.

"Did you say something, my dear?"

"I was just thinking of Matthew 10:29."

He nodded. "Yes, that one has been on my thoughts as well."

"He was a good horse," she said, squeezing his arm.

"Peter said it's lonely in the stable without him."

Anne almost started at the sound of his name. That evening in the stable never seemed to be far from her thoughts. She'd felt so comforted in his arms, and she relished in remembering how tender his green eyes had been in the soft lamplight. The kiss he'd placed on her forehead made her dizzy just thinking about it. And over the past week, he'd been very attentive to her, pulling out her chair at dinner and drawing her into the conversations between him and her uncle while they sat together in the parlor. It was as if he were courting her. Her heart leaped as she realized it, and she fought for control. *Stop it! Uncle Daniel may have decided to keep him on, but I'm still leaving.* She laid her hand at the side of her waist, feeling the crinkle of her letters tucked in her bodice, her resolve slipping. Maybe Peter was different. Unlike Sam, he'd seen her father firsthand, and it hadn't made a difference. Dare she tell him the rest? *No. I can't stray from this path. Besides, even if he understands, I can't do that to him. I love him too much.* Her breath caught in her throat as she finally admitted her feelings for him to herself.

It caught again, later, when she came down to dinner and Peter smiled at her. He stood behind her chair, as usual, and as he helped her slide it beneath the table, she happened to look at her uncle. His eyes twinkled and a smile played at the corner of his mouth. She bit the inside of her lip. Wasn't everything hard enough already without knowing that her uncle approved of Peter's regard for her?

"I hope you both had a good day," Peter said. He spoke to both of them, but he was looking at her.

"It was fine," Anne said, averting her eyes to serve her uncle. "It's actually been rather boring, now that term examinations are coming to an end. No one needs the library for now."

"You mean, aside from the other times when it's not?" he asked slyly.

Anne couldn't help looking up and smiling. He knew, so well, how tedious she found her job. "In fact, Emma told me to take the day off tomorrow."

"Excellent," Uncle Daniel said. "That actually fits right in with my plans." He turned to Peter. "Dr. Townshend came to see you today?"

"He did."

"Everything is arranged, then?"

"Yes, sir, everything's ready."

Anne looked at both of them quizzically. "What's going on?"

"Why Anne, I'm so glad you asked," her uncle said. Anne sighed. As if she could do anything but, what with the sly smiles on both their faces. Her uncle continued. "Peter wondered if you could help him with something tomorrow."

She knew it would be better to refuse, but her heart and her mouth turned traitor on her. "Of course, what is it?"

"A surprise." Peter's eyes shone as bright as a spring day. "I'll show you tomorrow, after we walk your uncle to the Main Building."

∽

The next day, Anne's curiosity peaked as Peter led her away from the Main Building. Especially when he stopped after a few steps and looked at her.

"Do you trust me?"

The playful look in his eyes was so charming she almost forgot to answer. "Yes—of course," she stammered.

"Close your eyes."

Anne looked at him momentarily then obeyed. He took her hands in his. Despite that they both wore gloves, the warm pressure of his fingers sent shivers of delight coursing through her.

He gently guided her over snow-covered paths and across what she thought might be Neil Avenue, which ran through the university grounds. She wasn't familiar with this part of campus, and she couldn't imagine where he was taking her. They came to a stop.

"Now don't peek," Peter said.

He removed her glove and guided her hand. At the same time her fingers made contact with something warm, soft, and smooth, the wind changed direction and a familiar scent reached her nose. Her eyes flew open. A sweet bay mare stood before her, hitched to a fence outside the university farm buildings. Anne took in the horse's markings, eyes widening as she recognized her.

"This is Spice," she said. "She belongs to Dr. Townshend. He brought her to our farm this past summer to breed with Scioto. What's she doing here?" The reason quickly dawned on her, and her jaw dropped as she looked at Peter. "He's giving the foal to Uncle Daniel?"

Peter nodded. He took her hand and smiled. "That's not all. If you want her, Spice belongs to you."

Anne looked at the mare with mixed emotions. She'd liked Spice while she was at the farm over the summer. She was so gentle and sweet tempered, Anne had jokingly told Dr. Townshend she should've been named Sugar. Stroking her neck, she wondered how she'd feel seeing her in Scioto's stall, when she remembered it didn't matter. She might as well say yes, and leave a note for Uncle Daniel when she left, giving Spice to him. Not trusting her voice, she nodded.

Peter looked down at her. "Are you sure? I know it's soon—"

She swallowed hard. "Yes, it's fine. Besides, Uncle Daniel said he was going to get another horse soon. It might as well be one I'm familiar with."

His smile warmed her and, for the moment, chased away the rest of her tears. "Then let's get her home and settled in."

With Spice loping placidly along behind them, Anne remembered she hadn't had a chance to speak with him privately since that evening in the stable. Her heart began to pound, and she yanked her focus to the question she had to raise.

"When do you plan to visit your friend Uncle Billy again?"

Peter looked down at her, his brows slightly furrowed. "Why do you ask?"

Anne chastised herself. She should've asked a less straightforward question. What had she been thinking? When she didn't answer, Peter's frown deepened, and she groped for an explanation. "I just wondered. . . ." Her voice trailed off and she looked away.

"The doctors at the asylum found Billy's family in Indiana," he replied quietly. "They contacted them and sent him home."

"Were they able to help him?"

Peter brought Spice to a stop, forcing Anne to do so as well. She felt his gloved hand lift her chin, and she looked into his stern but gentle face.

"I know what you want to do," he said. "I don't mind taking you to see him. But I won't do it until you tell your uncle that you know. No more sneaking around."

She nodded. She'd have to write to her father's doctor then. But Peter's words had sent her determination wavering again like a leaf caught by the wind. He was willing to visit her father? He didn't mind? *Father, I'm so confused. What should I do?* The answer laid on her heart only confused her further. No, it wasn't possible.

She was still pondering it when they got back to the stable. Once they had Spice settled in her stall, Peter brought out the grooming bucket. He smiled at Anne and handed it to her. She took it and gazed at it reflectively. Would this be the last time she'd do this? Or not? She looked at Peter.

"What's wrong?"

"Nothing." She started to work but winced as she found how hard it was to groom Spice today. She usually wore a simple skirt and shirtwaist when she worked in the stable. But the dress she wore now draped around her front, its bustle brushing the sides of the stable. Not to mention the sleeves were quite snug. She glanced at Peter. "I'm afraid you'll have to do it. I'm not dressed for this."

He grinned at her. "You do look as if you stepped right out of a fashion plate." He took the brush. "But then you look lovely no matter what you wear."

It took a full minute for her to organize her thoughts again. Once they were set to rights, she watched Peter groom Spice. He had an easy smile on his face.

"You look content," she said.

"I am." He gave Spice's coat one more swipe with a soft cloth, put it back in the bucket, and carried it out of the stall. He leaned against the door frame. "I'm very happy with where the Lord ended up leading me."

Her brows rose at his wording. "Where He 'ended up' leading you?"

"When I first came to Columbus and gave my life to Christ, I thought God wanted me to be a true 'new creation,' leaving behind everything from my old life." He rubbed Spice's nose. "I didn't think He would lead me to work with horses again." His eyes locked on to hers. "And I never thought He'd lead me to you."

Everything in the world fell away as she lost herself in the passionate green of his eyes. He reached out, toying maddeningly with one of the ringlets at the base of her neck before stroking her cheek with the back of his thumb. Cupping her face in one hand, he wrapped his other around her waist and pulled her closer. A roguish grin gently played across his face before his lips finally found hers.

Nothing else existed except the soft warmth of his lips, the faint scent of shaving soap, and the gentle pressure of his hand on her waist. Everything she ever wanted was in this moment, and she didn't want it to end. She refused to open her eyes when he lifted his head. She clung to him, their foreheads still touching.

"Anne," he whispered.

This time she kissed him, her hands buried in his chocolate-brown hair. Something prodded her at the back of her mind, something she should be remembering, something important. But the sweet forgetfulness of his kiss drove it far from her thoughts, until he finally raised his head again.

"Anne, I love you," he whispered in her ear. "Nothing else matters."

Sudden and painful remembrance gripped her heart and nearly stopped it. She backed away, her eyes rapidly filling with tears. Peter's face, full of shock and confusion, only added to her pain.

"I can't," she said. "I can't do this again. I'm sorry."

She turned and ran from the stable, not stopping until she'd reached her room.

Chapter 16

The words danced in front of Peter's eyes for the millionth time since he'd found the letters lying in the straw in Spice's stall.

> *The Topeka Insane Asylum will be happy to make room for your father, Robert Wells, at your earliest convenience. Please have his doctor at the Columbus Asylum for the Insane send us all necessary records. . . .*

He'd started after her then stopped himself. Mrs. Werner would wonder what was going on if she saw him chasing Anne from the barn to the house. He walked back inside and found Spice pawing at something and discovered two letters addressed to Anne Wells, care of the university library. He was more than willing to obey the nudge he felt God giving him to open them.

The first was the letter from the asylum. The other one, from some school district in Kansas, offered Anne a position teaching school as soon as she could make the arrangements. He shook his head at himself. Why hadn't he seen it? He knew that because of her father she didn't feel worthy of someone's love but hadn't imagined she'd take it this far. No wonder she wanted to go to the asylum again. She needed to talk to her father's doctor.

Peter rose from the bench near the harness room and ran his hands through his hair. He had to tell Dr. Kirby. He had no choice. She'd be angry, that was certain, but she'd get over it. There was no way on earth he was going to let her do this.

The stable door opened and Dr. Kirby walked in. He smiled at Peter, but it quickly faded.

"What is it?" Dr. Kirby looked toward Spice, who dozed in her stall. "Where's Anne?"

Saying nothing, Peter handed the professor the letters he'd found.

The more the professor read, the graver his face became. He looked at Peter. "You knew about this?"

"About her natural father, yes, but I had no idea she was making plans to take him and head out West." He explained how Anne had found out about her father. "Why does she feel the need to leave? I know most people can be unkind about things like this but—" He stopped at the look on Dr. Kirby's face. "What is it?"

Dr. Kirby motioned him toward the bench. "You should probably sit down, son."

∞

On Christmas Eve, Peter stood at the mirror in the professor's room, tying one of his famous four-in-hand knots. When he finished, he stepped back and looked at himself. He hadn't worn such fine clothes in—had it really been only months? It felt like years. He shrugged into the frock coat he'd borrowed from the professor and turned to face him. The professor stood just behind him, a small smile on his face.

"You know this is ridiculous, don't you? It's never going to work."

"Yes it will," the professor said, adjusting his own tie. He pulled at his vest to smooth out nonexistent wrinkles and brushed at his coat. "We should get downstairs. My family will be arriving soon."

Peter sighed and followed him down the stairs. He shouldn't have let the professor talk him into this. He certainly had a better understanding now of just why Anne felt she had to leave, but the solution Dr. Kirby had suggested—*Having me propose to her? In front of her family? Wouldn't telling her pa make more sense?*

They reached the bottom of the stairs and walked into the parlor. A yet-undecorated Christmas tree stood in the corner near the front window, and bunches of holly and fir boughs lined the mantel. But Peter's eyes noticed only Anne, who stood in front of the tree.

Despite that it was Christmas Eve, when he saw her, all he could think of was autumn. With her deep green dress, red hair, and doe-brown eyes, she looked like fall in all its magnificent glory. He'd never seen her so beautiful, yet the picture was marred by the way she looked at the tree. She had that sad, wistful look in her eyes again, and if it hadn't been for the professor adjusting the logs in the fire, he would've yanked her into his arms and kissed her until that look vanished. He walked over to her, hands clasped tightly behind him.

"Your uncle tells me your parents are bringing more decorations," he said. He'd helped Mrs. Werner bring down Dr. Kirby's small crate of decorations the other day. It sat on the floor next to the tree.

She turned to him, her eyes widening. There was no mistaking the admiring look in them as she took in his appearance, but she quickly looked away, as if remembering herself.

"Yes," she replied. "We'll start as soon as they arrive." She turned her head toward him but didn't look up. "If you'll excuse me, Mr. Ward, I better go see if Mrs. Werner needs my help with anything."

Peter frowned as she left the room. He was *Mr. Ward* again? "This is hopeless."

"Why Peter, I never knew you to be so faithless," the professor said, checking his pocket watch against the time displayed on the mantel clock.

"I have plenty of faith in God, sir, just not in this plan."

Dr. Kirby snapped shut his watch. "Don't worry. 'All things work together for good to them that love God.'" Outside, a carriage pulled up, and he walked to the window. "It's my brother and sister-in-law."

Peter followed the professor to the entrance in the parlor and watched as he opened the door and greeted them. He was relieved to see that Jonah Kirby appeared much more pleasant in person. The stern picture of him from the professor's mantel had haunted him ever since Dr. Kirby suggested this crazy plan. His wife and Millie, Anne's sister, accompanied him. A lanky young man with a shock of brown hair, who could only be her brother, Jacob, completed the group.

"How are you all, Jonah?" the professor asked, slapping him on the back. "How was your trip?"

"Fine." He handed his coat to his brother. "Are you too high and mighty to hang this up for me?" It must have been an old joke between them, because Dr. Kirby laughed.

"Jonah, don't treat your brother so," Mrs. Kirby said, smiling. She took the coat from the professor, and she and Anne's sister hung their wraps on the coat tree.

"Let me introduce you to someone," Dr. Kirby said and led them over to where Peter stood. "This is Mr. Peter Ward."

Mr. Kirby and his wife seemed startled for a moment.

"How do you do, sir?" Peter held out his hand, glancing at the professor, but Dr. Kirby simply smiled.

Mr. Kirby blinked then took his hand. "I'm well, thank you." He turned to his wife. "This is my wife, Mrs. Adele Kirby."

Mrs. Kirby's eyes were wide as she shook his hand. "I'm pleased to meet you, Mr. Ward."

Dr. Kirby introduced Anne's sister, Millie, and her brother, Jacob. As he finished, Anne came down the hall from the kitchen. She smiled when she saw her family.

"Ma, Pa," she said, hugging each of them. Noticing Peter, her smile faded a fraction. "I see you've met Mr. Ward."

"Yes." Mr. Kirby eyed him carefully and Peter found himself looking at his feet.

"I'm sure he and Jacob will have a lot to discuss this evening," Anne said pointedly. She gave Peter a meaningful, almost pleading, glance before taking her mother's arm. "Mrs. Werner is in the kitchen, Ma. She's eager to meet you and Millie."

"Take Millie with you for now, Anne," Dr. Kirby said. "I need to speak with your ma and pa for a moment."

"Sir," Peter said with rising alarm as the two young women left for the kitchen. "Don't you think—"

"Peter, why don't you take Jacob into the parlor?" Dr. Kirby interjected. "If you recall, he has some questions for you." He led his brother and sister-in-law into the sitting room across the hall and slid the doors shut behind him.

Peter looked at Jacob, who grinned at him.

"Uncle Daniel says you're a horse expert. What do you know about Percherons?"

Unfortunately, Peter knew little about the breed, but he was able to give Jacob a wealth of information about horse care.

"I haven't quite decided whether to commit to raising them," Jacob said. "I've talked to some people at Grange meetings, and now you. I hope to make a decision in the next few months."

"Let me know if I can help again." Peter's gaze wandered to the parlor door. He could just see the closed doors to the sitting room. What were they talking about? Dr. Kirby said this evening would be a surprise for Anne's parents.

"It's sad what happened with Scioto," Jacob said.

"Yes, I wish there had been more I could have done," Peter replied.

"How has my uncle been about it? And my sister? Uncle Daniel's letter to Pa was very brief."

Peter nodded. "They're doing pretty well. I'm sure you couldn't have heard yet about Dr. Townshend's Christmas gift to them." He told Jacob about Spice.

"Dr. Townshend is a good man," Jacob said, smiling broadly.

The sitting room doors opened and Peter swallowed, anticipating the look of disapproval sure to be on Mr. and Mrs. Kirby's faces. After all, he had hardly a penny to his name. How was he supposed to support Anne? But when they came into the parlor, they smiled at him, seeming curiously pleased. He tried to get Dr. Kirby's attention, but the professor ignored him.

"Well, if we are to decorate the tree before dinner, we'd better get started," Dr. Kirby said.

Mrs. Kirby went to the kitchen and gathered Anne, Millie, and Mrs. Werner while Mr. Kirby brought in their box of decorations from the vestibule.

They clipped candleholders onto the branches, strung beads, and tied bows all over the tree. In spite of his nervousness, Peter enjoyed it. Granddad had been generous in his gift giving, but they'd never had a Christmas tree. He reached up to hang a little toy drum and found himself standing very close to Anne. He looked down at her.

"This is my first Christmas with a tree," he said.

She kept her eyes focused on adjusting a string of beads. "Really?"

"Yes, Granddad wasn't quite sure of them. But I had stockings, growing up." Instead of getting another ornament, he continued looking at her. "Has your family always done this?"

"Yes, I think the first one was"—her hands stilled—"the year they adopted me."

Peter glanced behind him. The rest of the family was busy on the other side of the tree. He lifted Anne's chin, forcing her to look at him. "I meant what I said out in the stable, Anne, all of it. He doesn't matter. I love you."

Her eyes darted away from his, and she opened her mouth to say something, but her uncle's voice stopped her.

"Well, I think that looks wonderful," he said.

They all stepped back to look at it. Anne carefully moved away from Peter and stood next to her brother, who smiled down at her and squeezed her shoulders.

Millie cocked her head. "I think I see a bare spot."

"Whether you do or not, it doesn't really matter," her pa said with a smile. "We're out of decorations." He nudged his brother good-naturedly. "You and your big, fancy trees."

Dr. Kirby chuckled. "Yes, well why don't we all sit down?"

Everyone took a seat. Peter found himself next to Anne on the sofa. She twisted her hands in her lap.

Mrs. Werner was the only one who hadn't taken a seat. "I'll be going to see about dinner," she said.

"Let me help you," Anne said quickly and started to rise.

"No, lass, you stay with your family. It'll be ready shortly, Dr. Kirby."

Mrs. Kirby looked at her brother-in-law. "Where are Rebecca and Joseph, Daniel? I thought they would be here."

"They'll be here tomorrow. In fact, I have good news from both of them." He rose from his seat, picked up the picture of his children on the mantel, and smiled down at it. Looking at his brother, he said, "I'm sorry to beat you to this, Jonah, but Rebecca wrote to tell me that I should be a grandfather in the spring."

Amid exclamations of happiness, Jonah joined his brother at the mantel and hugged him. Peter glanced at Anne; her smile was strained. His heart ached for her. He fervently hoped the professor's crazy plan worked. Even if it took him his whole life, he was determined to make sure that look never crossed Anne's face again. Dr. Kirby spoke, and Peter turned his attention to him.

"As for my news about Joseph—" He took a deep, steadying breath. "As you know, after Katherine passed he felt it would be too hard to stay and attend college here in Ohio." The professor's beard bristled as he pressed his lips together. "But it seems he misses his mother even more keenly living so far away from home. He has decided to attend The Ohio State University, starting next term."

Peter offered his congratulations along with everyone else, but even over the noise, he heard a sigh beside him. He set his jaw. *You'll be here to see him, Anne. With me standing right at your side.* The merriment died down, and Dr. Kirby looked at him. If Peter had been nervous and un-sure of this before, he wasn't now.

"I have more good news," the professor said. "It concerns a young man whom it has been my pleasure to know for the past several months." Peter felt uncomfortable as Dr. Kirby looked him straight in the eye. "He

386

introduced himself to me as Peter Ward, but I have discovered his real name is Peter Tobias McCord."

Peter felt as if a horse had kicked him in the gut. In a daze, he looked around at them. Dr. Kirby, his brother, and his sister-in-law appeared calm, but the others looked confused, Anne most of all. The mantel clock struck the hour, and a carriage pulled up outside. Silently, the professor left the room. He returned, bringing someone with him. Peter's jaw dropped, and he stood.

"Jimmy!" he exclaimed.

Chapter 17

H ello, sir." The valet smiled and crossed the parlor to shake Peter's hand. "Actually my name is James Brooks." He glanced at the professor. "I'm a Pinkerton agent."

"What?" Peter exclaimed. "Who were you working for? My uncle?"

Dr. Kirby laid his hand on Peter's shoulder and urged him to sit. "Just listen to him."

Peter looked at the professor as he sat down. "You've heard this, then?"

"Yes. All of it."

Peter pressed his lips together and ran his hands through his hair in frustration. "I never wanted anyone to know," he said angrily. "It was all in the past."

"I had to know who you were for reasons that you don't understand yet. Please hear Mr. Brooks out."

Peter sighed and looked at James.

"Your grandfather hired the agency," James said calmly, "to watch over you."

"To watch over me? Why?"

"He'd been getting death threats."

Peter frowned and stared at James. "He never told me."

"He didn't want to worry you. The threats began years ago, while you were at Princeton, but he never took them seriously until one of them mentioned you. That's when he called us in. He knew you'd never agree to have a bodyguard around all the time, so that's why I posed as your valet."

"He didn't ask for anyone for himself?"

"No, you were his main concern."

"Then his illness—" Peter began.

"Unfortunately, the threats were not unfounded," James replied heavily.

Peter worked his jaw. "Who?" he asked, although in his heart, he already knew.

"Your uncle, with the help of your cousin Edward, slowly poisoned him. They also changed his will. Mr. Jamison, your grandfather's lawyer, helped with that." James pulled out some documents from his suit and handed them to Peter. "I found your grandfather's real will. Your uncle, your cousin, and Mr. Jamison have been arrested."

Peter slowly opened the will. It was the exact opposite of the document his uncle had shown him in May. As Granddad had always said, he left Peter nearly everything. An annuity had been set up for Uncle Randall and his family. He understood what had motivated Uncle Randall and Edward. They'd wanted the entire McCord fortune, not a yearly stipend. But what had motivated Mr. Jamison? Granddad had trusted him explicitly. Letty came to mind, and he looked at James. "How does Letty Jamison fit in to all this?"

A scowl crossed James's face. "It seems she did get herself in the family way, but your cousin Edward was responsible. Mr. Jamison took the matter to your uncle, who agreed to have Edward marry her, *if* the attorney changed your grandfather's will."

"But once he'd done it, Edward refused to marry her," Peter said.

"Mr. Jamison threatened to reveal the whole thing unless they provided a husband for his daughter. So they took advantage of your way with the ladies, hoping to trap you into marrying her." James grinned. "You leaving *before* the wedding complicated their plans, but I'm glad you got away."

Peter looked down, wishing James hadn't put it quite like that. What must Anne think of him now?

"What happened to Miss Jamison?" Mrs. Kirby asked.

"After Mr. McCord left, his uncle paid Mr. Jamison to keep quiet, and she was sent away. The child came early, stillborn."

"The poor girl," Mrs. Kirby murmured.

James shrugged. "At least, she didn't get ahold of these." He handed a velvet box to Peter.

"You found them." He opened the box to look at his mother's pearl necklace. He sighed with relief.

"Yes, sir, with the note you left me." He reached into his pocket. "I also managed to track down these." He pulled out mother-of-pearl cuff links. "Your trail ended at the pawn shop where I found them."

"That's the last time I bet on a sure thing," Peter said, taking them. He glanced at Dr. Kirby, shame-faced.

"That's who you used to be, Peter. Not who you are now." He nodded to James. "Please give him the letter, Mr. Brooks."

Peter looked up at them. "What letter?"

"Your grandfather left a letter for you, sir, to be read when the will was read." James retrieved an envelope from a pocket inside his coat and handed it to him.

"Peter," Dr. Kirby said quietly. "I know this seems like an intrusion, but it's important that you read it out loud."

Peter hesitated, but seeing the sincere entreaty on the professor's face, unfolded the letter and cleared his throat.

Dear Peter,

You are reading this now because I have passed and my legacy is now in your hands. I know that you never were one for business, but I trust your common sense and I am confident you will find an honorable man to run McCord Steel and Ironworks on your behalf.

But that is not the reason I am leaving you this letter. Guilt has a way of lying on a man's heart like a hot steel beam, and such is the case with me. For your whole life, I have kept a secret from you. Coward that I am, I have never been able to tell you, fearing your anger and what you might do when you found out.

As you know, your mother, Sarah, was my only daughter. She was a great source of joy for me, and I wanted nothing but the best for her. I sent her to the finest finishing schools. She was the most popular young lady in Pittsburgh society. But the War between the States began, and it was then that Sarah strayed from my carefully laid plans for her.

She met a young man by the name of Tobias Kirby, a private in a Union regiment being mustered in Pittsburgh. I do not know the specifics of how they met, but he swept her off her feet. They married secretly after only a few weeks. Eventually he was sent off for service, and when Sarah discovered she was with child, she revealed to me what she had done.

My anger toward your mother was terrible, even more so when

*I discovered the Kirbys were no more than farmers in Ohio. I imme-
diately sent her abroad, and when she returned with you, I circulated
the story that she had married someone who turned out to be a fortune
hunter and divorced her when he discovered he would get no money
from me.*

*By the time you and she arrived back in Pittsburgh, the war was
over. Sarah was heartbroken when she learned your father had been
killed at Cold Harbor and angry at me for not telling her. We fought,
and she left the house only to die in the carriage accident.*

*I had nothing left of my daughter but you, and afraid the Kirbys
would come and take you away, I decided to make sure you never
knew about your father's family. I destroyed the marriage certificate
and Tobias Kirby's effects the Union Army sent me and told you the
same story I told everyone else.*

*As time went on, I could not remain at peace with what I had
done, and yet I could not find the courage to tell you the truth. I have
since learned the Kirbys are good people, people I should not have been
ashamed to call my relations. I am ashamed of my actions, and I can
only pray that you, they, and God can forgive me.*

I remain your loving grandfather,
Hiram C. McCord

A second sheet of paper listed the address of the Kirby farm in Delaware. Peter let them both fall to the floor as he lifted incredulous eyes to
the professor, who now stood beside his brother in front of the mantel.
"This is why you had to find out who I was?" he asked.

The professor nodded. "Toby was our brother," he said, his voice
thick with emotion. "When Jonah and I left to fight the war, he was
supposed to have stayed behind at the farm to help Ma run the farm. But
he always was a headstrong young man. I guess the call to serve wouldn't
leave him alone, and he ran off and joined up. Why he went clear to
Pennsylvania, I guess we'll never know."

Peter stood up and walked over to them. "But what made you think I
was his son?"

"Your eyes," the professor replied. "You woke up and looked at me
with those eyes of yours."

Confused, Peter looked from him to his brother. Both of them gazed
steadily at him, and that was when he saw it—two sets of eyes exactly

like his own, as green as a spring meadow.

"I wasn't positive until I finally got you to shave that beard of yours," Dr. Kirby said.

"You look just like him," Mr. Kirby added.

The two embraced him, and Peter felt awestruck that of all the people he could have come across during his days of wandering, the Lord led him to his own family and restored him to them. Dr. Kirby—Uncle Daniel—pulled away and gave his shoulder a squeeze. "There is one more thing you're forgetting," he said, nodding toward where Anne sat on the sofa.

Peter started then looked at Jonah. He smiled. "It's not like you're related by blood," he said quietly.

Swallowing, he looked at Anne. She stared at him with saucer-like eyes. Spying the velvet box that contained his mother's pearls lying on the sofa next to her, he picked them up and sat down facing her. He opened the box, revealing the pearls.

"These belonged to my mother," Peter said. "I'd be very happy if you wore them on our wedding day."

He saw the shock in her eyes for only a moment before she fled the room.

∞

Anne shut herself in the sitting room. The news of Peter's wealth and his true identity had been startling enough, but his proposal left her completely undone. Ever since they'd kissed, she'd fought between running straight into Peter's arms and telling him everything to leaving in the middle of the night. She shook her head, trying to clear it, and as she did so, the doors to the sitting room opened and Peter walked in. He shut them and flashed her one of his most roguish smiles.

"You left before answering my question."

Anne stared at him. "I can't marry you, Peter. I can't marry anyone."

He took her by the arms. "That's ridiculous. Of course you can. You can marry me."

"No, my father—"

"I told you I don't care about his condition."

"You should." Anne pulled away and stood by the window, her back to him. "He's not just lost his senses, Peter. He's a murderer." She held her breath, waiting for the sound of the sitting room doors opening and Peter walking out the front door.

"I know."

She whirled around, certain she hadn't heard right. "You know? But—but how?"

He walked over to her. Reaching into the breast pocket of his jacket, he pulled out two letters and held them up in front of her. "I found these in Spice's stall."

She stared at the letters then took them from his hand. With everything that had happened, she'd never realized they were gone.

"I showed them to Uncle Daniel, and he told me everything. Your father wasn't in his right mind when he killed your mother and your pa's neighbor." He pulled her into his arms. "You've been running down the wrong path, Anne. God wants to lead you to green pastures and beside still waters. And if you search your heart, I think you'll find me right there alongside you."

Anne thought she couldn't stand the joy she felt as she finally let into her heart what God had been trying to tell her for so long. But it was quickly tempered by her next thought, and she raised apprehensive eyes to his.

"What if someone finds out about my father?"

His face hardened a little. "No one is going to find out. I'll bankrupt McCord Steel if I have to."

The relief she felt was so intense she laid her head on his chest.

"So you'll marry me?" he whispered into her hair.

Anne raised her head. Unable to resist, she gave him a roguish smile of her own. "Are you sure you know what you're getting into? I can't cook, I can't sew, and I'd rather be in a stable than the kitchen—"

Anne's words were stopped by a kiss that she returned fully with a restored heart.

Author's Note

Scioto's care and treatment mentioned in these pages is drawn from *Magner's Classic Encyclopedia of the Horse*, originally published in 1887. I apologize for any errors made regarding horse care in the nineteenth century. It was purely unintentional.

At the time of this story, what most Ohio State students and alumni now call University Hall was known as the Main Building, and Mirror Lake was simply called "the Lake." To see the dramatic changes that have taken place on the university campus from 1871 to the present, I encourage you to visit The Ohio State University Interactive Historical Campus Map at knowlton.osu.edu/historymap as well as the John H. Herrick Archives at herrick.knowlton.ohio-state.edu.

O–H–I–O!

About the Author

Jennifer A. Davids loves a good book. Not only does she read and write them, she gets to take care of them at her part-time evening job at her local library. She resides in central Ohio with her husband and two children, is a member of American Christian Fiction Writers (ACFW) and a graduate of The Ohio State University. She makes room to write in between being a busy wife and mom and despite the fact her cats like to walk on her keyboard. You can connect with her online at www.jenniferadavids.com